Iscariot

A Novel

By

Charles Barnett

iUniverse, Inc.
New York   Bloomington

iUniverse books may be ordered through booksellers or by contacting:

iUniverse
1663 Liberty Drive
Bloomington, IN 47403
www.iuniverse.com
1-800-Authors (1-800-288-4677)

Because of the dynamic nature of the Internet, any Web addresses or links contained in this book may have changed since publication and may no longer be valid. The views expressed in this work are solely those of the author and do not necessarily reflect the views of the publisher, and the publisher hereby disclaims any responsibility for them.

ISBN: 978-1-4502-3074-2 (sc)
ISBN: 978-1-4502-3075-9 (ebook)

Library of Congress Control Number: 2010906626

Printed in the United States of America

iUniverse rev. date: 05/12/2010

For
Carlyle Reginald Barnett

Chapter One

Spencer Quinn paced back and forth in front of the classroom. If only there were some feedback, not just that green grocer rack of cabbages in front of him— teenage heads, close to comatose. A few heads nodded, not asleep, just trying to disguise the fact that they were texting to one another and to other pubescent numbskulls down the hall.

"This will fascinate you," Spencer heard himself say. The only response was a squeak as one sneaker shifted position on the waxed floor. It was getting near the end of the period. Soon the bell would ring and the agony would be over until tomorrow.

Spencer kept pacing. A couple of heads followed his movement listlessly. As he reached mid-room, he tried not to look up the short skirt of the blond in the front row. She knew he was interested. It was a game. She shifted occasionally to change the view with a barely discernable, half-smile on her lips. Maybe it was his imagination. And what if it wasn't? The outcome would be the same— nothing. Maybe, he'd conjure up some lewd scenario about it later at home— one in which he would make a clever, non-threatening remark to her in the hall and she would suggest a rendezvous at his place. Actually, he was too paranoid to even pat her shoulder in public. He'd wait until tonight to develop the fantasy. Hopefully it would be replaced by some mindless show on TV.

The young blond shifted again and he thought he caught a glimpse of lime-green panties. He turned quickly on his heel without reaching his usual turn around point and looked away with a jerk.

Had she smiled at that? He didn't dare to look at her to find out. What the hell was he doing? He had stopped talking. No one in the room seemed to notice. He had suggested that he was about to reveal something fascinating to them, then swiveled and stopped talking as the fleeting

1

sight of lime-green panties, maybe just his imagination, fired a deadly shot through his cerebral cortex.

"As I was saying," he found his mental place, "This will fascinate you." He held up a small object delicately between his thumb and forefinger. It was a silver coin— not flat with serrated circumference like most coins, but thick with a boldly carved scene on its face. It also had an irregular notch on one edge.

A few heads followed the movement of his hand as he raised it high. Did they see it or did they just react like frogs, taking note automatically of anything that moved?   The blond looked up. It pleased him to imagine they had established some sort of intellectual connection. It might play a part in his later fantasy.

"Does anyone know what this is?"

A few heads wobbled. One hand rose.

"A coin."

"Right!" Now he had them. "What kind of coin?"

"Silver?" said the hand raiser.

"Right again, but a lot more than that. Does it look like other coins you've seen?"

The blond looked up. "No. It's thick and has a notch in it."

Spencer's mind gave a happy twitch. He was right. She was special. Later in his fantasy, he would show her the coin at home. She would lean in for a closer look, pressing her breasts against his arm though acting as though she were unaware of the contact.

"It _is_ a silver coin— a very unusual one— very old and very rare."

"Where did you find it? Maybe I lost it. I've got a hole in one of my pockets." The kid was half sprawled out of his seat and looked around to see if his clever effort to seize center stage had registered. There were a few chuckles, but as bored as they were, his childish effort at humor seemed no more entertaining than Spencer's efforts at the front of the room.

"You don't look that old, Art. If someone had a hole in his pocket, this coin fell out of it about two thousand years ago."

Perfect. Spencer had put him away, took on the mantle of superior wisdom and even got a bit of attention. Under his breath he muttered, *Thank you, Art, you little asshole. Suck on a sugar cube and maybe we'll be able to find your pulse.*

Out loud he said, "Good point, Art. Maybe someone did lose this coin. On the other hand, maybe he just died and left it behind in a dresser drawer. Until you spoke up I wasn't sure you were still alive, either. And how could anything fall out of your pocket when your pants are usually down around your knees?"

Spencer looked at the blond. She was enjoying this. He had a few more jabs ready to launch at Art but these days you have to be very careful not to cross the line. The kids are in charge.

"Back to this coin," said Spencer, holding it up again. "Why do you think it has a notch in one edge?"

Blank stares.

"How about you, Melissa?" He looked at the blond, careful to meet her eyes and not let his gaze fall to her thighs.

Melissa blushed. Was it his imagination or, at the edge of his field of vision, did he see her thighs take on a rosy glow as well? *Don't look. Keep smiling into her eyes.*

Melissa licked her lips and let them part just a bit, exposing perfect white teeth. After a moment of embarrassment, she recognized the teacher's attentive gaze and was smiling. She was back in control.

"I don't know, Mr. Quinn. Is it there by accident or on purpose?"

What a fine mind. "Good question, Melissa. Anyone know?"

Blank stares. Great. He held the whip handle of superior knowledge. He was master of the cabbage patch. Only the bell could save them from the weight of his superior intellect.

"In a way, it's both."

If he had expected jaws to drop he was getting a head start on his evening fantasy. There were no open-mouthed yawns, but that was about the best he was going to get.

"The notch was undoubtedly made on purpose, but made to appear accidental. Anyone know why?"

Melissa wagged her head, no.

Spencer didn't wait for the unlikely contribution from one of the cabbages.

"It's the reason most coins have serrated edges, not just for appearances. The serrations are added to coins so you can tell if someone has taken a little nick out of it. It was common for people to take a little sliver from coins before spending them. After a while, they could fill a bag with silver and gold after getting face value for their coins. Sort of like some banks today that charge you extra for lending your money to someone else if your balance drops below some fixed amount for five minutes during the month. Clever thieves are always with us."

"Nickels don't have serrated edges." It was Melissa again.

"Good, Melissa," Spencer beamed. "They weren't considered valuable enough for people to slice off pieces— only silver and gold coins. Now the serrations are only traditional. Our coins are made of junk. They're not worth anything. Look at chapter twelve. It talks about the signs of civil decline. One is the debasement of the coinage. That means it's one of the signs that a society is going down the toilet when their coins are worth nothing. We'll talk about it tomorrow— about the Great Depression and how Roosevelt took all the gold coins from the people and had them melted down into bricks and stored in Fort Knox so the people would have to depend on the government. In Europe, the Jews bought up diamonds so they could hide their wealth and make a run for it if they had to."

The boredom in the room was palpable. Only Melissa, bless her ravishing soul, was paying attention. She smiled as the bell rang, then rose to leave in a single sensuous movement. Was it Spencer's imagination or did she give him another little smile over her shoulder as she got to the door, her slightly wrinkled skirt tight across her perfect buttocks?

Chapter Two

Spencer Quinn sat in his little, home library. Instead of watching TV, he decided to listen to music. He liked to think he was a fan of classical music but knew his tastes ran within the genre to the schmalzier works— not the heavy stuff. He had once asked a serious, academic musician to recommend his favorite work. It turned out to be so dull Spencer had pitched the CD into the trash after listening for just a few minutes. He knew he would never listen to it again. He did appreciate a lot of important, classical composers but his favorites were always those that wrote sensuous, sometimes even mysterious sounding, pieces— people like Ravel, Debussy, and Pletnev. When he thought about it he realized there were lots of them— Goreçky, Tavener, Vaughan-Williams. He thought they must have been like him— introspective and sensuous, driven by a mix of intellect and hot pants. This evening he was listening to the *Violin Concerto in D, by Eric Wolfgang Korngold.* Now <u>that</u> was romantic schmaltz at its most saccharine. Marvelous!

Spencer liked to think of his obsession with sex as part of the complete man, the natural expression of an artistic soul. Look at Picasso. He was a mean little bull of a man driven by his pecker into a frenzy of creativity that the world could not ignore.

Despite his wish to identify with the creative geniuses of the world, Spencer was not a fool. He knew he was a high school history teacher in a small, co-ed, parochial school in Connecticut that depended more for its sound fiscal status on its ivy draped buildings than its academic excellence. He felt that his home library was the real measure of his personal depth and value as a special human being. He owned books, some of them unique, which had taken a good part of his financial resources to acquire. It was an eclectic collection, tending to the arcane— all sorts of books on magic, from stage illusions to card tricks, and on to more exotic, mysterious works about medieval spells and lycanthropy. He didn't believe in such stuff but loved the aura of mystery around the books and the realization through their writings that some intelligent people did.

Actually, Spencer was a very practical person, in love with drama and romance, but ideologically bound, hand and foot, by logic, historic fact, and scientific principle. He was an agnostic at best, but probably a bedrock atheist if pressed to explain himself. Like most atheists, Spencer dodged being categorized as such. He felt that people who openly professed atheism were usually on some ugly, personal mission to belittle others. He was not one to write off believers as simpletons clinging to their Bibles, nor as Karl Marx described them— members of a "non-descript mass of humanity behaving as automatons under the influence of an opium derivative called religion." To describe your fellow humans in such a dismissive way had to be the result of a deep-seated hatred. Where do such ugly emotions originate? Perhaps jealousy. Perhaps emotional impotence— an inability to love anything that didn't have genitalia.

That was Spencer's fear. Was he an atheist as the result of applying pure logic to the analysis of the physical world and humanity's interaction with it, or was he an emotional eunuch— incapable of experiencing a non-rational faith in God along with the joys and sorrows of being human? He saw himself as a live, breathing version of the Star Trek android, Commander Data, who longs to be human even at the expense of feeling sorrow, pain, and the broad spectrum of miseries that go with it.

Spencer Data— that's who he was, unwilling prisoner of his own sense of logic. Even the Star Trek writers were careful to avoid getting into the religious arena when it came to defining the cyber-persona of Commander Data.

Spencer had discussed all this with his brother, Ryan. The elder Quinn was a fun-house mirror image of Spencer. They were the same, inside and out, but with a twist. Ryan was a Jesuit, a priest. He was also, perhaps, an atheist, and probably not the only one. Most Jesuits are highly intelligent. Many join up just to make that point, like becoming a member of Mensa International, the genius club. Of course there was a lot more to it than that as far as being a Jesuit. There was companionship, opportunity to follow intellectual, non-religious pursuits. Some were astronomers, mathematicians, even politicians. Some countries denied them entry in fear of a religious takeover.

There was an inside joke. A couple of parents were concerned about the future of their child. They asked a child psychologist if he could give them any insight. He said he had a test and they agreed to it. He put the child in a room with a two-way mirror so they could observe him. On a table were a whip, a Bible, and a twenty-dollar bill. The psychologist told the parents that if the child picked up the money, he would become a financier, if the whip, a political leader, and if the Bible, a clergyman. They watched the child as he approached the table. He picked up the twenty-dollar bill and put it in his pocket. Then he picked up the whip, cracked it once, and stuck it in his belt. Finally, he took the Bible and put it under his arm. The psychologist let out a wail! Oh my God, he's going to be a Jesuit!

That was Ryan Quinn, Spencer's brother— more or less. He was an archaeologist of recognized excellence with a doctorate in Middle Eastern Antiquity. He was also very adept at securing great amounts of money to fund his research. In fact, he headed a private corporation to handle the large amounts of money and manage it in promoting work by others that interested him— the Chalice Corporation. As a Jesuit, he had taken oaths of poverty, chastity and obedience. Technically, the corporation owned all the money— so no conflict. Chastity was between him and God. As to obedience, no one tries to tell someone like Ryan what to do.

All this was going through Spencer's head as he sat at his desk. Ryan was a star. He was practically Ryan's double but he was a secondary school history teacher who lusted after pubescent coeds. He hadn't seen Ryan in a long time. It was a friend of Ryan's, another Jesuit named Habib Colophon, who had given him the coin he held up in class earlier. He wondered about Habib. He hadn't seen him in years. He had acted as though the coin was very important but never said why. Now it lay on the desk in front of Spencer. It seemed, in some respects to resemble a Judean shekel.

Spencer had seen many shekels. This one was different. On the front was the depiction of a man hanging by the neck from a tree. Very unusual. It looked a bit like a Shekel of Tyre, the coinage used widely at the time of Christ. But those had an image of one of the Ptolomies on the face and a feathered bird on the back. It didn't make numismatic sense— probably a forgery by some idiot who didn't know ancient coins. Also, Shekels were rarely very thick. As Melissa had noted in class, this one was. Perhaps it wasn't a coin at all but some sort of medallion. On the reverse, where there should have been a three blossomed flower stem surrounded by the Hebrew words, Jerusalem the Holy, though hard to make out, there was something like a stick figure hanging from a gibbet as in the French parlor game, Pendu. Circling it was a chain of sixteen links, or perhaps just eight, since every second one was connected to its companion by a crossover. Spencer stared at it. An eight on its side is the symbol for infinity. So it was either a chain of sixteen links or just a chain of eight infinity symbols. Ryan would probably know what it was all about but he hated to ask him. He loved his brother but asking for help was beyond his ability to manage his own sense of inferiority in the presence of his learned Jesuit brother.

Spencer pondered the strangeness of the coin. The nick on one edge broke the continuity of the chain. That made him smile. Had some greedy merchant broken the chain of infinity— severed eternity? He looked more closely at the nick. It wasn't the casual scoop taken out by a greedy merchant. It was actually quite intricate as though cut carefully to a specific profile. He continued to think about the unusual thickness of the coin, as well. It didn't seem heavy enough for its size— a very weird coin.

Slowly his interest in the coin dimmed as he thought again of young Melissa. In the fantasy he was fashioning, she had come to his apartment and a scene began to unfold. He had set her mind aglow with curiosity as he presented her with his learned observations about the silver piece. In his mind he felt her squirm with sensuous willingness as he held the coin to her gaze and slowly moved his other hand to her breast. She didn't resist. Her nipple grew hard and her breath began to come in short gasps.

He moved his hand down to the waist of her skirt, then down farther to its hem. He lifted it deliberately, never taking the coin from her gaze, and put his hand between her thighs.

Were they standing or sitting? He didn't know. The fantasy left him to deal with the details. He wanted to get her naked. She must be standing so he could take off her clothes, but how, with one hand holding the coin? He let it drop to the floor. It rolled under the paint-thick radiator beneath the window. He would get it later. She was moaning and reaching for his zipper. "Yes," she moaned, just as someone rapped sharply on the door.

"Damn," he said. "Damn, damn, damn."

"Hold on. I'm coming." He didn't notice the humorous connection between his words and his physical condition. He moved slowly to the door, trying to give his erection an opportunity to grow less obvious. But even before Spencer got to the door, there was another light series of knocks.

"Hold your horses. I'm coming," he said irritably. He turned the deadbolt, then the handle, and pulled the door to him, and let out a gasp. There stood the most beautiful woman he had ever seen— not a cliché phrase. She was actually, almost radiantly beautiful. She stared directly into Spencer's eyes.

"Do you have any wine?"

Someone was playing a joke on him. They were always kidding him about his "vow of involuntary celibacy." They had sent a hooker to make fun of him. Well, if that was the case, the joke was on them. He doubted they had seen this woman before they engaged her services.

"Yes." He heard himself answer in a half daze. "I have wine. Come in."

The woman wore a black cocktail dress that hung by spaghetti straps from her white shoulders so the bodice reached a level just above her nipples. Her hair, a natural blond that most women get only from a bottle, fell to her naked shoulders. A short silver chain circled her neck. Though taken aback by this sudden apparition, Spencer noted that she had "the eyes."

Since childhood Spencer had been victim to an erotic obsession with a certain type of eyes. Men as well as women had them but women with "the eyes" drove him into a state of romantic rapture. It was such a presence in his psyche that he had done some research into the matter. It got him nowhere in particular. "The eyes" involved a special crease in the lid, akin to the oriental, epicanthic fold. It can be seen clearly on an ancient portrait of Genghis Khan, but the eyes that fascinated Spencer were not oriental but those sometimes seen in northern European women. The first time he became aware of his obsession was on a high school trip to New York. On the second floor of the Metropolitan Museum of Art he discovered a small Flemish painting. For at least twenty minutes he stood mesmerized before the small tempera portrait that was labeled, simply, "A Young Woman." Next to it was a twin portrait, perhaps her brother, titled, "A Young Man." The pair was dated *circa 1583*. At age 15, Spencer fell in love with a 400-year-old woman. Spencer savored the bizarre aspect of such cerebral relationships. Years later, on a trip to Egypt, he fell in love again, this time with a woman more than three thousand years old— Queen Ti, wife of Pharaoh Amenhotep. She also had the eyes. He was obviously in danger of becoming a very strange man.

Now this woman stood in front of him, black dress, naked shoulders, sensuous lips smiling below a slender, perfect nose, and a pair of those eyes.

She broke his stunned silence and asked again, "Do you have any wine?"

"Oh. Oh, yes. Of course. Come in."

She walked past him as he closed the door. She moved with a grace that was not so much sensuous as athletic. She was perfect. What was she doing here? No. No. Don't ask such a question, even inside your head. She might sense it and leave.

"Please sit down. I'll get some wine. I don't have anything fancy. Do you prefer red or white?"

"Always red," she said. Her voice was low and throaty with just a hint of accent. Spencer prided himself on an ability to identify regional accents. He had never heard this one before, though the sound if it tickled the edges of his long-term memory. It sounded a bit like a smooth version of *click language*. Spencer had once heard that language spoken during a trip to Africa. Anthropologists claimed the strange language was a linguistic "echo of the earliest language spoken by ancient humans, tens of thousands of years ago." Today it is spoken only by the San People of Southern Africa and the Hadzabe of East Africa. The two do not live near one another and are thought to have been living far apart for forty thousand years. The connection had to be ancient. In any event, neither tribe was likely to have produced a beautiful blond like…

"Excuse me, but what is your name?"

"Maggy."

What a let down! A goddess named Maggy? Disappointment showed on his face.

"You don't like my name, Spencer?"

"No. No. It's a lovely name." But who had told her his name? He hadn't mentioned it. Not important. Probably one of the guys who sent her here.

"It's just short for a much longer, rather pretentious name," again that strange clicking sound to her words. "My father has a habit of picking very dramatic names for his children."

Spencer ran a few possibilities through his head and tossed them out to her— "Margaret? Magdalena? Marguerite? Magda?"

"No. Not even close. I said very dramatic. My name is Magnificent."

Spencer's jaw dropped. My God, how well it fit her. She looked pleased at his change in attitude.

"The wine, Spencer?"

"Oh, yes. Here we are." He brought over one of his prizes, a bottle he had brought back from Galilee— a 2004, late-harvest Gewürztraminer from the Sha'al Carmel Winery.

He placed it proudly on the little table beside her chair. "May I pull the cork?"

"Please."

He snatched it up again and ceremoniously uncorked the bottle. He sniffed the cork dramatically before pouring a bit into her glass. She, in turn, took the goblet, sniffed the wine's aroma while swirling it beneath her perfect nose. Spencer loved the performance.

"Anything else, Magnificent?"

"Do you have a bit of bread?"

"Bread?"

"To cleanse the palate before drinking, Spencer."

"Of course, of course. I'm so sorry."

Spencer went to the kitchenette and fetched a slice of bread. He brought it back on a small dish and presented it to his incredible guest. She took it, broke it into several pieces, and offered one to Spencer. He took it dutifully and they both consumed the morsels, then sipped the wine. It was a wonderful moment—ritual in its solemnity. Spencer's mind was spinning.

"Sit in that chair." Maggy did not ask. She pointed to an armless chair near Spencer's desk. He never even thought to object.

When he had taken his place as instructed, Maggy walked over to face him. Then she moved toward him and lifted her dress. She was wearing nothing under it. Spencer's heart was pounding violently. He could smell the aroma of her nakedness. She opened her legs and moved forward to straddle him.

As Spencer sat gasping, the woman, moist and moving rhythmically, massaged his engorged penis through his pants with her naked vagina. He was on the verge of passing out.

"Is this what you want, Spencer," that strange click language lilt to her husky voice?

"Oh yes," he gasped. "Yes, yes!" He felt a tingling rise from his legs and engulf his entire body, then a tugging jerk as he erupted into his trousers. He let out a groan of uncontrolled ecstasy and clutched the woman to him.

After a few moments, as Spencer fought to capture his breath, the woman disengaged herself, rose slowly, and let her dress fall back.

"May I give you a massage, Spencer?"

She didn't wait for a response but moved behind him and began to knead his shoulders.

"Does this feel good?"

Spencer was so drained he could hardly summon the energy to respond. "I wish I could just die and feel like this forever."

She kept kneading his shoulder with one hand. With the other, she withdrew a silver Beretta from between her breasts. Carefully, she placed the nose of the barrel about six inches behind the crown of his head— the area where a bishop would traditionally wear his skullcap. Spencer felt the hard muzzle of the gun on his head.

"What is that, Maggy, another surprise?"

"Yes, Spencer, it is. This is eternity," she said, and pulled the trigger.

Chapter Three

Korngold's violin concerto was still playing as Maggy went efficiently about taking care of what she had to do. The whole entrance, seduction, and execution had taken barely twenty minutes. She had known beforehand what she had to do so it went quickly. She drew a black cloth from the handbag she had left at the door and draped it around Spencer so only his head remained visible. It was slumped forward. She tilted it back against a small, black pillow she had also brought with her. There was no blood to speak of. The bullet had entered cleanly, plunging straight down. No ugly wound— just a small round hole hidden beneath a maroon patch of blood-matted hair.

Reaching again into her bag, Maggy pulled out a crimson skullcap and placed it over the wound— crimson, the symbol of the Church's highest political rank— a skullcap for a Cardinal, prince of the Roman Church. That done, she gave Spencer a strange look. It was one of pure love. Then she said a few words over him in a strange tongue. Only a linguist would recognize it as the ancient sound of mankind's earliest effort to communicate— archaic click language. Suddenly the room went silent. It gave her a start. The romantic Korngold melody had finished with a flourish.

Maggy drew herself away from Spencer as a gentle knock came from the front door. It was no surprise. She was expecting it. She let the slender, ascetic figure in. He was pale and blond like she, a handsome man but somehow sexless— perhaps a eunuch. His name was Hal. Like his sister, his name was short for a far grander one given to him by their father. At home, he was Hallelujah. The two exchanged a quick look. He glanced at Spencer, now just a motionless, black form, with a bloodless, white head on top, wearing a crimson cap. The man nodded approval, made a few clicking sounds and the two began to search the room. They knew what they were after and where to look for it. It would be in Spencer's small ebony chest, the one with velvet lined shelves and rows of slits to hold rare coins.

The initial search didn't take long. Spencer was proud of his ancient coin collection and kept the chest prominently displayed on a bookshelf. It sat between two Egyptian ushabti that served as bookends to hold back the leather-bound volumes on both sides. He liked the symmetry of it and felt lucky to have found two Egyptian figurines that were almost a match. They came from a grave robber's collection so he had no idea to whose mummy they had belonged. The coin chest was where he could get to it easily for his own convenience and so he could extract specimens to show his guests.

One after another, the couple opened and closed the slender coin drawers. The specimen slots were full in all but two— the lowest and the third one from the top. The bottom drawer was only half full, obviously awaiting new acquisitions.

There was no time to go through the collection piece by piece. The empty slot in the third drawer had to be it. The other coins were mostly from ancient Judea. Spencer had removed the coin they wanted and done something with it. The man and woman moved quickly about the room, so silently they almost seemed to be floating above the floor. They were certain Spencer would not have idly put the coin in some mundane place like the kitchen or bathroom. And they knew he had it with him during his history class earlier in the day.

Gingerly, Maggy lifted the black cloth covering Spencer's body and searched his pockets. A wry expression crossed her face as she felt the dampness in one pocket against which Spencer had ejaculated. When she withdrew her hand it bore the aroma of semen. She had smelled that odor many times before. In her experience, unlike that of most women, she associated it, not with the creation of life, but its termination.

The search of Spencer's pockets, pants, shirt, and jacket produced nothing but the usual— keys, a nail clipper, a handkerchief, some modern coins. Unfortunately, the handkerchief had been in the pocket near which he had climaxed. It was soaked in the life fluid of his last pleasure on earth. She pushed the handkerchief back into the pocket and wiped her hand on his pants. Then she carefully draped the black cloth about him again. Nothing!

They began a careful examination of the room— tabletops, the desk, everything in sight. They checked between the cushions on the couch. It was getting late and still nothing. They were bound by a rigid schedule. It was not a matter of choice. A flurry of hand gestures, a rapid exchange of clicking sounds, and the two went around the small apartment carefully wiping anything either of them might have touched— the wine glasses, the door knob, even the funereal cloth and skull cap. Forensics had grown very sophisticated of late. When they finished, they left, closing the door quietly behind them. Spencer was alone, a motionless mass of black cloth, with a silent, blood-drained head wearing the crimson cap of a holy prince.

It was weeks after the police had come and gone that the landlady swept under the radiator and discovered the missing coin. She had no idea what it was but suspected Spencer's brother, the priest, might want it. She put it in her kitchen cupboard in the coffee can with the rest of her spare change. Those two were a pair, she thought. Such fine Irish boys. Perhaps if both had become priests, like her own brother, poor Spencer would still be alive. She couldn't imagine what had happened here. Apparently no one else could either. She would pray the rosary for him tonight at Saint Brendan's. She loved the smell of the incense in the peaceful church. She felt secure with just the drone of the priest and the congregation for company as they worked their way patiently each evening through the monotonous tribute to the Mother of God.

Chapter Four

Reverend Ryan Spencer Quinn, S. J., sat on a slope high above the Hudson River. Someone had built an ornate bench that circled a broad leaved, ginkgo biloba tree. The shade was delightful on a warm day. Though the river was far below, a breeze always managed to climb the slope to this idyllic spot.

The ginkgo is a botanical oddity that has survived, virtually unchanged, over millions of years. Fossil ginkgo leaves, once buried in primeval ooze, are identical to those of the ginkgos alive today. Ryan wasn't thinking about that just now but he had in the past. It was fascinating to contemplate the anachronism of inhaling and exhaling summer breezes beneath a fossil tree. It made him feel a peculiar kinship with the planet. It also reassured him of the continuity of God's design, something he secretly doubted at times.

He wasn't sure he felt deeply about the theological conflicts posed by paleontology but he force-fit it meticulously into his clerical persona. Ryan was very aware of his image. He didn't consider it so much a vanity as his responsibility to present the Church to those about him in the best light. Priestly priests are the life's blood of a vibrant, credible Church. He wasn't exactly sure he held with that, either, but he was adept at finding a logical, even liturgical, basis through which he could indulge his elegant life style without guilt— or sin.

Ryan loved everything about being a Jesuit. In a way, it was like being a ginkgo tree— alive and breathing but unchanged, despite the ebb and flow of humanity for eons. A Jesuit is an anachronism, the personification of an ideology born in the self-flagellation sessions of St. Ignatius Loyola, and a scheme to conquer nations, ostensibly undergone a metamorphosis, into personae of benign educators, desiring only to enlighten and enrich mankind. Many have found the metamorphosis suspect. A number of nations have declared Jesuits to be Personae non Gratae. However, like the ginkgo, somehow the Order survives, essentially unchanged.

Most religious orders can be identified by their garb. St. Ignatius did not want to create such a simple target for his adversaries. Early Jesuits were encouraged to adopt the garb of all different orders. The world was to be his ideological masked ball. As someone once said, the best hiding place is in plain sight.

Ryan Quinn, S. J. sat in plain sight beneath a ginkgo tree high above the Hudson River. He was wearing the currently accepted Jesuit-style cassock wrapped around his torso, held closed by a broad woven band, or cincture. At his neck was a white Roman collar. A large crucifix hung from his neck in traditional Jesuit style, tucked into the cincture to keep it from swinging about. It also gave the wearer an air of deadly familiarity with Christianity's most sacred symbol, like a saber hanging from the belt of a cavalry soldier. Over everything, he wore a cape known as a ferraiuolo. Everything but the roman collar was jet black. Amerindians referred to the early Jesuit missionaries as The Blackrobes. If they wore a hat, it was a strange contraption like most Catholic priests, but it had a small black diamond shaped piece of satin-covered pasteboard at the apex rather than the silly little black pompom on the hats worn by parish priests. The Jesuit hat is called a biretta— with an "i"— no relation to the pistol, which is spelled with an "e." Jesuit garb was, and remains, impressive in its minimalist elegance. Perhaps it was that which provided inspiration for male stylist, Beau Brummel, when he designed the first tuxedo.

The day was warm even in the shade of the ginkgo tree— too warm for the ferraiuolo, but Ryan wore it anyhow. He fancied the image he presented, all in black in the middle of an immense lawn, sitting beneath the ancient ginkgo tree. His mind flew to a vantage point where he observed himself from the mansion's parapet. It was a surrealist tableau worthy of René Magritte's brush and palette— the perfect setting to receive his wealthy visitors. He had laid out a few props— old books taken from the mansion library and a couple of artifacts from a recent dig in the Middle East. He suspected his visitors might possess a great deal of money and follow an avocation of amateur archaeology. At least that was implied in their note requesting this meeting. The note had been hand written, using a real fountain pen. Ryan liked that. His own gold Écorce was a collector's item.

Its triangular nib was a French design that allowed one to write in either a heavy or thin line.

The note from his visitors had been written on a square of linen stock with a thin, black border. At the top was a single engraved word, Sarafian— no address or other distraction. No indication as to whether it was a business or family name. The note was square requiring a custom envelope. It bore no marks at all but the flap had been closed with dark red wax imprinted with an ancient Sasanian seal, the draped bust of a figure wearing a crown. Ryan had seen a number of such seals taken from Persian tombs. He even had one or two in a drawer back in the City. He thought he might adopt the whole idea for the corporation's stationery— just the word "Chalice" at the top. Using sealing wax might be a bit much and cause the post office to go berserk. They rattle easily but recover quickly when they find they can charge extra for something. He would look into it later. In the meanwhile, he suspected he would enjoy this afternoon's meeting. It sounded like the Sarafians had money to burn and The Chalice Corporation was a money oven. It had much good work to perform. The poor wait for help. The wealthy provide it— when and where they wish. The Chalice Corporation was very generous with people and projects favored by Ryan Spencer Quinn, S.J.

Recently, in honor of his deceased brother, Ryan used his middle name more often and conspicuously. Their parents had thought to create a special bond between them by swapping their first and middle names. Spencer's middle name had been Ryan. It worked. With Spencer gone, Ryan felt like half a person. Spencer never had the Jesuit talent for finance but he did have a mind every bit as keen as Ryan's. They had shared countless intellectual interests in archaeology, numismatics, antiquarian books, ancient maps, and manuscripts. Best of all, they shared a fascination with intellectual trails half-hidden in history that promised adventure. The loss of Spencer was the loss, not only of a brother and companion, but a soulmate.

The visitors would be here soon. Ryan toyed with the crucifix tucked into his cincture. He looked out over the Hudson River far below. On the opposite bank were the grand estates of legendary giants of American politics, wealth, and industry— Vanderbilt, Gould, FDR. Ryan couldn't actually see their mansions but he knew exactly where they were, hunkered down among huge, old trees. He thought with pride of his side of the river and his own personal contribution to its roster of architectural landmarks

— Gordon House. He had named it for his father, a simple New York policeman, but a man of intellect never given the opportunity to flourish.

Ryan sat near the middle of the estate's vast, east-sloping lawn. The Victorian mansion and grounds had been the bequest of a wealthy, Wall Street tycoon— a Catholic, of course, who had thought to buy a place in heaven when he realized his end was near. He had neglected to pay taxes on the estate for several years before he died but Ryan's Chalice Corporation was able to take care of those without too much strain. Once the property of the Church, it acquired tax-free status— no longer compelled to render "tribute unto Caesar." The Jesuits had a number of such estates scattered about the US and around the world.

Ryan was fond of telling people about "his side" of the Hudson. Just north of Gordon House, John Burroughs' awkward home was decaying rapidly and rotting its way back into the soil. Burroughs had been the foremost naturalist of his era, vying with John Muir for the title. A consummate egotist, he felt that only he could design and build the perfect house. His masterpiece, about a quarter mile north of Ryan's place, he named, Riverby. It turned out to be such a monstrosity he couldn't bear to spend more than moments in it. He left it to his fastidious wife to keep tidy and built a study down the slope in which he could relax and write. He built another, way back in the woods, which he named Slabsides. It was in the latter, actually a rustic little dump, that he entertained illustrious friends like Henry Ford, Thomas Edison, Walt Whitman, even the prissy wordsmith, Oscar Wilde. On one occasion, Theodore Roosevelt, always anxious to display his rugged, good health, docked the presidential yacht below Ryan's estate and hiked up the steep slope to lunch with Burroughs in his cabin.

In truth, Burroughs had another reason to build his little dump far away in the woods. It was not only to get away from the cold and uncomfortable Riverby house, but also to get away from his wife whom he openly declared to be frigid. The moans and wails that sometimes issued from the forest abode generally followed the arrival of some female environmentalist anxious for a private audience with the feisty old naturalist.

Father Quinn relished the salty details one could find in the footnotes of famous biographies. He liked to think it was part of his professional responsibility as an historian. He wasn't so naïve as to think this flimsy rationale for digging into historical dirt would fool anyone. Few had the temerity to challenge the "good father" on such matters as a little historical gossip. Besides, he was well known for his serious, academic work regarding the archaeology of the Catholic Church.

Now he sat mourning the death of his brother and awaiting the arrival of his guests with curiosity. The René Magritte image he had of himself under the ginkgo tree dissolved into a Salvador Dali— a moving image as three people crossed the lawn toward him. The one in the lead was Brother Augustus. The other two, a man and a woman, trailed far behind, probably at the suggestion of Brother Augustus.

The Jesuits created the lesser rank of "Brother" within the order. Brothers were not ordained priests and ordinarily not considered to be their intellectual equals. They served as domestics, doing the cooking, cleaning, gardening, and other such tasks, leaving the priests to follow their teaching, research, and spiritual tasks. The paths to heaven are many and the ways of the Lord can be quite mysterious.

Brother Augustus approached Ryan timidly.

"Your guests are here, Father— Mr. and Miss Sarafian— Hal and Maggy, I believe they said. May I tell them to join you?"

"By all means, Augustus, and thank you."

Brother Augustus didn't retreat, bowing like an oriental courtier, but his posture seemed almost that. He spoke with the couple for a moment, motioned them to join Ryan and hurried back to the main house. Father Quinn made him nervous.

Despite the fact that humility is a mandated practice among Jesuits, some fall short. Ryan was among those. He complied, uncomplaining, with standard Jesuit practices meant to bring down the haughty amongst them, but he understood that practicality might well intervene in special cases.

The final stage in the seventeen year ladder of Jesuit training is a return to the bottom rung— a year performing menial tasks as mopping floors, cleaning toilets, waiting on tables in the dining halls and so on— "and the last shall be first..."

Later on, as the newly ordained priests assume their regular duties, they are transferred periodically from place to place and job to job, lest they rise to a position of power and try to hold onto it. Ryan had seen his way around that— the Chalice Corporation. His vows of poverty, chastity and obedience were not in jeopardy. He owned no money— personally. He accepted the authority of those in the Order above him but they understood nothing of the Chalice Corporation except that it brought millions to their programs of good works. They dared not interfere with that. They could transfer him wherever they liked but Chalice had offices everywhere and could always open new ones if Ryan felt it necessary. As to his vow of chastity, Ryan had been there and done that, so to speak. He had been married and even had a son. His wife had taken her own life. He never understood why. It was only after her death that he entered Jesuit training. The boy, Paul, was raised by Ryan's parents, and better off for it. Paul was twenty-two now, and bore his father no ill will. They were friends. He had never had to deal with a new woman in his father's life. There was something mystical and marvelous having the Catholic Church for his foster mother.

Ryan observed his vow of chastity without rancor. He thought whimsically of the Eternal Triangle— priest, woman, and God. He would not get involved in that. He successfully managed his appetites with the same strength of will he brought to all his tasks. In fact, he felt he had outdone all but a few others within the Catholic Church. Of the Seven Sacraments, he had received all but Extreme Unction, the final anointment at death. He presumed that sacrament would be his as well in due course. Among the faithful, precious few receive all seven sacraments, Baptism, Confirmation, Penance or Confession, Holy Communion, then either Matrimony, or Holy Orders— marriage, or the priesthood.

Ryan rose as the two approached but did not extend his hand. It was not a haughty statement, just a habit. Priests are different. Their hands have been blessed. Hand shaking is not forbidden. It is simply a bit too colloquial in most cases. The couple seemed to understand completely and never offered their hands in greeting either. They all stood a bit awkwardly for a few moments.

"Please, sit down." Ryan motioned to several carved chairs Augustus had put under the tree for them earlier. Ryan's own chair was ornate, almost throne-like. He loved ceremony, especially when he was the personification of power in the tableau. The note he had received from these two indicated they had a taste for the same. His behavior should strike a chord with them.

"Unusual name, Sarafian," he pushed his first pawn to Bishop-Two.

The young man smiled. If he was aware of Ryan's subtle probe for information he dismissed it. He was handsome, clean-shaven, with short, black hair. His eyes were a piercing blue, almost luminous. He wore expensive, linen slacks as black as his hair, and a crisp, white shirt with short sleeves that hugged his biceps. His arms were hairless and pale, despite the summer sun.

"The name goes way back, Father." His smile twisted strangely, lending it a slight touch of arrogance. Ryan felt it at once, a bit of wry superiority—something he'd very rarely confronted.

"It is a very old name, of Middle Eastern origin," he explained, though Ryan had not asked. He said it with just a hint of an accent. It sounded vaguely familiar but certainly not Middle Eastern. Ryan would have known if it were.

"You don't look Middle Eastern and your sister certainly doesn't. She is your sister, I understand."

"Not exactly." It was she who spoke now.

She was the most incredibly beautiful woman Ryan had ever seen—blond, fair skin, slim, and shapely, in a black, linen dress that might have been cut from the same bolt of cloth as the young man's trousers. Her shoulders were smooth and pale like the man's arms. Her neckline dropped to just barely above her nipples.

Ryan found that he was fidgeting with the crucifix tucked into his cincture—and stopped. Did she smile at that? He wasn't sure. This meeting was not what he had expected. It seemed he was not the one in control. That needed to change.

"I'm not sure I understand. How is it that you are not *exactly* brother and sister?"

"We have the same father but have never met our respective mothers. For all we know, perhaps we had no mothers at all, just poor little waifs—weird products of an ex-utero, laboratory experiment." She smiled broadly at this and Ryan found himself smiling just as broadly. She was offering no information, just toying with him. What a marvelous woman! And again, that trace of a strange accent.

"OK. I'll stop asking personal questions. Your note suggested we have mutual interests and that you have lots of money you wish us to spend advancing them."

"Right to the point, Father. I like that in a man."

Ryan hadn't blushed in almost a quarter century but was afraid he had just done so. He tried to retake the high ground.

"Go on. Let's see if you can interest me." He regretted the choice of words at once but it was too late. This time it was *her* throat and chest that flushed a rosy glow. Ryan found her reaction exciting but quickly cast the sight from his mind. He had learned to pound his male instincts into pudding through raw will power. These were the potential sins of the flesh spoken of by the Church and dealt with during Jesuit training—"the occasions of sin" to be avoided at all costs. Ryan recognized them but had long since concluded he was more powerful than they.

Had she noticed his momentary struggle? She gave no sign of it and continued as though there'd been no animal exchange between them. Her partner had simply vanished. Actually, he was still there— a motionless Rodin sculpture. Neither the woman nor the priest was even aware of his continued presence. He stared at the two without expression. He had seen his sister at work many times before.

"You have been involved in excavations near El Minya," she said, all business now.

"Yes, the Middle Kingdom of Akhenaton. Interest is growing in the area. Archaeologists continue to dig in the popular areas around Giza in the north and Luxor to the south, but some of us feel the greatest discoveries are still to be made half-way between the two."

"My feeling exactly," she said. She seemed even more beautiful as her brow furrowed with intellectual intensity. "While I'm very interested in early Egypt, that's not what fascinates me about the El Minya area. It's what happened after Akhenaton and his wife, Nefertiti, were long dead, embalmed, and sent, bag and baggage, off to the underworld. I am particularly fascinated by the treasure trove of information to be uncovered in the desert caves where Coptic Christians first began to embrace the concept of hermit life and monasticism."

"You're right, young lady. We do indeed share a common interest, not only in a specific area but a particular aspect of Egyptian history."

Ryan tried to sound paternal and academic. He was under control but found it difficult to avoid looking at the smoothness of her exposed flesh and the promise of firm breasts below her black bodice.

Aside from his carnal instincts this woman had truly aroused his academic curiosity.

"We intend to fund an academic research effort into the history and physical archaeology of that area in a sizeable dollar amount."

"How sizeable?" Now Ryan was all business. Was it his imagination or did he see her nipples grow hard beneath the thin material of her dress as he showed obvious interest in her offer? Again, he marshaled his Jesuit training to force his return to the business at hand.

"Initially, fifty million dollars." She said it as though it were a trivial sum, "placed at once in the name of the Chalice Corporation at the Bank of Cairo in the belief you will be able to begin work very soon. Should results of initial research look promising, but remain incomplete, a great deal more will be available."

Even as the CEO of the well endowed Chalice Corporation, these were impressive sums. Ryan was fascinated on all levels— the area of research, the sizeable amount of the funding, and grudgingly, the woman.

"That is a great deal of money, Miss Sarafian."

"Please call me Maggy."

"A very plain sounding name for a woman of your exotic background— Maggy. Short for Margaret?"

"No," she added without offering anything further.

"And you, Mr. Sarafian?" He turned to the statue-like young man, silent until now.

"My name is Hal," he emerged from his apparent trance without the slightest indication that he had not been part of the conversation all along.

"Harold?"

"No, Father. Does our offer interest you?"

It was a relief to discuss business with this strange young man without the distraction of the woman's incredible physical magnetism.

"Such an amount would be of interest to any businessman. As a member of the clergy I cannot say that it makes much difference to me. The opportunity for funded research in my area of specialty, however, is quite compelling. As you might imagine, I have many questions— the reason for your interest, the source of your funds, the reason for seeking me out, and so forth. You must realize I have a great responsibility in protecting the image of the Church in all my dealings through the Chalice Corporation. Though it is an entity completely separate from the Church, the connections are obvious and the potential for embarrassment significant."

"That is well understood, Father Quinn," the woman rejoined the conversation. You will find no other organization on earth more dedicated to keeping a low profile than ours. We have been around for a very long time and have maintained our obscurity from the public eye very effectively."

"That is certainly so, Maggy. May I call you, Em? I find your given name, pardon my bluntness— I find your given name at odds with your image and I put a great deal of personal store in such things."

"As you wish, Father. I put no store whatever in the name I offer to the public. It is only a convenience."

"Fine, Em. For convenience sake, you may call me Ryan, except in the presence of others, when I will expect you to observe the formality of my clerical identification."

"Fine, Father Quinn. I take it from this exchange of name protocol that we will be discussing these matters further."

"I would be a fool, and a disinterested academician, were I to dismiss such an offer out of hand."

"Very good, then, Ryan. We will meet again very soon. May we call on you at your corporate headquarters in the City?"

"Yes, of course." He felt a strange tingle to hear her use his given name with such familiar ease. "Do you know how to reach me?"

"Yes."

"Em and the young man rose, and without ceremony, turned and left. Ryan could not draw his eyes from her retreating image as the two moved toward the house. They seemed almost to float above the close-cropped grass. He sat, silent for a long time, before heading in that direction. When he got there he found a nervous Augustus puttering with some baked goods and a teapot.

"What sort of car were they driving, Augustus?"

"I don't know, Father. They simply appeared at the door and knocked. I never heard a car on the drive. Perhaps they walked in from the main road."

"Perhaps, Augustus. Will you be serving tea? Those baked goods look delicious." Suddenly Ryan was ravenous.

"If you wish, Father."

Chapter Five

Reverend Ryan Quinn, Society of Jesus, sat at a small desk in a tiny room reading from a slim, leather-bound book. The austere room included few furnishings. There was a wooden bed, the chair on which he sat, and a small dresser with wooden drawer pulls. Above the desk was a portrait of Christ wearing a crown of thorns, a look of anguish on His face, and streams of blood running from the thorns that had punctured His forehead. The bed had been neatly made with a smooth coverlet of unbleached muslin. On the wall above the narrow bed was an ebony crucifix. A carved, ivory image of Christ hung from it. No other artwork or decoration conflicted with the monastic simplicity of the chamber.

Ryan sat at the desk, his Breviary in hand, reading his Daily Office, the obligation of all Catholic priests as tangible demonstration of compliance with St. Paul's command to "pray without ceasing." Ryan was not alone among Catholic clergy in finding the practice a nuisance. But perhaps that was St. Paul's intent. Ryan doubted that Muslims enjoyed constantly bumping their heads on the floor. What's the good of doing things for your salvation and the good of the world if it's all fun and games? It is basic to Catholicism, and to many other orthodoxies, that you must suffer to achieve brownie points in Heaven. Gym teachers say, "no pain, no gain." Whether in a gym or a cathedral, human rituals vary only slightly.

Ryan allowed himself one of his usual bits of aesthetic privilege as far as his Daily Office was concerned— nothing irreverent, but his personal breviary was a rare volume written in Latin, printed in Spain in 1806. It was a handsome little book, its red Moroccan binding stamped with gold leaf scrollwork around its edges. It was elegant, unique, and every bit as liturgically valid as any cheap version run off a high speed, Heidelberg press in Hoboken. In brown ink, in a precise hand, the flyleaf testified to the identity of its previous owner— Monsignor Obispo D. D. Andres de Torres. The Monsignor had lived in Barcelona in the late Nineteenth Century. As he handled the volume, Ryan conjured up a mental image of the long dead prelate reading his Daily Office, strolling past the construction site of Antoni Gaudí's just begun Sagrada Familia Cathedral. Over a hundred years later, Ryan had repeated the Monsignor's imagined stroll in Barcelona. The cathedral was still under construction. It reminded him of the temporal fragility of humanity. Stonework takes a long time to complete but follows the dictates of a far more lenient master as it faces the passage of time.

Ryan found the idea comforting. Even his modest contributions to the storehouse of human knowledge would live on long after he ceased to breathe. Like his Spanish breviary, he thought of his ancient coins as time travelers. Unlike the book, it was not so much the anonymous hands that had held the coins that captured his imagination. Rather, it was the concept of their temporal durability. One of his favorites bore a profile of the goddess Athena in beautiful bas-relief. There was a slight smirk about her lips. It gave her an enigmatic Mona Lisa expression. But what did she find humorous? Time, he decided. She had been smiling like that for almost three thousand years. She was smiling as they assassinated Julius Caesar, then as Christ was nailed to the cross. She smiled as Christians were devoured by lions for the pleasure of Roman spectators. Did she hide sometimes in the money pouches of merchants? Or did she drop out of sight for a long time, smiling to herself in the stygian prison of an earthen jar, buried for safekeeping beneath the soil of a Greek hillside? Wherever she was, she lay smiling. She smiled as they assassinated Archduke Ferdinand to set off World War One. She smiled as Hitler rose to power and slaughtered millions. She smiled even as the United States dropped atomic bombs on Hiroshima and Nagasaki. She lay smiling in Ryan's coin drawer during the birth of his son, then the suicide of his wife, and finally his rise to curiously anonymous power as head of the Chalice Corporation, the openly double life of both poverty-sworn Jesuit and wealthy ecclesiastical archaeologist. What might he do that would wipe the smile from her lips? Nothing. She would smile at his sins and his good works with equal mirth. She would smile at his death and hopefully at his spiritual rise to Heaven and eternal reward. Ryan, himself, smiled at the thought. He was uncertain of his ability to earn the reward of Heaven. Temptations were many and he was notoriously subject to vanities and secretly, to the yearnings of the flesh.

Thought of the latter brought the woman, Em, to mind. He set down his breviary and let his mind's eye scan her loveliness for a moment. With a shake of his head to rid himself of the image, he picked up the breviary again and proceeded to safer thoughts.

The room in which Ryan sat was only a short bus ride from a structure similar in many respects to the Sagrada Familia Cathedral in Barcelona. Construction began on the Cathedral of St. John the Divine on 110th Street on New York's West Side in 1892. It, too, was still not finished after more than a century. Few people are aware of the cathedral and rarely give American landmarks the same historical reverence they willingly lavish upon similar European structures.

Ryan visited St. John's quite often. It was not Roman Catholic but he cared little about that. Not only was the cathedral a magnificent edifice, but he had a special interest in what he liked to think of as his personal places, rarely noticed spots right in plain sight. Within the cathedral there was a small baptistry with an ornately carved font at its center. The room reminded Ryan of a limestone cavern with a puddle of holy water at its center. The ancient Maya of Central America would collect "virgin water" in ceremonial pots placed to catch water that dripped from cave ceilings. They also tore out the beating hearts of sacrificial victims in the same chambers. Ryan thought whimsically of the possibilities of such ceremonies in the center of Manhattan. No pain, no gain.

The small, monkish cubicle where Ryan now sat, was the modest accommodation provided him by the Jesuit Community when he tended to his charitable duties with old and sickly priests. The building was a multi-story structure located almost directly behind Carnegie Hall on 56th Street in Manhattan. Nothing at the front door identified it as belonging to Jesuits. Ryan loved the location. It was probably his imagination but he thought he once heard Luciano Pavarotti hit a high note right through the walls from across the street. Almost better, because it was not a matter of imagination, he found it convenient to walk the half block or so around the corner to get a cup of coffee and a pastry at the Russian Tea Room— advertised, tongue-in-cheek, as being, "Slightly to the Left of Carnegie Hall." The manager was a former student of his at Fordham College. He had taught him ancient Greek. Now, as manager of the famous dining spot, the student taught the master the value of knowing the right person in the right place. Regardless of your financial means, free coffee and cake at one of New York's most fashionable venues was a perk beyond measuring.

Ryan's taste for this neighborhood was not limited to his predilection for tasty treats. Almost across the street from Carnegie Hall was one of the finest coin dealers in the United States, Stack's Rare Coins. His father, though of modest means, had taken him there when just a young boy. It was in that elegant shop that he had first seen his goddess, Athena, smiling at him from the obverse face of a silver tetradrachma. It had been minted in Athens 450 years before the birth of Christ. It was expensive for a child but within Ryan's hopes of acquiring. After working odd jobs for a year and saving carefully, he had visited Stacks again with his father. This time they left the shop with his goddess in a cellophane envelope, then wrapped in a handkerchief that he clutched in his fist lest she somehow escape. She had been with him ever since. Now he sat just a block from the place where he had first met her. As far as he could tell, the shop looked just as it had when he was a child— a magical place, he thought, and went back to his breviary.

There was a gentle knock on the door. Ryan put down his breviary, rose, and crossed the small room to the door.

"Yes?" he said, and opened it.

There stood Damien, one of the community brothers, a concerned look on his face.

"You have a <u>very</u> important visitor downstairs, Father. He is from Rome, but came unannounced. He didn't tell me his name but I think I recognized him— Archbishop Pietro Gandolfo."

"The Papal Nuncio?"

"I'm not sure, Father. He didn't seem anxious to identify himself." Brother Damien was visibly shaken.

"Tell him I'll be right down."

"Of course, Father." Damien left, a nervous wobble to his gait, as he made his way down the narrow hall to the tiny elevator. They were on the sixth floor.

There was no mirror in Ryan's room but he did his best to straighten his cassock and donned the traditional Jesuit crucifix, which he tucked into his cincture. Satisfied that he was neat, if not elegant, he went out into the hall, headed for the reception room on the ground floor.

Chapter Six

Paul Quinn was Ryan's son both in appearance and temperament. He shared, not only his father's shock of raven hair and good looks, but also his keen mind and taste for elegance. Unlike his father, he was in no way constrained by vows of poverty or obedience— and certainly not by any rule that might put restraints on his exercise of self-indulgence, particularly those related to chastity. He was not wanton— simply smart, happy to be alive, and anxious to sample everything wealth and good looks had to offer.

Nepotism is an age-old rule of life on Planet Earth. Paul was not yet CEO of the Chalice Corporation but expected that someday he would be. For the time being, he received a generous stipend while he completed his doctorate in Middle Eastern studies at Columbia University. His father had been a star student of Moses Hadas, the classics scholar. Hadas had actually chaired Ryan's interdisciplinary, doctoral committee. Though Paul studied under a less stellar scholar than his father, he had already impressed the archaeological community with several published papers. Wealth and position had, of course, played a part. One does not generally receive a welcome in the academic community before receiving one's doctorate, but then, there was hardly a Middle Eastern scholar around the globe who was not receiving some financial support from Chalice. It was not that Paul's work was either shallow or shoddy. He simply received attention while others might stand in line— perhaps forever. In that regard, he liked to recall an anecdote about the renowned Professor Moses Hadas. Like many academic icons, Hadas often received treatises from young scholars hoping for a kind word they might add to their résumés. From his professorial bully pulpit he would reply with gentle disdain. On one occasion, upon receiving a document in the mail, he responded, "Thank you for sending me your manuscript. I'll waste no time reading it." The recipient of the response puzzled for some time as to its meaning but finally got the point when he heard no more from the learned gentleman.

The Chalice Corporation received funds from various sources. Its business was ecclesiastical archaeology, hardly a crowded field, nor one that might be considered a probable source of great wealth. Ryan, more perspicacious than most, had long ago recognized the lucrative business possibilities should one manage to tap the coffers of the world's religions. The wealth of the Roman Catholic Church was legendary. But it was just one of many such fabulously wealthy institutions. Rome simply got better press— or worse, depending on how one looked at it. Many religious institutions are less tight-fisted than the Vatican. A case in question is the Church of Jesus Christ of Latter-day Saints— the Mormons. Few realize the tremendous wealth of the Mormon Church, nor would suspect that it might be interested in funding archaeological research. The Chalice Corporation understood fully and had established a branch office in Salt Lake City. The Mormons have been subjected to decades of persecution by other Christian sects. The Book of Mormon has been considered by many of them to be heretical, the product of an hallucinatory charlatan from upstate New York. Indeed, the history of the Mormon Church does test credibility, but what orthodoxy doesn't? "Faith," is a password that opens doors to virtually all beliefs, including those that obviously defy reason.

The Mormons had poured millions into the coffers of the Chalice Corporation. They wished to maintain anonymity while they funded archaeological research in Central America. They hoped to uncover evidence among the ruins of the ancient Maya that Christ had visited America. If they found proof of it but had conducted their own fieldwork, their findings would be suspect. They desperately wanted to establish credibility with the other Christian orthodoxies. The Chalice Corporation managed the research money and, after extracting a sizeable fee, distributed the remainder to reputable archaeologists. Results would be untainted by suspicion of bias. At the moment, for example, excavations at El Caracol in Belize, were ongoing with quiet oversight by Chalice under the direction of a brother and sister team of archaeologists from a university in Florida— neither of them Mormons. This brother and sister team was not the only academic operation toiling in the jungles of Central America with Mormon funds.

The Chalice Corporation was a business, not a theosophical society. In its function as a business, its founder and staff were not bound by any specific orthodoxy. Like legal counsels, who proudly proclaim their obligation to work for clients without judging guilt or innocence, Chalice operatives limited themselves to performing their assigned academic and managerial tasks without prejudice. The company's logo was not the traditional Christian symbol it was thought to be. It was not the cup supposedly used by Christ at the Last Supper. It was a Chalice yet to be unearthed, whose existence was alluded to in an ancient papyrus read in its original by the Reverend Habib Colophon, S.J., close friend and mentor of Ryan Quinn. Quinn, in turn, had conveyed his belief in its existence to a few trusted corporation officers. Should Paul achieve his academic credentials, and a few more years of wisdom, he would be included among those privy to the significance of the chalice. Until then, like everyone else, he would simply believe the corporation's chalice was the famous Holy Grail of Christian lore and Arthurian legend.

Paul always dressed to suit whatever the occasion demanded. When possible, he chose to wear black— Armani, or such, with a white turtleneck. Those who knew both father and son suspected he was trying to assume his father's clerical gravitas without going through the ordeal of ordination. He would have dismissed that allegation but had to admit his father cut an impressive figure. He could do worse.

Now he sat, priest-like, his hands folded in front of him on a stone table, as though in prayer. The table was a massive slab of labradorite. It grew iridescent where sunlight from the huge, panoramic window fell upon it. A kaleidoscope of colors, mostly blues and violets, shot to its surface from the cleavage planes within. Seven hand-tooled, leather chairs sat around the table, unoccupied. The eighth, at the table's head, held the lonely figure of Paul Quinn.

It was a solemn sight, the empty room, the single, silent figure, and the incredible view of the East River through the panoramic window on one side. This was the penthouse apartment at Nyxos World Tower near the United Nations Building. It had several bedrooms and baths, but also a reception area near the elevator and some smaller meeting rooms. It was the New York headquarters of Ryan's corporation. Paul lived here but also kept a small apartment near Columbia University, convenient when attending classes. Except for him, the apartment at Nyxos World Tower was mostly empty at night. Just before dawn, a Jesuit appeared each day from the elevator and quietly went to take his place in the combination library and small artifact museum. There, James McAndrew, S.J. would toil all day, pouring over fragile manuscripts, making endless notes by hand, and occasionally using whatever bits of modern technology were readily available to him— a computer, a scanner, a printer, an ultraviolet lamp, and a few other items that looked more inspired by Archimedes than Bill Gates— a brass microscope, an ink well and sharpened quill, a pair of ornate tweezers, and a brass loupe. There was also an assortment of corked vials that contained oils, alcohol, glues, glazes, and paints — the tools of a museum conservator. The quiet was usually so profound that the slight buzz of the UV lamp sounded like a roar when he switched it on to examine a document.

The silence was usually broken at precisely eight AM. The elevator door would open and out would step Megyn Corbet, the slim, blond, Chalice Corporation receptionist. In the library, Father McAndrew was invariably startled by the sound despite its regular, daily occurrence.

On Megyn's desk, opposite the elevator, the phone was set to blink rather than ring. Monastic solitude was a mystique Ryan sought to create in this temple to antiquity, improbably set atop one of Manhattan's most elegant structures. Her desk had been carved from a single, huge, walnut burl. Hand rubbed and lacquered, it glowed as though from its own inner warmth. Above and behind Megyn's desk, in bas-relief, was the single, silver-leafed word, "Chalice," hand carved in a font known as Herculanum. The font, designed by Swiss-born typographer, Adrian Frutiger, was modern in its simplicity but spoke eloquently of classicism, as though ancient in mood but devised for contemporary eyes.

Megyn Corbet would capture attention amidst a crowd of super models. But like very few such beauties, she was more interested in intellectual pursuits than Klieg lights and Panavision cameras. She was a post-graduate student in archaeology at the City University of New York. It was free, the graduate center was in mid-town Manhattan on Fifth Avenue, and it was convenient to the "Met," the Metropolitan Museum of Art, where she was currently working with authorities regarding her work on the burial portraits unearthed near the Oasis of Fayoum, southwest of Cairo. Her life was neat and ascetic. She had her research and one extravagance, a one room, below-street-level, brownstone apartment on East 65th Street.

Ryan had run into her by chance at the Met. They were both attending a lecture on Coptic iconography. The audience was understandably small and Ryan, never one to dismiss a beautiful face, introduced himself. He was surprised and pleased to learn she had heard of him. One thing led to another and he managed to work two miracles in her life. He engineered a grant from the Brooklyn Museum to fund her field studies. He was personally connected with the heirs of Charles Edwin Wilbour, an American Egyptologist who had donated generously to that institution.

The second thing he did was offer her a low ranking, but well paid position as the receptionist at Chalice. The job was beneath her talents and education, but the salary made her little apartment possible and the connection to Chalice provided her the opportunity to use the library, it's equipment, and to make first-hand contacts with influential people associated with her interests. It was a plum of the first order. Her duties were light, to say the least, and she was rarely denied the temporary absences required by her academic schedule. She was a stunning, brilliant, industrious addition to the Chalice staff, and a very "happy camper." To himself, Ryan twisted an old joke to fit the circumstance. "Ugly girls go to Heaven. Beautiful girls go wherever they want."

Father McAndrew was a find of equal delight to Ryan. If Megyn was a blond goddess, he was her distorted, funhouse reflection. He was short and solid, with a face that bore the pits of childhood chickenpox. He was homosexual but not a twittering queen. He had run from his sexuality into academe and the Jesuits. He did not prey upon young boys and Jesuit novitiates. He was a good man, dedicated to God and his priestly vocation. If heterosexual priests could practice chastity, no reason a homosexual could not. Few people realized that, and concluded that all homosexual priests were child molesters. Bigotry finds its own answers to most everything.

Indeed, Father McAndrew was one of Ryan's rare and valuable finds. He was a double-edged sword in Chalice's arsenal. He was an art conservator of rare ability and a linguist capable of reading ancient texts in a variety of languages. In other words, he could handle and repair ancient manuscripts and read them in their original toungues, whether Greek, Hebrew, Sanskrit or Coptic Egyptian, to name just a few. His specialty was the repair, handling and reading of ancient papyri. He got little public recognition for his talents, but National Geographic always knew where to look for help. With no complaint from him, they invariably left his name out of the story when writing of "their work" at such sites as Agua Azul in Guatemala or Khirbet Qumran near the Dead Sea. He lived at Fordham University in the Bronx. It was a long trip to Nyxos Tower but allowed him time to perform his priestly duty of reading his Daily Office. On rare occasions, he spent time in one of several small offices provided for him in the Metropolitan Museum of Art and American Museum of Natural History. He had been offered something far grander but academic flamboyance was not his style. He wanted his solitude, his library, his conservator tools, and privacy to nurture his relationship with God. Chalice and the Good Lord had provided him with all of that. Providence had even given him the frequent company of lovely Megyn Corbet, sweet, gentle, and delicious to observe, without the nervous urgency he might have felt had he not been homosexual. He liked her a lot and she returned his affection. They were good friends.

When Chalice was entertaining clients, Headquarters could become far less than peaceful. The main conference room might well host a clutter of people and lecture easels. The massive stone table would invariably be strewn with documents of all sorts. Visitors, bold in the knowledge that they were paying dearly for the privilege, often stalked about, peering at the corporation artwork, even entering the library and other rooms without knocking. The permanent art display was spectacular. They had every reason to stare in awe. The pieces were subtly religious but obviously selected more for their historical than religious significance. They were extraordinarily valuable but most visitors held the purse strings to fortunes just as impressive, so there was little worry regarding mysterious disappearances. They could buy what they wanted. The collection, though religious in theme, would be offensive to no specific orthodoxy. It included Roman, Coptic, Greek, and Judaic items, including paintings on wood, cloth, gold-leafed, wall icons, and sculptures— the latter usually protected by freestanding, or wall-mounted, glass cases. It was, in essence, a small, working museum with an even smaller academic staff of well funded, highly educated, frequently published scholars and apprentices, relaxed in the knowledge that they were the best and need not compete for honors or grants. Objective research was both the goal and the reward. Ryan was the shepherd but these were not sheep.

† † †

There were no visitors today. Chalice Headquarters was very quiet. McAndrew was in his library. Megyn was in there with him pursuing some thread she'd uncovered in one of his papyri regarding Fayoum burial rituals. She had a wireless, encrypted connection to the front desk phone, so she could respond to its flashing signal should the need arise.

Paul, alone in the main conference room, was thinking about his uncle Spencer. He had hardly known him but knew he had been deeply treasured by his father. He felt guilty as the thought crossed his mind that Spencer's death would place a greater burden on him. Ryan shared a great deal with Spencer in spite of his unspectacular achievements. After a brilliant start he had been caught up in some child molesting scandal from which he had never recovered. The young woman had not really been a child. In some countries his transgression would have been considered trivial, if a moral transgression at all. But in matters related to sex, Paul believed US law to be held hostage by an undeserved reverence for its Puritan origins. Paul was certain that Ryan would disagree strongly. His father was a lusty male but believed that laws regarding morality descended from the hand of God, interpreted for mankind by Holy Mother, the Church. He might sin but he did not believe he could be relieved of guilt for that sin simply by arguing against the basic principle that labeled it as such.

So much for Spencer, his child-molesting uncle, and Ryan, his ordained priest/father. His immediate problem was more a matter of psychiatry than theology. With Spencer gone he was faced with taking on the role of being his father's best friend. No problem if Dad was an Irish cop on the NYC police force. But in this case, Dad was the super-achiever/priest/ archaeologist/linguist/corporation genius who operated around the world with the ease that Aristotle Onassis managed shipping schedules. He didn't mind being Ryan's best friend. Actually he liked the idea but he was not sure he could live up to the task. Dad was perfect. How could he be best friend to a perfect human being? Immediately, the analogy of a dog popped into his head— "man's best friend." Was that to be his role— perfect pooch to the perfect man? Paul gave a little bark in the silent room and then laughed. The sound bounced off the slab of labradorite and against the panoramic window. Paul put his head in his hands. After a while he sat up. He would go to the library and try to cop a look at Megyn's tits. Somehow, he'd manage to cope with wealth and position. But then he thought of his uncle's strange death again. It had baffled the police in the small town. Ryan had pulled some strings, and New York City police became involved. There had been a bit of a turf battle at first but the details of the crime scene were so bizarre the town police had given in with a minimum of grumbling. In the end, "New York's Finest" might well have spared themselves the trip. There seemed to be no clues and certainly no indication as to the motive for what appeared to be a strange, ritual killing. There were signs the apartment had been searched but no fingerprints, no sign that anyone but Spencer had walked on the carpet, and nothing missing. After a few days they let the landlady in, to clean the apartment, and they left. Ryan would have someone pick up Spencer's books, coins and art. His clothes would go to Catholic Charities.

Chapter Seven

As Ryan headed for the ground floor, the little elevator provided hardly enough room for him to adjust his cincture. New York City law demanded that buildings install an elevator if they were more than a certain number of stories. Grumbling landlords installed the cheapest, smallest lifts they could find. Like most Jesuit real estate, this building had been a gift. As it turned out, the elevator was a "godsend." The Jesuits had dedicated the building to the care of aged and sick priests. A climb of six or seven stories would have made it a holy death sentence.

Not only tiny, the elevator moved at an almost imperceptible rate. With a lurch, the tiny cubicle came to a stop and the door opened with grinding, arthritic slowness. Ryan stepped out to greet his prestigious visitor. He recognized him at once. It was, indeed, Archbishop Pietro Gandolfo— Papal Nuncio to His Holiness, the Pope. But he was wearing regular street clothes— not even neat ones.

A disheveled Nuncio? This had to be good, thought Ryan. He bowed slightly, took the man's hand and kissed his ring. "Your Eminence."

"Please. No formalities, Father Quinn." He spoke with an Italian accent. "Are you wearing street clothes beneath your cassock?"

"Yes I am, Your Eminence."

"Please, then— remove your cassock. We will walk outside. I wish to talk to you."

Ryan undid his cincture, removed his crucifix, then his cassock. He wrapped the crucifix in the cassock and placed the bundle on a chair near the entrance. Though he was wearing a shirt and trousers, he felt naked without at least a tie. But who argues with a papal nuncio?

The archbishop opened the door for Ryan, an unusual reverse of protocol. The two went out the front door onto the sidewalk and headed west. Gandolfo was silent. He had a limp that slowed him but did not seem to cause him any pain. At the corner, they turned north to Fifty-Seventh Street, then east toward Fifth Avenue. The number of pedestrians increased as they joined the foot traffic on Fifty-Seventh Street. New York pedestrian traffic unconsciously follows automobile rules. The flow stays to the right. Walking east put Ryan and the archbishop close to the store windows.

Gandolfo, more at ease within the moving crowd, gathered his words carefully. "I will get right to the point, Ryan. The Holy Father has sent me on a mission to secure the services of the Chalice Corporation."

Ryan was pleased but somewhat confused. "In what capacity, your Eminence?"

"Please use the English version of my given name— Peter." It was a command, not a friendly suggestion.

"In what capacity?" Ryan repeated the question.

"Archaeological field work and whatever academic investigations may be prompted by any discoveries you make."

"But, Peter," the use of the archbishop's first name, especially in English, made Ryan very uncomfortable, "the Church has a virtual army of highly qualified archaeologists. It has the libraries, the linguists, everything."

"Yes. It has everything but the one thing that is of utmost importance."

"Ryan raised an inquisitive eyebrow. "And that is. . .?"

"Anonymity."

Ryan was not surprised by the answer. It was the bread and butter of the Chalice Corporation— research conducted without the possible accusation of a vested interest in its findings. But in this case it made no sense. The Catholic Church had its supporters and its enemies. Nothing new was likely to swell the ranks of either.

Gandolfo continued, "There are things the Church has kept close over the centuries. It has taken seriously its role as shepherd, tending the Lord's flock of innocent sheep."

Ryan did not like the sound of this. He felt he was about to be made party to something in which he'd rather not be involved. He knew Church history. The people were not always made aware of the entire truth. Mostly he agreed with the Church's motives. Cremation had been forbidden, for example, not on theological grounds but because it had become a source of confusion to the uneducated masses. How could you arise on the last day if you were nothing but ashes? The Church might have made an effort to explain that resurrection was a matter of the spirit, not the body, and that the body could easily be reconstituted by the Almighty, but rather than risk the loss of followers over such a silly controversy, it simply forbade cremation.

It was something similar when it came to enforcing celibacy on the clergy. The Church loved to harp on issues related to human appetites. Sex was a favorite. Roman Catholic clergy were allowed to marry at one time, and among some eastern sects recognized by Rome, they still were. As a practical matter, Rome found it convenient to create a model in which its clergy would not be torn between their loyalties to the Church and to demanding women and their children. Nuns wore wedding rings. They were married to the spirit of Jesus. That was easily settled. As to priests— they were told to channel their hormone-fired wretchedness into hard work— and to take cold showers. The arrangement had many drawbacks but for the most part it worked.

Although Pietro Gandolfo's efforts at playing undercover agent were rather amateurish, Ryan felt that this was something quite different. And since the position of Papal Nuncio was without equal in Rome's political structure, Ryan reasoned that his secretive mission involved a matter extreme importance— to the Church and perhaps to its billion followers, or even to the world in general.

"I'm not at liberty to provide you with any details, Father Ryan. In fact, if things turn out as hoped, you may never know the full extent of the situation. You will be expected to conduct your research with no pre-conceived conclusion. In the process, you will undoubtedly encounter others working along similar lines of inquiry. If they uncover evidence that seems to be of cataclysmic significance, you will quite reasonably recognize it at once and it will be your responsibility to communicate with us at once so we can deal with it. Should you be the one to make such a find, we will expect you to ask us for further instructions."

"This is all very mysterious, your Emin... er, Peter." Ryan was extremely uncomfortable with this amateur gumshoe routine. He liked established protocol. It gave you a handle to maintain balance in an unstable situation.

"The mystery is quite necessary. In this case, open inquiry could prove disastrous. The Holy Father feels very strongly about this."

"Apparently. May I ask what we are expected to do and how we are to maintain contact with you?"

"There will be no immediate contact. We will be in touch. You will proceed as though involved in an independent, self-funded project. You will draw upon an account opened in your name at the El Azmi Bank in Alexandria."

"I take it, then, we will be working in Egypt."

"Largely, but wherever the trail leads you. I would actually suggest an initial visit by one of your people to France."

Despite his misgivings, Ryan was growing increasingly fascinated by the sketchy outline of this project.

"May I ask the size of the deposit at El Azmi Bank?"

"Fifty million US dollars as a start. More if it becomes necessary."

Ryan's stomach gave a twitch. It was no more than a few days since a similar amount had been mentioned under equally mysterious circumstances.

"You mention France. Anything particular in France?"

"The cathedral at Autun."

"Are we expected to conduct an archaeological excavation on consecrated ground in France? It's possible but the red tape would be extraordinary."

"No. The visit to Autun would be more in the way of an orientation exercise. The actual field work will likely be in the Egyptian Middle Kingdom, half way between Cairo and Luxor."

Now, Ryan's stomach really gave a tug.

"Near El Minya?"

"You know the area, Ryan?"

"Of course. I have worked in the area and an assistant at Chalice is just putting finishing touches on her doctoral dissertation about burial rituals near Lake Fayoum."

"About three days by camel from El Minya."

"You, too? I didn't think there were any beside myself who chose that mode of travel unless forced to."

"We are two of a dying breed, Ryan. Comfort denies us many unexpected rewards. I need not tell you the archaeological information one can absorb moving slowly across the desert, your eyes ten feet above the sand."

"Exactly! You're an Egyptologist, then... er, Peter?"

"Once— before I was called to Rome to serve the Holy Father, not the present one. I had published nothing. You will not find my name in the literature. I was on a mission similar to the one we've been discussing and found nothing of importance. The Holy Father was content with that. I hope you will be as fortunate."

As the two priests wandered back to the Jesuit house, they grew comfortable with one another— just two men in white shirts and black pants who might, ironically, be discussing the hopes and dreams of a billion people— if there was anything to this thing at all. The immensity of the possibilities was beyond Ryan's ability to put into perspective, particularly given the scant information provided.

Moments after they re-entered the building they'd left earlier, the older man departed with as little fanfare as he had when he arrived— just a final question over his shoulder.

"What do you know about angels, Ryan?"

"Not much. Do you want me to take a closer look?"

"Might be a good idea." And then he was gone, limping down the sidewalk, headed again for Fifth Avenue.

Chapter Eight

Ryan, back in the little room, sat and tried to gather his thoughts— interest from two different sources attached to a total of 100 million dollars with the promise of more. The research possibilities were marvelous and the financial aspects beyond immediate calculation. One thing was certain— something very special was happening on the Nile. Ryan needed some exercise to clear his head. It was only about 20 blocks from the Jesuit house to Nyxos World Tower.

Walking in New York is one of the great experiences in life— miles of merchandise displayed with taste and imagination in a parade of store windows that never seems to end, and the New Yorker's favorite pastime, checking out one's own fleeting reflection. Pedestrians, absorbed in the merchandise displays and their own images, course past you if you slow for any reason. You are invisible except for the occasional moment when one automaton collides with another. Little or nothing is said— perhaps an irritated glance but nothing more. The people of New York live in one another's faces but see no one unless there is a passing flash of extraordinary feminine or masculine beauty. Then there might be a sudden head swivel to evaluate the vision. That's when most of the collisions occur.

Ryan walked over to Fifth Avenue. He wanted to pass St. Patrick's Cathedral. He decided to drop in for a moment. He needed a massive symbol of Roman Catholic stability. Pedestrian traffic into and out of St. Patrick's is not usually dense but is constant.

Inside, the bustle of the City suddenly evaporates and gives way to the echo of the cathedral's immense interior— a shuffle of feet, the squeak of a rubber heel, the bang of a kneeling bench dropped into place— and the murmur of people praying quietly, but still audibly. Like people who call radio stations and ask the host, "Can you hear me?," silent prayer is rarely silent. The suppliant often seems to need reassurance that his, or her, words will be heard by the Almighty.

The aroma of incense is always in the air— that, and the smell of hot wax. Ryan anointed himself with water from the font near the door, then walked more than two hundred feet down the right aisle toward the main altar, passing thousands of melting candles that were flickering in front of side altars. The scent of hot wax and recently burnt incense comforted him. This was home— the home he had chosen during a time of turmoil in his life. He could be at home in these familiar surroundings wherever his travels might take him on the planet. The Catholic Church was everywhere.

He took a seat near the center aisle and let his eyes drift up to the vault, a hundred feet above. He always looked there. It pleased him for some reason to see the small cluster of galeros, hanging upside down from the ceiling— the ceremonial hats of pastm New York bishops who slept, now, in the crypt below the main altar.

Ryan thanked God for the peace this place brought him and left through the south side door, then walked over to First Avenue, and on south to Nyxos World Tower.

He thought about impending responsibilities and the structure of the Chalice Corporation. Everything was in place and worked smoothly but that fact never completely satisfied Ryan. How do you keep your hands off when you are a hands-on person?

Each Chalice branch office maintained a small staff to take care of necessary details— a receptionist, an office manager, and an accountant. All were usually trained, as well, in either archaeology or ecclesiastical history. Depending on the location, the staff might include someone trained in public relations or communications, and versed in local politics. Ryan wasn't stingy. He simply loved to create efficient systems. A multidisciplinary staff was the most efficient business model in his opinion. He had another advantage most businesses don't have. Archaeologists, artists, and historians are like actors. They are in love with their professions. They will support themselves, working "day jobs" if they can just have a chance to work, even part time, at their true professions.

Most Chalice offices were near universities. Doctoral candidates, even post-docs, were always ready and willing to "run around in the hot sun for a dollar a day," as the saying went. Ryan didn't have steady work for most of them but he did pay well when there was work to be done— definitely, no dollar a day. And there was travel. Rarely did a Chalice project require research at the local library. Chalice people might run into one another at some of the most interesting places on earth. While pampered slugs lounged by pools at fashionable resorts around the world, they were likely to rub elbows with working Chalice people at the Hacienda Uxmal, walking distance to the Pyramid of the Magician in Mexico, at the Oberoi Mena House, comfortably in the shadow of the Egyptian Pyramids, or at the Thiripyitsaya Resort in Burma, now, Myanmar, just beyond the ancient wall that circles the plains of Bagan and the temples that still bear the battle scars of Genghis Khan's attacks.

All this was churning about in Ryan's head as he walked south. He arrived at his destination sooner than he'd hoped. His mind was still in turmoil.

The elevator to the penthouse was fast and silent. When he got out, Megyn was not there— just the silver-leafed Chalice Corporation logo hovering above her empty desk. He was calm now, a bit sweaty from the walk, but composed. He went to the library. There they all stood, huddled together— Paul, Megyn, and Father McAndrew. Something unusual had happened. They all turned to him.

"Well? You all look as though you've seen a squadron of ghosts. What's going on?"

Father McAndrew answered. "We had several very unusual visitors today, Father."

"Yes? Go on."

Paul took over. "There was a gentleman— a priest, I think— but in street clothes. He had a limp and an Italian accent."

"I think I know who it was but it seems impossible," Father McAndrew added, somewhat befuddled.

"I think you may be right, Father, but we'll go into that later. Who was the other visitor?"

"Not visitor," said Megyn. "Visitors. It was a couple. They were here much earlier. You had said you didn't want me to contact you."

"That's right, Megyn." *And a good thing,* he added to himself. *If the couple were the two he suspected, he would have had his hands full— two Sarafians and the Archbishop at the same time— like backstage at the Jerry Springer show.*

"They seemed disappointed not to find you and asked where you could be reached. I said it was impossible. They stayed for a bit and looked around but finally left quite suddenly. They left you a note."

It was another of those elegant envelopes sealed with a dollop of blood-colored wax and an impression from a Sasanian seal. Ryan broke the seal and pulled out the now familiar, black-bordered card. No words were wasted.

Fifty million dollars have been deposited at the Bank of Alexandria in your name with your social security number for a password (more later if you are a good boy).

Yours,
Em

Ryan felt his testosterone level surge at the little joke. The most beautiful woman he had ever met had just pulled his chain. His Roman collar seemed too tight. This woman was dangerous.

"Is something wrong, Father?" It was Megyn.

"No. I'm fine. And what had all of you so upset?" He went on hurriedly to cover his momentary loss of composure.

"I can't speak for the others," said Father McAndrew, "but I know I met the Italian gentleman before and his presence here, unannounced, is unimaginable. I would stake my reputation that we just had a visit from Archbishop Pietro Gandolfo."

"The Papal Nuncio? Here?" Ryan was enjoying the priest's astonishment. "I can't imagine."

"But it's true. I'm sure of it."

"And well you may be, Father. I met with him earlier in the afternoon but I had no idea he intended to come down here. Calm yourself. It's good news. We are to take on a project for Rome and it may involve all three of you— and me."

That seemed to calm the waters.

"But what upset you about the couple who dropped in?"

"I can't say." That was Megyn. "The young man was extraordinarily attractive and his stare made me feel totally naked."

All but Father McAndrew enjoyed a fleeting image of Megyn naked. Paul made no effort to dismiss the image until Ryan addressed him. "And the woman, Paul?"

"Extraordinarily beautiful— and the same thing. It was quite an experience. I don't recall being mentally stripped naked in public before."

Ryan felt a flash of jealousy at his young son's experience but quickly drove it from his mind.

"So you all had an unexpected, libidinous interlude right here during working hours? Sorry, Father McAndrew. I wasn't referring to you."

Megyn was blushing. Paul was enjoying the memory, while Ryan tried to hold things together.

"It appears we may be undertaking a project for the Sarafians as well. You did catch their names, I imagine, or were you all too preoccupied, prancing about in your delusional birthday suits? We have some important plans to discuss," he continued in a business-like manner. "Let's meet in the conference room first thing in the morning. In the meanwhile, Megyn, please contact the Met and the Brooklyn Museum to find which of our Mid-East stringers might be available for an extended project. Father McAndrew, please do the same regarding conservators and people you might consider both expert and discrete in matters regarding iconography and ancient documents at the American Museum. Paul, see if you can get our accountant to select someone to handle international matters involving a considerable amount of money. We don't know yet what we're getting into. Talk together and see if you can made up a field team that I can look at during our morning meeting."

The small group snapped out of their confused reverie and focused on what had to be done.

With a broad smile, Ryan added, "See you in the morning. In the meanwhile try to keep your clothes on." Father McAndrew had already scurried off to set about his assignment.

Chapter Nine

Ryan had a busy evening ahead of him. He trusted his small staff to do as he had asked. Things would be in good order for the morning meeting. There were two other large orders on his plate. First, and foremost, was his old friend, Father Colophon— the Reverend Habib Colophon, S.J. He was dying. Not surprising, at this Jesuit home on Fifty-Sixth Street. Old Jesuits came here to pray and move on to their eternal reward in the company of their spiritual brothers.

Father Colophon was half Egyptian and half Russian. He kept his first name but chose a new last name when he entered the Jesuit novitiate some fifty years ago. His real name was virtually unpronounceable for English speakers— Habib Rutschowscaya. He chose the name Colophon as an intellectual joke. A colophon is a statement added to the end of a manuscript. With tongue in cheek, Father Colophon was telling his colleagues— in any argument over the interpretation of an ancient papyrus, his opinion would be "the last word."

Ryan sat by his bed and held his hand. He would be there to hear the old man's confession if he wished. Should he lapse into unconsciousness, or become too weak to respond, Roman Catholic doctrine provides for the forgiveness of all sins without confession, provided an ordained priest is present to administer Extreme Unction, the so-called, "Last Rites." It is the seventh and final sacrament recognized by both the Roman and the Eastern Orthodox Churches. The ritual varies somewhat but in general involves prayers spoken while the organs of the senses are anointed with oil. For Roman Catholics, the oil must have been blessed by a bishop. In the Eastern rite, the ceremony is performed by a group of priests who bless the oil themselves. In the West, the Eastern practice of anointing a male's genitals has been discarded. In neither rite have women ever been, "so blessed."

48

Father Colophon whispered to Ryan, "I wish to confess."

Ryan unfolded his stole, a scarf-like cloth that is the symbol of ordination. He kissed the cross at its midpoint and draped it over his neck. Then he leaned close to hear his friend's confession.

"Bless me father, for I have sinned." The ritual words were little more than a raspy exhalation. "It has been fifteen years since my last good confession."

Ryan drew back in surprise. Fifteen years? This was his friend, his own confessor, his role model for sanctity and dedication to the holy life. He leaned close again and spoke as a priest, "Go on my son."

"Long ago, I joined with others to withhold God's truth from His innocent flock— even from you, my dear friend."

"In what way, my son?"

Father Colophon's words grew so faint that Ryan couldn't make out what he was saying. He leaned close, his ear brushing the old priest's mouth. Instead of words, he felt only a light exhalation from the pale lips— then, no breath at all. He had not completed his confession. Ryan could not give him absolution. By Church tradition, if the sin he was about to confess was "mortal" in nature, his soul would be damned for eternity.

Ryan looked desperately around the room and found what he needed, the crucifix kept in Catholic sick rooms for such occasions. The crucified Christ is actually the lid of a cruciform container. Inside are the items necessary to administer the Sacrament of Extreme Unction— a vial of oil, blessed by a bishop, a vial of holy water, several wads of cotton, a couple of candles, and some matches. The base has a slot near the top into which the crucifix can be inserted so it can stand upright.

Ryan inserted the candles into the holes provided and lighted them. Then he took the vial of blessed oil and soaked one of the cotton balls. In the kit there was even a little scroll of paper with the appropriate ritual prayers. Ryan didn't need it. He knew the ritual.

In a stark room on Fifty-Sixth Street in New York City, Reverend Ryan Quinn, S.J. anointed the eyes, ears, finger tips, nostrils, and lips of the Reverend Habib Colophon, S.J., and sent his soul to Heaven, the nature of his lifelong sin unknown, but forgiven by the grace of God and Holy Mother the Church. Ryan sat for a long time, the aroma of the candles carrying him back to earlier in the day when he had stopped to pray in St. Patrick's Cathedral.

"Good bye, old friend. I'm glad I was here to send you on your way. I'm sure that was no accident. The Lord wished to call you to his bosom regardless of your fifteen year secret, and brought me here to be the instrument of His will."

After a long time, Ryan left the room and found one of the brothers to bathe and clothe his old friend in a shroud for the funeral that would soon follow. Back in his own room, his mind was in turmoil— first the Archbishop's suggestion, almost a warning, that he look into doctrine regarding angels— and now this new mystery, the fifteen year old sin of his friend whom he'd considered a paragon of wisdom and sanctity.

"Fifteen years," he thought. "That was about the time Habib and the Archbishop were excavating Coptic monastery ruins in the Egyptian desert. Ryan tried to put it out of his mind and went downstairs to the building's library. It wasn't a match for his own at Chalice but all he needed was a set of the Catholic Encyclopedia. He was sure they'd have one downstairs.

As the tiny elevator made its painfully slow trip to the main floor, Ryan thought about angels. They were a subject of on going controversy among theologians. They were not human, but not gods. They lived with God but nothing seemed to indicate that God loved them. He reserved that special emotion for His relationship with humans. The very name, "angel," was nothing special. It came from the ancient Greek and simply translates as messenger. One could not help but call up the image of those nameless people on bikes who weave through New York traffic, defying death, to deliver an envelope from someone who might not know their name, to another who wouldn't care to learn it— just a human device to deliver an envelope. Should you love your cell phone? According to liturgical writings, apparently God doesn't care about his angelic cell phones either. Do angels have brains? Do they have emotions? Are they content, or angry? Do they have sex organs? Are they straight, gay, or none of the above? Can they reproduce? Can they be jealous? If one showed up on your doorstep should you be happy, sad, or scared? Why did Archangel Gabriel say to Mary, "Fear not, for thou hast found grace with God."? And what is an archangel, if he, or she, isn't just an angel? *Inquiring people want to know,* Ryan joked to himself. *And what about Lucifer?* He stopped smiling. Lucifer— Latin for "bearer of light." So— a messenger whom nobody understands or loves but carries light for others. In the Garden of Eden, didn't he promise Adam and Eve the knowledge of good and evil? Did he have that power? And what were Adam and Eve before she fed Adam the apple— stupid, sexless, perhaps angel-like creatures? And was it the same warrior angel with a sword that kept them from re-entering the Garden, then went to Mary and said, "Fear not?" Ryan suspected this would not be a comfortable task, this business of looking into the matter of angels. He wished Archbishop Gandolfo had been a bit more specific.

Apparently the matter really got under the skin of a Syrian monk named Dionysius, around the year 500 AD. No one knows where he got his inside information, but he said there are nine ranks of angels, like the military. Angel is the lowest. The second lowest is Archangel. The top banana is a Seraph. The second highest is Cherub. In between there are five ranks that virtually no one ever mentions— Thrones, Dominions, Virtues, Powers, and Principals. Again, Ryan felt his sense of humor get the better of him— *If no one loves an angel, imagine how bad it is to be one nobody even heard of? I suspect Dionysius was nuts.*

The elevator opened and Ryan got out. He was right. The little house library had a Catholic Encyclopedia. He sat down to read. The entry under *angels* in the Catholic Encyclopedia was long and involved with a huge number of footnotes and references. Ryan skimmed it. There seemed to be a great deal of conflicting information, discussion of disagreements that had taken place, and in some cases had endured over the centuries. One thing was certain. The very idea of angels either pleased, frightened, or confused both the lowly and the learned. Being an image person, one thing that caught Ryan's attention was the matter cited in the Old Testament of a personal fight, a brawl, that supposedly took place between Jacob and an angel. A little more research in the small library led to a reproduction of a medieval volume, The Hours of Catherine of Cleves. Plate fifty-five was an "illumination" showing the actual fight, and the angel crying out, "Let me go. Soon it will be daybreak." That sounded more like the frightened cry of a vampire than an angel of God. What next? Apparently this strange episode had caught the attention of various artists over the years. Rembrandt painted his impression of it. So did Paul Gauguin. There were a number of others. In some, the angel is rather effeminate. In others he is heavily muscled, with almost a wrestler's physique. The variety speaks eloquently of the strong effect the reported episode has had on the minds of imaginative people— and their confusion.

The other thing that caught Ryan's attention was the idea of the angel as a meek messenger versus the concept of him as a warrior with sword in hand. Ryan thumbed back and forth among the encyclopedia entries and the few other references he found in the small library. The messenger to Mary who said, "fear not," was an archangel, depicted as frail and bowing before her. The angel who guarded the gate of Eden with a sword is depicted as big and muscular but identified as a Cherub. That didn't make sense. Cherubs are supposed to be little babies with fat cheeks and sweet dispositions, shooting love arrows into horny couples and blowing winds from the four corners of ancient maps.

It reminded Ryan of something that had caught in his mind a number of years ago. Carnegie Hall, on the next block, had undergone both major and minor renovations over the years. In the early seventies, an interior re-do had removed a number of plaster Cherub heads which were put out front on the sidewalk for the trash collectors. A friend had salvaged one and struggled for years to find the appropriate place for it. It's probably still in his basement on Long Island. That memory triggered another in Ryan's fertile brain. A major renovation of Carnegie Hall in 1986 had caused mayhem among aficionados. They insisted the acoustics had been destroyed. Whether or not it had anything to do with the acoustics, an investigation disclosed the fact that there was a huge concrete slab beneath the stage. It was jack hammered into chunks and removed leaving the fussbudgets without substantial grounds for further complaints. There had been rumors of bones and other strange artifacts sticking out of the concrete chunks but the whole business had little chance to develop into news items. The chunks had been quickly spirited away and dispersed to various locations around the country— some said, to the hundreds of Carnegie Libraries that the philanthropist had built all over the United States. Ryan had been in several— one in Las Vegas, New Mexico— not the gambling Mecca in Nevada. This Las Vegas is a strange Victorian town on the edge of the Rockies. On one side are the mountains. From the other side the Great Plains roll on, unobstructed to the horizon. Between the two is Las Vegas, a strange town with three village squares, all pretty much deserted. One has big trees and a bandstand nobody seems to use. The second one has a stone house on one side that looks like a Gorey drawing— haunted for sure. In the middle of the third one is a Carnegie Library, like a miniature Jefferson's Monticello. Are there bones from Carnegie Hall in its basement? It's doubtful anyone has looked. Ryan's mind was wandering.

Besides the matter of conflicting concepts regarding the nature of angels, something else struck a chord in Ryan's brain— the matter of Guardian

Angels. Once again, theologians were at one anothers' throats on the subject, but the consensus seemed to be that there were such entities as Guardian Angels, members of the host of angels who were assigned individually to every human on earth. *That's one hell of a lot of angels!* Ryan smiled at his own poor choice of words, even if only in his head. But something else was in his head, too. As a grammar school student at St. Brendan's, the Dominican nuns had taught them a prayer—

"Angel of God, my Guardian dear, to whom His love commits me here, ever this day be at my side, to light and guard, to rule and guide. Amen."

As the words went through his head, it surprised him how clearly he recalled them. *Put things into a child's head,* he thought, *and they're there forever.* He wondered just how much of the world is either at war or peace because of what some idiot put into a kid's head when he was in school. *Grammar schools are far more dangerous than military boot camps,* he thought. But back to guardian angels— *billions of them on earth? Eight and a half million just in New York City? Did they all get their assignments from God, or angel generals— archangels, or whatever? Did they stick to certain neighborhoods in a high-density place like New York? Were there Manhattan angels and Bronx and Brooklyn angels? In Manhattan were there some that only worked mid-town? And another thing— what if an angel got an assignment he didn't like? Was there an appeals procedure? Could he say, "Look, this guy you gave me is an asshole. I want a new assignment." Or could he simply go over the hill— leave the poor numbskull on his own? Or worse yet, could he just lead his assigned dork into a bad situation— a car accident, undertow at the beach, or into one of the Twin Towers on 9/11?*

Maybe there was something really sinister behind that Biblical reference to Jacob brawling with an angel. What was the angel trying to get Jacob into? Or out of? Jacob was leading a life full of potential problems— two wives and he was sleeping with their maids, too. More potentially homicidal twists to it than an episode of Law and Order.

A fire truck went screaming down Fifty-Seventh Street a block away and jolted Ryan out of his reverie. He had not found his cursory research into angels at all enlightening. It raised more questions than it answered and actually left him feeling a bit queasy— especially since he had become involved in it at the urging of an archbishop straight out of Vatican City. He would have to drop it for now. It was late and they had a big meeting tomorrow at Chalice.

Chapter Ten

After Ryan had left Chalice earlier, Paul and the others went over their assignments to make sure they understood what needed to be done for the next morning's meeting. Paul's task was the simplest. One phone call and he would have a commitment from the primary Chalice accountant to be present in the morning. Paul promised to provide him with the appropriate information from the banks in Egypt. That wasn't hard either. Despite the hour, it would be no problem. With seven hours difference, banks and accounting firms in Cairo would be opening at one AM, New York time. He could have a couple of drinks at the Sherry Netherland and take care of things before his usual bedtime. The tough part would be getting up for the meeting. He was not an early bird.

"I've got my end of things under control, Megyn. I'll have to make some calls at 1 AM. It'll be right after I have a couple of drinks at the Sherry Netherland. If you get your stuff out of the way, come join me. In the meanwhile, I'd be glad to help you get the people at the Brooklyn Museum onto the team for you. It may take some doing. They go to bed with the chickens."

"Thanks Paul. I can handle it. I know all their home phones if they've left for the day. I can work it from my own place if necessary."

"If I can help, let me know."

"Thanks. Why don't you give Father McAndrew a hand?"

"Sure. Need a hand, Father?" Paul understood he'd been brushed off. It wasn't the first time he'd gotten the cold shoulder from Megyn.

"No thank you, Paul." McAndrew was no dope. Not only did he not need any help, but he liked the way Megyn had put Paul away neatly.

✝ ✝ ✝

Things weren't exactly jumping at the Sherry Netherland but Paul didn't expect they would be. The hotel bar was more a quiet watering spot for New York insiders than a pick up spot. Paul didn't get lucky often at the Sherry but when he did, the women were invariably Fifth Avenue slim, cultured, and knew Prada from Banana Republic.

Time had begun to drag so he decided to wake up a few Egyptians even before Ra, the sun god, would be rising along the Nile, setting the Cairo pollution on fire.

"Hello? Dr. Abdul Ohouri? This is Paul Quinn in New York. Yes, from the Chalice Corporation. Yes. Thank you. He's fine. Have you received the deposit from the Vatican? Fine. Fine. And the amount? Yes. Exactly. I'll tell George Stone. He will be pleased. We are meeting in the morning. Yes. It's only midnight here. Yes. I will give everyone your regards. I hope you have a pleasant day. Give my regards to Hallah. Yes, Hallah Hamdi. I will undoubtedly see you very soon. Goodbye. Yes. You are welcome. Goodbye."

The call to Mohammet Kohlsoum, at El Azmi Bank in Alexandria, went much the same. Paul inquired about the traffic on the Grand Corniche. He felt that a sense of familiarity with the environments of his contacts was important in establishing his image as a world player. Sometimes it did. Sometimes it didn't. Egyptians are very astute and not easily influenced by showmanship. How do you impress an Egyptian banker who is living large in the midst of abject poverty and disease, as well as in the midst of the greatest archaeological treasures on earth?

Paul closed the cover of his cell phone and put it in his breast pocket. He leaned forward and took a sip of his gibson. He savored the hint of onion in the gin as it slid past his palate. It was almost time to return to Chalice. He would spend the night there instead of his own apartment. It was closer and it would be easier for him in the morning.

"Are you alone?" It was Em Sarafian.

Paul hadn't noticed her come in. Now she was sitting close to him. He could smell her perfume. No. It wasn't perfume. It was the scent of her warm skin. He didn't think he was that sensitive to aromas but it was unmistakable. He had experienced the perfume of her presence before, the aroma of her body. It was just hours ago at Chalice. The recollection of it had been nagging at his libido ever since. Now, there it was again. It had an uncanny effect on him. He felt the beginning of an erection start to lift the cloth of his pant leg.

"I'll have what he's having," she said to the bar tender who had wandered over. "What is it called?" This to Paul. She was so close her breath played about his face.

"A gibson. It's like a martini but with an onion instead of an olive."

The conversation was absurdly mundane. His erection had grown almost uncomfortable.

"I guess you checked on our deposit to your account at El Azmi in Alexandria?"

"Yes. Ryan wants everything to be in order for a meeting he's scheduled for the morning."

"And the deposit in Cairo?" She seemed to know everything. "How is Hallah Hamdi?"

How could she know about Hallah? "I don't know." Paul was feeling foolish, answering dumb questions, sitting at the elegant Sherry Netherland bar with a hard-on threatening to pop the buttons on his hand-tailored trousers. Her hand dropped to his thigh. He let out a gasp. This couldn't be happening.

"Here's your gibson. Care for an extra onion?" The bar tender put a small silver dish in front of her, several cocktail onions in it, each speared with a carved toothpick.

"Thank you." Her gaze did not leave Paul's face. Her hand had begun to massage him gently.

The bar tender glanced down. The action in Paul's lap was beyond the range of his vision but he could see the motion of her upper arm.

"I'll have another!" Paul blurted to get rid of him.

Em's hand continued. The aroma of her skin filled Paul's nostrils. He was floating, and then all at once he felt a whirlpool of firing nerve endings rising from his toes, engulfing his legs, his buttocks, and loins. His penis began to throb, then pump rhythmically, shooting dollops of semen along his leg as he ejaculated violently.

A smile pulled at the corners of Em's mouth. "Now, look what you've done, Paul. And I was going to ask you up to my room. I even had a little ceremony planned for this evening. Oh, well. It will keep. I wouldn't want to ruin tomorrow's meeting."

Her words, close to Paul's ear, had that same, strange, clicking sound he had heard when she first introduced herself to him at Chalice.

In a single, lithe movement, she rose, straightened her black cocktail dress, and left. She had been there only a few minutes. Now suddenly she made an unapologetic exit. Though abrupt, it was so smooth and effortless it appeared completely relaxed— not the image of a woman who, moments ago, had brought a man to sexual climax. As she walked the length of the bar, her feet hardly seemed to touch the carpet— and she was gone.

"Here's your gibson, sir. The lady seems to have left hers. Was there anything wrong with it? Maybe it was Paul's imagination but he thought he saw a smirk on the man's face. The pleasures of the serving class were few but savored deeply. A rich kid in fancy threads had just been turned on and dumped in the time it took him to polish a piece of stemware.

"Nothing. Everything's fine. Just bring me the check." Paul sat, completely drained, alone at the near empty bar, the dampness in his pants starting to feel cold and clammy. The walk to Nyxos was going to be uncomfortable. Frustration made his brain feel as soft and dysfunctional as his penis. He hadn't shot in his pants since high school. And with this woman of all women!

☥ ☥ ☥

Megyn had a dark secret. She had watched TV sympathetically as one beautiful schoolteacher after another went to the slammer for statutory rape. Megyn liked young boys. Not children— at least, not children as Megyn saw it. She was not a child molester. It was young, pubescent males that made her hormones rage. They were men, but innocent and harmless. They grew erections suddenly, tumescent organs they couldn't control. She would see her little men, slim hips, voices too husky for their just developing biceps, leaning forward in embarrassment to hide erections that simply would not subside. She would feign innocence while she helped bring their embarrassment to full size. No one was the wiser, when in front of one of them, she would bend over a waste basket, or an intentionally dropped pen, exposing her thighs, the crease of buttock at their top, perhaps even the mound between her legs of panties already grown damp at the thought of what she was doing. Then she would stand and turn casually to glance at the trousers of the young fellow behind her to see if she had achieved the intended results. If she had, and he returned her look boldly, she knew she had found an opportunity. She rarely even noticed his face, just the raw lust in his eyes.

Rarely had Megyn indulged her passion for young men— she refused to call them boys. She was too cautious to get involved in anything that might evolve into anything more complx than a single coupling. Opportunities were everywhere. Danger was equally ubiquitous and demanded her self-control. It wasn't a problem. She was strong. She looked at the teachers on TV who got caught. Every one of them had let things develop into "affairs." Debra LaFave made Megyn more nervous than any of the others. They were both approaching a "10" in physical beauty. Debra could have any male she wanted and so could Megyn. One problem— neither of them wanted men. They wanted young men— very, young men. She had pondered it many times. The problem as she saw it, supported by her studies in anthropology, was that adult/child sex was as natural as every other type of sex. For eons, various primitive cultures had recognized it. In some, it was customary for a father to deflower his young daughters before any other male had a chance at them. Emperors kept pre-pubescent girls by the dozens to satisfy their libidinous extravagances. Usually it was older men and young girls. The women always had similar urges but usually not the passive permission of a culture, or the absolute power permitted to many men.

US culture was born in the Judeo-Christian tradition with more than a hint of Puritan morality thrown in. Men still got away with a lot but were shown little mercy if caught. Women, on the other hand, had to be very careful about creating opportunities but if they were caught there would be embarrassment but probably light penalties. That was comforting. As Debra LaFave sat in court, the TV cameras creating tantalizing portraits of her on screens all over America, everyone sat mesmerized. The same thought went through every man's head, *That lucky kid!* Megyn had a different thought, *That dumb bunny! She could have had more sex than Kublai Khan if she had just kept moving from jock to jock.* Megyn had left no trails. *It wasn't that tough— pizza delivery boys, room service at hotels, fund raisers for basketball trips, collected by young guys who came right to your door. Sometimes it was even tax deductible.*

The last thought made Megyn squirm. Even to herself, she sounded uncomfortably like a predator. She wasn't. She gave some very lucky boys something to remember the rest of their lives— like Debra LaFave. She grew up pretty. She developed into a Victoria's Secret type beauty. It opened doors professionally, economically, and every other way one could imagine. It was even getting her through her post-doc project and a possible trip in a few days to Egypt. The Reverend Ryan Quinn was a good priest but she had a power that opened minds and wallets. She didn't use it, exactly. She just didn't turn her back on opportunities. Even old Father McAndrew, homosexual, sworn to chastity, and on the ugly side, was not totally immune. She liked him and he liked her— but even more than he would have if she had been ugly. It was just the way life was. She had been given a gift and knew it.

✝ ✝ ✝

It wasn't late when Megyn got to the Brooklyn Museum. The public doors were closed but she had a key to the staff entrance and knew that most everybody would be there well into the night. When you love your work, quitting time is the end of pleasure, not the beginning of freedom.

Megyn had her own little office in the basement. It was a mess— a desk covered with half-opened, stapled photocopies of current research papers, and small piles of books with slips of paper marking places between pages. On the walls were a number of reproductions of Fayoum burial portraits. None were framed. Many were hanging at odd angles. The faces of the dead stared into the room with round, unblinking eyes from faces uncannily alive. Most of the portraits were part of her research, not artwork tacked up for aesthetic reasons. One young boy, dead for five hundred years, was up there for another reason. His image was framed. Like the others, he appeared fresh and awake. It was as though his was the reflected image of someone staring into a mirror on Megyn's wall.

It had been this young boy's face that first drew Megyn into her archaeological specialty. Ancient Egyptian history, art, and surviving artifacts, presented an unrivaled source of tantalizing mysteries to tempt the doctoral candidate, and the Fayoum burial paintings, dating only a bit before the birth of Christ and a bit later, had a humanity about them, absent from the tombs and treasures of the pharaohs and their friends. These were the burials of people with whom one could identify— maybe better off than those who tilled the soil, but not kings and queens. Mostly they were expatriate Greeks and Romans, like Marc Antony, and Ptolemaic royalty, like Cleopatra. The portraits are images of olive skinned, attractive people, painted on wood attached to coffins that contained their mummified remains. Presumably, the practice of mummification had been picked up from the Egyptians by the newcomers.

The Fayoum boy on Megyn's wall was beardless— just a hint of peach fuzz on his upper lip. He was probably no more than fifteen. He turned her on. She had fantasized bedroom trysts with him countless times with no one but her own hand for a lover.

Megyn got on the phone as soon as she sat down at her desk. Within minutes she had reached everyone she needed to see. They were all still working as she expected. A few short steps down the hall and she had secured promises from the best people to be at Chalice in the morning— Doctors El-Akshar, Feinschutz, and Balanaq— Egyptologists and epigraphers, with practical experience in the Western Desert.

She returned to her office to check her mail. It would still be a lengthy subway ride back to Manhattan and her apartment.

There was very little mail and none of it important. She started to stuff a few things into her briefcase when she heard a light knock on the door.

"Come," she called out. She expected it was one of her colleagues from down the hall. It wasn't. Hal Sarafian stood n the doorway.

"Are you alone?"

"Yes. Please come in."

God— but he looked so much like the Fayoum boy on the wall. Why hadn't she noticed it this afternoon? She felt very nervous.

"I hope I'm not disturbing you." Odd choice of words considering the way she was feeling.

"Not at all. What can I do for you?"

"I presume you have taken care of all your business here. You have many fine connections among Egyptologists. Bedu El-Akshar has worked extensively in the area of interest to my sister and me." His words made a strange crackling sound—like a recording fed too much treble. Megyn had worked on a PBS show about Egypt. The sound engineer had taught her some technical stuff.

"Yes. I know. Are you familiar with the staff here?"

"We have a lot of contacts with museums and universities. Bedu is actually from a small community in the desert near Fayoum, but of course you know that."

"Yes." Megyn was beginning to feel very uncomfortable— not annoyed but fidgety. Once again, this man seemed to be undressing her with his eyes— and it felt good.

"How do you happen to be here this evening, Mr. Sarafian?"

"Please— Hal. After meeting you this afternoon I was anxious to see you again. I thought you might have some questions about our interest in the Western Desert."

"In fact, I do." Megyn felt more comfortable, moving on to business. "If it's not too bold— I know it's more Father Ryan's concern than mine, but whom do you represent?"

"That is hard to explain— not impossible, but difficult at this time. We Sarafians have connections all over the world with representatives most anywhere you might look. Our resources are extensive but so diversified, a single enterprise, or focus of interest, is too specific to define our organization. You might think of us as a matrix, or a socio-industrial hologram."

"Very mysterious, Mr. Sarafian— er, Hal."

"Not really, Megyn. May I call you Megyn, Dr. Corbet?"

"Of course."

"Thank you. Let me assure you, our interest in the Western Desert of Egypt is profound, our funding of this project more than sound, and our confidence in your own expertise, and that of Chalice, total."

Now Megyn felt a mix of emotions washing over her. His words filled her with a pride far beyond what she ordinarily felt when praised by a colleague— and completely unwarranted, considering her scant knowledge of him. Who was he? What were his credentials? Why were his words of praise of any importance to her?

The other emotion was lust. His eyes, round and innocent like the boy in the Fayoum portrait, continued to bathe her with their soft, unthreatening gaze.

Megyn was embarrassed. She felt her neck and chest grow pink in a rising blush that was luckily concealed beneath her man-tailored blouse. She was afraid, though, that her cheeks might begin to glow with the same rush of blood, to reveal an involvement she was not prepared to display.

They had stopped talking but he continued to gaze gently at Megyn. She felt something else. It was sexual arousal. Her vaginal lips had begun to receive the same rush of blood that was washing up to the skin of her chest and neck. She felt her labia part as they became engorged. A flood of lubricant began to bathe them and flow into the fabric of her underpants. It was beyond her control. Her breath grew quick and shallow. She was panting like a lioness.

Over years denying herself traditional sex in favor of rare encounters with young boys, Megyn had perfected an unusual technique of achieving self-gratification. She could bring herself to climax, totally without manual manipulation, by contracting and relaxing her vaginal muscles slowly and rhythmically. It was not a talent she was proud of, nor one had she mentioned to anyone— not even to any of her Lesbian friends.

Now she felt her vaginal muscles performing as she had caused them to before, but this time not at her direction. She was sitting at her desk, the young man's eyes on her, as she began to squirm with sensual pleasure, her vaginal muscles contracting and releasing with constantly greater insistence. She was bringing herself to orgasmic climax without any ability to stop it. She felt her uterus straighten. She felt her own hot breath rise from her lungs and force its way through her open mouth in a hoarse moan. Her organs began to throb and grasp at a non-existent penis. Her breasts were full and her nipples hard. Her anus grabbed and released the fabric of her underpants as a series of orgasms piled one on top of the other. She fought to control the volume of her moans. They had begun as whimpers but threatened to become screams of ecstasy.

Then it was over. She shuddered, and felt terribly weak. She collapsed forward, her head turned sideways so her cheek lay atop the scatter of papers and photos that covered her desk. A bit of saliva ran from one corner of her mouth.

The young man smiled at her gently, turned, and left, closing the door quietly behind him. Megyn didn't even notice. She had begun to sob softly. She was not crying out of sorrow or rage, or anything else she could identify. Her sobs were just the nervous reaction of a body that had reached its limit and had nothing left to give but tears. Her hands trembled as she pushed herself upright in her chair. He was gone! She was relieved but felt strangely empty and alone in his unexpected absence. Slowly, she gathered her things together.

Megyn was unsteady as she walked down the hall. It would be a long ride back to Manhattan.

"Are you feeling OK, Megyn?" It was Sharon Feinschutz, the epigrapher she had just enlisted for tomorrow's meeting.

"Yes, Sharon. Thank you. I missed supper and maybe lunch. I don't recall. Probably a touch of hypoglycemia."

"I'm finished for the evening. I'll walk with you. Here. Have a Twinkie." She fished around in her briefcase. Dr. Sharon Feinschutz, world authority on the papyri of peri-Christian Egypt, was a Twinkie addict.

☦ ☦ ☦

The Reverend James McAndrew, S.J. left Chalice after their meeting and headed straight for the American Museum of Natural History. It was across town and a good distance north, not too far to walk under normal circumstances but he didn't want to miss the staff in case the ones he needed to contact might start heading home. He would take a taxi. He didn't like taxis. It didn't give a good impression to see a priest riding in comfort past the homeless who were everywhere these days. But this was a necessity. Luckily the weather was good. Trying to catch a New York taxi in bad weather is virtually impossible. After just a few moments, a cab responded to his raised hand and pulled to the curb for him, but a young man jumped in front of him and grabbed the door handle.

"Excuse me, my son, I believe this cab is mine."

The young man was incredibly handsome, dressed in expensive clothes, and didn't seem impolite.

"Oh, I'm so sorry. I was in such a hurry I didn't notice. My bad luck. I apologize."

"No problem. Which way are you going? Perhaps we can share."

"Cross-town and to the north."

"Perfect. That's exactly where I'm headed. Get in."

New York cabbies are not delighted when New Yorkers become polite and share a fare. This guy was a priest so he'd keep his "tough trying to make a living" speech to himself.

The two sat in silence as the cab went north on Park Avenue past the Waldorf and on up to Seventy-Ninth Street. He intended to take the cross-town through Central Park. It took a little twist so that it ended up on Eighty-First Street on the other side of the park— right at the front door of the American Museum of Natural History.

James McAndrew was painfully aware of the attractive young man sitting beside him. He was used to controlling his libido. After years of practice it had become a reflex. The fellow was wearing some sort of cologne but very subtle. The thought crossed his mind that it was not cologne at all but the man himself. Quickly he sent the thought scurrying. He hoped the ride would go quickly.

The young man made a half-turn in his seat to face the priest. "I'm Richard."

"Nice to meet you, Richard. I'm Father McAndrew."

"Is your parish here in Manhattan?"

"I'm not a parish priest. I'm a Jesuit. We usually live communally, associated with universities and secondary schools, but many of us have individual careers and work outside of the community."

"Fascinating. When is a priest not a priest? — When he's a Jesuit." The

young man chuckled at his own, not very clever, riddle.

"Oh. I'm sorry. Did that offend you?" His eyes were unusually large and soft, thought McAndrew, as he grumbled a response.

"Not at all." He found his palms had grown sweaty. "I think we're almost there. I'm going to the Museum."

"I am, too. Is that where you work?"

"Sometimes."

The cab came to a stop at the traffic light on Central Park West. McAndrew spoke to the cabbie, "I'll get out wherever it's convenient for you. I can walk to the Museum." He had become very anxious to get away from his companion— mostly because he wanted just the opposite. He reached for his wallet.

"Please, Father, let me pay. You were so kind to let me share your cab. Perhaps I will look for you at the museum and we can chat sometime."

"I'm only there sporadically. I wouldn't want you to waste your effort."

"No problem. I'm fascinated with the whole idea of ancient papyri and conservation techniques."

"How did you know that was my profession?"

The young man just smiled and shrugged. The cab pulled to the curb and McAndrew fumbled awkwardly with the handle, and then practically sprang from the door. As the cab pulled away McAndrew muttered over and over to himself, *get thee behind me, Satan— get thee behind me—*

It was only a short walk to the semi-circular drive that descends from Central Park West to the museum's lower level, staff entrance. He used his key to enter. The door hissed as the hydraulic mechanism let the door close slowly behind him before the latch clicked shut. His steps echoed as he strode down the empty hall to the broad marble staircase that led up to the main floor.

Down the hallway to his office, he passed the familiar bronze bust of an Ndebele woman of South Africa. Her neck was long, stretched to an unnatural length by the customary stack of bead necklaces, in this case, sculpted in bronze. The priest had always found it amusing that although the bare-breasted bust had attained a dark patina over the years, the woman's nipples were bright and shiny. McAndrew rarely saw a soul in the hallway, and never saw anyone stopped in front of the sculpture. Obviously, countless perverts had stopped over the years, looked up and down the hall to make sure they were alone, then surreptitiously fondled the poor woman's bronze nipples.

Years ago there had been a TV show called, Candid Camera. They would hide a camera to catch people in the midst of embarrassing activities. McAndrew was tempted to contact the show's producer, Allen Funt, to have him do a piece on the Ndebele Woman. But how does a priest bring up such a subject?

Thinking about all this, McAndrew managed to get his mind off the strange young man in the taxicab. He opened the door to his lab. His office at the Museum was not exactly an office. He did have a desk, bookcase, and the usual accoutrements of a museum academic, but a conservator was a specialized craftsman. He applied his knowledge of ancient history and materials to repair artifacts in danger of falling apart. Nowadays it went further, involving x-ray machines, focused lasers, and so forth. One manuscript, rescued from a Central American Mayan tomb was a solid block. It had been written on bark pounded flat but had lain in a limestone cavern for seven hundred years. Saturated with calcium-carbonate-rich, drip water from the ceiling, it had turned into a solid limestone block. With focused lasers, Maya conservators were now attempting to read the document within the block of stone— no luck, so far, but perhaps eventually.

McAndrew stopped at his desk for a moment to use the phone. He was successful in reaching all the people on his list. They promised to stay until he had a chance to go up and down the halls and meet with each of them separately. He promised the meetings would be brief— no more than five or ten minutes with each. He would be done in less than an hour.

The people on his list included Dr. Hiram Benshaw, papyrus conservator, Dr. Nissim Timbavati, epigrapher specializing in Middle Eastern manuscripts, Dr. Leila Miller, desert geomorphologist, and Dr. Bint Farranha, Coptic iconographer. They all stayed as promised. McAndrew finished up with all of them within the hour. All agreed to participate in the project if summoned and would await further word from Father Quinn. McAndrew returned to his office/lab.

It was a bit late to get up to the Fordham Campus considering the early morning meeting. There was a convertible couch in the staff lounge. They all used it for overnights from time to time. Each took a turn changing the sheets and laundering them. There was a washing machine and dryer in the ladies room as well as a shower. A sign on the door could be flipped to show that it was occupied to avoid embarrassing encounters.

Father McAndrew decided to spend the night. One by one, the others left. He could hear them in the hall, their footsteps and conversations dwindling as they moved down the halls of the vast building.

The American Museum of Natural History is an eerie place at night. A few horror movies and several scary novels have used it as a setting. Dimly lit even during the day, the exhibits take on a seriously sinister aspect at night. The lights are never completely off. Hall lights pour dimly into the exhibit rooms actually making things worse. Dinosaurs, mastodons, and sabre tooth tigers— all become silhouettes of themselves and seem to come to life if one looks at them too long.

Father McAndrew found a can of soup in the staff lounge cupboard— chicken noodle. He hated chicken noodle out of a can. You can't find the chicken and the noodles are so soft it's a miracle they keep any shape at all.

The saucepan hadn't been washed. Luckily the stuff left in it had become too dry and crunchy to provide a breeding place for salmonella. A little dish soap, a swipe with the grimy towel on the rack, and he had his supper bubbling on the hotplate. There were Ritz crackers in the cupboard. He shook a few into a dish to check for mouse droppings. None visible. Chef McAndrew was all set for a feast. He carried everything over to the conference table and sat down. He had forgotten the pepper. Canned chicken noodle was chock full of salt but never any pepper. He got up and went to search for some in the cupboard.

There it was. He turned to return to the table and dropped the shaker on the floor with a cry of fright. There at the table, sat the young man from the taxi.

Chapter Eleven

The early morning sun fell across the Chalice conference table, igniting its natural, inner fire. Through the panoramic window, the East River was alive with activity— barges, tug boats, and private craft. Across the river the structures of Hunter's Point were dark shadows against the low sun.

U Thant Island, in the middle of the river, was alive with seagulls, squirming like maggots over its surface, battling for available space. The tiny, artificial platform had been built as a tribute to the former UN Secretary General. In Myanmar, Thant's homeland, a government marksman picks off birds that dare fly higher than the roof of the royal palace. It's a respect thing. In the United States, U Thant's memorial islet is six inches deep in seagull guano. American birds just don't respect authority.

Ryan Quinn, S.J. sat at the head of the table. He looked grim. He had not taken the death of his friend, Habib, lightly. And it had come so close on the heels of his brother's mysterious death. He hoped this project would involve him to a point where he might focus less on the sadness and confusion that had been filling his life lately.

The others began to trickle in. If he had hoped their presence would lift his spirits he was wrong. One by one they took their seats looking worse than he felt. He was sure the other invited participants would be along soon.

"I presume you all made the proper contacts and we will be able to proceed shortly," he began. "But before the others arrive, I have an unpleasant announcement to share with you. My close friend, and your colleague, Father Habib Colophon, passed away late yesterday. Besides my personal grief at this time, I am sorely disappointed. I had hoped he might provide his special insight regarding historical and archaeological aspects associated with this project."

Ryan waited to let the news sink in. There was a stunned silence, but not the intake of breath, the looks of shock, or flurry of concerned questions he anticipated. They all looked stunned, but they had already looked stunned before he spoke. Something strange was going on.

Father McAndrew and Habib had been colleagues for some time. "Friends," would be an exaggeration of their relationship. They were scholars, often working together, but just as often battling over some epigraphic interpretation to the point of open anger.

That wasn't it— not the loss of a friend or even a colleague. McAndrew looked numb. They all did.

"Apparently these morning meetings don't sit well with you. Let's perk up a bit before the rest get here. Two more things— I was in contact with Herb Flanders, our field manager. He assured me he would be taking care of travel arrangements associated with this project as he always does, smoothly and quickly. I have no reason to question that. The other thing is a name for the project. It seems trivial, I realize, but important for book keeping and filing of notes, artifacts, and to keep the various flotsam straight that can become mixed up with other projects underway. Since this work appears to be a revival of earlier work all of us have been involved in, to some extent or other, I thought it appropriate to call it "The Lazarus Project," or simply, "Lazarus." Any objections or suggestions?"

"Father McAndrew, your first effort will be a side visit to France on your way to Egypt. I would like you to visit the cathedral in Autun. It's the repository for relics of St. Lazarus, and named La Cathedral Saint-Lazare in his honor. I don't know what it's all about but the visit was suggested to me in a note from one of our clients."

"Which client?" Father McAndrew came out of his stupor for a moment.

"The Sarafian's."

There was a nervous shuffling of papers from around the table.

"Would someone please tell me what's going on here? You all seem to be off in another world. What is it, Megyn?"

She made a stumbling effort to respond but to her great relief the invited experts began to arrive. They all seemed in a far better mood than Ryan's core staff.

Things went smoothly. George Stone had double-checked on the accounts in Cairo and Alexandria. Sharon Feinschutz and Bedu El-Akshar from the Brooklyn Museum would be joining them in Egypt. So would Leila Miller, the geomorphologist from the American Museum of Natural History. The others were disappointed not to be on the "away team" but promised to keep themselves available in case they were needed later.

The meeting, which took less than an hour, was adjourned. The travelers were told to be at Chalice the following morning to pick up tickets, credit cards, and a few hundred dollars in cash. They would all be traveling separately on Egypt Air and rendezvous at the Safir Etap Hotel in Giza the following week. Egypt Air's flights out of Kennedy, Terminal 3, lay over for a few hours at Orly Field in Paris before continuing to Cairo— perfect for Father McAndrew. Ryan liked flying with Egypt Air. One moment you were in New York City— the next, on board the plane, you were already in Egypt. Coffee, though available, was a thing of the past. Tea was standard.

Although Ryan was a coffee drinker, tea somehow seemed to taste different in its own environment. In the desert, traveling with the Bedouin, he would watch as they heated a brass kettle over an open fire, then pour the dark tea from high up so the liquid would splash into the cup creating bubbles that floated on top. The bubbles disappeared almost at once, but for a brief moment they were a nomad's idea of luxury— a penniless Bedouin's cappuccino.

Ryan found that he continued to drink tea for weeks after returning from a trip to the Middle East. Then, all of sudden, he would think, *why am I drinking this stuff,* and return to coffee.

Megyn was asked to inform her usual stand-in to begin monitoring the phones and minding the front desk as soon as possible. She had already done so. She always kept Barbara Lenkowski up to date on what was going on. She too, was a trained archaeologist with a Ph.D. in anthropology but had made the choice of attaching herself romantically to a successful real estate broker who would not let her travel. Her specialty was ancient diets. She knew more about what the pharaohs ate than their own cooks or stool-examining physicians. Ancient excrement was an important part of Barbara's research. Once she had written a tongue in cheek paper to startle her colleagues titled, "Poking Through Pharaonic Poop." Actually, the study was so insightful she was urged to change the title and submit it for publication. In short, Barbara was a highly respected professional with a sense of humor and a heart too easily influenced by romance to allow her career to dominate. Without rancor, she would answer the phones at Chalice headquarters and take care of day-to-day operations with the other offices in a manner far beyond the demands of the job. Ryan paid her well and had often promised her a field position should her romance take a bad turn.

Chapter Twelve

James McAndrew deplaned in Paris and took a taxi to the Gare Saint Lazare. There he boarded a train for Autun. His connections worked well. He had little time to dwell on the strange events in the American Museum several days ago. Not that he could put them out of his mind. He had come to believe they had been an hallucination. Terribly unsettling, nonetheless. They cut deeply at the core of his struggle with Nature— his lifelong fight with his homosexuality and his deliberate quest for celibate sanctity, not only of body, but of mind and spirit. For years in his youth, then all through seminary and beyond, he had battled with his conscious desires but was unable to control his subconscious. It sometimes erupted uncontrollably in his dreams. But that plague had subsided over the years. There were benefits attached to aging and its diminished flood of glandular secretions.

If that young man had been a dream it was frightening. If he had been an hallucination, even worse. It had been only days and there had been no recurrence. But these were very busy days. He would keep them that way.

The coincidence struck McAndrew that he was boarding a train on track two of the first railroad station built in Paris, the Gare Saint Lazare— headed for the medieval city of Autun and the Cathédrale-Saint Lazare, built seven hundred years earlier. Christian Europe was constantly building and structures often shared similar saint names. There didn't seem to be enough to go around. It must still be the case. Saints of whom McAndrew had never heard were emerging constantly with letters asking for contributions. The other day he had received one begging him to support Saint Dymphna. Not only had he never heard of her, he didn't think anyone could even pronounce her name unless they had a cleft palate.

In the case of Lazarus, there is some confusion between the man Christ raised from the dead and Lazarus the Poor, depicted in a monastery illumination as a leper and friend to dogs. Father McAndrew was not sure which one was which or why the French had chosen to use that name for a cathedral and railroad station. Of greater confusion for McAndrew was exactly why he was headed to Autun and the Cathedral at all. He would wait for a miraculous revelation. He dressed in his clerical garb. In France, priests are a regular part of the urban landscape, and often receive special favors. Considering his state of mind, McAndrew could use all the help he could get.

Megyn had requested and received a ticket for the first Egypt Air flight available. She was in Cairo before the rest. It was familiar territory. She preferred the old terminal with its huge pharaonic bas-relief on the end wall and the mix of dust and cigarette smoke in the air. The new terminal was just another terminal, like one more fluffy towel in one more Holiday Inn, anywhere in the world.

But one step out the terminal door and Egypt descends on you like a dusty shawl. The sound of car horns is incessant— not the deep throated, or flat, blaring horns of New York, but the high beep, beep, beep of French and Italian cars— Fiats for the masses, Peugeot's for the better off, and for some up-scale taxis.

Egyptians drive with a madness that only another Egyptian can understand. Traffic is a mix of speeding cars, bicycles, pedestrians, and donkey carts. A taxi driver expects a special tip if he shows spectacular skill at weaving among the masses of animals and humanity without ever letting up on his horn. Traffic circles are a unique experience. A policeman stands high at its center on a pedestal, presumably for better visibility, but probably more as refuge from the weaving mass of flesh and machinery.

Megyn's driver was a champion. He drove at high speed, the hood of his Peugeot sometimes almost beneath the bumper of the truck ahead, narrowly missing pedestrians who would leap back without anger, as he pounded on his horn with a rhythm not born of New York impatience, but of the desire to make automotive music, Cairo style.

They made it from the airport to the suburb of Giza in excellent, if not record time. Megyn kept her eyes closed a lot of the time. As they screeched to a stop in front of the Safir Etap, the driver turned in his seat to face Megyn—

"You like? Pay the man." He was emphatically suggesting she give him an extra tip in recognition of his spectacular driving.

She did so rather than explain her true sentiments on the subject. She just wanted out. The hotel doorman, in a blue, knee-length coat and red tarbush, helped her out with a broad grin. He had seen many pale visitors hurriedly making good their escapes from taxis at his door.

The Safir-Etap is a comfortable place to stay even for those accustomed to Western luxury— not top of the line, but almost, and close to the desert and the Pyramids. Megyn had stayed there before. It was best to go where you were known if you were a gorgeous blond traveling alone. Despite the marble reflection pool in the lobby, there was also a house cat that wandered about with a possessive strut. It was a semi-elegant but homey environment.

Megyn made arrangements at the front desk for a taxi to pick her up early in the morning. She would be visiting the pyramids around dawn. She never tired of seeing them and early morning was the time for it, before the tourists were out of bed. Even in the twenty-first century it was still possible to be alone with history on the outskirts of Cairo if you weren't in love with your pillow. But that was not her purpose this time. Ryan had asked her to make arrangements with the Bedouin for a camel trek to Fayoum. He would be along in a few days.

The very idea of the nomadic Bedouin is one that fills westerners with a sense of romantic wonder. But these temporal misfits have fashioned a unique opportunity for themselves on the Giza Plateau. Up from the misty lowlands along the banks of the Nile, they arrive on camels at the pyramids around sun up.

Tourists are always game to spend a few dollars to have their pictures taken atop the complaining beasts and a few of the camel drivers have learned a nasty trick.

"Please, take your picture on my camel? It's free." After the tourist is seated, at the driver's command, the animal rises from its low squat to its full height. The tourist is suddenly aware of just how high up he is. That is when he finds out that the picture is free but it will cost ten dollars to get back down.

Megyn asked the taxi driver to bring her up close to the Pyramid of Khufu, the largest of the group, and wait for her. She got out and strolled about. The dusty mist of a purple dawn hung over the city. Suddenly a loud call came from the sunrise shadow of Khufu as a tall, thin silhouette of camel and driver approached.

"Megyn, my Princess of the Nile!"

It was Hadji Gamal Abu Pasha, sun-wizened caravan leader and patriarch of the Giza Bedouin— just the man she had come to see.

Chapter Thirteen

Ryan was in a down mood as he left the morning meeting. Everyone had been in a weird state and he still had a friend to bury. Too many people were dying around him. The project in Egypt would have been cause for high spirits if his brother were still alive, but he had just buried him. Now it would be Habib Colophon, a colleague and friend of many years, who must be buried.

Spencer's death had been a horrifying mystery. Ryan worried about his soul. Habib's death had not been unexpected. He was old and ill, but his final revelation had been more than unexpected. It had been highly disturbing. Now it was his job to sort through things and make order out of a life he thought he understood, but apparently had not.

Like most Jesuits, Habib's personal possessions were few. But like most scholars, his professional possessions were anything but. There were books, papers, and artifacts, that filled boxes and filing cabinets in several offices at different museums and academic institutions. Over the next few days, Ryan made quick trips to all of them. It would be a job impossible to complete before he was due to leave for Egypt. He tried to weed through things quickly to see if he could find material that would be of significance to his current project.

Habib was not only an epigrapher, but also a highly regarded authority on ancient Middle East numismatics. His expertise was so respected he had been allowed a small office at the new headquarters of the American Numismatic Society on Varick Street in lower Manhattan. Ryan found very little there— a small desk, a one-drawer filing cabinet, and a couple of books— not scholarly works, but apparently hand written diaries or trip notes. He took those with him to examine later. They might contain something of value regarding his work years ago among the Coptic monastery ruins.

✝ ✝ ✝

Paul Quinn was not excited by archaeological fieldwork. The whole Indiana Jones thing was not his style. *And make no mistake about it,* he thought to himself, *virtually all archaeologists share that image of themselves.* Paul liked New York, its theater, cocktail parties, designer clothes, art galleries, opera, and all the rest of it. He was not immune to his father's obsession for exotic travel. But archaeology was just one interest among what Paul liked to think of as his eclectic approach to culture. He liked alcohol, women, and a line of coke once in awhile. Nothing out of proportion— a balance of hedonism, intellectualism, and sex. He couldn't quite bring himself to tell his father who he really was. That's what he feared most about his new role as Dad's Best Friend. They were very different. What he didn't know was that Ryan understood completely. His own vocation to the priesthood had come relatively late in life. He had been much older than Paul when he lost his wife and ran to religion to save his sanity. Even then, he had chosen the Jesuits as a means of continuing with his macho image as fearless businessman and explorer in the heroic tradition. Like Clark Kent emerging from the phone booth as Superman, professor Ryan Quinn had entered the seminary and emerged as the Reverend Indiana Jones, S. J. It couldn't get any better than that. He was a little disappointed, but not surprised, when Paul came to him the day after the morning meeting.

"Dad, I think I could be of more use to Chalice if I stuck around here and managed things rather than join all of you in the field."

"It's OK, son. I understand. I really do. It's not like I really thought it would be wise to completely vacate headquarters for this project. With the people from Brooklyn and the American Museum, we'll probably be overstaffed in Egypt as it is."

Paul was terribly relieved. He loved and admired his dad. He just couldn't wear his shoes and make believe they fit. "I thought I might do a little more poking around Uncle Spencer's place and see if I can figure out anything about his death. I know it preys on your mind and with this project underway there's nothing you can do for a while."

Ryan suspected Paul's offer was made more to soften the effect of his decision to stay in New York than a pressing desire to play sleuth in his uncle's assassination, but he would play the same game.

"That would be great, Paul. There's so much more to Spencer's death than the police could uncover. They think with their eyes and something as visually bizarre as Spencer's death overloads their optic nerves."

Paul envied his father's clever use of words and images, another of his own comparative shortcomings. He would miss Ryan but having him nine thousand miles away would be somewhat of a relief as well. And then, there was that Sarafian woman. He couldn't get her out of his mind. While he was looking into his uncle's death he might go looking into the Sarafian family. If he encountered Em in the process, what harm? He felt he and she had unfinished business.

The funeral for Father Habib Colophon was a solemn affair. He had no family other than his adopted family, the Jesuit Community. There were friends, mostly museum people. The entire group was a total of less than a hundred people— hardly enough to warrant the venue chosen by Ryan for his friend— St. Patrick's Cathedral. Only a few city blocks from the Jesuit retirement house on Fifty-sixth Street, it was actually the appropriate parish church for the ceremony.

Those who know St. Patrick's are aware that there are often ceremonies being held there that are so completely dwarfed by the edifice that tourists come and go through the rear door and hardly notice that a ceremony is underway— just the smell of incense that is always present, and the tinkling of bells at the consecration. But with so many side altars, even those ceremonial sounds are so frequent as to go unnoticed. A funeral, such as that arranged by Ryan for Habib Colophon, does draw a crowd. It is the music. Passersby on Fifth Avenue are lured through the huge bronze doors by the sound of the organ.

Habib Colophon had a royal send-off, unusual for a Jesuit, courtesy of his old friend, Reverend Indiana Jones, S. J. During the funeral Mass, Habib's mortal remains lay within a cloud of frankincense, his feet to the congregation, his head toward the living presence of God on the altar, beneath the ceremonial galeros, hanging from the ceiling a hundred feet above him. No one but Habib, God, and Ryan Quinn knew that he had barely escaped the fires of Hell for a sin, un-confessed for fifteen years. But what was that sin? Only Habib and God knew— or perhaps, God, Habib, and some other, unnamed, and un-indicted co-conspirators.

✞ ✞ ✞

Ryan phoned Megyn in Cairo. He let her know that Paul would not be joining them on the camel trek to Fayoum but that Leila Miller and Sharon Feinschutz would be, and also Bedu El-Akshar. Megyn sounded relieved. Ryan was aware that Paul continually made attempts to hit on Megyn. He couldn't blame him. She was everything a man could want, beautiful, intelligent, and responsible. He understood her relief. The initial camel trek from Giza to Fayoum was more for fun than archaeological significance. He knew that Megyn shared his own romance with the desert and would cherish her privacy. It would not be fun camping in Bedouin tents for days without sanitary facilities while fighting off the unwanted advances of the boss's horny son.

Ryan and Megyn had once discussed their mutual approach to handling culture shift on expeditions such as these. You spend the first and last nights in an upscale hotel with the sounds and smells of Egypt safely beyond your balcony door. On the second or third day, you take to the desert or the river in a fashion as close to native as possible with someone still providing for the necessities— cooking, making tea, and that sort of thing. By the time you were deep in the desert and essentially on your own, both your mind and body would have achieved a truce with the shifting sands, the possibilities of deadly asps in your boots, and the prospect of no sanitary facilities for days at a time.

That was the purpose of the camel trek from the pyramids in Giza to the Oasis of Fayoum. It would take three days. Often your caravan would meander across the strip of asphalt that passes for a road between the two. The proximity of the road and the occasional roar of a passing truck are comforting at first but after only a day or so it becomes more a nuisance than anything else. By the time you get to Fayoum, the sounds of oasis humanity are a roaring intrusion. You have become a part-time nomad with little need for anything but sand and stars. Megyn would be happy to have Sharon, Leila and Bedu along. They were all desert rats like Ryan and herself, and Bedu spoke Arabic. Everything would be fine as long as there were enough Twinkies in the saddlebags for Sharon. Actually, Megyn thought, "Twinkies and tea in the desert by starlight sounded kind of nice."

Chapter Fourteen

All four chose to sit separately for the flight. They were all loners and liked window seats. Although the project money supply was fat, they traveled tourist class. That meant no special coddling, but tea and cookies with Arabic writing on the packages, right after lift off. None of the four were delicate. They would not be suffering, except for the inactivity. Close confinement during the long flight would be the most unpleasant aspect of the trip. The intermediate stop in France would be welcome. The continuation to Cairo would be just as uncomfortable as the first leg.

Ryan's field crew was exceptional in many ways. Secretly he wondered if he had not chosen them as much for their good looks as their credentials. It was a failing. He comforted himself with the thought that he would not have recruited them for appearances alone. Their academic backgrounds and practical field experience were beyond questioning. There was an old joke he remembered, ruefully— *If two women apply for the same secretarial position, have the same office skills, and the same work history, which one do you hire? The answer was, "The one with the big tits."*

Sharon Feinschutz was a "Distinguished Fellow" of the Epigraphic Society. She had co-written papers with both of the founders— Fell, of Harvard and Totten, of Bentley College. With a slim waist, ample bosom, and nicely rounded derriere, she was rarely taken for an Egyptologist. With her customary Twinkie in hand, the disguise was perfect— except it wasn't a disguise. Sharon was the genuine article, comfortable on a camel in khakis, and a knockout in a short cocktail dress. If only there were a French word for Twinkie, she could pass at faculty events for the standard, Ivy League, academic phony.

The name, Bedu, is singular for Bedouin. He was sun-black with Arab features. His mother was from Egypt, his father from Ethiopia. They were both attached to the UN in New York and enrolled him in prep school at Fordham University. At the time, James McAndrew, was a "scholastic," a Jesuit in training, not yet ordained, teaching Greek to high school students. Bedu fell under his academic spell and devoured the exploits of General Xenophon and the poesy of Homer as romantically presented by McAndrew. The young priest-to-be had a way of making history come alive through class readings in the original Latin and Greek. In his head, Bedu, could hear Xenophon's cry, Thalatta! Thalatta!— the sea! the sea!— as he and his band of a thousand topped Mount Theches and saw Euxeinos Pontos, the Black Sea, on their long journey home from a military campaign in Babylon.

Bedu went on to study other ancient tongues and the structural principles of linguistics that underlay them all. But it was in high school that his love affair with language had begun through the inspired classes of James McAndrew, S.J. Later, the Jesuit would introduce him to Ryan Quinn and help forge a connection between the two and eventually an adjunct position with Chalice. Now he was on a dream trip back to the continent where humanity, his own family, and language itself, had begun. It didn't hurt that his fellow workers included three of the most beautiful women he had ever met— and a priest to keep his libido under surveillance.

As a geomorphologist, Leila Miller was no "two olives in my Martini, please" gal. She could drink bourbon with the men and out arm-wrestle some of them. She was happiest in boots with an Estwing geology pick in her hand and a Brunton compass on her belt. She got into Egyptology through a back door. Her specialty was aeolian landforms, surface forms created by wind— in other words, deserts, and why they look the way they do. Egyptologists were always on the hunt for undisturbed ruins in the sand, but when does a dune look like a dune and not a buried ruin, or a limestone ridge just a ridge? Ask Leila. She had finished first in her geology class at the University of Arizona, then went on for a doctorate in geomorphology. It involved mathematics and fluid dynamics. Sand dunes are the result of the movement, all around us, of the fluid we cannot see— the wind. After school she won a competitive post-doctoral appointment to work on a sponsored research project at Lamont-Doherty Earth Observatory, a research arm of Columbia University. The research was funded by the Department of

Defense, which has its fiscal fingers in virtually everything— this time, things related to desert warfare. Lamont-Doherty is across the Hudson, just north of New York City, in Palisades, New York. That led to a dual career with Lamont and the American Museum of Natural History in the City. Ryan had run into her several years ago at Wadi Rum in Jordan. That was the beginning of her fascination with the application of geomorphology to the mysteries of Egyptology.

Leila wasn't in Sharon's or Megyn's class when it came to good looks but she was trim and muscular, with a beautiful face, more in the quirky style of Renée Zellweger than Miss California. She would be anybody's safe bet in a wet T-shirt contest— and she'd been in a few. She had also broken a few arms after winning one.

Ryan had himself quite a field crew. Lucky thing Father McAndrew would be around to keep a lid on things— and hear confessions if things got out of hand. He settled back and took one of Habib's diaries out of his briefcase. The handwriting was terrible. He must have written it while riding a camel. Ryan began wading through it as best he could. He'd leave Habib's other diaries for later. They would be a worthwhile tribute to his friend if he read them by candlelight in a desert tent.

Habib seemed to be talking in riddles. The diary was a mix of experiences in the desert and transcripts of disjointed conversations with various people— even Ryan, himself. In one passage he referred to Ryan as "the key." That would take some looking into— except, look where? With Habib gone, there was nowhere to look. Then he thought about one passage in the diary. It mentioned Pietro Gandolfo, the Papal Nunzio. But Habib wrote this long before Pietro had been appointed to that high office. Ryan had known that Habib and Pietro Gandolfo knew one another, and worked in the region where he was now headed. Ryan thumbed back through the pages to where Habib had mentioned him. No. Apparently it had not been Habib, but Gandolfo, who had called Ryan the key. The key to what? So, there <u>was</u> a place to look for answers— Rome. But it would have to wait. He was headed in the wrong direction.

After mind numbing hours of droning jet engines, a sudden change in pitch jolted the passengers back to consciousness. They were nearing Cairo.

The 747 began dropping slowly and would continue to do so for another half-hour before making its final approach into Cairo International. Ryan put the books back into his briefcase and looked out the window.

The sight of a Middle Eastern city from the air is surprising to an American. Even a modern megalopolis like Cairo seems mostly made of mud. The string of modern, high-rise structures along the Nile are at the center of the city, but not at the center of its soul. Egypt is poor and its people worse than poor. Mostly they live in uncomfortable looking, multiple dwellings that give way to clusters of mud houses farther from the city's center.

Poverty that goes back thousands of years, lives side-by-side with incredible wealth, much of it still buried in the sand. These were the thoughts that were passing sleepily through Ryan's head as the plane circled and the structures grew larger beneath them. He knew where to look and could see the pyramids and the desert stretching to the horizon beyond them. He and his team were gods and goddesses flying across the sky above the Land of the Pharaohs.

Megyn was waiting just beyond the customs enclosure. There was no need to have a taxi stand by as they collected their luggage and went through customs. There would be a crowd of them, squabbling among themselves, and calling for attention, outside the terminal. Hopefully, Bedu could speak to them in their own tongue and suggest they would like one with a weak horn and a healthy fear of traffic fatalities.

The cat in the lobby of the Safir-Etap walked directly to Ryan and gave his shin a long, friendly, sideswipe.

"Hello, Faruq. Did you miss me?"

No answer, but a turn, a flip of the tail, and a sideswipe from the opposite direction.

"I guess so. I missed you, too."

The others were busy handing over their passports and signing the guest register. Everybody was groggy from the flight and the time difference. It was 10 PM here and nobody except Megyn had had any sleep.

Ryan and Bedu would share a room. The three women would be in a room down the hall.

"Do you mind if we leave the balcony door open, Bedu? I like to hear the sounds of Cairo at night."

"I'm glad you do, Father. If you had asked me, I would have suggested the same thing."

"Please, call me Ryan. We will be spending a lot of time together. We're all on a fist name basis unless there's someone around we want to impress. Then it can be Father this and Doctor that."

Chapter Fifteen

The cabbie with the broken horn had promised to be waiting for them in front of the hotel before dawn— and he was. Any traveler will tell you that cab drivers in third world countries are incredibly punctual and pay no attention to the weird hours they may be asked to keep.

As the cab climbed the road up from the Sphinx to the top of the plateau, it passed a lonely camel or two ridden by drivers anxious to catch the first dollar of the day before their comrades. Once on the level above the city, the pyramids loom huge and dark against the distant lights of Giza. The driver was confused. He offered to wait and couldn't quite grasp the concept that they would not be returning to the city.

"I will wait. It will cost nothing extra."

Out of the shadows came twelve tall shapes. They moved steadily toward them as Ryan and his group stood in the sand, their luggage in disarray around them.

"FATHER!"

It was Hadji Gamal Abu Pasha. He loved to make dramatic entrances from within the shadows of the pyramids. This was his second in just several days.

"Abu Pasha, my friend!"

Ryan liked the drama, too, and was aware that two of the ladies and Bedu had not seen this performance before. After the crazy, scissor-legged descent of his camel to the ground, Abu Pasha leaped down and ran to Ryan, his dark blue gellabiya almost black in the twilight, but his spotless turban, a little white cloud rushing through the air toward the priest.

The two embraced. It was a grand performance. If any one of the group doubted Ryan's international recognition, this took care of that. With a look of resignation, the cabbie got into his Peugeot and left.

The other camels circled, then scissored down into their natural resting position. Immediately they began chewing. Camels at rest seem always to be either chewing, gurgling complaints, or spitting at those who would have them get up again.

Abu Pasha had brought three leathery-skinned drivers with him, as well as his son, Samir, about twelve years old who wore a white turban like his father. The other drivers wore blue gellabiyas and turbans of different colors— the loose ends hanging down in front so they could be drawn across their faces to protect them from sudden sand storms. Camels are protected naturally from the sand by long eyelashes and nostrils they can pinch down when necessary, to filter the air.

Abu Pasha barked at the helpers to load the camels. The beasts, as usual, gurgled loud complaints but did nothing to fend off their tormentors. Two of them were already loaded heavily with tents, poles, carpets, pillows, and provisions of all sorts wrapped in heavy, homespun blankets.

The field team was told to mount up. Ryan and Megyn had no trouble. Despite the fact that the others were not cream puffs, mounting a camel is not that simple. At rest, they are lumps about three feet high. Add a saddle and it's about five feet. For a novice, it doesn't seem right to stand on the poor beast's elbow but that's how you make it to the top.

The drivers smiled but did not laugh as they watched the awkward attempts of the team to mount their beasts. Abu Pasha gave a couple of them a helping boost— the ones in tight khakis with well-rounded buttocks. They realized they had just been felt up but this was not the time to cause a fuss. Bedu, of course, needed and got no help.

With a command from Abu Pasha, all the camels rose to their full height— a disquieting experience for a new rider. It happens suddenly, in two movements. The first is violent as the camel straightens his hind legs and is likely to throw the rider over the camel's head if he's not prepared. The next stage is relatively mild. If you make it through the first you're not likely to have a problem with the second. Once up, the rider becomes a giant, his head perhaps ten feet above the desert, with a view to the horizon.

Slowly, like a snake uncoiling, the circle of camels unwound and formed a long line, Abu Pasha at its head. They left the pyramids, still black silhouettes against the dawn, and headed off into— nothing.

For centuries people have commented on the peculiarities of the camel. Some have spoken of becoming sea sick due to the animal's peculiar gait. In fact, the camel has an unusually large selection of possible forward motions. Somewhere between a walk and a trot, is the most comfortable, causing the least swaying or forward-backward motion. Ryan had learned a trick from American cowboys to avoid painful abrasion. He had passed it on to the others— panty hose. The one-piece undergarment clings to the skin so abrasion takes place between it and the outer garment instead of the rider's epidermis. It had always struck Ryan funny that, unknown to Hollywood, the real he-man cowboys often wore panty hose under their chaps on the range. Even worse, were it to get out, would be the idea of a priest riding a camel to Fayoum in panty hose. He wondered, but never asked, how the Bedouin coped. They might be wearing virtually anything under those dress-like gellabiyas, but somehow panty hose seemed unlikely.

It wasn't long before the Giza pyramids were out of sight behind them. They were moving south towards Saqqara. Megyn had been here many times. It was in the shadow of the badly eroded pyramid of Amenemhet the Third, that, in 1888, archaeologist, William Petrie, had unearthed the funerary portraits that were the focus of Megyn's doctoral work. The portrait of the young boy on her office wall was one of them.

The caravan might have moved just a bit to the east and been in the green farmlands along the river, but this was to be practice for the isolated desert treks to come. After seven hours of plodding progress, Abu Pasha found a wind-scoured depression and circled the camels. This would be camp for the night. He asked the travelers to take a walk to get the kinks out of their legs. Actually he wanted to give his drivers a chance to set up camp without interference.

They all wandered about aimlessly while the Bedouin spread two beautiful carpets on the sand, then drove stakes into the sand around their edges. In just minutes, they had erected poles, tied them to cross pieces, and thrown woven cloths over them.

It was a very small camp but looked like it had been there in the desert for a hundred years. One of the drivers had staked and tied together a hitching pole to tether the camels. The camels had all assumed the usual lump-on-the-ground appearance and were chewing away. From out of nowhere, the drivers had produced bright green fodder and laid it, along with handfuls of grain, on another carpet where they were tethered. It was camel heaven— the day's work done, moist green salad and munchies on the carpet, and nothing to do but gurgle and growl at the setting sun.

The Bedouin had erected two tents. The sleeping arrangements would be by occupation, not gender. They would all eat in the tent with the drivers. The first class accommodations would be for the expedition team. Their beds had been made for them— thick mats and heavy blankets. Each had a second blanket rolled up to serve as a pillow.

Ryan and the others ambled about, peering toward the Nile and the distant lights in the farmlands along its banks. When that grew old they sat together in the sand at the edge of the depression and chatted, waiting for supper— all but Megyn. She had wandered off someplace with Samir, Abu pasha's young son.

It was cold when Ryan woke in the middle of the night. Someone had lifted the tent flap and come in quietly. It was Megyn. She had missed supper and was looking about with a little flashlight for an empty bedroll.

Ryan rolled over, took the blanket from beneath his head, and tried awkwardly to spread it down over his body. His legs had grown cold. Finally satisfied that he couldn't do any better, he lay back and put his head down on the "pillow." It felt as though it were made of stone. He had thought of calling out gently to Megyn but decided it was better to play dead. It was none of his business. Then he thought of Spencer. His brother had been his friend and companion on almost all of his uncomfortable field trips to exotic places. When things were the worst, they would laugh about it and make groaning sounds to emphasize their shared ability to find mirth in the midst of misery. Tonight he felt very alone.

As he lay quietly, Ryan realized his head was only a few inches through the tent wall from the mouth of one of the camels. It had begun to chew whatever it is that camels chew in the night. It was comforting. He dozed off slowly with the gentle sound of the closest friend he had in the world chewing in his ear.

Perhaps it was his imagination, but he thought for a moment that he heard the sound of muffled sobbing. It came from the direction where he had seen Megyn's flashlight. The next thing he knew, it was morning. The only clue in the pitch-black tent was a strip of dim light at the tent flap and a few unpatched holes in the roof that had been invisible during the night.

Morning hygiene was everyone's individual problem. The caravan master provided toilet paper. The Bedouin themselves had no need of such luxuries. Therein lies the origin for the taboo against dipping food from a common bowl with your left hand.

Breakfast was hardboiled eggs, cheese, pita bread, and hot, very sweet tea—poured in a cascade from a campfire-blackened, brass pot held two feet above red and green plastic tumblers. Everything was delicious!

The drivers broke camp even more quickly than they had set up the evening before. As the caravan rose out of the depression, it headed southwest. They had left nothing behind but a bit of disturbed sand that the wind would soon erase.

As the day proceeded, Ryan grew sore. He could only imagine how much worse it might be if he had not been wearing his panty hose. He wondered about the rest but thought it best not to ask. Their caravan, small by Bedouin standards, was a line about three hundred feet long. Near the rear rode Samir. He had a tape player that was blaring popular Egyptian music. Two things about that— first, contemporary Arab music is nowhere near as unpleasant as contemporary American music. It is an exotic sound played on instruments rarely heard in the western world, punctuated by the insistent sound of small drums beaten with gusto. Ryan found the undulating rhythm sensual and fit perfectly with the walking gait of a camel. They seemed made for one another.

On the last camel, enjoying the music, was Megyn. Her eyes were fastened on the young boy ahead of her. The rocking gait of the two camels created the impression their riders were locked in synchronous, pelvic thrusts.

Ryan was a priest. He had heard thousands of confessions. The Megyn/Samir thing had a strange and unholy feeling about it. But a priest's job is to understand and forgive, not to get in the middle of things that might not even be what they seemed. He would try to find an opportunity to talk to Megyn discretely when the time seemed right.

The second night went much the same as the first, and the following morning as well. The hard boiled eggs seemed a little too hard and the cheese, less than tangy. The tea, as always, was a cascade of tawny delight in the morning sun.

Toward noon the caravan arrived at the sand-buried ruins of Saint Jeremiah. Slabs of stone lay all about. A few remnants of carved columns poked up from the sand at odd angles. Some bore rudimentary architectural carvings— pedestal borders, that sort of thing. There were no archaeological finds to be made here. The ruins had been poured over both by treasure hunters and archaeologists for more than a hundred years. The only treasures that had survived were hauled away long ago, most of them safe in museums in Cairo, France, England, and elsewhere.

Nonetheless, there remained an aura of sanctity here, a holy graveyard pounded relentlessly by wind and sand for hundreds of years. Even Samir shut off his non-stop tape deck. The popular Egyptian music, entertaining at first, had grown cloying. Though better than Fender guitars and Roland keyboards, peace in the wind-blown desert is not meant to compete constantly with tambourines, arghuls, ouds, and mizmars. For the tape deck to have been running all this time, Samir must have had a huge stash of batteries hidden somewhere in his gellibiya.

Megyn would know where, thought Ryan. Then he shook his head violently to drive away that bit of unpriestly nastiness.

After another night with the camel by his ear and hard boiled eggs becoming more and more difficult to swallow, Ryan and the caravan were delighted to be moving quietly into the outskirts of Fayoum. Although, as he saw it, this trek was part of the hardening process for the work ahead, Ryan had to admit he was not sad to dismount in the courtyard of the Auberge Fayum, rural Egypt's answer to the Ritz-Carlton, on the banks of Lake Qarun, a highly treasured Egyptian landmark. The lake, 130 feet below sea level, takes its name from a man mentioned in both the Bible and the Quran. He had the ability to touch anything and turn it to gold, but rebelled against Moses. That annoyed God, Who caused him to be swallowed up into the earth with all his worldly goods. Egyptians believe his treasure lies hidden beneath the waters of the lake. Ryan and the others didn't care. Their butts were sore.

Hadji Gamal Abu Pasha said he and his band would camp nearby and head back to Giza in the morning. He made the rounds with big smiles telling each one how much he enjoyed their company, suggesting they might please both him and Allah were they to favor him with a sizeable tip. Ryan obliged. Bedu, Sharon and Leila apparently did not. Abu Pasha let forth a stream of guttural Arabic at them that was obviously not meant kindly. Megyn was gone again.

Elegant by Egyptian standards, the Auberge Fayum seemed dark and heavy to the travelers. This time, each had a separate room. The drapes were of thick brocade, as were the bedspreads. The furniture conformed to the same Middle Eastern concept of elegance. You see it all the time in news coverage of high-level conferences in Middle Eastern countries— lots of gold leaf, heavy upholstery, and thick carpets. Ryan and the rest did not find it pleasant but they understood it. For them, the simplicity of Bedouin tents was far more to their taste. Bathroom facilities were another matter. Hot showers would be very welcome. Hot soup instead of boiled eggs would be welcome as well. Ryan lay down on top of the rough brocade. He meant to take just a short nap. When the light knock on the door awakened him, he had no idea how long he'd been asleep— perhaps just minutes. It was Megyn.

"I hope I'm not bothering you."

"Of course not, come in. What time is it?"

"Not late. I noticed you weren't at supper and I needed to speak to you."

"You mean I missed supper? Blast! I was looking forward to a hard boiled egg."

"Actually, it was bouillabaisse. The locals catch all sorts of fish in the lake so it was fresh and home made."

"Now I *am* sorry I missed supper. I'll go get a cheese sandwich or something. What did you need to talk to me about?"

"I have a couple of gaps in the present paper I'm writing with Leslie Balanaq at the museum. We're not far from the site where I did my initial work— the hermit caves in the valley walls at Gebel al-Naqlun. They're just a short jeep ride from here."

"I'm aware of them. I dug around in a few of them with my brother a few years ago. But I've hired a truck to carry us and our gear to El Minya in the morning."

"I'm sorry, Ryan. I don't think I'll upset anything. It will just take a couple of days and I can join you in El Minya. The fact is, it will be a great side trip. I can hire a felucca and tack up the Nile to meet you guys."

"That really does sound great, Megyn. I'm jealous. If I weren't heading this thing I'd jump ship, er, truck, and join you. OK, go ahead, but take care of yourself. I know that you know your way around but you're a pretty spectacular woman to be traveling alone in these parts, even if you've done it before. Do you have a weapon?"

"I always carry a small Beretta. Don't worry."

"Is there anything else you want to talk to me about, Megyn?"

She looked puzzled. "I don't think so."

"I mean," and he stumbled over the next words, "as a priest."

Megyn's face flushed, but she nodded in the negative.

"OK. Take care of yourself and we'll see you in a few days. I'm going to look for a cheese sandwich."

"Between the research and the felucca trip, it could take me more than a few days before I hook up with you guys."

"I understand."

To himself, Ryan thought, *I hope I don't understand*

Chapter Sixteen

The truck was waiting in front of the hotel in the morning. Everybody loaded their stuff into the back and climbed in after. The driver had brought his brother to ride up front with him. El Minya was a long drive, at least fifty miles, and the road was pretty bad. It wasn't a lonely stretch. Trucks went back and forth constantly. That was the problem. Nobody ever fixed the potholes.

It was a marvelous morning. The sun was burnt orange on the horizon, poking sun daggers trough the palm fronds and across the green fields, sometimes setting farmers' turbans aflame as they dug with sticks and gathered vegetables from the irrigation-wet soil. You couldn't help but realize that all around you was a scene that had been going on with little change for more than five thousand years. The monastery ruins, buried in the sand, that hold such mystery for the archaeologists, were built, brick by brick, then torn apart and ground down by sun and wind— and the workers continued to dig and harvest vegetables in these very fields, just as they were today.

The truck lumbered past a tall, round-topped, mud castle riddled with holes in neat tiers and rows. Little white heads popped in and out of the holes. It was a pigeon farm, the birds flying off in search of food, then returning to feed their young. The birds, too, had been doing this, non-stop since before the birth of Christ. The middle of the mud castle was hollow so a farmer could harvest baby pigeons and eggs. Baby pigeons are an Egyptian delicacy, sometimes cooked, head and all, inside a tin cup of rice. Turn the cup upside down onto your plate and you have a cone of rice with a baby pigeon inside. It's not a dainty dish to set before the tourist, but quite tasty and the baby pigeons, a dependable cash crop for the Fayoum farmer.

The Chalice crew was bouncing about like numbered balls in a lottery basket. Sharon decided to stand with her face into the wind above the cab. She let her hair fly loose. Ryan had never noticed how lovely her hair was. She always kept it in a spinsterish bun for work. Now it whipped about and sometimes flowed like a river of burnished gold. It had taken on the light hue in the Egyptian sun. She half turned and noticed Ryan staring. A funny grin pulled at the corners of her lips. She liked being noticed by men, but rarely allowed herself that treat. To be noticed by a Catholic priest had that added tang of forbidden fruit. She enjoyed the innocent tease for a moment, but suddenly needed a Twinkie. She dropped down and bounced around awkwardly as she fished through the stuff in her duffel bag. She had learned as a Third World traveler, not to pack things neatly. Everything got scrambled anyhow. Just throw everything into a duffel bag and fish around for what you need. Twinkies came wrapped individually so they were almost indestructible. And you could fish and listen for the crinkle sound of its wrapper and know when you had located one— even in the dark.

Ryan smiled as he thought how cute Sharon looked, flowing golden hair, bouncing around in tight, khaki pants, munching on a Twinkie. It was a fatherly thought but Ryan was not a dope. He knew she looked sexy as hell— and she knew that he knew. She offered him a bite of Twinkie. Should a priest on his way to explore ancient ruins accept a partly bitten Twinkie from a sexy young woman? Oh well.

"Yes. Thanks, Sharon." He could taste her lipstick on the Twinkie.

✝ ✝ ✝

Megyn was up well before dawn. She bathed, packed her things and went into the lobby. It was still dark except for a night-light at the front desk. She had made a deal with Abu Pasha the night before. She would ride east with him and the caravan toward the Nile and into the valley of Gebel al-Naqlun. When she went out the front door, her old camel was waiting for her with the others. They were used to one another. The animal gave a little gurgle of recognition. Megyn mounted easily and the caravan headed off in silence toward the horizon. It was beginning to glow softly behind the pointy, black fingers of the palms. The sun would be up soon.

† † †

After the slow progress across the desert by camel, the old truck seemed to make short work of the distance to El Minya. They arrived before noon, beaten up by the combination of worn shock absorbers and the endless string of potholes.

Bedu had managed to sleep. Leila, always alert, kept moving from one side of the truck to the other, taking in everything she could along the way. Sharon found a relatively comfortable spot on top of the luggage, making sure first that the supply of Twinkies was not in danger of being squashed. Ryan wasn't exactly comfortable but he wasn't in pain. He couldn't sleep. His mind was in a whirl. He wanted to go back to Habib's notes but he could barely read the man's horrible writing. Trying to do it in the bouncing truck was out of the question. Two things kept gnawing at him. One was the thing about him being the key. The other was even more important. He realized that, like a happy puppy offered a ride in a car, he had jumped onto this expedition with virtually no background information. A hundred million dollars had been dumped into his lap with virtually no explanation— with the promise of more if he were successful. But successful at what? One client was the oldest, and possibly wisest, organization on earth— the Roman Catholic Church. The other was a mysterious family whose financial resources were dependable according to Mohammet Kohlsoum, the banker in Alexandria. He had assured the Chalice accountant that the deposit had indeed been made in Chalice's name. Even if the Sarafians disappeared as mysteriously as they had appeared, the money was real and it was there for Ryan's use. But again— to be used for what?

Other things were bothering Ryan, too— all the recent deaths, his brother's, particularly, with all the mystery surrounding it, his son's last minute decision not to come along, and now the unexpected departure of Megyn. He was not her parent but as expedition leader, he did feel she was his responsibility.

With a bump and final cough, the truck stopped in front of the Ibn el Khassib Hotel. Chalice had arrived in El Minya. The hotel looked as old as the pyramids, sort of dingy, but all things considered, not so bad for the Egyptian Middle Kingdom where tourists rarely ventured. When making the reservation from the Auberge in Fayoum, Ryan had asked the clerk,

"The Ibn el Khassib, how many stars?"

The clerk shrugged. "I think, maybe no stars at all."

The interior of the Ibn el Khassib mirrored every bit of the dinginess of the exterior. It wasn't so much run down as it was frozen in time with a light veneer of dust over everything. It made Ryan think of a Fellini movie set.

Before they left the front desk, Ryan laid out the plan for the rest of the day. "Let's meet in the dining room in about forty-five minutes. After we eat, we'll do a little sight seeing. I'll find us a taxi for a tour of town."

The wooden floor squeaked as they walked down the hall to their rooms. Not far from the lobby a low arch on one side opened into a sitting room with several high back, overstuffed chairs, and a heavy table covered with an embroidered cloth. Above it hung a dusty, crystal chandelier. The Fellini set kept gathering detail.

Ryan glanced in as he struggled past with his luggage and his heart gave a start. In one of the big dusty chairs sat Hal Sarafian. Ryan stopped dead and dropped his bags.

"What's wrong?" It was Sharon.

Ryan looked at her, then gestured toward the room with his chin, but now the room appeared empty.

"Are you alright?"

"Of course, Sharon. I'm sorry. I guess it was the ride in the hot sun. I thought I saw somebody I knew."

"Here in El Minya? You probably just need some Twinkie," she chose the words with impish intent and smiled innocently.

"That's probably the last thing I need," but he returned her grin.

They and the others continued down the hall, peeling off, one by one, as they came to their rooms. The keys were the round-shank, iron ones that went out of use in the United States about fifty years ago.

† † †

Megyn felt uneasy. It was a short way, even by camel, from the Auberge Fayoum to Gebel al-Naqlun, but it seemed endless. The ruins were extensive— some hermit caves low, near the ravine floor, others cut into the cliffs up and down the walls of the main and side canyons. They were everywhere— almost a hundred of them. They had been scoured out of the rock over the centuries through the tireless efforts of ancient holy men, the first around the middle of the Fifth Century. Inside the cliff dwellings the walls of many had been plastered and painted with images of Christ, the apostles, Mary and a host of other iconic figures. Megyn was interested in locating a specific one. She asked Abu Pasha to make camp in one of the side ravines and bring her to the river the next day. She figured she would find what she was after or give up by then. She would hire a felucca to take her south to El Minya and join the others. He agreed. He had been well paid.

While the drivers went through the usual routine of hammering stakes, spreading carpets, and putting out feed for the camels, Megyn began to climb the cliffs and enter one chamber after another. Some were simple with just a single, shallow room. Others were extensive, extending deep into the rock, with many rooms, interior courtyards and antechambers— subterranean palaces. She knew what she was after but there were so many places to look, so many rooms, crevices, niches.

She was searching for a wall painting of a man, probably Christ, holding a chalice. Presumably it was a depiction of the Last Supper, but maybe not. It had a different aura about it. She had only seen a pencil sketch of it. Christ looked amused and the chalice was extremely large, not something to simply hold one man's portion of wine. There was a ring of medallions embossed around its rim. In the field drawing one of the medallions was missing— as though it had been plucked out— or perhaps just dislodged and lost. That was what she was here for. Could it be that somewhere in the dust and debris of Gebel al-Naqlun the actual medallion might still lie hidden? Or at least on some wall, could she locate another mural in which the medallion was still in place on the rim of the goblet? She wanted desperately to see the image carved on it. She didn't know why but felt it was terribly important.

Megyn knew she should have told Ryan about this obsessive quest but she was afraid he might say she could look into it later and must come along with them to El Minya. She could not explain the compulsion that was driving her to do this at once. The feeling had descended on her the night of that psychologically devastating experience in the museum. She could still see the smile on the face of that fantasy child as she writhed and convulsed in sexual ecstasy. She had seen a woman, only once, who had an expression on her face that matched what she had felt. That woman was made of stone, a marble sculpture by Giovanni Bernini in the Cornaro Chapel of Santa Maria della Vittoria in Rome. The sculpture is called, The Ecstasy of Saint Theresa. Hovering over the saint, her head thrown back in wild pleasure, is an angel, a young boy with wings. On his face is the same smile she saw on the face of the Fayoum boy in her office as she writhed at her desk, her underpants soaked with desire, her organs trying to clutch a phantom male organ, not actually inside her.

The memory of that experience both excited and repelled Megyn. She was terribly confused, immersed in an unholy riddle, a mix of academic curiosity, unexplained religious fervor, and shameful sex, all wrapped together in an untidy bundle that threatened to drive her berserk. Now in a deserted, Egyptian valley, riddled with ancient monastic caves, she was feverishly going from chamber to chamber searching the walls for a painting that might not exist, kicking dust about on the cavern floors in hopes she might uncover a two thousand year old medallion, miraculously overlooked by centuries of greedy thieves and probing archaeologists.

The sun was beginning to change from a bright yellow disk to a glowing orange ball. Soon it would sink behind the sandstone cliffs. Megyn returned to camp without success. She could not leave tomorrow as planned.

When she got to camp, hardboiled eggs, little cakes, and tea were waiting. As they ate, Samir kept looking at her. Now, it made her uncomfortable. She was ashamed that she had made use of the boy and was now done with him. She told Abu Pasha she would need more time in Gebel al-Naqlun. They could stay to provide a place for her to sleep or leave. She would find a place to pitch her own tent. The Nile wasn't far. There were farms all along the banks and ditches that carried irrigation water inland to the fields. There was no way she could get lost.

The Bedouin said they would stay. She had money and they had time.

☥ ☥ ☥

Ryan decided they were moving faster than necessary. It was not a difficult conclusion to reach since he didn't have any idea what they were doing here in the first place. He said they could rest after lunch and take a cab through town when it grew cooler. He received no argument.

The cab turned out to be a cart with leather-upholstered benches along its sides. It was drawn by a plump donkey. In a bin below the driver's seat was a stash of bright-green alfalfa, Egyptian gas tank for a one-donkey-power engine. Probably many of those, familiar to the world through the Bible, traveled like this.

One of the great things about touring a strange city in a donky cart is that you move slowly. We are so accustomed to moving quickly in our automobiles that speed seems normal. Things flash by and we think we have seen them, but we haven't. We've seen a blurred image that conveys a sense of reality, but is only that, a sense of reality, nothing more. We have used only our sense of sight, and even that, a blurred caricature of itself.

Before computers, Hollywood animators would blur their drawings so theater audiences would not be uncomfortable with what they saw on the screen. Sharply defined animation images look unreal. American life is a blur.

Suddenly tossed into a living tableau of biblical life, the Chalice troupe had a marvelous time, clop-clopping through the streets of El Minya. Sometimes the air smelled like donkey manure, at others like hot oil, as they passed a street merchant pouring batter onto a hot drumhead to make fresh noodles. The smell of baking bread was everywhere, and so was the aroma of tobacco smoke. Egyptians smoke all the time— mostly cigarettes, but when there is time, the shisha, or water pipe. The Turks call it a hookah. Tobacco smoke is drawn through a reservoir of water so it reaches the smoker, cooled and filtered.

The most common aroma on the streets of El Minya is wood smoke. Small fires burn everywhere, to cook food and heat blacksmith forges. Some are kept glowing to ignite corncobs, which are used to light other substances, usually tobacco.

Ryan paid the cart driver and asked that they be let off at a shisha bar. On the sidewalk, Egyptians sit at small tables, elaborate water pipes in front of them, as they suck in the cool smoke and watch the rest of the world go by.

Ryan took one table. Sharon sat with him. At the next table sat Leila and Bedu. A waiter soon put a shisha before each of them, filled their bowls with tobacco, and touched a glowing corncob to each, indicating they should suck on the flexible hose while he held the smoldering corncob in place.

Sharon coughed when the smoke, even though cooled and purified, came bubbling through the water, up the colorful hose, and into her lungs. The waiter smiled patiently. Sharon was a delightful sight for any male. Bedu sucked at his hose like an expert. He probably was. Leila smiled, but refused the shisha politely. Ryan enjoyed his smoke but also the sight of his group, sucking away like seasoned Egyptians, on a sidewalk in ancient El

Minya. But all at once the sobering thought came to mind of Megyn, off alone, or worse. He hoped she was not doing something foolish that might jeopardize not only her dignity but even, perhaps, her life.

Men walked by in flowing gellabiyas and colored turbans as the Chalice group smoked and talked. The passing men stared openly at Sharon and Leila. A few women passed, totally imprisoned in burqas, only a grid of small holes over their faces to observe the world. Perhaps they smiled but their garments were a two-way prison, a filter against life that locked them inside, but locked out the world as well.

The waiter returned a number of times with tobacco and glowing corncobs as the sun set.

Chapter Seventeen

Father McAndrew was having a splendid time in Autun, but had received no divine revelation as to why he was there or what he might be looking for. The cathedral was magnificent and he was intrigued by the assertion that somewhere in its bowels it sheltered relics of Lazarus, believed to be authentic. Supposedly, Lazarus and Mary Magdalene traveled to France where he became the bishop of Marseilles but was assassinated, thereby dying for the second time, after being raised once from the dead by his friend, Jesus of Nazareth. Eventually, Autun shared his remains with other influential cities. Supposedly, Marseilles kept his head.

Fact, fiction, or religiously inspired myth, Father McAndrew was ecstatic to be in the midst of ecclesiastical history. He could spend years examining the wonders in this place.

It is hard for an American, even a Roman Catholic priest, to fully grasp the antiquity of Church architecture in Europe. The village of Autun was founded by Emperor Augustus around the time Christ was born. The cathedral was built a thousand years later to cope with the crowds that were pushing one another around to get a look at the relics of Lazarus.

Though a true believer, Father McAndrew always had a queasy feeling about sacred relics. He had seen too many crime scene dramas on TV in which they make a big thing about evidential "chain of custody." Relics had passed through too many hands over centuries to suit McAndrew. His own mother wore a scapular, a religious necklace that contained pieces of Christ's cross. A nasty friend of the family had once said to her, "If all the pieces of cross around the world were gathered together in one place there would be enough wood to rebuild Chicago after the fire."

McAndrew, himself, had chuckled when he was digging among the Buddhist temples in Burma and heard that the whole nation had shut down for a week because they were transporting one of Buddha's teeth from Yangon to Mandalay. He would go and take a look at the remains of Lazarus, but he had his doubts. Beyond questioning was the beauty of the cathedral and the incredible sculptures attached to it almost everywhere one looked. Among the most notable, were those created by a man named Gislebertus. In 1130, he hammered his name into a sculpture of the Last Judgment. It says. "Gislebertus hoc fecit," Gislebertus made this.

James McAndrew, attired in Jesuit black, a crucifix stuck casually into his cincture, and his hands clasped behind his back, examined the sculpture with the eyes of both priest and archaeologist. He was still searching for a clue as to why he was here.

Perhaps he'd found it! Suddenly he noticed something in the Gislebertus sculpture that reminded him of an Egyptian papyrus, a drawing in the Egyptian Book of the Dead. In chapter one hundred twenty five of the funerary text, there's a drawing of a ceremony referred to as The Weighing of the Heart. Osiris, god of the underworld, looks on as the heart of a deceased noble is measured against the weight of a feather. A horrible beast, Ammit, waits to see the result. It has the head of a crocodile, the body and front legs of a lion, and the hindquarters of a hippopotamus. If the heart is heavy with sin and outweighs the feather, Ammit will stretch his ugly neck up to snatch the heart in his crocodile jaws and devour it. He is known in the Book of the Dead, as Ammit, The Gobbler. Above the horrid scene, sit forty-three gods and goddesses. They watch without emotion.

Now here, above the west door of the Autun Cathedral, on the right hand side of what has been called, "the magnificent Last Judgment tympanum," Gislebertus carved a similar, Christian ceremony. Art critics have named it The Weighing of the Souls. Archangel Michael is shown leaning on the scales to help someone fake his way into Heaven.

The angel is cheating God! thought McAndrew. He had recalled that Ryan suggested he pay special attention to things involving angels. Was this what he was supposed to be looking for? Had he found a clue to angelic dishonesty?

He had asked Ryan what he meant but he had just shrugged. "I haven't the slightest idea. Someone important told me to look into angels. I'm just passing it on. Maybe it has something to do with this whole mysterious project of ours."

"Who told you to look into angels?"

Ryan had a curious look on his face. "It was the Papal Nunzio."

"Archbishop Gandolfo?"

"Thou hast said it," Ryan smiled, quoting the words of Jesus to Judas at the Last Supper.

Now they were both confused. In Egypt, Ryan remained confused. In France, so did James McAndrew. In Gebel al-Naqlun, Megyn was covered with dust and sweat as she ran from cave to cave in confusion, looking for something that might not exist. In New York, Paul Quinn sat at a posh bar sipping Lafroaig on the rocks, hoping desperately to catch the aroma of a certain woman's flesh he'd experienced once and now craved constantly.

Chapter Eighteen

James McAndrew, S.J. could not be certain he'd found what he came for in Autun. How could he be? He'd been sent by a man who didn't know why he was sending him here. He had to keep looking.

The sculptures adorning the cathedral are so numerous and diverse they defy meaningful examination in the time allotted for James' side trip. There are scenes from virtually every biblical text. There are signs of the Zodiac, caricatures of beasts, both real and apocryphal. There are depictions of humans working at every imaginable task. The sculptures are not smooth and lifelike, but rude and bizarre, almost a frenzied statement by the artist that he had to sculpt everything in Heaven, Hell, and on Earth, before he, himself, would be summoned to judgment and have his own heart weighed for value before God. Many of the sculptures are gargoyle-like. James felt he was on a wild goose chase. With a silent chuckle, he thought, *If I look long enough, I'll probably find a portrait of an evil looking, wild goose. I wonder if that would satisfy Ryan as mission accomplished?*

McAndrew examined his own whimsical thought and realized something important might have been buried within it— "evil looking." Perhaps that was the sub-text of this whole cathedral and its decorations. He shied from the thought. This was a highly revered edifice, a center for devout worship for more than a thousand years. Could he, a Catholic priest, in a few hours, find a flaw that had escaped millions for eons? First he had questioned the idea of relics, and now highly-revered art work that others considered masterpieces, perhaps even divinely inspired. He decided to question himself rather than those wiser than he. He kept scanning the sculptures to see if he had missed anything of importance. But he couldn't get rid of the feeling that there was something strange about many of the grotesque images.

He began to examine the carved capitals, the pieces that adorned the tops of the many columns. At one, he stopped dead in his tracks. It was truly ugly. A man with a rope around his neck was hanging from a tree. The man's eyes bulged and his tongue hung far out of his mouth. The rope had been thrown over the branch of a palm tree. On the ground, pulling down on the other end of the rope, were ugly, half- human, half-beasts with open mouths and beady black eyes. They had apparently hoisted the figure into the tree by his neck. One was either pulling down on a second rope, or more likely, propping up the branch with a pole so the branch would not break and allow the figure to survive. Both of the beast creatures had wings. Were these angels involved in assisting a suicide, as the archangel at the Last Judgment had been involved in deceiving God? James found this last sculpture particularly revolting.

He searched the cathedral for a docent-priest who might give him an explanation of this apparently very unholy sculpture. He found one just exiting a confessional booth at the rear of the church. He beckoned to the cleric to come walk with him to the column he had been examining. Probably because of his Jesuit garb he got a broad smile from the man who came along at once. In his faltering, French, James asked him about the scene.

"Mon Père, quelle est la significacion de cette scène, là ?" (Father, what is the meaning of that scene?)

"C'est le suicide de Judas Iscariot." (It's the suicide of Judas.)

"Mais, mon Père, il y a là deux personages aidant. On dirait plutôt un meurtre qu'un suicide, non ?" (But, Father, there are two figures helping. It looks more like murder than suicide, doesn't it?)

The priest smiled gently and gave James a French shrug. *It's in God's hands. The matter is closed.* He left quickly before James could challenge him with another silly question. As he left, James thought he heard him mutter, "Les Jésuites !"

James hadn't examined the north door of the cathedral yet. By the time he got there another priest was pointing out the artwork above it to two old ladies.

James walked over and looked at the sculptures. Above the door was a famous piece, the depiction of Eve— naked. It was reputed to be the first sculpture ever allowed in ecclesiastical art of Eve displayed in the nude. Like the other Gislebertus works, it had strength, but lacked enough detail to be considered at all pornographic. James noticed that a piece of an adjacent sculpture was missing. He didn't want to upset the priest and waited for him to finish with the ladies.

"Excusez-moi, mon Père ! Je vois que plusieurs parties de la sculpture manquent." (Excuse me Father. I see that many pieces of sculpture are missing.)

"Oui, c'est dommage, n'est-ce pas ?" (Yes. A pity, isn't it ?)

"Où sont-elles?" (Where are they?)

"Partout." (Everywhere.)

"Et cette partie là ?" (And that piece there?)

"New York – aux Cloîtres. Vous connaîssez ce musée ?" (At the Cloisters. Do you know that museum?)

Oui, bien sûr. Merci, mon Père. (Yes, of course. Thank you, Father)

James didn't know if he had anything to bring Ryan, but this might give him something to think about. He remembered Ryan's reply when he had asked about angels— the words of Jesus to Judas at the last supper. Now he was seeing murderous angels, cheating angels, and gargoyles with wings. He had a funny feeling the missing piece of sculpture in New York might just be one of an angel.

It was time to go someplace where he understood at least a bit of what was going on— Egypt.

Chapter Nineteen

Ryan asked the clerk at the Ibn el Khassib if there was a phone he could use. There was, but it seemed more for decoration than communication. It had a layer of fine dust on it. The clerk gave it an official wipe with a cloth and handed it to Ryan.

"Thank you."

"Most pleasing, sir."

To Ryan's delight, when he lifted the receiver he heard a dial tone. The next series of hurdles was no worse than he expected. There was a routine to which he had become accustomed over the years— contact the local operator, ask for the long distance operator, state the desired overseas contact, provide your own number, then sit in the lobby for an hour or so to wait for the operator to call back after making a connection. As long as you knew the routine and did not expect anything different you were OK. Ryan had learned to bring reading material with him. It was sort of like going to the doctor. Whether MD's, dentists, or Egyptian telephone operators, once people realize they can make you wait, they do.

Ryan had meant to bring one of Habib's diaries with him. They had taken on a disquieting aspect in his mind. He was afraid of them. They contained statements he needed to explore. He was sure of that from the little he had seen. He had kept turning the phrase over and over in his mind— the key— "Ryan is the key."

He didn't run back to his room to get the book. The phone might ring and he would have to go through the whole thing again. Who leaves a doctor's waiting room, even to go to the bathroom, if they know they're "next"?

Fifteen minutes passed, twenty. Finally, after a half hour, the phone rang. The clerk picked up the receiver.

"Khassib! Na-rham. A-jal. OK. Shukran.*"*

"Pleasing, sir. It is for you."

Ryan took the receiver. There was a lot of crackling and popping.

"Father Quinn?

"Yes. Is this Barbara?"

"Of course. With all of you off playing— who else? I'm the only breathing soul here in this temple to ecclesiastical bank accounts. I can hear my own heart beat."

Ryan liked Barbara Lenkowski's sense of humor. He and she were among the few who realized you didn't have to be dull to be a brilliant scholar.

"How about Paul? Isn't he there?"

"I haven't seen him for days. He talked about going to your brother's place and that was about it. Oh, yes. He did phone a few days later to say he had to visit the Cloisters. He didn't say why."

New Yorkers are singularly blessed. There is a bit of everything cultural in the world at their fingertips. The Cloisters is a perfect example— a conglomerate of medieval artifacts housed in a structure built in a hybrid style, part Romanesque and part Gothic. New Yorkers could visit the Middle Ages for the price of a subway ride. It was the incredible accomplishment of the Metropolitan Museum of Art with money from several sources, principally John D. Rockefeller, Jr.

"Has Megyn called in?"

"No. Not a word."

It wasn't time to worry about Megyn. She was not in telephone country. He knew that. He knew she was a tough gal despite her looks, and had a lot of field experience. He was uncomfortable, nonetheless.

"How about Father McAndrew?"

"I thought you'd never ask. At least I've got some news there.

"Yes. He called from Autun, wherever that is."

"It's in Burgundy."

"He said he doesn't know what he found but needs to talk to you. He'll be catching a flight out of Paris tomorrow and connect in Cairo with a flight to Luxor."

"Why Luxor?"

"That's what I asked. He said, "No reason." He said he needed some peace and quiet to think. He said he knew a felucca sailor in Luxor and intended to float down the Nile for a few days and catch you someplace in the Middle Kingdom."

"What?"

"Don't ask me. Talk to him."

"Sure. I'll call you again in a few days. If you need us, you can leave a message at the Ibn el Khassib, in El Minya. We'll be here for a few more days. Try to find out what Paul's doing, would you?"

"OK, boss."

Ryan went back to his room and dug out Habib's notebooks. He looked for the passage where he mentioned Gandolfo and the "key" thing. Habib's handwriting was tiny, cramped, and virtually illegible. He took it to the window where there was more light. It seemed to say, "Ryan is the key," but something was scribbled after it in Arabic. Ryan's Arabic was not great but he did know a number of common phrases. He was sure it said. "Insha'allah", God-willing— but maybe not. Arabs say that all the time, for everything— "Today it will rain- God willing." "Today it won't rain, God willing." The worst is when your Egypt Air pilot says something like— "We will be landing safely in Luxor in one hour, God willing."

Only Gandolfo could straighten this out. Maybe he could add something to clear up his suggestion about angels, too.

Paul wasn't that hard to find. Barbara Lenkowski knew he wasn't at Chalice. He wasn't picking up the phone at his own apartment. That left the bar at the Sherry-Netherland. She often left messages there for him. The bar tender never sounded friendly. I guess it gets to you, tending bar where the women are either old and ugly, or young and beautiful, but wearing jewelry that cost more than your father's funeral. He knew Paul but never let on that he was aware of his name. He always referred to him as "that rich priest's kid," not loud enough so anyone could hear him. He had been tending bar the night that gorgeous gal had jacked the kid off right in front of him. It had been fun making believe he hadn't noticed so he could watch the asshole try to sneak out the door hiding his wet pants.

"Has Paul Quinn been in?" It was Barbara Lenkowski.

"Who?"

"You know. The priest's kid."

"Oh— the rich priest."

"Cut it out. This is important. Has he been in?"

"I'll say he's been in. We could stand him in the corner and get rid of the potted palm. He's here every evening and stays until lights out. I think he's waiting for someone."

"Who?"

"I don't know. But if it's who I think it is, I would, too."

"Never mind that. Tell him his father wants to know what he's been doing and to call me. I'm Barbara at the office. And there's a message for him from Father McAndrew who called in from France. Got a pencil?"

"Go ahead."

"Go up to the Cloisters. There'll be message for you at the entrance gate. Just tell them you're from Chalice."

"From whom?"

"Chalice. It's a company name. Got it?"

"Got it!"

"Thanks."

"Are you single?"

"Taken."

"Figures. Probably rich, too."

"No. Just taken."

✝ ✝ ✝

Paul got the message later that night. He didn't like the idea that everyone knew they could find him at the Sherry Netherland. That meant that Em could find him if she wanted. Apparently she didn't. He sat there until closing anyhow. The bar tender had a smug look on his face as he polished glasses and glanced over at him every once in awhile.

"Another one?"

"No. Thanks for the message."

"No problem. What does that Barbara look like?"

"She's hot. Why?"

"Just asking. She sounded hot."

"She's taken."

"Oh?"

The Cloisters don't open until 9:30. No problem. Paul rarely got up before 10 unless he had to. It's a short trip by public transportation but you have to transfer from the subway to a bus— too much trouble. Paul took a cab. He was sleepy and cranky when he got there.

The woman at the entrance didn't seem to know anything about any note. Paul told her again who he was and emphasized that his father was <u>the</u> Reverend Ryan Quinn who had provided a number of priceless artifacts to the museum.

The woman was not impressed. Every second New Yorker thinks he or she is someone special. "Wait here. I'll go get a supervisor."

The woman came back. "They're all in a meeting. You can wait in The Trie Café. It's in the French Trie Cloister, but you'll have to pay the general admission to get to it— twenty-dollars."

Paul dug a twenty-dollar bill out of his pocket, slapped it down, and glared at the woman. She seemed unruffled, accustomed to rudeness— less here at the Cloisters than at her last job with the Transit Authority. "Straight ahead and downstairs."

Paul had no idea why he was here and would have preferred to be somewhere else but had to admit that the Cloisters was a magnificent museum. He knew it had been built in the thirties with Rockefeller money but it felt like medieval Europe.

The Trie Cloister is a composite of French architectural pieces from the Carmelite convent at Trie-en-Bigorre, a monastery at Larreule, and the Abbey of Saint-Sever-de-Rustan. Most of the pieces are authentic. Some are accurate duplicates of originals. Only an expert can tell which were which. It isn't important. The whole museum was meant to recreate the mood of a bygone era, not represent itself as anything but a tasteful setting for the display of medieval art. In that, it is more authentic than numerous other venues around the world. It has become customary recently to present replicas of famous settings to the public to save wear and tear on the actual sites. Tourists now visit a copy of Stonehenge, not the real thing. The same is true of the caves of Lascaux with their prehistoric drawings. Even the murals in jungle ruins at Bonampak in Central America were found to be deteriorating from the carbon dioxide in visitors' exhalations and the constant flashes of tourist cameras.

Paul made a conscious effort to put away his impatience and enjoy the surroundings. New York museums, once dark places intended for serious scholars and students, became meeting places for urban sophisticates. Why have a high-priced watercress sandwich at a mid-town restaurant when you could munch delicately on a ham and brie baguette amidst priceless artifacts, and at the same time, impress your friends with the elegance of your choice in dining? Always pressed for money, the museum directors learned that there was a rich crowd that preferred to pay for food and beverages than make donations. The menu items were always light, rather expensive, and chosen to sound as dissimilar as possible from food that might appeal to the lower classes.

Paul ordered a Turkey - St. André on ciabatta with cranberry mustard. It came with a roasted pear and a few leaves of arugula. To drink, he ordered a bottle of water from Fiji. He would have his cappuccino afterwards.

Half-way through his turkey sandwich, a very slender, probably gay, gentleman came to his table. "I'm so terribly sorry, Dr. Quinn. "I am Jeremy de Borquist with the Cloisters. No one told me you had arrived until just moments ago."

"Not doctor yet, Mr. de Borquist. Soon, I hope."

"Of course. I have a note for you from Reverend McAndrew in France. He is well known to us and highly respected. He said it would be most convenient to deliver it to you here since you will want to examine some of our artifacts with regard to it."

"That makes sense. Thank you very much. What does it say?"

"I have no idea. It came in by FAX and was placed in an envelope immediately by my secretary. I didn't think it appropriate to examine it."

"I'm sure it would have made little difference, but I appreciate your delicacy in handling it. May I see it?"

"Of course, of course. What am I thinking? Here." He withdrew a Metropolitan Museum envelope from the inside pocket of his jacket and handed it to Paul.

"I'll leave you to it then, Mr. Quinn. Please ask for me if you need any help. And once again, I apologize for keeping you waiting."

"Not at all, Mr. de Borquist."

Paul tried to hide the fact that he had gotten cranberry mustard on his fingers and onto the envelope. He was relieved when the obsequious de Borquist left hurriedly so he didn't have to wipe his hands before shaking with him.

The note was short.

Strange connection between Lazarus, Autun Cathedral, and angels. That's all I have , but learned there is a sculpture at the Cloisters by Gislebertus from here. I believe it's in the Langon Chapel. Take a look at it for me. Your dad didn't give me much to go on. Maybe all this makes sense. Thanks. Give my best to Jeremy de Borquist.

Father James

Hardly worth getting up early for, thought, Paul. He wouldn't rush his lunch. "Waiter. You can bring my cappuccino, now."

Paul sat looking at the way the light played on the rows of double columns around the Trie courtyard. They were truly magnificent, from a period when art meant more than time. Each of the double columns had twin, carved capitals, but not copies of one another. There were no two alike. In fact, even the marble columns were different colors, probably chosen by ancient stonecutters for their unique qualities.

When the waiter retuned, Paul asked how to get to the Langon Chapel, then sat back and slowly sipped the froth from the top of his coffee. When he was done, he left a generous tip and went upstairs and worked his way through the various chambers, finally entering the Langon Chapel through the massive oak doors from the Romanesque Hall. At the far end, behind an altar, was a carved wooden statue of Mary. The label identified it as having come from Autun, but McAndrew had said nothing about Mary.

Paul walked around the chapel looking carefully at all the artwork. Then he saw it— a block of carved stone stuck on the wall— an angel in flight. The plaque beneath identified it as the work of Gislebertus, taken from the Cathedral of St. Lazarus in Autun, France. But what of it? He stared at it. Something about it struck him as familiar. He had never been to Autun, nor to this chapel at the Cloister. A voice behind him whispered near his ear, "Does she look like me?" Paul turned on his heel and caught the sent of her. It was Em.

Chapter Twenty

This was just what James McAndrew needed— peace and quiet, away from everything and everyone except the oarsman, floating down the Nile. The trip out of France and then out of Cairo had been the usual mayhem. Finding a room at a cheap hotel in Luxor was no problem. In the morning he had gone in search of Ghadalla, a felucca sailor he had met years earlier.

Jusef Mohamet Ghadalla had been a man just out of his teens, a dark-skinned youth with teeth as perfect as his flowing white gellabiya. He was a con man, flashing his smile at tourist women, luring them to board his felucca for a sail on the Nile, a brief journey among the thousands of lotus plants that had made it past Aswan Dam, now bobbing their way toward the Middle Kingdom.

When they first met, McAndrew had asked Ghadalla, "How much?"

"Ten American dollars."

It was robbery and Father McAndrew had told him so. Ghadallah had smiled— guilty, but so what? There would be a fat old woman by in a moment who wouldn't care.

"For how long?"

"A half hour."

"No. Thank you."

"For you, Father, an hour." McAndrew had been wearing his roman collar.

James McAndrew and Jusef Mohamet Ghadallah ended up sailing for almost three hours. The young entrepreneur had brought along pita sandwiches and bottled sodas that he drew from beneath his rowing bench as they sailed through noontime and beyond.

"Would you care to share my lunch, Father?"

"Thank you. You are very kind."

"It was prepared for me by my very old mother. It seems she is dying so I had to pay the doctor with my last pounds and she had to make my lunch."

"How much, Ghadallah?"

"Ten dollars?"

"Five."

"OK. At least I will be able to buy a little bit of that expensive medicine the doctor ordered."

"OK. Ten."

"Allah will bless you— I mean Jesus."

The two men smiled. The sun was bright, the Nile smooth, and the lotus plants, an undulating carpet around the felucca as they drifted past green fields and wading water buffalos, just as pharaohs had for five thousand years.

† † †

That was ten years ago, thought James. Would he find Ghadallah still here, the fast-talking youth with flashing white teeth? Yes. He recognized his voice. He was sitting beneath a canopy with other sailors, near the river, waiting for tourists.

"Ghadallah!"

"Father!"

The face that turned to James was his old friend but deeply creased by the sun. The smile was as broad as before but several front teeth were missing. He was probably no more than 28.

This time there was no bargaining. McAndrew wanted to float downstream for more than a hundred miles to El Minya in the Middle Kingdom— food, drinks, everything.

Ghadallah suggested a ridiculously high price.

Father McAndrew said, "I think twice that much would be better. How is your mother?"

"She died when I was born."

The two men laughed and were happy they would be heading down the Nile in the morning.

Chapter Twenty-One

Seasoned travelers know there are two ways of indulging their wander lust— go where the tourists go, be comfortable, pay a lot, and see the things everyone will ask you about when you return home. The other way was— go where few people go, risk discomfort, and see things you will remember as uniquely your own.

Ryan and his group fit into neither category. They would go where they thought they needed to go, try to be comfortable, and hope to find what others have never seen, and may not believe. El Minya offered a bit of everything, the hoped for New Kingdom of the renegade pharaoh, Akhenaten and his beautiful wife, Nefertiti.

Akhenaten rejected the Egyptian god, Amun, and built a new holy city near El Minya, dedicated to his chosen god, Aten— the shining disk of the sun. The long-entrenched, powerful priests were dismissed as misguided. They were furious. But how do you fight the Pharaoh? On the other hand, how does anyone dare dismiss the high priests of the established religion?

There are no pyramids around El Minya. There are no massive temples. There is no Valley of Kings, riddled with the opulent tombs of pharaohs, priests and dignitaries— no Valley of the Queens with remains of royal women. All those trappings of wealth, dignity, and power were, and remain today, either to the north near Cairo, or to the south, near Luxor. The splendor of the Middle Kingdom is little more today than a row of painted, rock tombs in a cliff, a few toppled temple columns, and rows of adobe bricks near the Nile, working their way back into the soil. The son of Akhenaten and Nefertiti was named Tut-Ankh-Aten to honor his father's chosen god. With the demise of the pharaoh even that did not survive. The child was renamed to honor the god favored by the priests. He became Tut-Ankh-Amun, and was eventually buried in the Valley of the Kings with the rest of the great pharaohs near Luxor. Akhenaten's image was chiseled off wall carvings wherever they were found and even the hieroglyphs that extolled his virtues were scratched over and made as illegible as possible.

Reverend Ryan Quinn, the priest, accepted the divine origin of The Church. Dr. Ryan Quinn, the historian and archaeologist, always felt there was some connection between the heritage of the ancient pharaohs and the beginnings of Christianity. He also felt it was possibly here in El Minya, that clues to that connection might still exist.

Was that the reason behind this mysterious mission, funded heavily by two separate organizations? Was the purpose of the one to uncover the connection and proclaim it to the world— and the purpose of the other, to uncover the connection and stamp out all evidence of its existence? Was that why Ryan was The Key, or at least possessor of the key? Had he been sent into battle to fight for opposite sides of a controversy? Or was it possible that they both had the same objective but for different reasons?

Em and Hal on one side, and Pietro Gandolfo on the other, had the answers. Were they aware of one another? Ryan had been too excited by the well-funded research opportunity to examine that aspect rationally. Foolish, he thought. The other possible source of information had been Habib Colophon, but he died, confessing a transgression against the will of God— or so it seemed. But he had left illegible diaries describing Ryan as the key, if that was actually what it said.

Ryan mused cynically, whether or not a key inserted into a lock had any idea of its importance? Keys don't have brains. But then, neither do plants. Yet some Japanese scientists had thought "good thoughts" over one potted plant and "evil thoughts" over another. The good plant thrived and the cursed plant withered and died. Some other nut, probably with a government grant, had set up super-sensitive recording equipment and captured audio of plants screaming when they were uprooted. *The realms of possibility are infinite*, he thought. *Perhaps I am like a dumb key, or a plant about to scream if somebody pulls me up to Heaven by my hair. If possibilities are infinite, then they are like God.*

Ryan was tossing all this around in his head as he tried to sleep on his lumpy mattress at the Ibn El Khassib. He didn't feel his musings were profound but he nurtured them to keep his mind from wandering to the vision of Sharon's butt in tight khakis. He wondered if, down the hall, she might be rummaging about for a Twinkie in a shorty nightgown. This was getting dangerous. He was a priest and meant every syllable of the vows he had taken at ordination. He got up and paced around the room. His briefcase lay on the table near the window. It was dark outside. He pulled back the heavy drape and looked up at the sky. The stars were a bright salt and pepper even through the dusty window glass. Stars are bright like that in rural New York, but only during the dry night skies of autumn. Here in the arid desert, the night sky is always a majestic canopy of twinkling lights.

Ryan unzipped his case and took out one of Habib's diaries. If only the man had taken some classes in penmanship. James McAndrew, an epigrapher, could undoubtedly decipher Habib's hen-scratch with ease— and so could Sharon. But one was not around, and the other was not an option under the circumstances. Besides, he was not yet ready to share Habib's thoughts with anyone.

He opened the diary gingerly. What a mess! There were inkblots, grimy splotches, and coffee rings. Habib, like Ryan, wrote with pen and ink, but had hung onto a dull-tipped, old-friend of an instrument, more like a crow quill in need of trimming. Besides all the normal mess of a much-used diary, this one was full of sweat stains from midnight scribblings by kerosene lamp in 120 degree tents in the desert. And then, worst of all, there was Habib's habit of wandering back and forth among English, Arabic, Greek, Russian, and Hebrew. He was a scholar too comfortable with his talents to imagine they might not be shared by others.

Ryan thumbed quickly through the maze of scrambled entries, stopping at times to look at a few crude drawings. One popped out at him. He recognized it! It vaguely resembled a coin Habib had once given his brother after one of their field trips. It looked somewhat like a Shekel of Tyre— the only coin accepted for payment to enter the Jerusalem Temple in the time of Christ— the same coins that lay on the tables of the "money changers" despised by Jesus, and also the coins probably used to pay Judas for handing over Christ.

Shekels of Tyre are not rare among ancient coin collections. They are valuable, but not worth more than couple of hundred dollars each. A great many have been unearthed in ancient ruins— some even found by farmers working in their fields. The Jews were good at hiding their personal treasures for protection against bad times— with good reason.

There had been something different about the coin Habib had given Spencer. He hadn't paid attention at the time but here it was in the sketch. It appeared to be a Shekel of Tyre, but the face of a Ptolomy, a Greek ruler, should have been on its face but wasn't. Instead, there was a scene with several figures, a palm tree, and some Hebrew lettering. Habib's sketch, like his handwriting, was not easy to figure out. The Hebrew was beyond hope— at least as far as Ryan was concerned.

He puzzled over it for a while, then tried to read the notes above and below it. It seemed Habib did not believe it was a coin at all but a medallion— the notch in it, not a haphazard slice taken by an avaricious cheat but something purposely carved in detail. Did that mean it was a forgery? Habib didn't think so but that left it as a mystery.

Ryan tried to read further but there was a knock at the door. He threw on a robe and went to open it. It was Sharon.

"I thought you might be in the mood for a Twinkie."

Chapter Twenty-Two

Megyn was exhausted. Her startling good looks were undiminished by the grimy sweat that poured down her cheeks. Her hair had come undone and hung about her shoulders. Her blouse was transparent, soaked with sweat. As always, she wore no bra, so her breasts appeared totally naked. She was alone and didn't care. She was proud of her body and probably wouldn't have cared even if she weren't alone. She was gasping for breath. The cave she was in was large and hot. The air was completely still. The only light was what little came down the passage from outside into the large chamber where she sat breathing heavily.

As she tried to calm herself, her eyes slowly adjusted to the dim light. Then they opened wide in astonishment. This might be it! Not the medallion. Maybe better. Fifty feet long and eight feet high, all across the back wall, was a magnificent Coptic mural.

Eight figures, bigger than life, sat staring into the chamber. They were all seated, each with a huge chalice in his left hand, the base supported on his left knee. All of the men were dressed alike in a brown garment that hung to their sandals. Over their shoulders, each wore a white shawl that fell open to expose the brown garment covering their knees. In an identical gesture of blessing, each held up his right hand with two fingers held straight up as though to make the sign of the cross. Despite the uniformity of their garb, the positions of the chalices, and the hands conveying the blessing, each wore a unique hat. They were different shades and shapes.

Megyn noted that the figures did not have golden halos traditional in Coptic murals to imply sainthood. These figures were empowered to convey blessings but they were not saints. Who were they? She had a small flashlight in her pocket and went close to examine them. Starting at one end, she examined the artwork carefully. The figures were so large, the rims of the chalices propped on their knees, were at her eye level. The heads of the figures loomed above her in the half-light.

The rim of each chalice bore a round emblem that faced the observer. All were different. On one, the last to the right, the image had been scratched out. Only its outer edge had survived the vandalism— a circle marred by an irregular notch. It did not appear to be a slip of the artist's brush but a purposeful depiction of an important aspect of the image. Whatever the significance of the eight figures, their chalices, and the emblems, medallion number eight had been erased.

Megyn could not reach high enough to examine the headgear of the eighth figure. Perhaps it might convey some clue to the vandal's intent. She knew it was customary for ancient Egyptians to chisel away and deface the images of those whom they wished erased from history. It was partly ritual but partly practical. Out of sight, out of mind.

She couldn't see anything peculiar about the headgear. They were all different colors. This one was brown. It looked as though it might have been purple at one time. No help. Megyn stood back. It was still terribly hot but she was so excited by her find that she was anxious to get back to the group and report her find. She had a small flash camera with her. She stepped back again and took a picture, then another. Then she started taking a series of closer shots, moving along the mural so she could reconstruct it later using a computer "stitching" program to create a panorama. When she was done, she sat down on a chunk of rock that must have fallen from the roof. She looked up to see where it had come from and was startled again. The ceiling was covered with ancient art. There was an image of Christ at the center. His hand was raised in blessing like the figures on the wall. Around His head was the traditional, golden halo. In His other hand He held a huge chalice. Around its rim were eight medallions— the same as the ones on the chalices on the wall. Seven were distinct. The eighth, once again, had been defaced by some vandal. All around the figure of Christ, angels stood with their wings folded. There were eight of them. One had the face of the boy from the tomb in Fayoum. Megyn gasped when she saw it.

It was growing late. The light coming down the passage from the outside was taking on an orange glow. The sun was about to set beyond the dunes of Gebel al-Naqlun. Megyn made her way slowly up the passage. Near the entrance she could hear men talking in the valley below. They sounded agitated. She carefully moved to the entrance making sure not to be seen.

They seemed frustrated, going from one cave entrance to the next, calling out. She understood the guttural desert Arabic.

"Where are you, whore from Hell? You have defiled the son of our leader. We have stones to smash your skull and silence the moans of your whorish ecstasy."

Megyn was terrified. She thought Abu Pasha and the rest had left. What did they know and why had they come back to search for her? No one had seen her with the young boy. Had he boasted to the men about their sexual encounter? Didn't Arab men laugh and slap one another on the back about such stuff?

The men kept yelling. "Come out, yellow-haired demon— raper of boys. My son is dead, his hand held between his legs, calling your name as he struggled for his last breath. Where are you, spawn of a she-camel?"

Luckily for Megyn there were hundreds of cave entrances all up and down the valley and its tributaries. She was in a deep cave with many rooms high above most of them and the sun was about to set. They would never find her. She withdrew to the interior and down a narrow passage where she could hear them if they entered her cave. She hoped there might be a side passage that cut around to the entrance so she might use it to escape if she heard them getting too close.

Now she squatted on the floor in the dim light, panting like a trapped lioness. Her survival instincts had sharpened her senses and pumped her veins full of adrenaline. If she needed to, she could run, jump, and claw her way past them. Part of her knew that wasn't true, but she clung to the thought. It was all she had— that and the knowledge that she had done nothing but make a young boy very happy. She remembered his astonished panting as he wrapped himself in the softness of her breasts and plunged his penis deep into her. Such a liaison was forbidden in her own prudish America, but here? She had made love to a boy. She had hurt no one. She didn't know what they were talking about. Maybe they weren't looking for her, but for whom, then? She had made a lot of young boys happy over the years. Many had probably bragged about their experience. Very few had convinced their friends that anything had actually happened. Nothing unpleasant ever occurred afterwards, either to her or to them— as far as she knew.

Megyn thought she heard the men's voices growing closer. She tried to make herself smaller, to keep her thigh muscles taught to spring up and away if necessary. Then, all at once, she heard a soft voice at her ear that made her leap to her feet, her heart pounding.

"Don't be afraid. I am here to help you."

The words were in English but with a strange accent, the clicking sound she'd heard once before. She couldn't see him but she knew it was Hal Sarafian. It was his voice and the strange fragrance of his breath.

Now the men had entered the passage leading to where Megyn stood. They were growing closer and closer. They seemed to sense that their prey was near and grew louder, yelling disgusting references to her womanhood, threatening to tear out her organs and feed them to wild dogs. They were carrying torches. The light of the flames began to flicker on the walls. The ugly sounds of the enraged men bounced about in the hollow chamber.

Suddenly, Meghyn felt Hal, or whoever this was, fold her in his arms— but they didn't feel like arms— more like wings. But there were arms, too— and hands. One hand worked its way down over her breasts and into her pants, coming to rest between her legs, cupping the mound of her sex.

Megyn was terrified but somehow aroused at the same time. The wings, if that was what they were, kept her tightly enfolded in a rustling cocoon of what? Feathers? Hal's breath within the cocoon filled her nostrils with an unearthly fragrance that made her head swim. His hand between her legs moved gently, a firm finger caressing the groove between the folds of her labia, moving to her erect clitoris, then into her vagina, rubbing and caressing with slow determination. The finger moved up into her and became warm and swollen, moving rhythmically in and out of her like an engorged penis. This was impossible. Megyn felt herself squirming with passion even as an angry mob of men with flaming torches came roaring into the room.

They thrashed about in the chamber, cursing and swinging their torches back and forth to throw light into all the corners. In the middle of the room, overwhelmed by a throbbing, violent orgasm, Megyn stood, wrapped in a protective shield of feathers, moaning loudly, thrusting her hips and rotating them slowly, then more rapidly, as a rush of incredible pleasure coursed through her whole body. The angry men neither saw her nor heard her gasps and moans, though she stood right there in their very midst.

Apparently angry at yet another empty chamber, the men left, cursing and yelling as they went up a side passage. Megyn collapsed to the floor as the sound of their retreat diminished. She could tell after a while that they had left the cave and were outside. The sound of them eventually disappeared completely into the distance. The angry mob was gone. They disappeared into the desert, the men's shadows stretching longer and longer across the dunes beneath a purple sky pierced above by the first silent stars of evening.

✝ ✝ ✝

Megyn lay on the dusty floor as though dead, her legs parted slightly, her arms at her sides where they had been pressed close by the enveloping wings. Now the chamber was deathly silent. She was alone.

It was many hours before she stirred. When at last she did, the light of dawn had just begun to creep down the floor of the passage to where she lay. It illuminated her body, casting its silhouette along the lower edge of the opposite wall. She gathered herself slowly and sat up. Her feet and ankles were in the light. Her torso and above were still in the shade. She remained like that a long time, not moving, just hugging her knees to her chest.

The sunlight moved up her body until it shone into her eyes. She shaded them with her hand and rose to her feet. Clumsily, on sleep-numbed legs, she made her way toward the sun. As she moved, she looked down at the floor. Every pebble and ridge was accentuated by the horizontal light, so the pebble-strewn floor looked like a rocky landscape as though seen from the window of an airplane.

After a few steps she stopped to look back. She saw nothing but her own footprints and the disturbed dust where she had lain. There was no sign that anything had taken place other than her activities entering the chamber, taking pictures, and now leaving. Had it all been an hallucination? As a scientist she could hardly deny the evidence of the undisturbed dust on the floor. Nothing had happened here! And yet, she had never had a dream so explicit or vivid. She had been exhausted, dehydrated, and hypoxic. Perhaps, she had fainted and slept. That had to be it. She needed to get out of here, get some air and water. Despite the evidence, she found it hard to dismiss the possible reality of what she had experienced. It was all too real in her mind. She dared not relax. Physical danger might still be lurking. She <u>had </u>slept with the young Bedouin. That was a fact. She might have violated some ethnic taboo that she was unaware of— one that required public stoning. She needed to get away from Gebel al-Naqlun as quickly as possible. She made her way to the entrance, taking great pains to observe everything around her, moving like a cat, ready to sprint from an enemy should one appear.

From the cave entrance, high on the canyon wall, she could see far up and down the valley. It was deserted. The men, if there had been any, were gone. She had thought ahead and left a cache of water and bread in one of the lower caves. She would have to go there first. It was not an option. From there it would not be a long trek to the broad band of irrigated fields that flanked the Nile. There she could find a felucca sailor to take her down a canal and out onto the river where they could tack slowly against the current to El Minya.

Back in the cavern, a gentle breeze washed out of a side-passage into the chamber where Megyn had slept. The dust on the floor barely stirred but in one corner a small feather fluttered about for a moment.

Chapter Twenty-Three

Father McAndrew was in a marvelous mood. He and Ghadallah had shared some of the most peaceful and idyllic moments of his life— at least, he had. Ghadallah had spoken mostly of his family. He had a wife and two children. They had a little piece of land irrigated by a small canal fed by the Nile. Everything in Egypt is fed by the Nile. It is the source of all life. The priest, in tan shorts and a white shirt, lay on the deck of the felucca. He was barefoot. Ghadallah, in a bright white robe and turban, sat at the tiller guiding the craft this way and that to keep full the cheeks of its great white sail.

McAndrew looked up into the sail, thin enough for a single sailor to manage, yet tough enough to fight the sun and wind. The priest could see the disk of the sun through it. It was bright, but not so bright he feared looking directly at it. The disk was like a hypnotist's bauble, hanging there in the puffed out sail, drawing his gaze, luring him into a waking dream.

The Nile flows through some of the most arid country on earth. From a jet at thirty thousand feet, it looks like a multicolored ribbon— the open water, a stripe in its center, with bands of green on both sides the irrigated fields that hug the river's winding path through the desert.

At Luxor, the river is narrow and cluttered with huge boulders, some as big as houses. A thousand miles to the north, at Alexandria, the irrigated fields spread out to form a giant triangle as the Nile shatters into a complex pattern of interlaced streams, all seeking the final goal, the Mediterranean Sea. Beweeen the two ancient cities, the Nile flows smoothly, the green of the irrigated fields on each side growing narrow at times, disappearing entirely in a few places where the river cuts through hard rock, and leaves no room for life-giving alluvium.

McAndrew and Ghadallah were sailing north down a broad stretch of the ancient river. Green pastures and tall palms offered a peaceful scene on both sides as their felucca drifted with the lotus blossoms. Here and there, water buffalos stood, stomach-deep in the marshes, munching lush reeds and grasses along the west shore. Some were hidden within tall stands of papyrus. None seemed concerned by the passing felucca. The little boats had been sailing by for five thousand years.

Occasionally, a young boy would brave the waters and wade close to the boat in hopes of extracting a few coins or at least a friendly greeting. McAndrew was generous with both. Each gift of money raised a wrinkle on Ghadallah's brow. A coin handed from the boat was money he would have no way of extracting later from the good priest, despite any eloquent tale of personal poverty and woe.

Slowly they slid past eons of human history. Some ruins were visible. Most were beyond the broad marshes and shoreline screens of tall date palms. Even in the treetops the waters of the Nile were at work, feeding the plump dates that would feed the brown workers who dwelt in the mud huts below.

In McAndrew's mind's eye, it seemed they were toy figures in a model sailboat atop a green carpet of lotus plants all drifting north together—past Dendera, Asyut, Hermopolis, and past the monasteries he'd visited in his younger days. Some were grand and some just half-hidden caves— St. Shenute, St. Pshoi, Muharraq, Bawit. He would visit them again, he hoped, but today it was his joy to feel the sun on his face, smell the perfume of the lotus blossoms, and observe the Biblical purity of the figure in white at the helm of his little craft.

Did he love Jusef Mohamet Ghadallah? Yes. But to his great joy, he realized that he loved the handsome young man as a priest loves one of his flock. He could see Ghadallah at the tiller as though in a print from a child's Bible history. He could even imagine a caption below the hand-colored drawing— "Nile Boatman in the Time of Moses." He saw the reeds on the shores as those in which the baby had been hidden from the Pharaoh.

McAndrew rejoiced in the fact that he was a human, driven by base appetites, but through God's grace, given a calling to the priesthood, where he had been able to control them and seek a union with the Divine. He was a man floating down the Nile toward the ancient city of El Minya with one of his children. He was Reverend James McAndrew, S.J.

Chapter Twenty-Four

Megyn Corbet, disheveled and not yet feeling at all at peace, sat near the bow of a felucca, tacking with the wind. She was headed up the Nile against the current. Earlier, she had found her stash of supplies and slipped out of Gebel al-Naqlun without incident. As she had anticipated, she was able to make the hike to the river even exhausted as she was.

Egyptians can smell money through walls, or in this case, across fields of vegetables. It was hardly fifteen minutes from the moment she approached cultivated fields that she had collected a curious crowd of children, all babbling at once. Many held an open palm to her, pointing to it with the forefinger of the other hand. The message was clear. Put something there—anything, a stick of gum, a pencil, a ballpoint pen, some food, or best of all, money.

Megyn tried to be gentle with them but she was tired. She finally exploded when they started pinching her and pulling her hair. Blond hair was a rarity. A single strand yanked out and brought home would be a source of delight to its new owner, and of interest to all who might get the opportunity to look at it. There may have been blonds in ancient Egypt but very few today. The mummy of Amenhotep's mother-in-law still retains a mat of reddish hair. The blond gene pool was swallowed up long ago with the invasion of Muslim Arabs.

A heavy man in a voluminous white robe and immaculate white turban came to Megyn's rescue. He chased away the children in guttural Arabic that, unfortunately, Megyn understood. Then with a sweet smile, he turned to Megyn and addressed her with courtly deference.

"Would the lovely lady be needing transportation by any chance?" On foot, and limping a little, Megyn's need was obvious. There was some money to be made. "Perhaps a donkey? Or if the lady can afford more, perhaps a cart with a cushion on which to relax?" His English was perfect.

Megyn's response was a gift from Allah. "Yes. I am very much in need of transportation. But I am headed a very long way and am afraid you may not be able to provide what I need." She spoke in Arabic. This meant his bargaining would be more difficult. A lost blond would be desperate. One who spoke Arabic might still be desperate but probably not lost.

"What did you have in mind? He continued to speak in English.

"I have a very long way to go and wish to use the river as my highway. Perhaps you have a friend with a felucca?" She spoke in Arabic.

"No problem. You happen to be addressing Captain Nemo, master of the finest felucca on the Nile. You will be heading to Cairo?"

Megyn doubted both his name and the accuracy of the claim, but it was a felucca she needed, not the sailor's credentials or those of the craft. "No, not Cairo— the other direction."

Captain Nemo's eyes opened wide. Perhaps she did not know Egypt, after all. "That is against the current. A very difficult journey, dear lady."

"Ana mish merakem dil" (I am not a stupid donkey).

The captain's eyes narrowed. "To be sure. Sailing against the current is one of my specialties. I was taught by my father who once sailed from Cairo to Luxor wth a boat full of camels."

"A noble feat, captain. Would you then be able to manage an eighth that distance with a small, blond archaeologist?"

Ahah! An archaeologist, he thought. *That explains it. Deserted by her workers at some dig, able to speak Arabic, and undoubtedly able to pay.* "Of course, dear lady. How far?"

"I must meet my friends at El Minya."

"That is, indeed, very far— not beyond my skills, but of course, there is the round trip to be considered. Very expensive."

"The trip back will be with the current, captain. How much?"

"My felucca is the finest on the Nile— very trim and light, perhaps the quickest as well."

"Haste is not my main concern. Perhaps you know a sailor with a more cumbersome ship who is in need of money to make repairs."

Nemo smiled broadly. Egyptians are astute businessmen but most of all they enjoy the banter of the bargain. He knew he had an unusual woman on his hands, beautiful, intelligent, and with the mind of an Egyptian.

"How many days," she continued, "and how much?" Megyn knew when to shift bargaining gears and get to the nitty gritty.

Nemo did a quick calculation in his head. It had nothing to do with wind, currents, or number of days. He was calculating in rice, tobacco, new clothes, food for his camel, paint for his felucca. It was a calculation based on the adversary's innocence and need as measured in tangible goods. Megyn had removed innocence from the equation and also urgency. Nevertheless, he named an astronomical sum.

Megyn didn't blink. She countered with a sum so low it was equally ridiculous. Nemo liked her pluck. They bargained for a bit when Megyn asked innocently, "In a riverside community like this, there must be many feluccas. As I said, I need only an old, badly worn craft to make the journey. Do you have any friends with feluccas in need of repairs?"

Nemo had met his match. Egyptians hold no grudges at being outmaneuvered. They admire the talents of a shrewd bargainer. The price dropped drastically. Megyn had her ship and its master.

Egyptians are tough about bargaining, but once the deal is made their generosity is enormous. Nemo opened his house to Megyn as though she were a beloved relative come to visit. She dined with him and his family and spent the night on a comfortable cushion in a small room with his three daughters. They had been warned not to pull her hair.

In the morning they gathered supplies for the trip— rice, fresh vegetables, bread, charcoal to feed a small stove, and clean water. Meat and fish would be available along the way. It might be four to six days. Nemo, heavy and jolly, seemed no threat. All men found Megyn beautiful. Men like Nemo had lived long enough to know the limitations of their possible success at seduction— zero. He would mind his manors. Megyn also had insurance. They had made their bargain without any money.

"My friends at the Ibn el Khassib in El Minya will pay you handsomely."

He had no doubt she spoke the truth. Nemo knew the Ibn el Khassib. He had been there once and was overwhelmed by the thick carpets and heavy drapes. He could smell money dripping from every tapestry.

"They are all museum people from New York. Two are Jesuit priests."

Though a semi-devout Muslim, Nemo smiled broadly and made the sign of the cross, touching his forehead, heart, and shoulders. He got the shoulder part backwards but close enough to make the point.

Museum people and churchmen! There would be more work. After all, he had the finest felucca on the Nile and it was docked a short camel ride from the hermit caves of Gebel al-Naqlun. And who had a bigger, stronger camel than he?

Chapter Twenty-Five

The Nile, an undulating, carpet of lotus plants, was even more versatile than the magic carpet in the Thief of Baghdad. This one carried, not a little prince, but two archaeologists travelling in opposite directions— all at once. They both rode the same, sun-drenched carpet to El Minya, desert kingdom of the once powerful Pharaoh Akhenaten.

☥ ☥ ☥

In El Minya, Ryan had survived a serious test of his priestly vows. He was more afraid of his own potential weakness than of hurting Sharon's female pride. He found her terribly attractive and apparently she found him equally so. He resorted to psychological cunning. Besides hormones, he and Sharon shared a fascination with manuscripts and Egyptology. He had invited her in but immediately went to his briefcase and withdrew one of Habib Colophon's diaries. A retreat into Habib's notes would provide both of them with the otherwise impractical cold shower suggested by medieval clerics to control raging libidos. A mental picture actually flashed through Ryan's head of taking a cold shower with Sharon, but he cast it out at once.

"Here, Sharon. Look at this. I need your help. I think there is some very important stuff in these diaries but I can barely read most of what's here. You are the most accomplished linguist and expert in deciphering decaying manuscripts that I know of. This should be a snap for you. Sit over there where the light is better and see what you can get out of this one."

He had caught her full attention. She might have a great body, but she was a scholar of the first rank. Focus her mind on work and she became an intellectual laser beam. Ryan paced around the room as Sharon sat near the light and took out a small magnifier she kept stashed improbably somewhere in those tight khakis.

"A snap? I don't think so. Wow— talk about hen scratch! This looks like the guy was writing with a nose hair dipped in crankcase oil."

Ryan was relieved that Sharon's earthy sense of humor had replaced the potentially dangerous mood of sensuality that had been there moments before.

"He was never known for his penmanship, Sharon. He probably wrote most of his diaries either riding on a camel, sitting in crowded subway, or in the back of a beat-up truck."

"Don't get defensive. I know he was your friend. Even so, this stuff is a real challenge. I'm used to working with ancient, crumbling documents. For the most part, they were written by professional scribes. The documents are often in bad shape but once you're able to piece them together, the writing is usually quite distinct. This is different."

"Just try, Sharon. That's all I'm asking. Hopefully, McAndrew will be along soon and can help out."

The subtle challenge of another epigrapher, possibly more talented than she, provided the incentive Ryan had hoped for.

"He seems to be talking about Alexandria and the Great Library."

Ryan was not surprised. Habib might have written about anything in these diaries. He had not given Sharon the one he had been looking at— the one with the drawing of a medallion. Nor had he handed her another one possibly even more sensitive. A note had been folded and stuck between its pages. The note was so thick it had partially split the binding of the old diary. Ryan had pulled the notes out and was startled to see what Habib had scribbled on its outside leaf—

To be read only by my lifelong friend and colleague, Ryan Quinn. This is my final word, my "colophon." Forgive me, Ryan. God will not.

—HABIB

Ryan sucked in his breath when he read the words. Not only did they sound ominous, but also reminiscent of Colophon's dying words. What was so horrible it would keep a priest from confession for fifteen years? Or prompt him to write a secret note to a friend citing the same conviction, that he had deeply offended God?

Ryan would have to solve this mystery when there was more time to deal with it appropriately. His old friend was dead. There was no rush. Besides, it would be up to him to struggle with the poor penmanship by himself. He would not willingly violate his friend's wish that the message not be seen by anyone else. If only he were better at reading Habib's horrible scrawl. How do you keep something to yourself when you need help just to read it at all? In any case, Sharon was certainly not the person he wanted at his side working on the note. He was afraid he might become entangled in an unforgivable sin of his own.

"He says something about the burning of the great library and that it was no accident. Then he talks about other book burnings around the world— especially the destruction of the ancient Mayan codices in Yucatan. I'm sorry, Ryan. This isn't going to be easy. He may tie it all together but when you can only catch a word here and there it certainly seems disjointed. In the midst of it all, he says something about angels, and then something about Lazarus and something else about the apostle Judas."

"Habib had a mind as sharp as any I have ever known. Rambling was not his style, Sharon. You're right. This isn't going to be easy. You'd better go on to bed. We can work on it tomorrow. I think it's important."

Sharon realized she was being dismissed and took it without any sense of emotional rejection. She realized she was putting Ryan in an uncomfortable position by being alone with him in his room. She didn't understand the Catholic hang-up with priests and vows any more than she could figure out why religious men in her own, Jewish faith, thought it was a good idea to wear braided sideburns and funny underwear. Science rarely provided the consolation afforded by religion, but at least it seemed to make sense. She handed the diary back to Ryan and headed for the door.

"Thanks Sharon. I really appreciate your being here on this trip." It was an awkward thing for Ryan to say but Sharon understood. He was apologizing for being both a man and a priest alone in a room with an attractive Jewish woman who might not realize the torment his dual role posed. Actually, she did, and felt a moment of compassion for him.

"Thank you, Ryan. In this expedition, you have given me an opportunity that many Egyptologists would kill for. Good night. See you in the morning."

She had brought the issue down to one of professional courtesy. He knew she had accepted his apology. In hot, dry El Minya, he hoped the shower in his room would be cold enough.

Chapter Twenty-Six

After a fitful night, Ryan was happy to see daylight poke its fingers beneath the thick, window drapes. Egyptians equate thick with rich. The Ibn el Khassib caters to the rich. Ryan rose and took another shower, this one warmer than the last. There was still a great deal on his mind but it would all settle into some sort of manageable order. It usually did once the monsters of the night had been driven back by Aten, the sun god— at least for a while.

In her room down the hall, Sharon was sleeping peacefully. Passions rise and fall more slowly in women than men. Her fascination with Father Ryan Quinn was growing but without any urgency. It did not upset her. Besides, unlike Father Quinn, she was not subject to arcane traditions and draconian rules imposed by crusty old men in Rome.

Was it premonition? Before leaving New York she had bought a slender book at a shop on Barclay Street that sold Catholic religious articles— a "catechism," a book of doctrine for Catholic school children. She often bought books written for children. It was the quickest way to get the basic facts of a subject, presented simply and succinctly. Anything of interest could be researched in depth if need be. This book was titled, "A Pocket Catechism for Kids." The salesman had smiled unctuously at Sharon and asked how old her children might be. He looked puzzled when she smiled back and said she had none. "It's for me. I'm single and Jewish." She added the last with a sense of impish glee. To punctuate her mock-hostile reply, she took a Twinkie from her purse and began to munch on it as she handed the clerk her Visa card.

The book was just what she wanted. It began with a series of succinct questions and answers, meant to be memorized by children. Bit by bit, it put forth the basics of Catholic belief and ritual.

Q. Who made you?

A. God made me.

Q. Why did God make you?

A. God made me to know and love Him in this world and be happy with Him in the next.

The questions and answers went on and on— very simple and direct. A quick read that promised to give Sharon all she might want to know. Basically she was an atheist, though more probably an agnostic. As a scientist she was aware that it is virtually impossible to prove a negative. If there were a God she was sure His presence would be physically manifest— an eternal flame, an indestructible hunk of metal with His name on it— that sort of thing. The Kabah, that big black stone in Mecca, seemed to provide such proof for Muslims, though she doubted they ever tried to take a chisel to it. They say it is "the right hand of Allah with which he shakes the hands of his people." An interesting idea, with a special twist. They believe it came down to earth white as snow but was turned black by the sins of man. *You should be careful who you shake hands with*, Sharon thought irreverently.

The Ark of the Covenant seemed to provide similar physical evidence of God's existence to her Jewish ancestors and for her own orthodox parents— a box endowed with fearsome powers that could be carried around by handles like a sedan chair. It could generate thunder and lightning and devastate hordes of enemy combatants. *Conveniently*, she thought cynically, *the Ark had mysteriously disappeared before modern technology had emerged, leaving the Jews to fend for themselves while Arabs worked feverishly to develop atomic weapons to level Jerusalem. Of course, modern Israel already had nuclear weapons, but feared to use them lest they enrage the whole world that was always looking for another excuse to hate Jews. Had they, perhaps, hidden the Ark away in a secret crypt, quietly sizzling with ancient fissile material, its physical proof of the Divine, poised to blow Israel's enemies to smithereens and lift a mushroom cloud above them for all to see?*

She had let her mind wander as she walked down Barclay Street, away from the Catholic religious articles shop and its smarmy clerk. If there were a God, and Catholics held the key to the eternal question of creation, it would take more than a Roman Catholic catechism to convince her. In the meanwhile, she would glean what she could from the book. She didn't want an inside look at Roman Catholicism. She wanted to get inside Ryan Quinn's head. In El Minya, down the hall from him, she slept soundly.

Chapter Twenty-Seven

With a population of over 4 million, Alexandria is the second-largest city in Egypt. It was founded by Alexander the Great in 331 BC and remained the nation's capital for more than a thousand years until the Muslim conquest in 641 AD.

Author, Lawrence Durrell, who loved the city, described its climate in rather melancholy prose—

"…there is no spring in the (Nile) Delta, no sense of refreshment and renewal in things. One is plunged out of winter into a wax effigy of a summer too hot to breathe. But here, at least, in Alexandria, the sea-breaths save us from the tideless weight of summer nothingness, creeping over the bar among the ships, to flutter the striped awnings of the cafés upon the Grande Corniche."

Borg al Arab Airport is about 15 miles from the center of town. Once a military base, it sees relatively little traffic, mostly corporate jets from the oil rich nations of the Middle East. A few of the sleek machines were sitting silent on the tarmac as a Falcon 2000EX circled and landed. On its tail, the papal insignia of Benedict XVI shone brightly in the sun— gold and silver keys crossed behind a red and gold shield, topped by the papal mitre. The plane landed quietly, just a chirp as its wheels touched the runway, then a rush of reversed jets to slow its forward motion.

The engines whined for moment as the pilot increased thrust to turn toward the terminal. As the plane came to a stop, an airport worker, legs pumping hard with the effort, pushed a set of stairs against the plane just as its door opened to reveal the dark interior. A man in a light suit stepped out, blinked for a bit in the sun, then struggled clumsily down the stairs, holding carefully to the handrail. By the time he reached the bottom, a black Peugeot had stopped a hundred feet away. The driver jumped out and opened the rear door. The man limped directly to it and got in. They drove away without going through the formalities of customs. The plane and its occupant were well known.

At the El-Salamiek Palace Hotel, the man in the light suit limped up the hall behind a bellhop. He found his room a bit too ornate for his taste though he had grown used to overblown displays of luxury over the years. He had found that old age is far more tolerant of excess comfort than the opposite.

Pietro Gandolfo decided to soak in a tub before venturing out. He was in no hurry. The meeting was still a number of hours away and the subject for discussion was one that had been dealt with many times over a period of two thousand years.

He had selected the meeting place— Kom El-Dikka, the Roman Theater. Built in the Second Century, the amphitheater has thirteen semi-circular tiers of white and gray marble benches and original mosaics still visible in some places between them. During the days of the Ptolomies the theater was dedicated to Pan, the Greek god of shepherds and flocks. Actually, Pan was most noted for his indulgence in worldly pleasures, but to Gandolfo it was the shepherds and flocks aspect of its nature that seemed more appropriate to the theme of this rendezvous.

☥ ☥ ☥

Elsewhere in the city, another old man arrived— this one very simply. He came by train from Cairo— Third Class. He wore a simple, black dishdasha and kufi— the featureless cassock and skullcap worn by millions of Egyptians. Other than his massive, gray beard, nothing distinguished him from the rest of the travelers in Misr Station. Even the beard did not truly set him apart. There were many such in the crowd that poured from the station onto Nabi Daniel Street.

The man was old— very old, but he walked briskly in the direction of the Grand Corniche. He carried himself with an air of aristocratic dignity out of keeping with his age and simple garb. The walk to the Normandy Hotel would be no more than ten minutes for a young man. It would have taken no longer for this energetic old man except for the fact that he fell into a slow pace to take in the sounds and sights around him. For him, such a walk had become a rare treat. He had been subjected for years to a level of pampering he detested. The aromas and boisterous foot traffic of Alexandria evoked pleasant memories of his youth. They carried him back to a time when his stride had been even stronger and his devotion to God just beginning to ripen. Even at eighty-six, he was not soft. He had been hardened in the Western Desert where he had lived in a cave for many years as a hermit. He had been comfortable with himself there and assumed a new name to symbolize his detachment from the world. He became Anthony the Syrian. Only religious discipline and devotion to his faith induced him to return to civilization. The end of his austere existence had come at the command of Pope Cyril, Patriarch of the world's fifteen million Coptic Christians.

This straight-backed, old man, easily lost in a crowd, was Nazeer Gayeb, born three-hundred miles north of Alexandria, in Asyut, on the banks of the Nile. He was now, Pope Shenouda, successor to Cyril. His appointment to that lofty office, came after internal church squabbles in 1971.

His Holiness stopped for a few moments at a vendor's cart. On it was a huge, brass, coffee machine. For a few coins, the vendor produced a demitasse full of frothy, brown coffee. The old man took the little cup in his gnarled hands, like a child reaching for a toy. After tilting his head back to savor all but the dregs of the thick, sweet brew, he resumed his stroll, a contented look on his face.

Like the man himself, the Normandy Hotel was of the people, plain to look at, not even a separate structure, simply the fourth floor of a building at Eight Gamal el-Din Yassen, a hotel in which the bathrooms were "down the hall."

Content to be in this place he knew so well, His Holiness, Pope Shenouda, decided to take a short nap. His meeting would not be for several hours.

The sun was an orange disk that hung over the ancient theater, bright but not dazzling, behind a silhouette of sharp-leaved palm trees. It cast a warm glow across the tiers of marble benches that descended to the ancient stage. It was quiet and deserted when Gandolfo arrived, except for the lone figure of an old man seated near the stage. The man was dressed in a black dishdasha and kufi. As usual, His Holiness had arrived early and without fanfare. He had sat in silence for some time before he heard the approaching footsteps of his old friend.

Archbishop Pietro Gandolfo, in a stylish Italian suit and elegant calfskin loafers, hobbled down the marble stairs, his leather heels an irregular staccatto against the stone slabs as he struggled to manage his limp. Finally, he reached the tier just above the stage where his friend waited patiently. He side-stepped along the aisle until he reached the seated figure. Shenouda would have chosen a seat easier to reach had he known Gandolfo would enter the theater from the upper level. In addition, he did not recall that Pietro had a limp when last they met.

"Masaa' alkhayr, Nazeer— good evening, my friend. It was kind of you to meet with me."

"Saluti, Pietro. It has been a long time. We were both young and fascinated with the incredible secrets the desert sands might reveal."

"We were not wrong, your Holiness."

"Your Holiness? Should I then address you as Archbishop?"

"Of course not."

"Then, as before, to you I will always be Nazeer, the country boy who grew up on the banks of the Nile."

"And I, Pietro Gandolfo, too rich for his own simple tastes but grown accustomed to gold and silver."

The old man rose. In the orange glow of evening the two hugged one another for a long time. When they finally separated there was a tear on the old patriarch's cheek. The eyes of the Italian were misty as well.

"Now, what is it that has brought you from Rome with the insistence I journey from Cairo without a word to my flock?"

"The same thing that most likely brought your Pope Cyril to meet with our Pope Pius the Twelfth at Castel Gandolfo fifty years ago."

"Aha! And why this time do they send an underling like you to meet with me?" There was a twinkle in the old man's eye.

Pietro took up the gambit.

"Benedict is German, you know. He has never come to grips with Egypt's primitive plumbing."

The two laughed loudly, their outburst echoing off the marble slabs in the empty theater. The eerie sound of it jolted them to an uncomfortable silence.

"Let's get out of here, Pietro. I don't care how vital our meeting is, I need the warmth of humans around me. Let's go to a café and share some coffee as we used to. Do you need a hand? I see you walk poorly. What happened?"

"I fell while trying to climb into a nuns' bedroom."

The two roared again with laughter.

"No, seriously, my friend."

"I was up on a scaffold, sketching the sanctuary ceiling at Saint Pshoi, south of Asyut. It felt as though someone pushed me. I suspect one of the angels."

This time neither of them laughed.

"I could have been killed but only broke my leg. One of your incompetent doctors in Aswan set it badly."

This time they chuckled lightly but without conviction.

"I'm sorry, my friend. Let's go."

† † †

It was noisy in the Patisserie Delices. A mix of locals and tourists had kept the café constantly bustling since 1922. Nazeer Gayeb was delighted with the rattle of dishes and cutlery. Pietro Gandolfo felt at home. It was very much like a Roman espresso café. He ordered cappuccino and a Greek Baklava. The Patisserie was noted for its Greek Baklava, similar to the Egyptian variety but with an added drizzle of cinnamon and honey. Nazeer ordered a dish of Cassata, the café's own ice cream creation, and an Egyptian coffee, one of those small, sweet concoctions like the one he had enjoyed on his way to the hotel.

The clatter of dishes and cutlery mixed with the babble of chatter was perfect for the discussion of sensitive matters. No one beyond their table could possibly hear their discussion, and should anyone attempt to record them, the effort would be a dismal failure.

The two men seemed divorced from the importance of their meeting. They were truly enjoying the evening, the ambience, and the luxury of indulging themselves with tasty treats. The fact that they were enjoying their hedonist behavior together lessened Nazeer's guilt. Pietro had long since forgiven himself his lavish indulgences. Rome is anything but a hermit's cave. Yet it was Gandolfo who was the first to wipe his lips with a linen napkin and assume a serious air.

"I've been told to ask you for a favor, Nazeer."

"I suspected as much. I hope it is within my power— and conscience— to oblige you, my friend. Go on."

"In fact, it is our friendship, not mismanaged protocol, that suggested I, not the Holy Father, meet with you."

"I suspected that as well. We old men of the cloth understand the value of friendships in our world devoid of feminine companionship."

"It has happened again, Nazeer, and this time I was an accomplice to the transgression. My involvement is not known to the Holy Father. But that aspect of it is not the reason I am here."

"What are you referring to, Pietro?" The concern was clear on the sun-darkened face of the Patriarch.

"Once again, the Chalice has been unearthed."

"I know. But that was many years ago and it disappeared again, just as Rome has always wished."

"You knew?"

"The desert winds carry more than sand into the caves of our far flung monasteries. It was before my time as Patriarch. I was myself living in the desert when it happened."

"You know, then, that it was my old friend, Father Habib Colophon, who made the discovery?"

"Yes. And that you were nearby, perhaps sketching some mural in one of my sand-buried monasteries."

"Exactly. I happened to learn of the find from an illiterate laborer who was working for Habib, clearing sand from the site."

"And you made no mention of it to Rome?"

"Worse, Nazeer. I never mentioned to Habib that I knew and he never mentioned it to me. As both theologian, historian, archaeologist, and priest, he was apparently aware immediately of the dangerous significance of announcing his find. Coward that I was, I chose not to share his dilemma. I said nothing and he said nothing. I left to examine some murals to the south— left Colophon to announce his discovery or make it disappear. He chose the latter."

"It was to St. Pshoi that you retreated, wasn't it?"

"Yes. How did you know that?"

"And was it not there, that you had your unfortunate fall from a scaffold— perhaps pushed, as you said in jest, by an angel?"

Archbishop Pietro Gandolfo's face grew ashen.

"Until this moment, I never made such a connection. If it's true, the Holy Father's elaborate precautions to maintain the secrecy of this meeting were pointless. Those who might wish to know, already know."

"Precisely, my old friend. So, it is far better a jolly café than a somber Roman theater in which to share secrets, no?"

"As usual, your wisdom trumps my feeble attempts at clever political manipulation— your Holiness."

They both smiled.

"Out with it then, Pietro. What is gnawing at your gut— recently grown quite large, I might add?"

This attempt at wit fell flat. Pietro was truly disturbed by his mission and the request he was now forced to bring to the table.

"Representatives of the Holy Father," he began in a low voice, "feel that the Artifact would be best protected were it kept under close supervision in the Vatican as it once was."

"That is debatable, Archbishop."

Pope Shenouda, pushed his dish of ice cream to the side and folded his hands on the table in front of him. "But in any event, what have the Vatican's opinions in this matter to do with me?"

"They feel, your Holiness, that the Artifact may presently be in your possession." There! He had said it. He had accused the leader of fifteen million Coptic Christians of clandestine shenanigans.

Nazeer tossed off the accusation. This was his friend. Besides, verbal jousting was not his strong suit. It had gotten him thrown into exile for a long time by President Anwar Sadat. Only that man's assassination, and a later pardon from Hosni Mubarak, had returned him to the Papacy of Alexandria.

"The Holy Father's manipulative operators are wrong. I don't have it. Strange that you should accuse me, Pietro. It was you who were on the scene when it was uncovered."

"No, Nazeer. I admit I was nearby but never saw it, nor do I know what was done with it. I didn't want to know. You, of all people, know why."

"It would have set you either on the side of God or on the side of your Church."

"That's putting it bluntly, but yes."

"So we have the same old problem, eh, my friend? It has always been solved through your church's unilateral actions to obliterate all evidence of its existence."

"Blunt again. Yes. And now the task falls to me."

"I cannot help you, Pietro. I cannot because I do not have it. If I did, it would be a far more complicated matter. I would have to make a very difficult decision. You ran from such a decision in the desert. I now run from it over dessert."

Despite the momentous nature of the issue, they both chuckled at the word play. Nazeer continued, "As you know, the followers of my Church have possessed it for moments. But it has always been snatched away by yours, then hidden away with all evidence of its very existence expunged, to the point of defacing some of the murals in my monasteries to keep silent the truth that its nature would demand explanation."

"I am torn, your Holiness, between the practicality of my Church's actions and the possible heresy they represent. The Holy Father and the two-hundred-sixty-five popes before him, have all come to the same conclusion, and found justification for their actions in the dichotomy of Christ the Man and Christ the Son of God."

"Don't lecture me on theology, Pietro. I am not a first year divinity student."

Pietro's face flushed at the rebuke. I apologize, your Holiness."

Nazeer sat back and thought for a moment.

"No. It is I who should apologize, old friend. You are undoubtedly just as learned in theological matters as I. We simply find ourselves on parallel paths with certain differences of opinion. As you know, our churches have been joined at the hip, so to speak, for hundreds of years. Though "the Pope" to the faithful of my Church, I am also considered a bishop in yours. But let's get on with it. I do not know the whereabouts of the item, nor have I ever. I thought you or your Pope, did."

"I'm afraid I do not, Nazeer. I willingly recused myself from that burden by galloping off on a camel to Pshoi when Habib Colophon made his find. He told me nothing and I asked nothing. If he recorded its present whereabouts, he did not include me among his confidants."

"That is a disappointment. I was hoping to convince you that perhaps the time had come, after two thousand years, to include the faithful in the meaning of the Chalice. I realize the Church, starting with Simon Peter, has had a valid practical reason to withhold the information. The idea that suicide was a sacrament might well have decimated the early ranks of the faithful."

Pietro Gandolfo blanched to hear the facts spoken out loud in a public place. They had only been whispered behind huge, bronze doors for millennia. Pietro's mind was racing.

Christ wanted His subjects to follow the surest path to His Father by any means they chose. The Church, on the other hand, needed a growing population to preserve the structure that would ensure the enduring population of "faithful." It was a terrible dilemma. Christ the Son of God delivered himself for execution with the help of His best friend, Judas. Christ the Man, chose Peter to build his church and perpetuate broad acceptance of His Divinity.

The key was the Chalice. He had commissioned a silversmith in Galilee to fashion it according to his specifications. At the Last Supper, He had carefully chosen His words when he commissioned His apostles—

"Hoc est enim corpus meum."— this is my body. He did not follow by saying, this is My blood. Instead, He said, "Hic est enim calyx sanguinis mei"—this is the <u>Chalice</u> *of my blood. And finally, "Do this in remembrance of Me."*

He transformed the bread into His body but he instructed them to follow the directions He had laid out on the Chalice. There, for the world to see, were eight medallions depicting the eight sacraments, including the depiction of Judas being hanged by two angels— a voluntary, assisted suicide.

All these things were tormenting Pietro's head for the thousandth time as he sat across from his friend, the Patriarch of Fifteen Million Coptic Christians— a man who knew and understood the meaning of the Chalice as well as he.

"One more thing, Pietro, the old man added. I doubt that either Christ the Son of God, nor Christ the Man, expected the message of the Chalice to remain secret forever. I believe that in the very nature of the Chalice, is not only a liturgical instruction but proof for all time that He was Who He said He was— and the vehicle of his return to the world of humans. I think we may be blessed, or cursed, my friend, by the reality that this is the time to reveal all and herald a Second Coming."

While they had been speaking, a beautiful young woman took a seat at the next table. Though not close enough to hear their conversation, she nodded her agreement with the last words. Just then, a waiter approached her.

In perfect Egyptian Arabic she said she would have an order of asabi'gullash bi-l-lahma. She was hungry. It had been a very long time since she had been allowed to sit in a restaurant and order food. The waiter noted that her Arabic was perfect, but had a strange clicking sound to it.

Chapter Twenty-Eight

The Chalice group were all in the dining room of the Ibn el Khassib to plan their day over American-style breakfasts, bacon and eggs, warm rolls with butter, and hot coffee.

"First of all," Ryan spoke up, "we should not just go around playing tourist. I'm not certain what our job is yet but several organizations are paying us a lot to be here. I presume we will find out soon what it is."

"In the meanwhile, what do we do, Father?" That was Bedu El-Akshar. He and Leila Miller had been out in a jeep looking for suspicious landforms where perhaps undiscovered ruins might be lurking. The two had grown quite close, she with her quirky, beautiful face and trim body, he a handsome, dark Arab. Ryan suspected he was observing the beginning of a "relationship." These things were inevitable on archaeological expeditions. As long as they did not interfere with the agenda he didn't care. Since there was no agenda as yet, there was no problem. For his part, it seemed he would be paying strict attention to the management of his own time and situation to avoid the development of a relationship of his own. Sharon had chosen the seat next to his at breakfast.

"We're still missing Megyn and Father McAndrew, Sharon. Neither is a tourist and they know we are waiting for them. I suggest you and Leila spend some time at the quay. I hope both of them will be along soon. I'll stay at the hotel and work on some things. You should canvas the local shops and let it be known you're interested in unusual antiquities. Dealers should come falling out of the palm trees."

Sharon loved shopping and this was a rare opportunity to go shopping for stuff she loved with a wallet full of other people's money. On the other hand, the fact did not escape her that Ryan was essentially telling her to leave him alone. No. That was putting it too harshly. Not leave him alone.

149

Allow him to cope with what she felt was his uncomfortable interest in her. She contented herself with the old adage that "absence makes the heart grow fonder." There was no rush.

† † †

Whether by accident or Divine Providence, the two feluccas docked at El Minya within minutes of one another. Bedu and Leila waved furiously at them from the shore as the Arab sailors maneuvered their crafts smoothly through the currents and came to rest gently in a space long ago cleared of papyrus reeds for such landings.

Megyn was the first off her boat. She looked awful. Her clothes were torn, her hair wind-dried and shaggy. Very unlike Megyn. Bedu eyed the dark Arab at the tiller suspiciously. Nemo smiled back broadly, white teeth in a very dark face. He moved quickly to tie up his craft. He did not want to let Megyn get anywhere out of his sight until the bill was paid. The aura of the two on shore was not reassuring. One was another good-looking woman, the other an Arab. This might not be as easy as he had thought.

Father McAndrew took his time coming ashore. He seemed to do so reluctantly. The handsome Arab at that tiller seemed unconcerned. McAndrew, strangely, was in shorts and a black shirt, but wearing his Roman collar. Apparently he had been traveling behind the protective shield of his religious persona. This time it was Leila who was suspicious. She eyed the handsome, Arab sailor, waiting for her woman's intuition to give her psyche a nudge. Everyone connected with Chalice was aware of Father McAndrew's sexual orientation.

Soon all four were onshore together. As they started to leave, Nemo came running up, panting heavily.

"The young lady assured me I would be paid when we arrived."

""He's right, Bedu. I was in desperate straits and offered him a great deal of money."

Bedu scowled again at Nemo.

"And he was always a perfect gentleman," she added hastily. "He and his family fed me and provided lodging for me before we set sail."

"Bedu's scowl softened into a smile."

"Shukran." Thank you.

"Aafwaan." You're welcome.

"Ahlan wa sahlan al el Minya. Titakellem ingleezi?" Welcome to Minya. Do you speak English?

"Yes. Very well. I went to a Christian school taught by nuns. They were all ugly."

All five of them laughed. Father McAndrew shot a sad glance at Gadallah who was already untying his felucca for the long voyage up-river to Aswan.

"As the lady said, she promised me a great deal of money." Nemo got back to the point.

"And you shall be paid, my friend. The leader of our group is at the hotel. Come with us."

Bedu hailed a passing carriage. They would return to look for Sharon after they took care of this business and had given Megyn a chance to take a shower and tend to herself. Leila put her arm around Megyn with motherly tenderness. Nemo sat up on the bench with the driver and chattered away in Arabic.

☥ ☥ ☥

Sharon was enjoying herself immensely. She had found her way past the open bazaar to the back streets where serious buying and selling took place. A number of small shops displayed artifacts, mostly fakes, in dusty windows with cracked, black sills. She entered one after another and looked at the wares in the glass cases and on shelves that looked like they might collapse at any moment.

"We have the finest antiquities in Egypt." The merchants all made similar, opening remarks.

"I'm looking for items that date from the time of Akhenaten," Sharon replied with little variation to each of them.

As though choreographed for the same dance production, each would give a slight smile, a turn of the head as though looking for listeners, and reply in hushed tones. "We have many rare objects but not for public display. You understand."

"Of course. I am a collector and know what may be said and what may not."

On and on it went from shop to shop. After the routine performance had been played by each shopkeeper, he would produce a tray of imitation scarabs and ushabti from under the counter, or from a back room— ushabti, the little figurines that were wound into mummy wrappings and believed to perform tasks for the deceased in the next life. The name ushabti means, "the ones who answer." Scarabs were also wound into the wrappings, replicas of beetles thought by the Egyptians to be immortal and appropriate symbols to follow the deceased across the threshold to the afterlife There are so many scarabs and ushabti in antiquities shops, both real and imitation, that it is hard to tell which are which. The same type of artisans who made them thousands of years ago are still making them at the same skill level with the same materials.

Sharon was not looking for ushabti or scarabs. Actually, she didn't know what she was looking for. Ryan had simply sent her off with the cryptic implication that she might find something of interest.

Sick of the repetition of one tourist shop after another, she turned down a narrow alley and came to a little shop with a window so dusty it was almost impossible to see through. She opened the door gingerly. A tiny brass bell tinkled lightly.

She was already inside and the door closed behind her before a wizened old man in a white turban came out of a back room through a beaded curtain. He looked as though he were surprised to see anyone actually in his place. Tourists rarely wandered this far from the main thoroughfares of El Minya. Of those that did, even fewer were determined enough to enter his place, unable to see through the dusty window.

"Welcome," he said. "You are English?"

"No. American."

"Ah. I see very few Americans in my shop. They seem more attracted to the perfume shops and the purveyors of medicinal herbs in the souk. You must be a special sort of American— a writer, perhaps?"

Sharon loved the idea that she was easily identified as someone special.

"No. I am an archaeologist."

"Ah," the man's expression took on the delighted smile of one comrade to another. "I, too, am an archaeologist. Many years ago I attended the university in Cairo but circumstances led me to this less than honorable vocation— one who deals in antiquities rather than studies and writes about them— existing only at the fringe of my original intellectual ambitions."

"Circumstances?"

"A wife and five children, the usual circumstance that leads a man from books to hard labor."

Sharon smiled. She understood. Unmarried at thirty-one, she was an oddity by Orthodox Jewish standards. She had forgone marriage to pursue her doctorate first, then museum work she loved with a far greater passion than the idea of a dull marriage and noisy children. She didn't bother to explain all this to the shopkeeper. She extended her hand. "I'm Dr. Feinshutz from the Egyptology department at the Brooklyn Museum in New York City."

The man looked delighted. "I am Gawdat al-Meskeen, once a student at Cairo University. I have some authentic scarabs and ushabti, if you care to look at them."

"I don't think so." Sharon was direct and it did not seem to bother the shopkeeper. "My specialty is epigraphy. You are familiar with the field?"

The man's eyes shone with delight. "You are looking for papyri?"

"Perhaps. But not bright, shiny ones pounded out by factories for the tourists. You understand."

"Yes, indeed I do my dear lady. And you have come to the right place."

Sharon was ready for this sort of reply. She suspected it would have been the same had she asked for Tutankhamun's mummified testicles.

"Wait. I'll be back in a moment."

The old man struggled through the beaded curtain. He appeared to be suffering with severe arthritis. Sharon could hear the opening and closing of old wooden drawers in the other room. Finally the man reappeared with a felt-lined tray on which several, partially-fragmented, papyrus sheets lay side-by-side. He put the tray on the counter in front of Sharon but made no move to touch the old document. Sharon was relieved that he did not. She knew about such things. The slightest touch might do the pages irreparable damage.

"Please don't touch it, my dear lady. It is very fragile."

"I won't. And I am grateful that you show such great respect, yourself, to a potential treasure of this sort."

A broad smile lighted the old man's face. This was truly an exceptional woman. He noticed, too, that she was very beautiful, and wearing tight pants. The arthritis had not spread to his libido.

"Do you know what it is," Sharon asked gently?

"Not precisely. I know that it is very old. I know that it is written in the Coptic language, so it is not as old as some of the authentic ushabti in my shop— and I assure you, my ushabti are both ancient and authentic."

Sharon smiled. She believed him. In a land of fast talking merchants, she knew she had found an honest man. She leaned close to examine the document. Her Coptic was not as good as her Hebrew, but the document was brief, the text clear and precise. It had obviously been written by a trained scribe, perhaps a monk.

It was not long after Our Lord was crucified that an old man covered with sores came to the door of Lazarus, the Rich. The old man kept striking a stick against a piece of wood so it made a loud sound while he called out, "Unclean, Unclean. " All the people withdrew from him in fear, for they knew he was sick with a terrible disease and did not wish to come close. Yet dogs from the street approached him and licked his sores without fear, and he stroked their heads.

Inside the house, the rich man sat at a table piled high with food, eating and drinking with his friends. There was far too much for them to eat, and yet he did not send any food to the door for the sick man.

A simple monk who was passing offered to take the man to his cave and the man went with him. There, the monk gave him to eat and drink and even bowls of food and water for the dogs.

Then the monk made a bed of straw for the man and gave him a blanket to cover himself. The dogs slept with the man but in the morning all of them were gone.

On the blanket where he and the dogs had slept was a cloth bag drawn tight at the top with a leather thong.

The monk opened the bag and was startled to find that it contained a magnificent silver cup of intricate design. It had a double spiral of wrought silver for its stem and around its rim there were eight medallions.

The monk had no use for the cup. It was far too magnificent for his simple life and he knew no one to whom he might give it. So he placed it in a niche at the back of his cave and placed a rock in front to hide it.

The next night, an angel came to the monk in his sleep and told him he had done well to give food and drink to the sick man for the man had been a messenger of God. The angel also said that he should keep the cup safe until God sent for it again.

When the monk awoke the angel was not there and no one ever came for the cup. He decided that it truly belonged to God and he would leave it where he had hidden it. For the rest of his days, he spent all of his energy painting the walls of his cave with portraits of the elders of his church. He depicted each sitting with a cup like the one the poor man had left behind, but each with a different medallion facing forward.

And these things took place in the desert, at Gebel al-Naqlun, near the River Nile.

The old shopkeeper had brought Sharon a chair and a cup of tea while she examined the papyrus. He was happy this long treasured artifact, that had lain in his cabinet for many years, was receiving professional attention— and from one so beautiful as this young woman.

"Are you able to read it?"

"Yes. It's fascinating. Where did you get it?"

The old man's eyes narrowed. This was a dangerous question these days. Zahi Hawass had eyes everywhere. Appointed Secretary General of the Egyptian Supreme Council of Antiquities in 2002, Hawass was tireless in his efforts to promote world interest in Egyptology, but equally driven to keeping Egypt's antiquities out of the hands of foreigners.

Gawdat al-Meskeen admired and agreed with Dr. Hawass, but he also had a responsibility to his family to make a living.

"I got it from an illiterate farmer who said his uncle had discovered it far from here— to the north, near Fayoum. I have no way of knowing more than that."

"From Gebel al-Naqlun, perhaps? That is mentioned in the document."

"Possibly."

This was getting dangerous. Gawdat was very taken with both the woman and the idea of being part of some actual academic research.

"Actually, I believe you are right. He said his uncle lived near Gebel al-Naqlun. But this must be kept strictly between us. I know the document is valuable. Are you interested in buying it?"

"Quite possibly but there are strict rules these days about the purchase of such materials. I am associated with an organization that has highly respected connections within the Council of Antiquities. We might be interested in purchasing it in association with them."

Gawdat was trapped. The great value of the document had suddenly become obvious, but his price for it almost nil if the government was involved. They could just take it and pay him nothing.

"Must you involve the Council, dear lady?"

"I'm afraid so, but the director of my organization has access to a large amount of money and would see to it that you were well paid, regardless of the govrnment's involvement."

The smile on Gawdat's face broadened into a delighted grin. This was truly a happy day.

"I must go now, mister— " she had forgotten his name.

"You may call me Gawdat."

"And you may call me Sharon. Would you like a piece of cake?" Sharon took a Twinkie from her purse and offered it to the merchant. Like a cloud passing across the sun, his expression changed from joyous to one of concern. Had he misjudged this woman?

"No. Thank you, Miss Sharon."

"Very well. I must go now. The leader of my group is back at the Ibn el Khassib. I will return with him as soon as possible to look at the papyrus— but it may not be until tomorrow."

"Of course." The old man carefully picked up the tray and went back through the beaded curtain. From beyond it, Sharon heard him slide the tray back into a cabinet. Then he returned. They shook hands very formally and Sharon went out the door into the alley, the little bell tinkling again as she closed the door behind her. It was already late afternoon and the alley was growing dark. Black shadows on the walkway were sliced into angular shapes by blades of orange sunlight bouncing off windowpanes from above.

Ryan, alone in his room, was getting anxious. As usual in dry, dusty Egypt, the evening sun had become a flat, orange disk, sinking rapidly behind spikes of palm fronds and silhouettes of minarets. The muezzin had long since sent their evening calls-to-prayer echoing across the city, never completely synchronized with one another so the sound of one was picked up a moment later by another, some close, some far in the distance. As an orderly person, Ryan admired Muslim dedication to rigid routine.

It would be dark soon and Sharon had not returned. Sharia Law imposed horrible retribution for crime so one is usually safer at night in a dingy Muslim city than San Francisco. Nevertheless, darkness carries with it an aura of mystery and a cargo of unspoken terrors.

As he stood by his window, Ryan was forced to admit that he cared a great deal for this feisty, Twinkie-munching woman. He would wrestle with that problem later. For the moment he was simply worried about someone who was important to him. He had sent her on this pointless mission to protect himself from his own frailties. Now he was paying the price for his lack of self-discipline. Soon it would be time for supper and an evening conference in the dining room with the Chalice crew.

Earlier, things had been lively at the Ibn el Khassib. Ryan had greeted Megyn, then Father McAndrew, with equal displays of relief and delight. He had been more troubled by their extended absence than he had let on. He held court in the dining room with the help of the hotel staff— small sweet cakes and soft drinks. Alcohol could be found when necessary, but with difficulty in a Muslim country.

Father McAndrew had little to say. The reason for his trip to Autun had been a mystery to him and he left France feeling he knew little more about his mission than when he had arrived. He had seen sculptures by the medieval artist, Gislebertus, that he thought might have some bearing on things. And he had a gut feeling that Lazarus was more important in the scheme of things than he had anticipated.

That side trip to France was a mystery to Ryan as well, but Pietro Gandolfo had suggested it, and he was paying the bill. As to the trip down the river from Aswan, McAndrew had little to say.

"It was a chance to spend time with an old friend," he'd said and did not elaborate. No one pressed him for anything further.

Megyn was another matter. She had arrived looking as though she had been tossed in a blender full of instant tan and peroxide. Her skin was café-au-lait, her hair, the color beauty parlors call platinum. The Egyptian sun had made her more beautiful than ever, just a bit disheveled and sporting a few bruises. She would have inspired a New York ad agency— "Bruised Blond Jeans #4, Felucca, take 14. That's a wrap. Print it."

James McAndrew was very quiet. He too wore a heavy tan. It did little for his rough complexion an small stature. He went to the front desk and got the key to a room near the others, then quietly withdrew.

Megyn had spoken quickly with Ryan, Captain Nemo hovering close to her. Ryan peeled off a great number of Egyptian treasury notes and gave them to the felucca owner. Nemo retreated in a hurry, afraid Ryan might change his mind and try to renegotiate the deal. He had delivered the woman, safe and sound. He had no bargaining chips left to defend the enormous payoff he'd just received.

Megyn waved fondly to him as he left. He had been good to her. She would tell Ryan about it later. Bedu took her to the front desk and got her a key for a room down the hall from the rest where she could get cleaned up and catch a short nap. She still had her satchel with her and some slightly cleaner clothes.

✝ ✝ ✝

Now it was almost suppertime and Sharon was nowhere to be seen. Ryan suddenly realized he cared more for this woman than he dared admit even to himself. The others seemed unaware of it. Things were bad enough with Bedu and Leila making cow eyes at one another, Megyn off for days to the north, and James punting down the Nile with a handsome Arab boy. They didn't need Father Ryan nesting with the beautiful Jewish epigrapher from Brooklyn. This was looking more like an episode of The Loveboat than a serious, well-funded, archaeological expedition. That realization did nothing to lessen Ryan's concern over Sharon's absence.

He left his room and went out through the lobby to the front portico. He tried to look nonchalant as he walked slowly through the front entrance and out beyond into the lengthening shadows. He had only been out in the night for a moment, with its aromas and insect sounds, when he heard the noisy clatter of a horse-drawn carriage approaching. It appeared suddenly out of the dark under the hotel lights, the horses' hooves clop-clopping loudly. When it stopped at the entrance, the carriage rocked for a moment, its springs demanding oil— and Sharon jumped out. Ryan tried to walk over slowly as though unconcerned but there was an obvious urgency to his steps.

"Where have you been?" he called out, trying to sound like a stern father.

"Just where you sent me, Ryan Quinn!" She was excited as she fairly bounced toward him. She had great news.

For a second, neither paid any attention to the orange glow on the horizon, the carriage driver, the horse that had begun munching a handful of alfalfa, or anything else. She grabbed the priest in glee and hugged him soundly. He stood frozen like a statue then suddenly, as though released from hidden bonds, returned her embrace warmly. They stood like that for no more than a moment or two, but the world had gone topsy-turvy. When they released each another it was without urgency, or embarrassment. It felt completely natural as he looked into her face and asked again, "What have you been doing?"

Her eyes were bright. Her mouth twitched, hardly able to contain the news she was about to blurt out here in the Egyptian night. "I've been off doing the king's bidding," she giggled, "and boy, did the king know his stuff when he sent this Jewish American Princess out shopping!"

"What are you talking about, Sharon?"

"Everything! Now I know why we're on this trip, why you sent me shopping— everything!"

Sharon had actually started to jump up and down like a little girl, too excited to control herself.

"Calm down and tell me, because if you know why we're here and why I let you out of my sight without a chaperone, you know more than I do."

Sharon looked a bit puzzled but still continued to babble about El Minya, the Middle Kingdom of Akhenaten, the marketplace, and a little shop in a back alley.

"Put a Twinkie in it, Sharon, and start over."

Ryan was afraid his remark was demeaning but Sharon hardly heard it. Instead she suddenly jumped up and kissed Ryan on the cheek. Ryan reeled back, not at Sharon's sudden act, but the flash of reality that shot across his consciousness— he loved this impish, brilliant, beautiful woman.

In the next instant he took control of himself, and Sharon. He took both her hands in his and looked into her face sternly.

"Tell me!"

Sharon slowed down, the pressure of Ryan's gaze and his grip on her hands pulling her back down to earth.

"OK." She did not pout but there was peevish submission in her tone. "I discovered an ancient codex— several papyrus sheets, in remarkable shape, that say too much for me to tell you out here in the road."

Now Sharon was the Egyptologist, rational, objective and in control. It was Ryan who fought the urge to beg like a schoolboy for more information.

"Would you be more specific?"

"Later. Let's go inside. The others must be waiting for supper and I still have to take a shower."

Whether scientist, mother, co-worker, or employee, somehow women always end up in control. Ryan had a lump in his brain— the same idiot lump that always left men begging. They went inside and blinked at the bright light in the lobby.

"I'll be back as soon as I can. Ask the others to please dawdle over their appetizers. I'll hurry."

Ryan stood in the lobby, his hands at his sides, struck dumb by the events of the past three minutes. He was a priest, a powerful corporate executive, an Egyptologist, a theologian, and a blah, blah, blah. In the end, he was a man who just discovered he was in love and faced with a terrible predicament— what he had referred to jokingly once, as "The Eternal Triangle— Priest, Woman and God."

He shook himself loose of his thoughts and went into the dining room. The others were already hungrily dipping pita chips into a bowl of bab-ghanoug, a puree of tahina, eggplant and spices. Ryan announced that Sharon was back and had some news but wanted them to hold off for a few minutes before ordering supper. There were no actual groans of impatience, but the dipping and munching went on with added enthusiasm.

Chapter Twenty-Nine

When Archbishop Pietro Gandolfo returned to the El-Salamiek Palace Hotel, the concierge at the front desk sent a bellhop scurrying to intercept him before he could reach the bank of bronze, elevator doors.

"There is a message for you, your Excellency."

Gandolfo turned and went back to the desk. The concierge waited with a smile. With a grand air he extracted a note from its pigeonhole and presented it to the Nuncio.

"Your Excellency."

"Thank you." Gandolfo fished a pound note from his pocket and placed it in the outstretched hand of the concierge.

"Many pleasures, your Excellency."

Gandolfo didn't open the hotel envelope but returned to the elevators and went up to his room. It was quiet inside, just the slight rush of air as the air conditioner did its work. He sank into a plush, overstuffed chair and thought for a while before looking at the envelope. He thought with sadness that his meeting with Nazeer was probably his last. Not only were they old, but apparently on opposite sides of a sensitive matter. And now, a note. This wasn't good. Very few knew of his whereabouts. He opened the envelope slowly.

As he feared, it was from Rome. The words were direct and carefully chosen to provide no one with unnecessary information. Return to the site where last you spent time with Reverend Habib Colophon."

The Archbishop loosened his collar and exhaled slowly. He was old. He was tired. And he did not relish the mission on which he now found himself being sent.

He disrobed in the bedroom, donned a bathrobe, and limped, barefoot, to the shower where he stayed a long time beneath a cascade of hot water.

Is this what it has all been about, he thought, *fancy hotels and good plumbing? Did I give up the life of a simple priest and my childhood dream of digging among the tombs of the pharaohs— all for the pomp and dignity of a position in Rome and a title that will eventually pass to another?*

Beneath the cascade of hot water, he never heard the door to his suite open and close. He shut off the water and stepped carefully out onto the Carrara marble floor. Wet marble is a hazard for crippled, old men. He had taken a spill earlier in life, one he dared not repeat at this age. He toweled himself slowly as he hobbled to the bedroom door, leaving his bathrobe behind on a hook by the shower.

Pietro Gandolfo, Archbishop and Papal Nuncio, stood in the door, naked. He sucked in his breath in surprise. Across his bed lay the most beautiful woman he had ever seen. Her breasts were full, her nipples erect. Her legs were slightly parted revealing a rose-hued cleft, barely hidden within a cloud of light blond hair. The room smelled like gardenias.

"I've been sent to spend a bit of time with you."

Her words were spoken in perfect Italian, just a slight clicking sound to them.

Almost four hundred miles to the south, Sharon Feinschutz wriggled nervously under a barely adequate shower at the Ibn el Khassib Hotel in El Minya. She was in a hurry. People were waiting. She soaped herself quickly and rinsed before squeezing a dollop of shampoo into her bronze hair and working it in vigorously. Her hair was her most urgent task. She felt as though she had half the Sahara lodged against her scalp.

When she was done, she didn't bother to dry her hair but tied it in a ponytail with a beaded, elastic band. The rest of her, she hastily patted dry and climbed into clean underwear and a pair of khaki jeans. Sandals completed her wardrobe as she headed for the door. She was tempted to stop and grope through her bag for a Twinkie but resisted the urge. People were waiting.

All the baba-ghanoug was gone by the time she got to the dining room. She spotted the empty bowl and exclaimed, "Thanks a lot, gang. What about "the last shall be first?"

Leila laughed out loud and quipped back, "So? You're the last one to get here, and now, the first one not to get any baba-ghanoug. Sit. Stay. Where the heck were you and why weren't you there with the others to welcome Megyn back from the jaws of death?"

"Or me?" That was James McAndrew. He was starting to enjoy the idea of being accepted as just one of an elite, energetic, expedition team.

They all turned to him, surprised at his levity, and laughed. They liked him a lot but had never felt they could treat him like the others. He was always, "Father McAndrew."

"Did I hurt your feelings Father McAndrew?"

"Not at all, Sharon. I doubt I could have held down my tabouli within sight of a Twinkie after my long sea, er, river voyage— and please call me James."

Everyone smiled as though an old draconian law had been revoked.

Everything's coming together, thought Ryan, *whatever everything" might be.* He raised his voice above the banter. He had an announcement to make. "Somebody, please order before they run out of goat."

✝ ✝ ✝

Back in Alexandria, at the El-Salamiek Palace Hotel, Pietro Gandolfo covered his groin with his hands and continued to stand in the doorway.

"I believe we've met before, young lady."

"Perhaps. I do travel a great deal. My work takes me to many out of the way places."

"To dangerous places, like a scaffold at the monastery of St. Pshoi fifteen years ago?"

"How good your memory is for your age. I had no idea the damage would be so severe, and permanent. I apologize."

"Put on some clothes. I may be a man, not immune to the sight of your naked body, but I am also a priest, and I know that you, beautiful as you appear, are not a woman. Put on some clothes. Why are you here?"

"Like you, Nuncio, I have a job to do. My visit to your room was just a chance to have some fun. My job often grows boring."

"And what is your job this time? Have you grown tired of throwing priests off high places?"

As she dressed, she laughed and it was the sound of sleigh bells in the snow. "I said I was sorry."

"Go on!" Somehow Pietro had summoned an air of stern authority despite the fact that there were only his cupped hands between privacy and the world. Someone had once said— "If a person seems intimidating, just imagine him naked and you will be able to get through the ordeal." Gandolfo was naked but had somehow managed to demand respect from this temptress.

"It is my present mission," she said with that clicking sound, "to slow your pursuit of the people you're looking for."

"Why?"

"So they can get on with the wishes of the Almighty."

Gandolfo was stunned. He almost raised his hands to his mouth and the beautiful creature laughed again.

"And those plans are?"

"I think you know them as well as I, Pietro Gandolfo."

With those words she seemed to grow diaphanous and her image to waver as though behind a sheer waterfall.

"Just stay a few more days in Alexandria, Pietro. Do not be in such a rush to travel up the Nile where others are best left alone for a bit."

The air grew chilly and the sound of bells filled the room. Were they sleigh bells or that cluster of little brass bells that signal to the congregation that the Transubstantiation has taken place?

She was gone.

Pietro dressed hurriedly. He found the envelope he'd been given by the concierge. By habit he had opened it with the expertise of a former museum conservator. It was completely undamaged. He looked around for the note and found it on the side table beside the overstuffed chair. He put it back into the envelope, licked the undamaged flap, and resealed it.

At the front desk he found the concierge still bowing and scraping over his distinguished hotel guests. Pietro approached him directly.

"Ah, your Excellency. May I be of further help?"

"Yes, my dear fellow. I never had a chance to open the message you gave me. I have a great number of important matters on my mind and now I find I have to go in search of Pope Shenouda."

"Of course, Excellency, you have a meeting with the esteemed Patriarch?"

Pietro stifled the temptation to laugh. This man was an ass. "Yes, we planned to meet this evening. Would you be kind enough to put the envelope back into the slot for me. If anyone inquires, I will pick it up later. If I forget, you can forward it to me by mail, to the Ibn el Khassib Hotel in El Minya. Do you know the place?"

"Yes, Eminence. Not a place I would choose for you, but adequate considering the level of accommodations available in El Minya."

"Not five stars?" Pietro was enjoying the man's snobbish behavior. He also wanted to prolong the dialogue to fix the details in the man's mind should anyone come asking about him. He'd been instructed to go to a place near El Minya. Best he indicate that he was doing what he'd been told.

"The Ibn el Khassib? No, Excellency. Not five stars. Perhaps, regrettably, no stars at all."

Pietro forced a snobbish pout to please this fool, and added, "I will be traveling by train so it may take some time. Did you know that my friend, the Patriarch, travels by train, third class?"

"No!" The man's jaw dropped in astonishment.

"Don't forget about the note," Pietro put a large denomination bill in the man's hand and left.

Despite the momentous events of the last hour and the incredibly important decision he had made the moment the woman left, Pietro felt a tremendous lightness to his steps as he went out onto the street. He went in search of Nazeer. He wanted to tell him of the recent events and inform him of the good news, that after almost a lifetime, they were probably on the same side at last. Hopefully, the Patriarch would still be in Alexandria, in residence at St. Mark's Cathedral. If not, so be it. Pietro Gandolfo was in no hurry. The slower his progress, perhaps the closer he might be to following the will of the Almighty.

† † †

Nazeer was not hard to find. In fact he did not need any finding at all. Walking down the crowded street in the direction of the Cathedral, Pietro was engulfed in a cacophony of car horns, thrumming engines, footfalls, and loud, Arabic conversations. Arabs always seem to be yelling to emphasize this point or that. At an intersection, cars and buses were rushing by when he heard a familiar voice behind him.

"Let's go for coffee."

The Patriarch took Pietro's elbow as they crossed the street. A bus nearly ran them down. There were passengers hanging from its rear platform and bored faces at every window, faces whose expressions would not have changed in the slightest had the bus been successful in flattening them.

"My people," grinned Pope Shenouda.

"Our people," the Archbishop smiled back.

Chapter Thirty

Only hunger kept the Chalice group's mouths too full to blurt out the news that threatened to explode from within more than one of them. Megyn was the first to swallow hard, take a drink of orange soda, and speak up.

"I can't tell you everything that happened to me. I'll reserve that for the confessional."

Most of them smiled. The two priests tried, but had some difficulty with her jest. James had heard Megyn's confession once and wasn't anxious for a repeat performance. Her secret was safe with him, of course, but any repetitions of the same sin would put him in dangerous territory, not only as a matter of religious propriety, but civil law. Ryan had not heard her confession but had suspicions about Megyn. Unless she chose to talk to him as a priest, it was none of his business. He was grateful she had not chosen to do so.

"Remember," she began, "that I am a scientist and historian like the rest of you. I find what I have to say, incredible, to say the least. I would have my doubts were it one of you speaking."

Megyn had their rapt attention. Even the munching stopped and there was a clink here and there as one, then another, put down a fork.

"I will start with the wackiest part. I assure you it gets better, not worse."

A waiter stopped at the table for more orders. Ryan put his finger to his lips, a universal sign to be quiet. The waiter picked up a few dishes and left.

"Some time ago I had a vision in the middle of the night. It was one of the figures I had been studying from the Fayoum burials. He spoke to me about a medallion, an artifact of great importance that must be found.

He suggested I search the hermit caves at Gebel al-Naqlun. That was why I hung back rather than coming along with you to El Minya."

Megyn had been right. The disbelief was becoming evident among the group at the table. A few rearranged their chairs nervously but made no move to interrupt.

"What makes this a little less whacky," she continued, "is the fact that Spencer Quinn, Ryan's brother had shown me a medallion, once, that fit the description given me by the person in my dream— if it was just a dream."

Ryan sat up. This was getting a bit too close to him for comfort.

"Forgive me, Father, but I paid little attention to Spencer and his medallion. He had lured me to his apartment under the pretext of showing me his collection of coins and books. It was apparent as soon as I got there that he was interested less in books and coins than he was in more physical pursuits. Again, I'm sorry, Father. I only mention it because he did show me that medallion and said it had been given to him by one of your friends, a priest with a strange name."

"Habib Colophon?" asked Ryan.

"Exactly. I never took a close look at it. Spencer made me nervous and I made a clumsy excuse to leave. Now, out of nowhere, here was this Fayoum phantom."

Megyn made a silly face as she exaggerated the alliteration. She wanted to let everyone know she realized how fantastic her story must sound.

"I thought it was nothing more than a dream, the medallion part dredged up out of my subconscious from the earlier episode with Spencer. Yet it was so compelling that I felt obliged to search the hermit caves at Gebel al-Naqlun. I didn't ask anyone to stay and search with me or I would have had to tell this story and I doubt any of you would have done more than laugh and drag me off to El Minya."

Megyn's earnestness recaptured their serious attention. The story was ridiculous, but compelling.

"I searched every cave I could get to, kicking up the dust in every corner, searching up and down the cave-lined canyon. Do you know they estimate there are over a hundred caves in Gebel al-Naqlun? I think I searched most of them looking for that dumb medallion. And then," she paused for dramatic emphasis, "I gave up."

They all smiled. You could hear them exhale with relief.

"But I found something more incredible. In the last cave I searched, I discovered a large mural with a depiction of eight elders, each holding a chalice. And around the rim of each was a row of medallions. Each figure sat exactly as the others and held a chalice in the same way but with a different medallion facing front. The problem is, when I examined them, one by one, the medallions were all clearly drawn but the last. It had been defaced. I'm sure it must have been the very one I was looking for."

Megyn sat down, exhausted. She had told her wild story and it turned out to be little more than that. There was an uncomfortable silence. Her story had begun with a phantom apparition and ended with what was probably a phantom painting born of fatigue and desert heat. They resumed talking amongst themselves to cover their embarrassment.

"Oh yes," Megyn caught her energy again. "I took pictures."

Pietro Gandolfo and Nazeer Gayeb found themselves once more in a café, this one off the tourist track. The room was huge, the walls hung with thick tapestries, faded paintings, and enormous, tarnished mirrors. Perhaps there were a number of people in the room, but it seemed almost empty, the diners swallowed up by the room's size. A white, damask cloth covered the table where the two priests sat. A waiter arrived from a great distance, carrying a brass tray with demitasse cups, cloth napkins, and a couple of tiny, silver spoons. He made the long round trip again, with a brass pot on a wooden handle, and filled the cups carefully. Unlike the desert Bedouin tradition of pouring tea from a great height, the intention here was to cause as little turbulence as possible so the finely ground coffee would remain in the pot and not find its way into the waiting cups.

Nazeer took his cup at once and drained it. *He's obviously a caffeine addict,* thought Pietro. He would remember that. It might come in handy some time.

"I hear you had an unusual visitor, Pietro."

"You hear a great deal for a man who wears his hat down over his ears, my friend."

They both chuckled. It was good to be here, two old friends drinking coffee together again. For the moment, the world was safely at bay beyond the tapestries and mirrors of this marvelous room.

"Yes. I had a visitor. She was very persuasive."

Nazeer's expression changed. It seemed a dark cloud had passed between the two.

"Calm yourself, your Holiness," Pietro continued, after taking a moment to enjoy his friend's discomfort. "I told her to put on some clothes and go home. I meant to say that her words were persuasive. She said very little, but indicated that it was the wish of the Almighty that I dally a while in Alexandria. Considering who she is and Whom she works for, it seemed a suggestion worth heeding."

Nazeer was visibly relieved.

"And considering for Whom she works," Nazeer added, "her methods do seem strange, I'll admit. She and I have had our encounters as well— you say she convinced you to stay here in Alexandria for a while? Why? Did you have other plans?"

"I'm not sure why, but yes. I was planning to leave at once. I received a message from Rome. It told me to return to El Minya."

"Return? But you didn't come from El Minya. You just came from Rome, no? Return to El Minya? Is that what the message said?"

"No. Not exactly. It said to return to the place where I last spent time with my old friend, Father Colophon."

"And that was El Minya, Pietro? I am becoming confused."

"I'm sorry. Once again I was only speaking in general terms. Actually Colophon and I were out in the desert, living in tents. Our excavation site was closer to El Minya than any place on a current map."

"On a map of archaeological sites?"

"No. We were fifty miles from El Minya at an isolated site near Tuna el-Gebel."

"I know Tuna el-Gebel very well— a few columns and preserved shrines, mostly buried in sand, once an important religious site near Tel el Amarna, the Middle Kingdom of Pharaoh Akhenaton."

"Your knowledge of places and events is impressive as always, Nazeer."

"Remember, my friend, I was born not far from there."

"Of course."

Nazeer had begun to stare into space, mentally revisiting the land of his youth and its marvelous archaeological sites. He recalled how frightened he had been as a child by the almost intact mummy of a woman named Isadora in a shrine at Tuna el-Gebel. Yes. He knew Tuna el-Gebel very well. Much later he had ventured with a kerosene lamp through the miles of catacombs beneath the sand where tens of thousands of mummified animals, falcons, ibis, baboons, and crocodiles, had been laid to rest in niches. There were tunnels and side tunnels that seemed to go on forever. *Humans are the strangest of God's creatures*, thought Nazeer.

"Where did you just go, my friend?"

"Excuse me, Pietro. I was thinking about my childhood adventures in the desert. When do you plan to resume your itinerary to the south?"

"In a few days. I intend to go by train. That should make you happy. Any suggestions? But please don't tell me about the joys of traveling third class."

"Traveling by train is the essence of the experience, Pietro. Whether you go first or third class is immaterial. I like the sounds of humanity around me. But the vendors who walk the aisles in third class serve the best coffee."

"Aha," said Pietro. "Now I understand."

When Pietro got back to the hotel, the concierge waved another note at him from the front desk.

"I'll look at both of them tomorrow, my good man. Just keep them and any others that come in for the time being. If anyone asks you why I didn't pick up my messages, please forget you saw me return. Would you be so kind as to do that for me?"

"Most pleasurably, your Excellency."

The extra service cost Pietro another large treasury note.

✝ ✝ ✝

Megyn pushed back her chair and hurried off to her room to look for her camera. In all the excitement, she had forgotten it.

During Megyn's short announcement, unlike the others, Sharon took none of it lightly after first mention of the mural. As soon as Megyn left the room she grabbed Ryan by the sleeve and whispered in his ear. "I have to talk to you in private. It is very important. Secrecy may not be an issue but I want to talk to you before I speak to any of the others."

Ryan had no idea what this was about, but Sharon seemed genuinely concerned. "As soon as we look at Megyn's pictures, if she can find her camera."

Megyn returned with a triumphant look on her face. She had found it, a small digital, pocket camera with a two-inch viewing screen. She sat and began to push its buttons. The others crowded behind her, all trying to get close enough to see the small screen. The images were bright and clear but far too small to see any details like the all important medallions to which she had referred. Nevertheless, one thing was certain. The mural she had described was no illusion. It was a beautiful example of First or Second Century Coptic cave art. Except for the possible connection to near invisible medallions, they did not seem exceptional. Obviously some hermit, or a group of them, had spent countless hours, maybe years, in a dimly lighted cave, working with religious fervor to produce them.

Sharon pulled at Ryan's sleeve again. She seemed even more agitated. "OK, Sharon. Let's go to one of the back sitting rooms. He was anxious to avoid the privacy of either of their rooms. They left the dining room and went down the hall. The others were taking turns holding Megyn's camera to examine the images more closely. It was unlikely the Ibn el Khassib would have a computer to which they might attach the camera to bring up larger images.

In a sitting room half way down the hall, Sharon pulled Ryan over to a game table and sat down. Ryan sat across from her.

"I know who painted that mural!" she blurted out.

"What?"

"It's related to what I wanted to tell you out on the road before, but I had no idea Megyn would come up with this story and those pictures."

"Slow down, Sharon."

She took a deep breath and tried to relax, then told Ryan about the papyrus in the old man's shop.

It was dark on the back streets of El Minya. Sharon and Ryan had left the hotel abruptly without telling any of the rest. Now they were the only souls in the alley that led to the antiquities shop of Gawdat al-Meskeen. When they found it, it was already closed. But unlike daytime, when the grimy window hid the interior, they could see a dim light through the doorway into the back room.

Ryan knocked on the door. The little brass bell inside tinkled from the vibration. That was all. There was no response. He knocked again, harder this time. He and Sharon could hear someone moving about. The light in the back room winked as someone came through the doorway towards them.

"Yes?" The old man's voice came from close to the front door. He spoke in English. He expected the woman to return. He had seen the fascinated excitement in her eyes when he showed her the papyrus.

"I am Father Quinn," Ryan called through the door. "I'm the leader of a group of archaeologists. You met one of them this afternoon."

"Yes. Yes. Can you come back tomorrow? The shop is closed."

"We are prepared, perhaps, to make a purchase."

They could hear the old man working in the dark to undo the lock. "Just a minute."

He disappeared and returned after a few moments with a kerosene lamp. There was more noise as he found a place to set it down before coming back to the door. After some more rattling of hardware, the door opened. The old man looked like a ghost in the halo cast by the lamp.

"Come in. Come in" He picked up the lamp and led them directly through the beaded curtain into the back room. "Please sit." He motioned to a small table covered with ceramic figurines and faience ornaments. He set the lamp down in the midst of them and cleared some space on one side of the table.

Satisfied there was enough room, he went over to a wooden cabinet against the wall. On top was a bust of Queen Nefertiti. It was nothing rare, just an often-reproduced copy of the famous sculpture in a Berlin museum, which is also believed, now, to be a fake. Al–Meskeen kept the bust there for atmosphere, nothing more. It was too well known even among tourists for him to lay claim to its authenticity. And after all, El Minya was in the Middle Kingdom, once ruled by the beautiful lady and her husband. Gawdat's replica was covered with dust, set too far back on the cabinet for his feather duster. The walnut cabinet had many drawers like those used by engineers to store maps. He went immediately to one, several down from the top, and pulled it to him. Inside, in a slim tray, lay the papyrus he had shown Sharon earlier. He took the tray out and brought it carefully to the table. He stood above them, arms folded, a look of pride on his deeply creased face.

"My grandest treasure," he said in almost a whisper, "and very valuable," he added, always the Egyptian salesman despite the natural drama of the moment.

Ryan peered closely at the papyrus sheets laid flat beside one another. He dared not even breath. He turned his head to the side every time he exhaled so as not to disturb the delicate pages.

Sharon sat back. She had examined it closely that afternoon. She waited for Ryan's reaction. It didn't take long. The document was short, written in Coptic, which he understood, in a hand methodically precise and legible. He pushed back from the table carefully and finally let out a deep breath.

"It's authentic. I'm sure of it."

Sharon grabbed his arm and squeezed it. He put his hand over hers and they sat that way for a long time. The smile on the face of the man above them threatened to split his old face in two.

"I assure you. It is authentic. I know my land, its history, and the feeling one has when one looks at something that has lain hidden for centuries beneath its sands. It is authentic, my dear friends."

Ryan turned to Sharon. "It's not just the document but its reference to the chalice. But, of course, that's what you were talking about, and now the whole thing with Megyn and the medallions." He sat for a moment and added, "William Burroughs, a friend of Jack Kerouac, said that in the magical universe there are no coincidences and there are no accidents. Nothing happens unless someone wills it to happen."

Sharon squeezed his arm harder. "I didn't think you'd be into quoting Beat Generation dope addicts, Ryan."

"There's a lot about me that might surprise you, Miss Twinkie Gobbler. And besides, it's something that would even sound right from a pulpit."

"You are interested in purchasing my treasure? But I must be assured you will not keep it to yourselves. It has remained hidden in the dark too long. It belongs in a museum, no?"

"Yes. I know Zawi Hawass very well. I will see to it that it is displayed prominently in the Cairo Museum. And when it is placed there, it will be marked with a plaque that says, *A Gift to the Egyptian People From the Private*

Collection of Gawdat al-Meskeen. I promise you that, my friend," said Ryan. "Now, what is your price?"

Unexpectedly, the old man began to cry softly. "No price. It is yours. Take it. You have been sent by Allah. I'm sure of it."

Ryan stood up and embraced the old man. "Perhaps, but Allah understands the needs of this world." Then he whispered a huge sum in the man's ear and took the man's shaking hand in his own. "It will be placed in the local bank in your name— the El Minya Branch of the Bank of Alexandria, correct?" The old man nodded silently.

Sharon stared at this exchange and realized she loved this priest with all her heart. What a horrible predicament.

Al-Meskeen placed a glass plate directly onto the documents to secure them from jostling and closed the tray's hinged lid. Then, in the way of Egyptian merchants for all sales, whether a cheap photo of Hosni Mubarak or a priceless artifact, he cushioned the item with layers of newspaper, wrapped it in brown paper, and tied the package securely with rough twine made of braided hemp. He handed the bundle to Ryan as though putting a baby into his arms.

When Ryan and Sharon left the shop the little bell on the door tinkled in the night. At the sound, a man in the alley retreated quickly into a doorway and did not emerge until he was sure they had gone.

Chapter Thirty-One

The package sat on Ryan's desk like the proverbial elephant in the room. He was not prepared to baby-sit a national treasure. Sharon shared his discomfort. The two of them sat in his room just staring at the package.

"Put it under your bed. It'll be safe there. No one ever gets near it but you," she giggled.

Ryan laughed out loud and did as she suggested. For the time being, he could think of nothing better.

"If it disappears and I see a trail of Twinkie crumbs leading out the door, I'll know where to look for the thief."

It was Sharon's turn to let loose a throaty, feminine laugh. Then they both started to laugh until they felt the tears rolling down their cheeks. The realization hit them both at the same time. Here they were, a Jesuit priest and a Jewish old-maid in the priest's bedroom in the middle of the night, not worrying about their reputations but about a crumbly old papyrus under the bed. It wasn't that funny but they were worn out. Ryan stopped laughing first. "Let's go to bed."

Sharon was startled.

"Me in mine, and you in yours, down the hall. Good night."

"One last thing, Ryan."

"What?"

"What is Transubstantiation?"

"What? Where did you come up with that?"

"I bought a Catholic catechism in New York before we came here. I know what it said— When the priest consecrates the bread and wine at Mass, it becomes the Body and Blood of Jesus. So, you can do that, Ryan?"

"Yes."

"You believe that?"

"Yes."

"Whew! That's pretty heavy. Could you do it right here in this room?"

"Are you making fun of me, Sharon?"

"Sort of, I guess. Sorry."

"Why did you buy that catechism? Were you interested in becoming a Catholic?"

"No."

"Why, then?"

Sharon got an impish look on her face. "I wanted to figure out why a good looking guy with a high I.Q. wanted to run around in a black dress."

Ryan smiled. "To hide my knobby knees. Now let me ask you a question."

"Shoot."

"Why does a nice Jewish girl, from an Orthodox home, wear such tight pants?"

"I didn't think you noticed."

"Now you know. So, why?"

"Because I've got a great butt, and I was wondering if a man who wears a black dress would notice."

"Go to bed. I'll see you in the morning."

✝ ✝ ✝

Bedu El-Akshar was a member of the Chalice team. He was a respected member of the Brooklyn Museum's Department of Egyptology. He was a Coptic Christian. And now, he was a spy, standing in a doorway in a deserted alley in El Minya, spying on his friends. He ducked out of sight when he heard the tinkle of the doorbell. Neither Ryan Quinn, nor his colleague, Doctor Sharon Feinshutz, were aware of his presence. They seemed excited as they hurried away with a parcel Father Quinn carried as though it were a delicate child.

When he was sure they were gone he came out of hiding and went down the alley to the door they'd come from. He didn't try to go in. He took a flashlight from his pocket and played it across the lintel above the door. In gold leaf it said, "Genuine Antiquities- G. al-Meskeen, Egyptologist." Bedu had been instructed to observe Ryan Quinn's activities and report back, to take notes if necessary, but nothing more. In the dark, holding the flashlight in his teeth, he scribbled the name, G. al-Neskeem. Then he hurried away to the main street to look for a carriage to take him back to the hotel. The shisha parlors were busy, men sucking on water pipes and playing backgammon. The carriages were lined up waiting for customers, their horses munching on alfalfa. He took the first one he came to. He told the driver to go first to the Hotel Mercure Nefertiti, then search for a drug store. He was only in the hotel for a moment to leave the scribbled name of Gawdat el-Meskeen in an envelope at the front desk. As for the drug store, in the event his friends had missed him, he had his excuse ready, a migraine. He'd say he had gone in search of a chemist to compound a special combination of herbs he had found effective in the past in treating his headaches. The guilty often see danger where none exists. No one noticed his absence, except perhaps, Leila. But if she did, she would never let him know that she missed him when he wasn't around.

Bedu went to bed as soon as he got back, but slept poorly. He was a spy and hated the role. He didn't even know what was at stake or why he was being asked to observe his friends. If he was on some side, he didn't really know there were sides at all, or why. The reason he was involved was simple, money, lots of money. He had been offered a sum that made his eyes pop just to watch and report the activities of Ryan Quinn and the others. A man had approached him that morning in the market place. Bedu had become separated from Leila when she had gone off to shop for jewelry. The man said there was nothing sinister involved. The Chalice group was working for his superiors and they wanted to be certain they knew at once if any important finds were made.

"What kind of finds?" he asked.

"Anything at all that seems important or seems to excite Ryan Quinn. We have paid him an immense amount of money and we trust him but we believe in double-checking on our investments. Just watch, listen, and report back to us. You will be paid five thousand dollars a day while you are working for us and a bonus if something important is found as long as you let us know immediately. As proof of our good intentions, there are twenty-thousand dollars in this package."

"And how do I report to you, and receive my payments?"

"Just ask the clerk at the Hotel Mercure Nefertiti to put a note in the slot for room thirty-six. Do you know the hotel? It is on the Corniche al-Nil. Payments to you will be made in the slot for room thirty-seven. You have been registered to that room and the rent paid in advance for a month. If you have to leave El Minya, we will know and contact you with further instructions. You will have no cause for complaint with our punctuality, generosity, or efficiency, I assure you."

And that was that. Bedu was a spy, soon to be a lot richer, and he hated himself.

✝ ✝ ✝

Everyone was together at the breakfast table. Sunlight was pouring through the tall windows of the dining room. Everyone knew Ryan and Sharon had been up late together but no one mentioned it. Leila knew that Bedu had been out late, too, and resisted the pang of jealousy she realized she had no right to be feeling. *If he had to go out at night in search of company, he was a lesser person than she thought. Of course, if it was in search of sex, she had been rather prudish and perhaps driven him to it. She was anything but a prude and found him very attractive both physically and intellectually. Perhaps she would lighten up a bit. After all, they weren't holed up in a nunnery. Even the boss stayed up late with Sharon, and he was a priest. God knows what went on with that?*

Ryan raised his voice to get attention. "Sharon uncovered a very interesting artifact in town which may have some bearing on our mission here in El Minya. Last night we went back to the shop where she discovered it and it is now in our possession. We may need help from all of you to figure out how it fits into the puzzle of our being here. You, Megyn, will be especially interested."

Leila felt like a worm for suspecting Father Quinn and Sharon of midnight shenanigans. Bedu felt worse than she. He had spied on his friends, and now, right in front of everyone, Ryan was about to give an account of what happened, undoubtedly in more detail than he had obtained with his dumb, gumshoe operation.

"It is a very old papyrus which both Sharon and I believe to be authentic. We believe it must date to sometime around the First Century, written in Coptic, describing a chalice with eight medallions around its rim and the efforts of a hermit monk to cover the walls of his cave with a mural depicting eight elders holding eight chalices."

Megyn was all but overcome by the revelation. She sat dumb, one hand to her mouth as though trying to stifle a gasp.

Bedu sat, fascinated, with something of such unexpected intensity churning in his gut that he felt close to vomiting. He was a traitor and that made him also an outsider within a world he had chosen as his own. Something momentous was going on and he, through his petty greed had placed himself on the outside. It was all happening so fast he felt he could not be blamed, but he knew that was not true.

Everybody rose and circled Ryan and Sharon, firing questions at them.

"How did you discover the papyrus, Sharon?" That was Leila.

"Why do you believe it's authentic, Ryan?" from McAndrew.

"Where did you find it?" That was Bedu, his voice quavering.

"I think you know, Bedu." Ryan fixed him with a steady gaze. And everyone turned to look at Bedu El-Akshar, whose Arab tan hid what otherwise would have been a deep flush of embarrassment.

"I need to talk to you in private, Father. Can we go for a walk out front?"

"Of course." The two left a bewildered group behind them.

Out the front door, the two men walked down the curved hotel drive, dwarfed by the tall palms that hung over them. "I have a terrible confession to make, Father."

"I am not Coptic, Bedu."

"I know, Father. This is a different kind of confession, a sad admission of how a friend has betrayed another."

"Is it about following Sharon and me into town yesterday evening?"

"Yes."

"No need. I saw you. I wondered why you didn't join us in the shop. You would have been welcome."

"Please. Don't make this even harder for me. I didn't know you were aware of me. I was being paid to follow you."

Ryan stopped dead. He had been startled by that admission.

"Paid? By whom? And why?"

"I don't know, Father, but it was a great deal of money. He didn't identify himself or give me a reason. Greed took hold of me and I betrayed you. I must give the money back, but I don't know if I can regain your friendship and trust after behaving so miserably."

"Bedu, my friend. You need no forgiveness. You did me no harm. You hurt only yourself. If I trusted you before, it may have been a mistake. I know I can trust you now. We share the knowledge of your infidelity. As to friendship, you have displayed the depth of yours by telling me this. I hope I am equally worthy of yours. In a practical sense, you have done me, and the rest of our group, a great service. Now I know we are being watched. We will leave El Minya as soon as possible."

Ryan took Bedu's hands and drew the man to him in a bear hug. He could feel the young Arab shaking with emotion.

"You must tell me whatever you can," Ryan continued. "As to returning the money, let's use it instead to buy equipment and supplies. We will be going into the desert and I don't know for how long."

"I have enough money to buy a lot of stuff," said Bedu with a sheepish grin.

Chapter Thirty-Two

Wadid Hamza was a rich man. He had made a fortune selling large pharaonic antiquities, both legal and illegal, to collectors and museums all over the world. It had been a family business for over a century. At first, when he took over the pillaging of historic sites, it bothered him. When he analyzed his emotions, he found it wasn't so much the raping of history that bothered him but the danger of getting caught. In Twenty-First Century Egypt the illegal portion of the family trade, the most lucrative, had become very dangerous. A crooked dealer was almost certain to be caught and jailed. Bribery was getting more difficult with any degree of safety, and punishment, if caught, was even more severe than for simple theft. Egypt did not practice Sharia Law as generally understood, but transgressions did not receive Western style wrist-slaps either.

Small time crooks still dealt in contraband artifacts, ushabti, scraps of ancient papyrus, scarabs, and such. Wadid's family specialty was big stuff, obelisks, stelae, statuary, temple façades, sometimes, entire temples. Even the government recognized his expertise and called upon him to broker deals with foreign museums and municipalities in legal transactions. He played a significant part in managing the transfer of the Temple of Dendur, in 661 crates, aboard the US freighter, S. S. Concordia Star, to New York for installation in the Sackler Wing of the Metropolitan Museum of Art on Fifth Avenue. The deal was lucrative and all perfectly legal. The small temple was a gift to the United States from Egypt in recognition of its help saving other structures from the rising waters of Lake Nasser. Wadid had a special interest in the matter. He was not often given to performing "good works," but he was a Coptic Christian. He knew that the temple once served as a secret, Christian chapel, away from the prying eyes of Muslim persecutors. Wadid chuckled to think that, like a US medical marijuana salesman, he had done well by doing good.

When Wadid first took his place in the family business, trade in authentic artifacts was already illegal, but the law was something to which one rarely needed to pay much attention. Egypt had yet to develop true pride in its national treasures. Its history was for sale and the world was buying, as well as stealing. Archaeologists were usually foreigners. They came from everywhere, Italy, England, Germany, Switzerland, Russia, France, and the United States, to name just a few. Virtually every major city on earth proudly displays an artifact taken from the deserts of Egypt, an obelisk in New York City's Central Park, another in Westminster, another at the center of the Place de la Concorde in Paris, and several in Rome. The thieves have been, not only jack-booted municipalities, but with an air of righteous, academic privilege, highly respected museums. They have been among the Hamza family's best customers, vying with one another for international recognition of their collections, New York's Met, the Louvre, the British Museum, even Sharon Feinschutz' Brooklyn Museum. But collecting Egypt's historical treasures has not been solely a pecadillo of wealthy nations and museums. Many priceless artifacts have "found their way" into private collections. One of the most bizarre examples is a mummy, now believed to be that of Pharaoh Rameses I, found in a "Freaks of Nature Exhibit" in what National Geographic described as "a tacky museum in Niagara Falls." Along with a few other specimens, Rameses was bought in the mid-1890's from Wadid's great-grandfather, Abdullah, by a man named Thomas Barnett, for display in his tourist sideshow. It lay there until recently, its importance unrecognized for 140 years. It has been returned to Cairo and the waiting arms of Zahi Hawass.

The past disrespect shown Egyptian mummies now seems incredible. It was a popular practice among wealthy families during the Victorian era, to give "mummy unwrapping parties." Even worse, was the use of mummies as fuel to stoke steam trains on the British–run, Egyptian railroads.

Nineteenth Century history left little reason for Wadid Hamza to consider any of his artifact sales to be egregious crimes against Egyptian nationalism. What others did in the name of academic research, made his, and his family's, activities look exemplary.

Whether through larceny, or simple indifference to rules, regulations, and propriety, Wadid Hamza was a wealthy man. Like many wealthy men,

Wadid indulged his fancies, sex, of course, a fine estate, naturally, an expensive car, without question. But in Wadid's case, not just an expensive car,but a fleet of them, not just numerous, expensive vehicles, but machines of unique, historical significance. He owned the largest private collection of World War II desert vehicles in existence, many camouflage-painted trucks and half-tracks left in Egypt by Field Marshall Erwin Rommel, "The Desert Fox," who had been defeated by the Americans at El Alamein, near Alexandria.

Wadid restored the vehicles and maintained them in excellent working condition. They were garaged in a huge structure on his estate beside the Nile. His prize possession was an open touring car, Rommel's personal half-track, his command vehicle, known to history buffs as "Rommel's Rod." It is a massive, khaki-colored vehicle with tank treads. It was the ultimate desert machine, now in Wadid's garage, still sporting Afrika Korps logos on its side panels, black Swastikas within red circles against gracefully-leaning, palm trees. On the rear of the vehicle, in bold black letters, it says, "Abstand Halten"—Stay Back!"

Wadid's one problem with his collection was its irrelevance. He didn't believe that artifacts should sit silently in museums. They should be fondled and enjoyed by enthusiasts. That went for everything he treasured, from famous gems to famous automobiles. He insisted that his beautiful, ex-bellydancer, wife conspicuously display the extraordinary jewelry he bought for her, and sometimes, he drove Rommel's Rod through the desert wastelands around El Minya. He boasted that he was his own best security force. As a super burglar of sorts, he knew everyone on the wrong side of the law. As a very wealthy man, he knew everyone on the right side of the law. As to his beautiful wife, he was fond of saying she wore a golden burqa. She wouldn't cheat and lose her fabulously sweet life, and anyone who did more than silently lust after her, would never look at another beautiful woman again, with only sockets left for eyes. No great philosopher, he would happily expound on his life theories after a drink or two.

"Mostly," he would say, "men make their wives wear burqas to hide their ugly faces. I'll bet lots of them make their women wear burqas when they screw them." Then he would laugh loudly. Muslims don't drink alcohol but as a Coptic Christian he was free to indulg his taste for booze.

Considering his contacts on both sides of the law, and around the world, it was not surprising that Wadid knew it, the minute Ryan Quinn and his troupe set foot on Egyptian soil, and everything that had transpired since—

everything. He was no moralist, so he cared nothing about Megyn Corbet's transgressions with the Bedouin child, nor the gay priest's float trip down the Nile with the well known tourist swindler, Jusef Mohamet Ghadalla.

He had met Father Quinn several times. He respected both his knowledge of Egyptian art and his business acumen. If Ryan Quinn was here in El Minya with a troupe of epigraphers, geologists, and artifact conservators, something big was afoot. That suspicion was confirmed when he learned that huge sums of money had been deposited in Quinn's name both in Cairo and Alexandria. The T's were crossed and the I's dotted when he learned that the Roman Catholic Church was one of the depositors. He had never heard of the other. That bothered him. Was there a new "player" on the board? He alerted all his informers to keep him current regarding any developments. He wasn't surprised to learn that several high ranking clergy from Rome had come to El Minya within the last few days, dressed in sports clothes, obviously trying to look like anything but priests. They were staying at the Mercure Nefertiti and playing undercover agents with one of Quinn's group.

Wadid was not prepared for what came next. It was a note, by messenger, from the Patriarch of his Church, Pope Shenouda. He knew members of Shenouda's family, in nearby Asyut. He had dealt with a number of them. They were rotten artifact dealers, always worried that their famous family member in Alexandria would find out about their less than legal enterprises.

Wadid had met the Patriarch. He was a very impressive old man. Wadid had made some very generous contributions to the church. He also sensed at once that the size of his contributions meant nothing to the holy man. That door to Heaven was not for sale. It didn't matter. He respected Shenouda and though his gifts were sizeable, they were insignificant compared to what he routinely spent on jewels for his wife.

Receiving a note from the Patriarch startled Wadid. He never expected the old man would need him for anything. Maybe the door to Heaven might still be open after all.

The note was short and to the point—

It would please me greatly were you to provide Reverend Ryan Quinn any assistance he might require both with his research and with the handling of any artifacts that might be involved.

—Shenouda

Wadid whistled through his teeth. Something very important, and therefore very valuable, was involved in the Jesuit's visit to El Minya. Great! There had been little excitement in his life since the government had grown sticky about antiquities.

After taking some time to let the matter settle in his mind, he went out to the garage and fired up his magnificent Bugati Veyron. He had captured it in a competitive bid against designer, Ralph Lauren. The roar of the powerful engine echoed through the huge garage and set its windows rattling. That pleased Wadid immensely. What followed, of necessity, did not please him at all, the drive along the poorly maintained streets of El Minya. Each pothole, each rut, tore at his gut even more fiercely than they tore at the carefully machined parts of his magnificent automobile.

The entrance to the Ibn el Khassib was better maintained than the municipal streets so he pressed his foot to the floor and roared up the driveway, between the rows of palms, almost running down two men who stood talking in the middle of the road.

† † †

"How were you going to return the money, Bedu?"

"The man gave me a room number at the Mercure Nefertiti where I was supposed to drop notes about your activities. I actually did drop one there, with the name of the antiquities shop, after you returned to the Ibn el Khassib last night."

"Let's go there together, Bedu. We'll see what he's up to."

"From what he said, he was not alone. It might be dangerous."

"I'll risk that. And so will you, Bedu," he said as a mischievous afterthought.

No sooner than those words had left Ryan's lips, than a powerful car came rushing up the entrance road so fast they both had to jump out of the way. The car came to a screeching halt, feet from where the two had been standing.

"Good morning, Father Quinn. And a good morning to you, too, Doctor El-Akshar. You remember me, Reverend?"

"I do, indeed, Mr. Hamza. How are you, Wadid?"

"Rich, good father. Very rich. And you."

"Sworn to poverty, my friend, but wanting for nothing."

The two shared a hearty laugh.

"And you, Doctor Bedu El-Akshar? Recently a bit richer, I hear."

Bedu was completely taken by surprise. Who was this man? How did he know Bedu's name, and most disturbing, how did he know about the money? Was he one of the group that had approached him?

"Please explain, my dear friend, Ryan." He was still speaking from the open window of his Bugati.

Ryan turned back to Bedu. "This is Wadid Hamza, one of the richest, most powerful men in Egypt, perhaps the world. He knows everything, sometimes even before it has happened. He is neither clairvoyant nor blessed with pre-cognition. He buys everything, including the very souls of the fellahin who are unfortunate enough to cross his path." Then back to Wadid, "Nice Bugati. A Veyron?"

"Would you like one like it, Ryan?"

"I don't think there *is* another like it, but no. Ralph Lauren offered me one in exchange for some work last year. He wanted me to secure some stained glass windows for him from a cathedral in France, but had to back off when he lost the bid for the Bugati at auction. I planned to say no, but I'm sad to see the Bugati fell into hands no cleaner than his."

The two men laughed again. Bedu stood dumbfounded, his jaw agape. Who was this boss of his, so friendly and unassuming, who apparently moved comfortably among the super rich and famous?

"Come, Ryan. Walk up to the hotel. I'll be in the bar. It was you I was coming to see. I'll go first so I don't run you down. I'll have a drink waiting for you. I know it's early but I so rarely find a drinking partner in this Muslim country of mine." And off he went with a tortured chirp from his Pirelli Rosso tires.

"Wake up, Bedu. Wadid is an old friend of mine. Well, maybe not exactly friend. Sometimes we've been adversaries. Gold is his god, and his prayers are probably answered with more regularity than mine."

"I'm sorry, Father. It upset me to hear him speak of my transgression. It was less than 24 hours ago that I betrayed your trust and already all of Egypt knows. It will be comforting to return to my small office at the Brooklyn Museum. Did you know that Brooklyn has a sizeable Arab population? I think the food is probably more authentically prepared than in Felfella's in Cairo."

"Bedu— you must get a grip on yourself. Now you are talking about Egyptian comfort food in Brooklyn while we are walking along a street in Egypt." As though nothing had taken place, Ryan had cut to the soft place in his companion's heart and made him feel comfortable. "Will you join Wadid and me for a drink? You Coptics do drink, don't you?"

"Not within site of papist priests." He was feeling better. The two of them laughed.

"If I see a priest I'll warn you. Let's hurry up before Wadid buys the hotel and has us kicked out with no place to spend the night."

As promised, Wadid was waiting at the bar, a small snifter of brandy and a glass of ice water in front of him, a shot of bourbon and an ice-water chaser at the next place for Ryan. They knew Wadid at the Ibn el Khassib and always kept a bottle of his favorite brandy handy.

"I had no idea if you would be joining us. Would you like something, Doctor El-Akshar?"

"No thank you, Mr. Hamza. I think I will join my friends and leave you two alone to discuss whatever you need to discuss."

Wadid nodded and turned back to Ryan who moved his bourbon and water closer. Ryan spoke first. "I've known you long enough, Wadid, to realize no meeting is ever limited to idle chit-chat. What do you need?"

"This may surprise you, Ryan, but the answer is, nothing. In fact it is quite the opposite. You need me."

"And why would I need you, old friend?"

"That's your second surprise. You do need me but I actually don't know why."

"This will require more than a little explaining. I have known you to be devious but never obscure. Give me a few hints."

Wadid laughed easily and tossed down the shot of brandy. Then he apologized.

"I know it is poor form to toss down brandy, but my throat was dry. I will show the next one greater respect." He signaled the bartender.

Ryan sensed that the man was being completely honest. He would have to play sleuth for both of them. "Do you know why I am here with my team from Neew York?"

"Yes, and no. I know that a great deal of money has been put at your disposal to carry on an investigation. I know everything about all of your team members, and where a couple of them have been dallying for the past few weeks, but the actual purpose? No. Will you keep me guessing? I hate to be kept guessing."

"I'm afraid I can't help you with much. The truth is, like the mystery of how and why you are here, I'm afraid I'm as much in the dark about my own mission as you about yours. It became a little clearer within the past 24 hours."

"You mean because of your visit to Gawdat al-Meskeen's shop? He is such a small-time operator. I'm sure that can't be it. Perhaps the two priests that have been following you?"

"Priests?"

"Aha! I've got something on you. Of course. Two priests were sent directly from Rome to dog your footsteps. They're the ones who lined your friend's pockets with silver. I'll agree it doesn't make much sense, since it was Rome that put all that money at your disposal in the first place. Weren't you told what you were being paid to do?"

"Actually, no. But I think I may have figured it out, at least partially. I believe I was sent to look for an artifact. Only yesterday I think I figured out what it is. But why priests to follow me?"

"Perhaps they think you have some clues as to where to find that artifact, but are not convinced you will be willing to relinquish it if you're successful. Do you have some special clues as to its nature and whereabouts?"

That was too direct for Wadid to imagine he would get a straight answer, but he found that sometimes, when you hoist a blank flag, some idiot may get caught in a reflexive, half-salute.

"Before I answer that, you must tell me why you think you should help me without knowing why."

"That's an easy one, Ryan. I was asked to."

"By whom?"

"An important friend of a friend."

"Must be a very good friend, and a very important friend of that friend."

"Not that good, regarding the first but, as to the other? Yes, very important."

Ryan had finished his bourbon and placed his hand, palm down, over his glass as the bartender approached. Both men were enjoying the cat and mouse game but Ryan was ready to get to the meat of the subject.

"That still sounds a bit too altruistic for the man I've known all these years. Something valuable must be involved."

"Very astute, Ryan. But there is no money in it for me."

"Now you truly have me puzzled. Something valuable, important for some reason other than its monetary value to you, and an important friend, who expects you to give it to him?"

"No. He wants me to help you to keep it and get it out of Egypt."

"Alright, Wadid. You win. What is it and who asked you?"

"I don't know what it is and hoped you did. As to the important gentleman— his name is Nazeer Gayeb."

"The Patriarch, Pope Shenouda?

"Exactly. Want another bourbon?"

"Yes."

"Now, does that give you some clue as to what we might be talking about as far a any artifact is concerned?"

"Yes. It does. I think we're talking about a goblet, a very special goblet. I only learned during the past few days that it might be located somewhere near here."

"A goblet important enough to warrant hundreds of millions of dollars in up-front payments to your corporation from Rome, and from some mysterious family whose members keep showing up unexpectedly? A goblet important enough to send the Pope into a frenzy, sending his Nuncio around the world, and another squadron of priests to chase after him? A goblet important enough to prompt the "Wise Old Man of Alexandria" to call in a favor from someone like me, whom, I'm sure he doesn't hold in very high regard? I think we know which goblet we must be talking about. I need another brandy."

Bedu returned. He found the two men sitting as though they had been hit by something strong and silent. They had.

"Should I leave you two alone?"

Ryan came out of his trance. "As a matter of fact, we do have some things to discuss in private. I'm sorry."

"I'll be in my room if you need me. The others are still in the dining room. I'll tell them you have business to attend to with an old friend."

"Thank you." Ryan turned to Wadid. "You and I may not be the most likely bedfellows, especially considering a matter of this importance and potential value, but I have no choice. We must be partners."

"Not a heart-rending declaration of love and trust, my friend, but straightforward. I'll give you that. Now let me say where I stand. I no longer need money. I have trouble finding things on which to squander what I already have. I do love the thrill of the search and the intrigue involved in disposing of my treasures under the noses of those who would hang them around my neck and push me into the Nile. We shall be partners, Ryan, the most dependable of partners, two clever gentlemen who need one another more than they need anyone or anything more than one another. It will be a new experience for me. I hope Pope Shenouda has some pull in Heaven. Frankly, considering everything I know at this point, I don't put much faith in your Holy Father."

"They are both just men, Wadid. What powers they have beyond this earth, I don't know. I'm beginning to wonder, myself."

"OK. Now that that's settled, let's compare notes. You first. Who is this family that goes by the name of Sarafian, a very beautiful woman and a brother, handsome but with more the air of a vampire than a womanizer?"

"Sorry, Wadid. They are as much a mystery to me as to you. They made a deposit to an account in my name. I was assured by the bank that the money was there. I have already made withdrawals without incident. What do you know of them?"

"Virtually nothing. That is not a normal situation. When I ask questions, people give me answers. I do know that the woman has been in Alexandria, and had a meeting with your Nuncio friend, Pietro Gandolfo. Strangely though, I received the impression, from what I've been told, that they are not in league with one another. Just the opposite. They seem to be adversaries on some level. The confusing thing is that it would seem the Vatican is interested in obtaining the artifact for itself, while the woman, and probably her brother, are interested only in blocking the efforts of the Vatican. I find no record of any Sarafians among the worldwide ranks of art and artifact collectors, legitimate, or otherwise. They seem to come and go out of nowhere, and use money as though it comes with similar ease, out of thin air."

"I don't doubt the facts as you present them, nor your assessment of them, Wadid. They do, however, put me in an awkward position. But you know that. I am a Catholic priest sworn to obedience."

"You are also sworn to poverty and chastity, if I recall the rules of Rome correctly."

"Yes."

"As with the artifact business, my friend, there are technical ways of avoiding the letter of the law without violating either the law, or the conscience."

"You are a devious soul, Wadid."

"It is not my soul that is devious, Ryan. I was cursed with a complex brain, like yours. I have never noticed that you suffer from outward indications of poverty. I know nothing of your battles regarding chastity."

"It is a battle, my friend, because I take my vow seriously. On the other hand, I feel that poverty and obedience are less personal, and promises to the Church, rather than to God. There have been very rich bishops, cardinals, and even popes. Little disapproval has been voiced regarding their wealth and displays of independence, as long as they fell in line with the aims of the Church. In fact the wealth and political activities of some have proven to be the keys to its earthly prosperity and survival. But we are wandering way off track. My vows should not concern us at this point. I'd be glad to discuss them at length with you, some other time."

"I apologize, Father Ryan. My life certainly bears no scrutiny. I certainly have no right to examine yours. As you say, let's get back to issues of importance in the matter before us. It is my observation that, although you have been entrusted with a great deal of money by your church to go in search of something, it did not tell you what, and seem actively involved in spying on you. Hardly a vote of confidence. Perhaps it is not you, they mistrust, but perhaps they fear the mysterious Sarafians. They, on the other hand, seem far less inclined to keep an eye on you."

"So, Wadid, I think we can agree that the priests who have been sent to watch me are more of a problem than the Sarafians, but neither pose much of a problem."

"My conclusion as well."

"One thing, Wadid. How do you know they are Catholic priests?"

"Ryan, my friend, do you think you, yourself, can enter a mosque without drawing curious eyes? People wear their personalities, and nationalities, on their sleeves. Is that the right expression? Catholic priests look like Catholic priests. They always seem to have very white, well-scrubbed hands, and look like they would scream if a woman patted them on the ass. What can I say?

You can just tell. They look innocent, but not necessarily comfortable with their innocence. You are different. Why, I don't know."

"OK. I think I know what you mean, but what about black priests, or Indians, or Australian aborigines? We come in all shades and colors, you know."

"You win, Father Quinn. But on this one, trust me. Now I have a question for you. You said you figured out what you were looking for within the last few days. How?"

"A couple of things. One is the experience of one of my group, along with photographs she showed us. The second thing is a papyrus another of my group uncovered at a local antiquities dealer."

"Gawdat al-Meskeen?"

"Yes."

"Well, that sly old devil. For years he has been peddling phony ushabti and scarabs that he turns out in his back room. He had something genuine? Are you sure?"

"I'm sure. The colleague with me is a renowned epigrapher and I am no amateur."

"You mean the pretty gal with the tight pants?"

"The papyrus is authentic. The main reason I know, is the fact that Sharon and I read it in Meskeen's shop together and it bore out the experience and photos of my other colleague, photos obtained completely independently."

"And the papyrus said?"

"It was a parable, or gospel, written by a monk who lived in a cave at Gebel al-Naqlun. It told the story of a leper who left the goblet with him under peculiar circumstances."

"Peculiar circumstances?"

"The account speaks of angels, dreams, and that sort of thing. It also parallels accounts of a leper and a rich man mentioned in other gospels."

"Not my area of expertise, Ryan."

"It says he made drawings of the goblet on the walls of his hermitage. The photos taken by my colleague, are of those drawings in a cave, not mentioned anywhere in archaeological, or Coptic literature, to the best of my knowledge."

"Does the papyrus say what he did with the goblet?"

"He hid it and waited for an angel to come for it."

"No one showed up, I suspect."

"Don't be such a cynic, Wadid."

"So, it is still in Gebel al-Naqlun?"

"Perhaps. But I don't think so. Another priest, perhaps you knew him, may have found it. I have some of his notebooks and feel it might be urgent that I go through them as soon as possible."

"Who is that?"

"Habib Colophon."

"Yes. I know him, but you spoke of him in the past tense."

"He died in New York, practically in my arms. I only found his notes because I knew where he used to spend his private time."

"The notebooks— they are in New York?"

"No. They are here in my room."

"Those dumb priests from Rome might be snooping around, to say nothing of your friend, the Nuncio, who is headed this way."

"Gandolfo is coming to El Minya?"

"Yes. But for some reason I'm told he is doing so at a snail's pace. That may be why Rome decided to send those other numb skulls. We must get those notebooks to someplace safe. I have a well-appointed guesthouse with enough room for you and your group. Get them together. There'll be a horse and carriage waiting out front for you within the hour. You shall all be houseguests of Wadid Hamza, the Coptic Patriarch's favorite grave robber. "

With that, Wadid left the bar, walked through the lobby, and out the front door. After a moment or two, the windows rattled to the roar of the Bugati as it laid rubber down the driveway.

Chapter Thirty-Three

There was a carriage waiting in front of the Ibn el-Khassib when Ryan and his colleagues were ready to go. It was only about an hour since Wadid had left. Ryan offered no reason to the group, but urged them to hurry, and not to discuss the departure, even with one another. He did not want the hotel staff to have more information than they already had.

"I hope you had a pleasant stay, Father Quinn?" It was the clerk at the front desk.

"Marvelous. Thank you so much for your hospitality. And please compliment the chef. The food was excellent."

"May I have a forwarding address? A few gentlemen asked me to keep them informed in case they needed to reach you. They were Italian, I believe. Excellent Arabic, but definitely Italians."

"I wish I could give you an address, but we will be headed into the Western Desert to visit a number of Coptic monasteries. I don't know where we'll start, or where we'll finish. Please give the gentlemen our apologies, and tell them we are flattered that they were so anxious to keep in touch, and grateful for their generous contribution toward our expedition expenses."

"Of course. And you will be returning to our hotel?"

"Even that is not certain. We hope so."

Bedu was within earshot and smiled. He had grown tremendously fond of this priest whom he now considered his role model, if he dared even think of himself in the same league. Leila stood very close to him and wondered at the new bond she felt Bedu had developed with Ryan since the private conversation the two had shared. There was a lot going on and she hoped to be part of it but decided this was not the time to ask. Sharon, Father McAndrew, and Megyn, had all come to the same conclusion. They exchanged glances with one another, but had gotten their things together hurriedly.

Out front, Sharon made a quick, last-minute grab for her duffel bag, which was about to be put onto the carriage. She fished out a Twinkie. If there were to be surprises, she did not want to be forced into survival mode without appropriate fortification.

It wasn't a long ride. The carriage headed south out of town, then to the east, toward the Nile. Before long, the road curved, then straightened to run parallel with the river. They were in the lush, green pastures, fed for eons with loam-rich soil from Sudan, contributions left by the river's annual floods that had occurred with clockwork regularity throughout recorded history, but no longer. The Russians, to curry favor with Egypt, had provided money and expertise to build Aswan Dam, a bad mistake according to those who understand economic geography. The floods that nourished the wetlands along the Nile were now under control and could perform their sloppy but necessary task no more. To add insult to injury, the damn began to fill with sediment from Sudan, so it became almost useless, while the water level of Lake Nasser, created by the dam, began to rise and swallow priceless temples, once safe on its shores. The United States, and other nations, rushed in to save the treasures. Russia stood back, red faced, as it lost influence in the area.

Several benefits did derive from the debacle. Some of Lower Egypt had electricity courtesy of the dam's generators, and some green fields were made safe from flooding, permitting the safe establishment of rich estates like that of Wadid Hamza.

The Chalice team rattled along in silence behind a well-fed mule. The adobe wall beside the road seemed endless. It went on for at least a mile before it was interrupted by a section of wrought iron fence. The tips of its tall pickets were plated with gold. A gate at the center of the fence was supported on each side by an obelisk. Ryan was sure they were authentic. There was an inscription within a cartouche above the gate. In ancient pictographs it said, "Hamza." All of the Chalice group could read it, even Leila, the geomorphologist. She had been with the American Museum of Natural History, dealing with Egyptologists daily and did not want to be left out of department discussions. She had made Egyptian language and hieroglyphs a priority in her spare time. Her huge Egyptian Grammar, by

Sir Alan Gardiner, was always on her desk amid a chaotic scatter of fossils, minerals, and aeolian concretions.

A pair of gatekeepers, in matching black and gold dishdashas and turbans, drew the gates wide to admit them. The road ahead was lined on both sides with palm trees. At regular intervals along the way, stood armed guards in black, ornate jambiya blades hanging from chains around their necks.

Some people deserve to be rich, thought Ryan. *Wadid really knows how to spend money.*

If the others had similar thoughts, they didn't express them. It was a time for silence as the carriage rattled on toward a stone structure still in the distance. When they arrived at the front steps, Wadid was there in traditional Egyptian garb, a white dishdasha, embroidered with gold. On his head was a pure white turban.

"Greetings, good Father. And welcome, to the rest of you. The carriage will take you around to the guesthouse. Later you will join me and my wife for dinner. I hope you like lamb. Until then, make yourselves comfortable. Do not hesitate to ask the guesthouse concierge should you need anything not already provided." He made a slight nod to punctuate his words and swept his arm to the left to signal the driver to proceed around the house.

If the main house was impressive, the guesthouse was a treasure in miniature. Ryan recognized it at once— not an ancient artifact but a replica of one— the Temple of Khnum at Esna. It's outer walls leaned inward slightly, hinting at Egypt's long fascination with pyramids. The walls, true to the original, but in miniature, were adorned with images of ancient gods as well as Greek and Roman rulers. One column at the entrance showed the Roman Emperor Trajan dancing before the goddess Menheyet.

The guest rooms lay to both sides of a central hall, its roof supported by papyrus-shaped columns. Between the columns, a wall of fitted stones created a screen similar to those in the temples at Dendera and Edfu. The hall was open at one end to invite the evening breezes from the Nile.

Traditionally dressed servants took the group's bags and hurried with them down the main hall, leaving them in separate chambers. How they determined which bags belonged together, and which ones belonged in different chambers, only they knew. None of the Chalice team was inclined to question anything at this point.

The team members were ushered into their appropriate chambers. The rooms, although within a stone temple, lacked nothing in the way of contemporary luxury, wall-to-wall carpeting, concealed incandescent lighting, even the background susurrus of modern air conditioning couold be heard at work.

The beds were luxurious. On each lay a traditional Greek, Roman, or Egyptian garment. The temple of Khnum was built over a period of time that included all of those regimes. Wadid was determined to see that supper would be an event to remember.

The Chalice group all agreed to meet in the central hall around sunset, as suggested by a servant from the main house. A carriage would be there to pick them up. The idea of a carriage seemed superfluous for a trip of less than two hundred yards, but Wadid liked to do things in style.

After several hours, the group members trickled out of their respective rooms, one by one, wearing the costumes provided by the host.

Megyn was incredibly beautiful, her blond hair falling in a cascade about her naked shoulders. She had been given a white, gossamer gown that she had tied at the waist with a golden cord. Around her throat was an elaborate necklace of coral and azurite in the form of a falcon. On her feet were golden sandals. Ryan understood at once that she was meant to represent the goddess, Hathor.

Sharon was the avatar of Nut, the dark-haired goddess of the evening sky, her diaphanous gown studded with gold and silver stars, tied at the waist with a black, velvet band, studded with white and blue crystals. Her sash was the Milky Way, a circle just above her slender hips.

Leila, like her name in Hebrew, was the expression of night, the goddess Anentet, enveloped in a cloud of midnight blue chiffon. On her feet were black sandals. On her head was an ebony coronet, a silver crescent at her forehead.

The men stood as though in a trance, even McAndrew, who understood feminine beauty perhaps even more deeply than the others, though denied by nature the pleasure of plumbing its physical delights.

Wadid had played host with unusual taste, but with more than a bit of mean-spirited humor. While the women were portrayed as visions of desire, the men had been given costumes totally uninspiring, if not silly.

Ryan wore a robe of brown monk's cloth tied with a length of hemp. Bedu was in a floppy robe that looked as though cut from a bolt of awning material. Father McAndrew was in a shapeless, chartreuse robe, a purple tarboush on his head.

Ryan was certain that Wadid would be wearing a magnificent outfit. He had to laugh at how they had been played for idiots. Despite his understanding of the silly game, he found the vision of Sharon disturbing. She was the goddess of the night sky and he felt the strength of that image in his gut. Luckily a rogue thought flew for a moment through his head. *I wonder where she has a Twinkie stashed in that outfit?*

Right on schedule, they heard the rattle of the horse and carriage approaching the open portico of the central hall. The women turned and began to walk toward it. The men followed in silence.

Ryan was unable to control his gaze. He found himself staring at Sharon's rear, twin mounds pressing insistently through the diaphanous gown toward him. He felt a pang of possessive jealousy. He did not want other men's eyes to see their motion as she walked toward the carriage.

Suddenly, Sharon turned her head to look back over her shoulder. She saw where Ryan was looking. He was caught! But she smiled and surprised him with a mischievous wink. To his dismay, he found that he was not embarrassed by the event, but relieved that he and she shared a humorous complicity in this drama neither of them understood.

The carriage ride lasted less than three minutes. It was all about pageantry. It left the guesthouse, circled the main house, and stopped in front.

If the guesthouse was a miniature gem in imitation of the temple of Khnum, the main house was no imitation. Stone by stone, column by column, paving brick by paving brick, Wadid Hamza had disassembled, then reassembled, the Temple of Hibis from the Kharga Oasis in Western Egypt. It was not the largest, best-known, nor most frequently visited temple in Egypt. It was far from being the oldest, built by Pharaoh Psamtik II, barely six hundred years before the birth of Christ. But the beauty of its decorated columns was second to none in the kingdom. It had been decorated by the Persian conqueror, Darius I. Later the smallish edifice had been increased in size by the thirtieth dynasty kings Nectanabo the First, and Nectanabo the Second.

During many renovations, it had grown quite large while retaining its elegant simplicity. The radiant beauty of its decorated columns was legendary. Now it was the home of Wadid Hamza, encircled by a stone apron on which the Chalice troupe's carriage rode. The sound of the horses' hooves mixed with the grinding of metal-rimmed wheels on stone seemed appropriate to the setting. As they rounded the final corner, the sound of their carriage was drowned out by a cacophany of gefs, ouds, zurna snake flutes, bamboo nays, and finger cymbals. Wadid had assembled a a native orchestra.

As the carriage came to a halt, two attendants in gold turbans rolled a red carpet down from the top stair. Measured in advance, it stopped dramatically at the side of their carriage. Men with huge musical horns, like Swiss alpenhorns, blew a basso continuo of great volume at them as they climbed the red carpet to the main level of the temple. At the top, as Ryan had anticipated, Wadid stood in princely attire, his beautiful wife at his side. She was dressed as the goddess Isis, he as her consort, Osiris. Ryan and the other men felt like they should be clanking along in chains with bits of straw falling from their shoulders.

Isis and Osiris drew to the side to make way for Hathor, Nut, and Anentet. They followed them into the temple leaving the men to follow clumsily behind. Ryan, despite his religious calling, and his lofty station in life, was still an Irishman and was beginning to feel his blood pressure rise. Just in time to avoid mahem, Wadid turned, walked back, and grabbed him in a big bear hug.

"You look terrible, Father. Who the hell invited you and these bedraggled, infidel dogs, to this high class get together?" Then he laughed and gave the priest a second hug. Ryan really liked this silly man and joined in the laughter. Bedu and McAndrew didn't quite get it, but smiled dutifully when they saw the boss lighten up.

The entrance of the temple was a hypostyle hall, lined with immense, painted columns. The farther reaches of the temple had been made comfortable to serve as Wadid's residence. They never got that far. A striped, canvas tent had been erected in the entrance hall, carpeted in thick Orientals, and strewn with plush cushions. In the center was a low table surrounded by low seats that had intricately-carved backrests. Dinner would be served on the low table. The utensils would be those of the desert, the diners' right hands.

The loud music never stopped. The dinner courses seemed to come one, after the other, without interruption, for an hour. Everyone was laughing and coping as best they could with hands shiny with lamb grease, until a waiter arrived at last with hot, wet towels on a gold platter.

No party of such spectacular opulence would be complete without a fitting star performer to entertain. Tonight's event would be unique. Wadid asked his wife to dance for his guests. Once the best-known dancer in Egypt, the beautiful woman, dressed for the occasion as the goddess Isis, removed her dress in front of everyone, to reveal the traditional garb of the bellydancer. She disrobed with such ease and grace it was not erotic, nor was the dance, despite the gyrating of hips and artful undulations of her beautifully tanned midriff.

Wadid, completely confident, looked with pride at his half-naked wife and even glanced around to assess the possible lust he might detect in the faces of his male guests. He thought he saw a glint in Bedu's eye. Good. He would hate to think his trophy wife had lost her touch.

With the dance over, she drew a robe around her and sat by Wadid's side. He signaled for the musicians to be quiet, and stood.

"Thank you so much for joining us this evening. We have been truly honored by your presence. And thank you ladies, especially, for allowing me to experience the reality of four goddesses dining at my table. As to you men, my apologies. Osiris allows for no rivals in his realm." He laughed again, goodnaturedly, and everyone joined in.

"I am aware," he continued, "that you are all here on a mission in Egypt because you each possess unique expertise in some specific specialty. I expect you will be here with me for several days before we depart for the Western Desert, if indeed, that is our eventual goal. In the meanwhile, I hope you will enjoy the accommodations I have provided for you. But most important, in this house I have assembled one of the finest libraries devoted to Egyptology existent in the world. Excuse my lack of modesty, but it happens to be the simple truth. I now offer you complete access to that library and to my laboratory which is fitted with all the best and most modern equipment required by a professional conservator." He made a small bow to Father McAndrew.

"And now, my friends in crime, I bid you goodnight. I believe we must ready ourselves to go rob a tomb. I think you can walk back to the guesthouse. The horse was hungry, so I sent him back to the stable for a bag of alfalfa."

All but Ryan were confused by Wadid's reference to tomb robbing. He would explain it to them back at the guesthouse.

Chapter Thirty-Four

Everyone was quiet during the short walk to the guesthouse. The Chalice people knew how to party but they were all essentially post-doctoral eggheads. After hours of the non-stop cacophony of competing native instruments, it was a relief to be engulfed in the silent, sultry, Egyptian night. The only sounds were those of mating insects, and their own footfalls on the stone causeway between Wadid's residence and the guesthouse.

Ryan broke the silence, "Before we return to our rooms, let me explain Wadid's tomb-robbing remark. He was making a bad joke. With the help of Wadid Hamza, I expect we will leave shortly in search of the chalice mentioned in the papyrus uncovered by Sharon and depicted in the mural photographed by Megyn. It would seem that is the unstated purpose of our mission, mysteriously funded by several benefactors. That's all I will tell you because that's really all I know. How I know, is another matter, and I will discuss it with you all tomorrow after breakfast when we meet in Wadid's library. He will become a member of our party both physically and intellectually. I have reason to believe he can be trusted. I hope I am correct in that assessment."

Father McAndrew was the only other to speak. "But what's that got to do with the side trip you sent me on to France?"

"That was suggested to me by the Papal Nuncio, James. I don't know why, either. Apparently you found some relevance since you contacted Paul in New York. Correct?"

"Relevance, perhaps, but a mystery to me as to why I felt it was relevant. I was desperate to find anything to justify an admittedly delightful visit to a marvelous religious edifice at company expense."

"Thank you, James. Maybe we can clear that up before all this is over so you won't go to Hell for it."

Everybody was laughing as they came to the guesthouse.

"Now I suspect we all need some rest. There are a couple of disturbing aspects to this mission. We'll discuss them tomorrow, as well."

They were too drained to demand anything further and headed off to their rooms.

"One thing," added Ryan speaking to Sharon and James, "could I see both of you for a moment before we go to bed?" The others went on ahead. "I am in possession of some private papers that belonged to my old friend, Father Habib Colophon. You knew him, James. His papers may be of importance to our expedition. The problem is that he was the sloppiest writer I ever knew. There are notes he left to be read only by me. That is impossible. I can't read them. I need the talent of an epigrapher, you Sharon, to read the darn things, and the spiritual assistance of a priest, you James, in the event there are matters discussed that are possibly of ecclesiastical significance that must be kept under wraps. The others may be told of our work but not of the contents unless I decide afterwards that it is appropriate. Understood?" The two nodded sleepily. "Now, off with you. And no Twinkies, Sharon. I hear Wadid serves big breakfasts. We don't want you to be rude and pick at your food in the morning."

† † †

Apparently, Wadid Hamza did not believe in catering to late risers. At Six AM, Chef Rashid Nefooz, came down the central hall of the guesthouse rattling a goatskin deff (tambourine), crying out, "dee-noor." All meals to Mr. Nefooz, were dinner.

There was no kitchen in the guesthouse. The chef prepared all meals in the main house and delivered them on a colorful street cart that had a number of insulated drawers like an airline kitchen. It also had a brass kettle on top with a spigot so he could dispense hot water into either a teapot or through a mound of freshly ground coffee.

In the drawers were warm rolls, scrambled eggs, crisp bacon, semi-sweet pastries, and a huge variety of Egyptian delicacies. Though the drawers were well insulated, hot, fresh food was hot, fresh food. Rashid Nefooz was not about to have his meals grow cold and leave him open to criticism. Hence, the tambourine and the loud announcement about dee-noor.

After a few moments, the sleepy Chalice team members stumbled from their rooms and into the dining alcove. There, Rashid was busy ladling various things onto plates and into bowls.

Ryan was relieved to see that everyone was in bathrobes provided by the host, no gods, goddesses, sheepherders, or camel drivers. He and James would have the privilege of opting for either civvies or priestly garb. Neither was inclined to go clerical. At least Ryan had no such intentions. From this point on, all of them were Egyptologists, no more deities, or peasant outfits. He hoped Wadid would not push the fancy dress code any further for himself, either.

After serving everyone, Rashid came over to Ryan with a pad in his hand. He read from it carefully— "Meester Hamza in libroory, ten oh-gluck. OK?"

"OK. Shukron." Then to the others, "You have lots of time. We'll all meet with Wadid in his library at ten o'clock. Finish your breakfasts and walk around the grounds if you wish. I suspect there's a lot to see. We'll all get together here in the central hall at nine-forty-five and walk over together."

Ryan asked Sharon and James to come to his room as soon as they had showered and put on whatever they planned to wear for the day.

Ryan had hardly finished dressing when he heard the first knock on his door. It was James. Ryan was relieved.

"I want you to take possession of the papyrus Sharon and I brought back from the antiquarian dealer in El Minya. It's in good shape, but I want you to do what you can to stabilize it further, and prepare it for some possibly rough travel. Also, as I will explain to everyone later in the library, I have reason to believe there are some agents anxious to take it from us."

"Agents?"

"I know it sounds dramatic, James, but there have been people following us. Wadid is aware of them. I believe his estate is probably the safest place for the papyrus and for all of us, for that matter."

"These agents are antiquities thieves, Ryan?"

"Not exactly, James. It's complicated. I think they're Catholic priests."

"What?"

Just then, Sharon knocked on the door. She was back to wearing tight, khaki, field pants. Ryan looked at her for just a bare moment too long, then hurriedly turned back to James who was already undoing the package that contained the papyrus.

"Come in, Sharon. James will be doing what he can to stabilize the papyrus and repack it for our travels."

James spoke up from where he already had the artifact out of its wrappings— "It seems to be in excellent shape. I should get it right over to Mr. Hamza's lab to work on it."

"No, James. Please stay with us. We aren't due to be over there until ten. I want you to hear what I am about to tell Sharon." He went to the campaign style desk against the wall and opened the drawer where he had put Colophon's notebooks the night before. "Come, let's sit down." James and Sharon each dragged over a chair.

"These are notes made by Father Habib Colophon some years ago. I discovered them where I think he knew I would, in his office at the American Numismatic Society in New York. The problem is, my dear friend Habib wrote like a physician, in a hand almost completely illegible. Tucked into one of the notebooks was a sheaf of papers, marked clearly, to be read only by me. Fine, except, try as I have, I've been able to read almost none of it."

"The fact that it is for my eyes alone implies that there may be some material involving theological matters he wished to remain undisclosed to the world. I didn't reach that conclusion simply because of the "your eyes only" aspect. I was with him when he died and he indicated that he was guilty of a grievous transgression of some kind. I am not revealing the content of his confession. He never had the chance to make one. I was forced to administer Extreme Unction before the spirit had left him."

"You're talking a lot of stuff I don't get," said Sharon.

James didn't say a word but looked grim. He understood fully.

"It's not important that you do, Sharon. In fact, it may be an advantage that you don't. If I were puzzled by the writing of an MD, I would ask a pharmacist to read it for me. You, Sharon, a Jewish epigrapher with vast experience reading messy documents of great importance, are the perfect pharmacist to read these notes. I want you to prepare a transcript in your own hand for me to read. If there is a problem with concepts that puzzle you, do your best, or ask James for help. I trust you both completely to keep your work, not hidden, but to yourselves. If there is anything to be shared with the others I will do so. Incidentally, Wadid Hamza is aware of the notebooks as well, and was the one who urged me to keep them safe. His guards with the curved knives are not just for show. They are trained in martial arts."

"Several more things. Although Wadid undoubtedly has computers, please do all your work by hand, Sharon. And James, please make a clear hand transcript of the papyrus as well. No computers there, either. And neither of you must let these items out of your hands until you're done, no walks with them, except between this building and Wadid's library."

Sharon was tempted to ask, *how about when we go potty,* but thought better of it. Ryan's stern tone conveyed the importance of the matter. There was no smiling or light banter.

Wadid's library was everything he promised, a large room flooded with flat, white light from a scatter of skylights. The lofty ceiling was supported by a number of hand-hewn beams, marks of the woodsman's adz visible. The end of each was supported by a corbel, carved in the image of Horus, the falcon god. Two tiers of bookshelves, separated by a beautifully carved beam, were packed with volumes. all the way to the ceiling. A teak ladder ran on wheels along a brass rail attached to the beam. In the middle of the room was a massive table with carved, falcon legs. Around it were ornate chairs with seats of scarlet, Moroccan leather. A couple of study carels, on two sides of the room, were equipped with similarly upholstered chairs. The research team was seated around the big table, Wadid and Ryan at each end. Ryan spoke up.

"I hinted at several concerns earlier. Here is what I know. None of this is to leave this room. It is apparent that both Megyn's and Sharon's discoveries fit together neatly to define our mission. We are here to search for a very special artifact, a goblet of historical, perhaps greater significance. With information from both Bedu and Mr. Hamza, it is also apparent that we are being followed and observed by people sent to do so for reasons as yet unknown. Do you have anything to add, Wadid?"

"Thank you, Ryan. Yes, I do. This venture of yours has been funded by two sources with virtually unlimited resources. You know that of course, Ryan. I don't know about the rest of you, but Ryan has told me to speak to you with complete candor. One of the sources is the Roman Catholic Church. The other is a family, unknown to anyone on earth as far as I have been able to determine. The family name is Sarafian. I think several of you have met their representatives. We have two mysteries. The first is the anonymity of the Sarafians. The second is the fact that it is your one benefactor, the Roman Catholic Church, that is having you followed. My sources indicate their instructions, if not from the Pope, were at least sanctioned by him. I have a third mystery to add to the soup, one that I revealed to Ryan only within the last twenty-four hours. The Patriarch of the Coptic Christian Church, my spiritual leader, and Bedu El-Akshar's, Pope Shenouda, is apparently aware of your mission and has asked me to assist you in any way I can."

There was stunned silence around the table. Bedu shifted nervously. Leila took his arm, sensing his unrest. Ryan spoke again. "I have asked Father McAndrew to do what he can to stabilize and prepare Sharon's papyrus for travel. I have also asked Sharon and Father McAndrew to work on deciphering the impossibly sloppy notes of a departed friend of mine, to see if they have any bearing on any of this. The notes are a private message to me. I only asked them to do this because I think they can, and I know that I cannot. I've tried.

Please respect my privacy in this matter, as I expect Sharon and James will. If all goes well with the work of your two comrades, I expect we will be going deep into the desert in search of a treasure of great importance."

Wadid spoke up again, "As to a journey into the desert, I have a grand surprise for you and a rare opportunity for me. I have long nurtured a special treasure very dear to my heart. At long last it will live again to perform a task for which it was equipped but never intended. I own the original command vehicle that once belonged to Field Marshal Erwin Rommel— the perfect desert transport machine. It will carry us into the Western Desert." Wadid was beaming as he finished his remarks. One almost expected him to raise his arm in salute and scream, Heil Hitler! He didn't, but obviously this aspect of the expedition was even more important to him than the quest, itself.

Working with the best is always a marvelous experience. By the following morning, James had the papyrus in as good shape as it ever would be. He made a hand transcript of it in a clear hand and an English translation from the Coptic original. The latter two, he folded and kept among his personal effects. They would be with him wherever he went. The original papyrus he pressed between layers of acid-free matting cardboard, then thick sheets of acrylic, all bound together along the edges with acid-free mounting tape.

Once secure, he wrapped the package in plain, brown paper and tied it again with twine made of locally grown hemp. He had found everything handy in Wadid's conservation laboratory. His needs had been simple but he had been amazed at the variety of high-tech equipment in the lab.

More and more, Egyptologists were applying modern medical and forensic techniques to the examination of ancient artifacts. Wadid even had an MRI machine to examine the bone and other tissue that lay hidden for millennia within the mummified remains of ancient Egyptians. He had made his equipment available to the Egyptian authorities as they became more and more anxious to probe the nature of their fabulous history and its inhabitants. In return, when Wadid needed a favor, he was rarely refused.

Deciphering the personal note from Habib Colophon was a simple task for Sharon. She didn't need James' help. The contents, however, were startling both in their historical import and their implications regarding theological matters and world history. She knew she had no choice, but dreaded giving Ryan her carefully handwritten transcript.

At the morning meeting, James proudly presented the packaged papyrus to Ryan. He had also made one more English transcript and handed it to Ryan. Ryan decided the package might best be given to Wadid to store. He surely had a place for the safekeeping of archaic treasures.

Sharon approached Ryan gingerly. "It was pretty easy, Ryan, and fascinating, but I suspect you will want to read it alone, or with James. It makes pretty clear what's going on."

She looked so distraught that Ryan wanted to comfort her but resisted the urge to hold her, especially here in the library. He took the neatly written pages and sat at one of the carrels. Sharon watched him nervously.

Chapter Thirty-Five

Sharon's hand was strong and clear—

† † †

Hopefully, it is your eyes, dear friend Ryan, and not those of someoneelse who reads these words. I will not commit them to one of my diaries lest they be read accidentally by one of my many colleagues. Instead, I will scribble them on these scraps of paper. I can see you smile, Ryan Quinn, as you read my admission about scribbling. I know that my penmanship has always been a source of great pain to you. There are several other possibilities. Someone with good intentions might possibly read what I have written and destroy these pages. His or her crime will be no less than mine. The other possibility is that an evil person may publish what I have written in hopes of doing harm. That is my dilemma. My feeble attempt to achieve the correct solution is to write on these pages, then tuck them into one of my diaries and leave them where hopefully you are likely to find them. Let me begin, as both friend and priest, to one who is also a priest and my dear friend—My agony, Ryan, is that I am torn between loyalties to two masters— the Divinity and the earthly custodian of that same Divinity. Simply put, I am tormented by my love of God and my devotion to the Church— one is my Master, the other is my Shepherd. They are not exactly in conflict but close to it. By God's very design they cannot be or we would be forced to doubt His wisdom, and therefore His divinity. And yet, there is a third entity to be considered— the Flock. Excuse me for talking as though I were in a pulpit. It's a bad habit. I have not made a valid confession for more years than I care to count. The reason is not that I spurn the sacrament of Penance but that I dare not share the nature of my sin with another soul, especially a priest, or he would be bound by Canon Law to keep my secret and therefore share in my sin by so doing. You see, mine has been the sin of silence in defiance of a possible obligation to make known what I believe to be truths— truths that concern all of humanity. I suspect by now I have caught your attention, Ryan— if indeed it is you, my friend, who is reading this. Simply put, I chose to follow the commands of the Church in preference to those I believe to possibly be those of God, Himself. The torment lies in my confusion as to my trust in the Holy Church and my personal conviction that I think I know God's wishes. It is not simple arrogance. I believe He made His wishes known to me through my studies of ecclesiastical history and my very own archaeological fieldwork. All things considered, I believe the very improbability of my discoveries, could have been brought about by no other than the Almighty. You will recall that it was I who brought to your attention the probable existence of a very special artifact, a chalice. You honored me greatly when you chose my allusion to it as the inspiration for your corporation. Let me tell you now that THE CHALICE DOES EXIST! I have held it in my hands, secretly pried a very important medallion from its rim, then hid the cup carefully, where it remains today as far as I know. The medallion, I took back to America with me and hid it in plain sight where you would most likely be the only one to understand its significance. When I found the Chalice, my colleague, Pietro Gandolfo, was occupied with his own work at a nearby excavation. As you know, he is now the Papal Nuncio to His Holiness, the Pope. Pietro's later part in this remains unclear to me. I did not share with him the fact that I had unearthed the Chalice, nor the fact that I had hidden it again. He never indicated he knew anything of my find though I suspect one of the workers may have told him. I think he may have been similarly confused and tormented by the unparalleled significance to the world of my find and didn't want to be involved. I accept my guilt, if there be any. God will judge Pietro Gandolfo, not I. My possible sin lies in my decision to hide the Chalice and maintain silence about it— two acts not frowned upon by the Church but perhaps by God. Hints of its existence have been with us all through history yet always efficiently dismissed as either rumor or unfounded legend. Any written evidence of its actual existence has been methodically destroyed, leaving nothing for serious investigators but those rumors— and romantic tales of mediaeval knights on holy quests. I believe the efforts to keep things hidden have been orchestrated by Rome. I even fear it may now be Gandolfo's job to eradicate existing evidence. It may be yours to do the opposite. Pietro is not the first to find himself caste in this unenviable role. I believe there's been an unbroken succession of search and destroy missions for two thousand years, sent forth by one pope after another to scour the world for documents, and to investigate rumors of documents, ever since the death and resurrection of Christ our Savior. It is unfortunate that you, my dear friend, came to be just that— my friend. And then, that you exhibited a unique set of talents that prompted you to create a corporate structure such as Chalice. You, Ryan Quinn, are the key, the single individual in history to the best of my knowledge, with the intellect and quasi-ecclesiastical corporate structure behind you to deal with the perhaps unholy campaign by Rome to expunge any tangible evidence of the Holy Grail and its true importance. Forgive my arrogance, but I feel they may have been justified at first but no longer. You were born, Ryan, during a time when technology has finally achieved maturity envisioned, but never alluded to, by Christ, Himself. As you read on, you will understand. Contrary to what I told you at the time— forgive me dear friend— the Chalice in question is indeed the Holy Grail, the cup that Christ used at the Last Supper to change bread and wine into His precious Body and Blood. But it is not its historical or even religious nature that makes it so terribly important. It is the Chalice itself. And it is the physical nature of the Chalice, itself, that is the reason why it has not been allowed to be found and made public despite ongoing human efforts to do so. I believe it was Christ's wish that it be used as the pictographic guide to the sacramental structure of His Church. That sounds complex but is not. I will explain later. It was not Christ but the Apostle Peter, and all the popes who followed, who chose to avoid the destructive arguments that would certainly have been raised over the meaning of the Chalice's design. That is my sin, Ryan. I consciously joined with the Church to thwart what I believe were the intentions of Christ. The Church rationalized its behavior by holding to the concept that it followed the wishes, not of Christ the Man, but of Christ the Son of God. The Church buttresses its position by pointing out that it was Christ, as God, Who commissioned Peter to act in His stead after the crucifixion. I have always accepted the validity of the Church's ecumenical decisions, Ryan, as do all priests including you, I presume. But faced with the message of the Chalice I came to realize that I was not completely convinced. I don't know if Pietro was better informed than I and might have doubts of his own. Fortunately, he does not know where the Chalice is, nor do either of us know of any existing text that describes its true meaning. Perhaps in Rome. Pietro would know, not I. Here it is, as best I can convey it in writing. As doctrine openly admits, Christ did not come to the Last Supper by accident. Nor did He do so without a plan. My own research has led me to uncover the long hidden fact that, months earlier, He commissioned an Arab silversmith in Bethany to create a cup to His very specific design criteria. He was living in the house of Lazarus and visited the artisan repeatedly to be certain his design was being followed precisely. When it was done, he arranged to enter Jerusalem on a donkey borrowed from Lazarus, the Chalice wrapped in a blanket tied behind his saddle. He brought it with Him with the express intent that it be there on the table at the Last Supper and presented to the world after His crucifixion. It was the disciple, Peter, who had other ideas. For years I trembled at the immensity of my emerging conclusions. Then, unexpectedly, I actually uncovered the Chalice. In one sense I felt fulfilled but I also felt terribly depressed, robbed of my innocence and even of trust in my own vocation, the very core of the orthodox religious life I had chosen and to which I had dedicated myself. Had I followed a deceptive master? Had I followed the Church instead of the true Master, the Son of God? I have never been able to resolve that dilemma. I believe with all my heart that the Church followed its best instincts in preserving and spreading belief in the True God. On the other hand, the Chalice is proof that it has been hiding a major truth whose broadcast to the world was the express wish of Christ our Lord. Forgive me, Ryan, for passing my confusion and torment on to you. Perhaps you will be more successful in unraveling the threads of logic that have had me bound and helpless for over fifteen years. I will try to be brief— not one of my virtues. My hand shakes as I put my conclusions in writing. It was not the Transubstantiation that was the message of the Last Supper. It was not the changing of bread and wine into the body and blood of Christ to which Jesus was referring when he said, "Do this in remembrance of me." It was the whole series of events that ended with His crucifixion, the hanging of Judas, and the later crucifixion of St. Peter. It is violent, voluntary death that is the message— the message dutifully accepted by Judas Iscariot, eventually accepted by Peter, and later by thousands of the faithful in the arenas of Rome. If you have read these words without anger and disbelief, dear Ryan, you are not the man of faith I believe you to be. But bear with me. I am convinced that it was not Peter who was the favorite of Christ, but Judas. I have recently seen an ancient papyrus, a treatise written in Coptic, found in a cave by farmers near the village of Qarara. You know the place. The papyrus has been bouncing around among greedy antiquity dealers and self-appointed aficionados for years. I have seen it and believe it to be authentic. Naturally, like most of the Gnostic gospels, Rome has denounced it. The gospel, if that's what it is, supports the idea, though not explicitly, that it was Judas whom Jesus truly loved and to whom He gave the wretched task of handing Him over for execution. One can only conclude that Christ knew that Peter would never have the stomach for it. Instead, He told Peter to undertake the work for which He knew Peter was best suited, the management of an organization— to found and manage a durable church of vast proportions. Now perhaps you understand my dilemma, Ryan. God chose Peter to create a structure able to manage human hearts and minds. He chose His best friend, Judas, to return Him to His Father in Heaven. To guide Peter, He designed a Chalice that symbolically outlined the structure of the church He wanted. It had around its rim, eight medallions to represent the eight sacraments that would be the skeletal structure of that church. "Eight sacraments, you say, Colophon? Have you lost your mind? There are only seven." No, Ryan, my friend. There were to be eight. They are depicted on the Chalice. The initial act of Peter, as the first Pope, was to hide the Chalice. He must have felt the eighth sacrament would unravel the proposed organization before it ever had a chance to succeed. Where he hid it no one knows. Into whose hands he may have passed it, or to whom he may have entrusted its secret, also unknown. All the details have been lost in time— not by accident. We must assume from subsequent events that the secret of the Chalice's existence and purpose has been passed down through the centuries from one pope to the next. Rome got wind of my discovery in Egypt. How? I do not know. I suspect now that it may have been Pietro Gandolfo. I even suspect he may have been sent by Rome in the first place to monitor my work in the event I might find something Rome might prefer left alone. I really don't know the answer to that. I do know that I felt a compulsion to hide the Chalice, even from Gandolfo, and keep its whereabouts to myself. Before I did so, the same compulsion prompted me to pry off one of the medallions from its rim. As an archaeologist, I felt dreadful at committing such an act but as I said, I felt compelled to do so— and am now glad I did. The medallion I removed was that which depicted, the Eighth Sacrament, the suicide of Judas Iscariot. The medallion was easy enough to keep out of sight. I planned to give it to someone with whom you would have normal, casual contact— contact unlikely to arouse the suspicions of anyone. By now, you must have had that contact and all this will make sense. If not, I deeply regret the damage I did to the Chalice. I will not tell you where the Chalice is. Others might read this and rush to get to it before you. Its location is for you to determine. I will simply present you with a riddle that hopefully you, and no others, will be capable of deciphering—

Seek the prize where darkness rules within the kingdom of the sun. It rests unseen below the timeless home of one who would inhale the blood of the lotus rather than the fragrance of its blossom. You will find the prize within the heart of a Shining One, but be not misled by Maa-atef-f, Kheri-beq-f, or Horus-Khenti-maa. Look rather to their fellow defenders of Osiris, the sons of Horus. But even then, reach beyond Imset, Hapi, and Duamutef— to Him who refreshes his brothers. He will stand in the dark amongst them, waiting beyond the deceptive well of death, along the hidden path of beastly sepulchers. You need not venture far though the journey may seem so in the dark— merely five lengths of a pontiff's crook, then left for another five.

The Shining One waits, the prize held safe at his heart, within a chamber above four others where sacred beasts still slumber undisturbed.

One last note, Ryan. Be very wary of angels! They have a role in all this, but I do not know what it is.

God Bless You— HABIB

Chapter Thirty-Six

Ryan was visibly shaken. He went over to James who was at the big table chatting with the others.

"We need to talk in private, James. Can you come to my room in about fifteen minutes? First I have to find Wadid."

With the help of one of Wadid's servants, Ryan found him in the garage, his rump sticking out over the front fender of a 1935 Rolls Phaeton.

"Wadid! I need to speak with you."

"Of course, Ryan." Wadid yanked himself back to his feet, grease on his nose. "What is it?"

"I have seen a note among the papers from Habib Colophon. You were anxious that I keep them out of harms way. You were right, my friend. The note explains a great deal. I am now certain why we are here, possibly where to search for the artifact, and perhaps why we are being followed. But I must ask for your indulgence. I will tell you everything you need to know. But some things I must keep to myself for a while, maybe forever. It is theological stuff. I hope you understand."

Wadid made a wry face and seemed about to object, then smiled. "Pope Shenouda asked that I help you in every way. I'm sure you wouldn't cheat my Pope any more than you would cheat your own, correct?"

Wadid Hamza was not only a very rich, very intelligent man, but he had a sixth sense about where to fire darts to find an opponent's vital organs.

"Correct?" he asked again.

"Don't press it, Wadid. I will tell you everything your Pope would want you to know." Ryan's response was as cleverly phrased as Wadid's challenge. Stalemate!

"Of course, my friend. May I show you around my stable of automobiles?"

"I would love it, Wadid, but not right now. I must meet with one of my colleagues. I'm sorry. Please excuse my rudeness."

"Of course. Will this new information involve our leaving soon for the desert?"

"Probably, but after some research in your library and discussions with my team. You are welcome to join us."

James was waiting at the door to Ryan's room. They went in together.

"You look terribly worried, Ryan. What is it?"

"Nothing, James, just the end of everything you and I, and a billion others have held sacred for two thousand years."

"That's not funny, Ryan."

"It wasn't meant to be. Come sit down at my desk and read this."

Ryan paced while James read. It didn't take long .

"No. You weren't joking, were you? I'll need time to sort this all out."

"We both do, James, but there is no time. We must find the artifact first and sort things out later, if it's possible to sort it out at all. We are apparently stuck between a rock and a hard place."

"You mean, between Peter, "the rock," and some apocryphal hard place?"

"Exactly, James," and the two started to chuckle, then laugh out loud, as they tried to comprehend the magnitude of the dilemma that had been thrust upon them.

"Let me try to get it straight, Ryan. You and I have dedicated our entire lives to a church that is now trying to hunt us down so we cannot do the will of God?"

"That's they way I read it too, James." And the two started to laugh again. "Well, that's a fine kettle of fish," and they guffawed again for a full five minutes.

"And watch out for angels! They're behind every rock and tree!"

"But, apparently not behind the rock, called Peter!" Another paroxysm of laughter.

Finally the two grew silent. They just sat and looked at one another.

Ryan broke the silence. "This looks like a disaster, James. But maybe it is just the opposite. Perhaps we have been given a great gift. Let me play God for a moment."

"Shouldn't be a problem for you, Ryan." More laughter. Ryan never realized that his unattractive, seemingly dull conservator, had a wry sense of humor. Already there were some blessings emerging from this disaster.

"Knock it off, James." They were talking like old pals. "Let's stick to some basic principles. You and I have dedicated our lives to the belief that Christ was God, right?"

"Yeah. Ask me another tough one."

"And he was put on earth by his Father on our behalf, presumably to save us from ourselves, right?" He didn't wait for a flip retort. "But He didn't put him on earth as a god-figure but as a man."

"I'm with you so far, Ryan. When do you startle me with the divine wisdom you promised a moment ago?"

"Right now, James. God put his spiritual Son on earth as a man. That means he gave that man free will like the rest of us. What does an entity do that is omnipotent, yet also just a man with free will?"

"This is not new, Ryan. Eggheads in the Church have been pondering this for two thousand years."

"That doesn't mean they are any smarter than either you or I, James. Here's the thing. Just as Colophon and others have struggled with that dilemma, perhaps Christ, too, was struggling. Maybe he found Himself to be both God and Man, not in harmony, but in conflict. Perhaps it was not a smooth relationship, but an internal dogfight beyond our ability to even imagine. Even when He was baptized, remember we're told a voice came from Heaven saying, "This is my Son in Whom I am well pleased," or something like that. God was letting everyone know He loved this man-god, so don't mess with Him if He screws up occasionally."

"That rings a bell, Ryan. It reminds me of the words of Pharaoh Amenhotep II when he presented his commoner wife, Tiye, to the people. As I recall, he said something like— I am the ruler of all the lands from horizon to horizon. I own everything you see. My armies are numbered in the thousands. And this is my wife, Tyie. That's all he said, but everyone knew he was leaving out the last words, "any objections?"

"Great point, James. That's what any powerful entity might say when he or she was claiming kinship with a possible disaster child. I can imagine a state's governor called into a principal's office because his son threw mouse turds into the air conditioner— You called me in, Mr. Dork? I believe we know one another. I'm the fellow who OK's your annual budget. Now what's the problem with my son?

"You said you were going to play god, Ryan. What's the point? Are you saying that God was expecting Christ to make a bunch of blunders?"

"Maybe, but I don't think that's what happened. I think Christ was God, but also had a great, practical mind. Perhaps that part was accidental. As with the rest of humanity, God wasn't pulling the strings. Christ might have remained content to build furniture with his dad in the carpentry shop. The problem was that God sent His Son to save humanity in an act of spiritual sacrifice. But the Man part of Christ saw the practical need for a human structure to help His human brothers through the chaos they kept stirring up. The Last Supper was the Main Event, time for God and Man to implement a unified plan. The crucifixion was the theological necessity. The Church was the practical one. Christ had to work within the framework of the time period to which He had been sent. He chose Judas to sell Him to the judicial system that would assassinate Him, and later, Peter, to create the structure that would perpetuate His church. If we can believe Colophon, in the case of Peter, perhaps He chose too well. Peter saw the flaw in the man-Christ's plan for a corporate structure and modified it. He hid the blueprint, the Chalice, and built a church according to all Christ's plans except the eighth sacrament, which he believed had the potential of collapsing the whole srtructure. We are witnesses to the two thousand year old result of Peter's decision. He was right. What if every time things got tough people just took the pipe?"

"Took the pipe?"

"Suicide, James. You can't build a stable, corporate structure when you never know if the staff will be back in the morning."

"Isn't that a bit extreme, Ryan?"

"Maybe, but think about it. Until recent times, the larger the population of your group, the greater the likelihood you'd be able to overrun your adversary. It's only modern technology that makes it possible to leverage the strength of a small force to the point where it can destroy a larger adversary."

"I don't think the analogy extends to competing religious orthodoxies, Ryan."

"No? What about Christians versus Muslims today? Do I need to point out the recent work of a few men with box cutters who were able to take down huge buildings and almost destroy the economy of a vast nation?"

"Box cutters are not high technology, Ryan."

"Those were just the means of intimidating the ones with the technology. The mistake was to allow those planes to fly at the whim of a couple of men up front in the cockpit."

"Ok. You win, Ryan. You're pretty good at playing God. But what about successful groups that have accepted suicide? The ancient Maya thought of it as an act of devotion."

"Yes, James, and their civilization melted into the Central American jungles and disappeared. They're still trying to figure out what happened."

"They all committed suicide? I don't think so."

"I guess not, but maybe it's a factor overlooked when they discuss the mysterious disappearance of the Maya."

The two priests had gotten so involved in the quasi-theological discussion they had forgotten the reality of the dilemma they were facing when there was a knock at the door. It was Sharon.

"I heard you two laughing. It certainly couldn't have been that transcript I gave you, Ryan."

"Actually it was, Sharon. Sometimes there's nothing left to do but laugh."

Sharon smiled softly. The compassion for her two priest-friends was apparent in her expression.

"I'm not sure I understood the nuances of the dilemma posed by Father Colophon, the duality of your Christ, nor the apparent brutality shown at times by your Church. Then there's its claim to papal infallibility, and so on, but hold on. I don't need a lecture on Roman Catholic theology. I had enough out of my father and his obsession with the nuances involved in the Talmud. I just want you both to know I understand that you may be in pain, that I love you both, and am here for you if you need me."

The two priests were dumbfounded. Ryan thought he saw a tear on James's cheek. He wasn't far from tearing-up, himself.

"Thank you, Sharon. You are a dear person," said James. Ryan nodded.

"If you'll excuse my interrupting your deliberations, the document ended with a riddle that affects the next steps we must take soon, regardless of theologies."

Ryan snapped to. "You're right. I almost forgot. We were about to head off into nowhere without a clue. I'm not sure we're any better off now, but at least we've got a clue. Let's go to the library and see what we can do to figure out where we should be headed."

"One other thing, Ryan." This time it was James. "What about that medallion Colophon mentioned? We know about that from Megyn's photos, but Colophon said he had hidden it in plain view where you would find it. Have you?"

"No. Maybe it will turn up. In the meanwhile, let's get on with the riddle."

The three left Ryan's room in silence and headed for Wadid's library. He was there with the rest of the group when they arrived.

"You all seem more than a little depressed. Is there anything I can do?"

"Thank you, Wadid. No. We have work to do. If you want to sit in you are welcome." Ryan stopped and reconsidered. "Yes. You could give us a quick tour of your library so we can save time searching for research material."

"Of course. Volumes are not arranged according to standard library techniques but to suit my interests. The lower tiers are primarily devoted to works related to ancient Egypt, dig sites, artifacts, et cetera. The upper tiers are devoted to post-Pharaonic Egypt, Greek occupation, Roman, et cetera. The west wall is specifically related to Coptic matters, first century material on the lower shelves moving upward to the present. That's about it. The cabinets along the east wall are obviously meant for maps, large documents, and in certain cases, original papyri. If you have questions, just ask."

"Thank you. We will. Ladies and gentlemen, we have a riddle both real and intellectual before us. My old friend and colleague, Habib Colophon, passed away recently. He left behind a mystery of world significance and a riddle that does not unravel it. In fact, it creates a huge dilemma for people like me and Father McAndrew, while presenting a possible solution to the whereabouts of the artifact I believe we were sent here to find. I know this sounds confusing. You don't know the half of it."

"We will attack our mission in an orderly fashion, starting with facts, leaving philosophical and theological matters until later, perhaps not even to be dealt with by us, but by others better suited to the task."

"Let's begin. I will put it to you succinctly. It would appear that, during a dig, Habib Colophon unearthed the fabled Holy Grail."

There was stunned silence. Even among those who were already aware of Habib's discovery, it was electrifying to hear it put into words.

"The Grail," Ryan continued, "is most likely the same goblet depicted on the mural photographed by Megyn and mentioned in the Coptic manuscript uncovered by Sharon. There are aspects to all of this, as I mentioned, that are of special interest to myself and to Father McAndrew. They are matters of religious doctrine. They need not concern the rest of you, at least for the moment. What is important to you, in that regard, is the fact that we are being followed and our activities monitored. I believe the agents following us are associated with the Roman Catholic Church. Though I am not prepared to characterize their intent as a threat to our well being, I must allow for that possibility. There is a great deal at stake for the Roman Church. Momentous issues may, at times, suggest radical solutions. Rome does not want the Grail to fall into any but their own hands. I don't know to what lengths they will go to secure their objective"

"Our host, Wadid Hamza, has generously offered to throw his lot in with ours in arriving at a conclusion, perhaps not favored by Rome. In addition, as some of you know, he has been asked by the Patriarch of the Coptic Christian Church, to assist us in any way he can. He has offered us the protection of his personal guards and any equipment necessary to accomplish the successful recovery of the Grail."

"We will begin in this room. Father McAndrew and Sharon Feinschutz will make legible transcriptions of the notebooks left by Father Habib Colophon. Bedu El-Akshar, with the help of Megyn Corbet, will investigate Coptic reference sources to see if any mention is made of a special cup, chalice, goblet, or whatever, fabricated in Galilee, or moved from one place to another. Leila Miller will consult our host's collection of topographic, historical, and geomorphology maps, to determine the most likely routes of land travel and settlement between the Nile Delta and the hermitages of the Western Desert, between the time Christ was crucified and the present. Concentrate, if you can, on trade routes around the First and Second Centuries. It's a hunch. "

"I will coordinate your efforts and attempt to guide each of you in view of any progress made by the others. One more thing. Let me know if you come upon any references to angels. No. I'm not nuts. I'm serious. Both the Papal Nuncio in New York and Habib Colophon, in a personal note to me, warned of angels. I'm not sure why. Please tell me right now of any strange encounters any of you may have had with persons, even if they seemed hallucinations, involving what seemed to be supernatural entities. The encounters need not have been sweet, touchy-feely events. I'm not referring to New Age, feel-good stuff, or Victoria's Secret, soft core, porn pageants. I'm talking about dreams or events that may have either been pleasant or unpleasant. Angels seem to figure into this whole matter and I have no idea exactly how."

Ryan looked at his colleagues, one by one as he completed the last remarks. He noticed at once that Megyn was blushing deeply. Her fair skin made it obvious.

"Megyn, you will help me look into any historical evidence of angels."

She nodded mutely and continued to blush. Father McAndrew looked uncomfortable. "May I speak to you privately, Ryan?"

"Of course, James. Anybody else? If you are uncomfortable, let me state up front that I have come to the conclusion that I, myself, have had such an encounter, and suspect you all have, some perhaps more personally than the others. We'll discuss it later. I'm looking for information. That's all."

Chapter Thirty-Seven

One man's trash is another man's treasure. Among the majority, that saying is perhaps clever, but basically of no importance. To archaeologists, it is a concept upon which professional research is often almost entirely dependent. To make things sound more academic, archaeologists do not talk of garbage dumps. In the halls of academe they are known as "middens" and sometimes as "stratified mounds." It's all the same thing.

One of the most valuable garbage dumps in Egypt was uncovered in a place called Oxyrhyncus. It was named for the fish in Egyptian mythology that ate the penis of the god, Osiris. What connection the town had with that momentous event is unclear, but the settlement was once the third-largest city in Egypt. No documentary evidence has been cited regarding the relative size of Osiris' penis.

Unlike most sizeable cities in Egypt, Oxyrhynchus was not located on the Nile, but on a tributary canal, "Bahr Yussef." As a result, it was not subject to the annual floods that inundated most of Egypt's major settlements. From the archaeologist's point of view that was a plus. Another was the custom of Oxyrhynchus inhabitants to dump their garbage at sites in the desert outside of town where rain was, and still is, a rare event. With no rain and no floodwater, there was relatively little to encourage the growth of destructive organisms. Dry refuse is very durable. For a very long time, the middens of Oxyrhynchus have been the perfect playground for academic dumpster-divers.

The actual town site has never been excavated. Over eons, structures have been built on top of one another, making orderly excavations potentially fruitful but difficult and confusing. Why bother? Since the 1800's archaeologists have been much too busy rooting around in the town's garbage dumps to care.

The finds have been extraordinary. They have unearthed public and private documents, municipal codes, edicts, registers, census returns, tax assessments, petitions, court records, sales leases, wills, bills, accounts, inventories, horoscopes, and private letters, as well as copies of literary works such as the plays of Sophocles, the comedies of Menander, and political documents such as the Constitution of Athens, penned by Aristotle.

To date, seventy-one huge volumes have been filled with just the listings of important papyri found at Oxyrhynchus. They are the essential references relied upon for the reconstruction of Egyptian life between the 4th Century BC and the 7th Century AD. They are also the references that document the history of the early Christian Church, listing fragments of non-canonical Gospels, epistles of John, the Apocolypse of Baruch, even what purport to be portions of an unknown Christian Gospel. The list is virtually endless. In fact, since excavation is still underway, so far it is endless.

Ryan knew all this, and was also aware that at least forty more volumes were anticipated as work in the Oxyrhynchus garbage dumps continues. Presently, the work is under the direction of Oxford University and University College London.

He was not surprised, then, when Sharon came to him excitedly with the discovery that she had found a passage in Habib's notes that said he had personally uncovered some fragments of a controversial nature at Oxyrhynchus.

"Controversial in what way, Sharon?"

"I'm not certain. I'll have to read further. It seems related to his personal statement to you about a silversmith in Galilee."

Ryan perked up his ears. "That could be very important. Is James working on that passage with you?"

"No. He's on another notebook."

"Ask him to work with you. It will be of great interest to him. Perhaps you can move faster together."

Sharon was slightly miffed, but realized that Ryan did not mean any disrespect. "Right on it, Boss," she said, letting Ryan know she was not entirely happy with his executive decision. She turned and walked off. As she went, she gave her hips a toss, certain that Ryan was watching. Ryan glanced away immediately. He didn't want to be caught a second time, ogling her butt.

Sharon's announcement followed right on the heels of Megyn's embarrassed admission to Ryan that several times she'd had dreams or hallucinations of a sexual nature involving what she believed to be an unearthly figure. One, she said, had actually taken place in the cave where she photographed the mural. The other event was not as likely a candidate to be identified with angels, more likely an hallucination, one of the young men whose portraits she had been working on among the Fayoum burial portraits. The encounter, or whatever it was, had occurred in her office back in New York.

As a priest, Father McAndrew was accustomed to hearing detailed accounts of perversions of all sorts, whispered to him within the shadows of the confessional. So he was less embarrassed than Megyn to admit to Ryan that he had, indeed, had a suspicious encounter with someone, or something, he doubted was an angel, but otherwise inexplicable. With a bit of hesitation, he admitted that his hallucination had had homosexual overtones. Ryan was neither shocked nor surprised. He patted the priest on the shoulder and thanked him for his candor.

Ryan had admitted to the two that he believed he had been tempted as well, if that was the right word, by a beautiful woman they had both met, Em Sarafian. When he mentioned her name, they understood at once. They had both experienced an overwhelming sense of sensuality about the woman and her brother when they had met them at Chalicc headquarters. Ryan remembered now, the state of confusion he had encountered among his staff when he returned to Chalice just after the Serafians had left. Now, a new worry flashed into his mind, his son, Paul. Paul had seemed in a state of total hormone overload after the Sarafian visit. Then he recalled that it was James who had last been in contact with Paul. He would have to talk to him about that.

In general, Ryan was glad that most of the dirty linen was either out of the closet, or brought to the surface, where future events of a supernatural nature would be acknowledged openly. He felt that the team was moving in the right direction. Soon there would be answers, he hoped.

Leila was pouring over a mosaic of ancient maps she had assembled when Ryan approached her for a status report.

"Check on any geomorphologic indications of foot traffic between Galilee, Oxyrhynchus, and Benedictine hermitages in the Western desert. It's a long shot and you'll probably find such a criss-cross it'll prove useless, but it's worth a shot."

Chapter Thirty-Eight

Italians have a familial relationship with the Catholic Church. It is not uncommon to see priests in clerical garb walking among the crowds on the streets of Rome. Egidio Scarza, S.J. was scurrying down the sidewalk beneath one of the arches above Via della Pilotta. He was moving so forcefully his cassock billowed about him like the undulating fins of a black, Siamese, fighting fish. He was neither angry nor anxious for a fight, just the bearer of disturbing news. He needed to speak at once to the rector of the Instituto Biblico.

The Via della Pilotta is just a short distance from the Fontana di Trevi. Of interest to tourists is the papal palace at number 17, built by Pope Martin V in the 15th Century. Since 1703 it has been the home and art gallery of the Colonna family. In the "throne room," an empty chair is kept turned to the wall. It waits patiently for the unlikely visit of any pope who might decide to drop in.

At number 5 is a lesser-known structure, the Pontifical Biblical Institute. A quarter-million volumes fill library shelves that occupy most of its four floors. All the material is related to the Bible. The building also contains a number of offices, laboratories and classrooms.

Founded by Pope Pius X, the Institute offers degrees in biblical studies, including a highly regarded doctorate. All academic work is done from a Roman Catholic perspective, of course. Since its founding, a hundred years ago, the institute has always been staffed and managed by Jesuits.

Reverend Scarza, in his early sixties, was a slender, wiry man with a short beard and full head of closely trimmed, white hair. Except for his clerical garb, he might be a military figure.

Father Scarza was born in Tuscany in a poor but picturesque village that smelled of cow dung. He left for the seminary as soon as possible and never looked back. His interest was canon law. Whether by chance or heavenly design, in 1972 he was assigned by Pope Paul VI to a professorial post at the Biblical Institute. In 1977, he was given the heavy responsibility by then rector, Reverend Carlo Maria Martini, S.J., of becoming one of only five men in the world allowed access to the "Stanza Speciale," the Institute's equivalent of a military "top secret" vault. Since its inception, entry has required a huge, brass key kept in the personal possession of the Institute's Rector.

The Institute offices, classrooms, and laboratories are equipped with modern conveniences such as computers and high speed Internet connections, but some things remain, anachronistically, bound to tradition. The brass key was one. For a century, there has been only one, always held by the current Rector, and relinquished only for specific needs, to a handful of highly placed clergy, the Pope, the Rector himself, several important theologians, and Father Scarza. The two most recent theologians were biblical archaeology specialists, Habib Colophon and Pietro Gandolfo.

Scarza didn't slow his pace as he came to the Institute's entrance. He rushed through the ironwork doors and bounded up the stairs with the energy of a man a quarter his age. He burst in on the Rector, Clemente Brava, who sat in his office on the top floor, behind a desk full of papers and books, his aristocratic face lighted by the screen of an Apple iMac. He looked up at the sudden intrusion. He was not angry. He was a man blessed with patience, despite his high rank and brilliant intellect.

"Che cosa, Egidio? Calmi giù ! Calm down Father Scarza! Parle me."

"La vostra Eccellenzza, scusimi. È il Calice da Consacrazione. Penso che possa stare circa per essere riscoperto. The Chalice. I think it is about to be unearthed again."

"Mio Dio! What about the Nuncio?"

"Quello è un grande mistero, Eccellenza. A big mystery, Excellency. Apparently he met with the Coptic Patriarch, Shenouda. Why? Who knows? Then he disappeared onto a slow, third class, train from Alexandria to El Minya. Despite urgent messages to him in Alexandria, he did not answer but left his hotel and chose to take a slow train, a very slow train. Perché? Chi sa? Who knows why?"

"And the priests you sent to keep Father Quinn's activities under observation?"

"Uomini stupidi! They offered bribes to a Coptic Christian for information. He went straight to Father Quinn with everything. Quinn even kept the money. At least those dumb priests sent me the latest information that I bring you, no thanks to their "spy." Apparently, Quinn has joined forces, in his quest, with a wealthy antiquities dealer, an unprincipled man with time, money, and a flock of mercenaries, anxious to guard Quinn and his band of meddlers."

Do not speak so harshly of Quinn, Egidio. Remember, it was the Holy Father, at our suggestion, who ordered the Church to provide funds for Quinn's trip to Egypt. None other than the Nuncio, one of our very own, managed the negotiations."

"I know. I know. It made sense at the time. I think we still agree that Habib Colophon may have discovered the Chalice many years ago and hidden it again. I think it was you who decided that the Nuncio, working nearby, may have learned of it and decided to turn a blind eye to the whole business, two good and holy men, perhaps infected with heretic inclinations of their own."

"Perhaps not completely their own, Egidio. One must always allow for the possibility of mischievous interventions by angels."

"Of course, Excellency. Angels! One can never be sure why they do what they do."

"We agreed, Egidio, and the Pope along with us, that it would be prudent to put the three together, Pietro Gandolfo, Habib Colophon, and Ryan Quinn, two with knowledge from within the Stanza Speciale, the third, a brilliant archaeologist with the right organization to accomplish things that would be difficult for us, if not impossible. With the guidance of the first two, Quinn might well have a chance of finding the Chalice, providing us the opportunity to recover it for the Church. We must submit to the possiblility that events might be unfolding according to the wishes of the Almighty."

"It is unnerving, Excellency, to even contemplate that possibility. But you make a point worth considering. First Colophon dies, leaving no indication of what he knew. Or did he? And now, the Nuncio has disappeared while Ryan Quinn teams up with an antiquities thief and a private army of cut-throats. Are we to also consider the possibility that we have to contend with a few deranged angels as well?"

"Mind your tongue, Egidio. Their methods may seem strange to us but we must remember they are the messengers of God. The Nuncio will turn up, Egidio. We all bear a heavy burden in the matter of the Chalice. The Nuncio may be dealing with a mind and soul in turmoil. Since the death of Habib Colophon, he and the Pope are the only ones besides the two of us, who realize the full importance of the documents in the Stanza Speciale. He may be having personal difficulties sorting things out. We all have our moments of sorrow over what we must do to defend Christ's Church on earth. I do. I'm sure you do as well my dear Egidio. What is it you suggest, my old friend? Not since the Middle Ages have we resorted to physical methods in dealing with such matters. Certainly not now."

"We must take strong measures, Excellency. It is unpleasant business, but too much is at stake."

"That has always been the excuse, Egidio. The heresies of the Albigensians and the Bogomils led to the Inquisition. That was not a happy chapter in our history."

"Not led by Jesuits, but Dominicans."

The Rector smiled. Put two men together, even those devoted to God, and territorialism arises almost at once.

"You have an idea, Egidio?"

"I hate to even mention it, Excellency, la Mano Nero, the Black Hand."

"Like the Inquisition, they also began in Spain, not Italy, Egidio."

"Yes. I know, as La Mano Negra. But neither in Spain nor Italy was there ever such an organization. It was simply the name given to a procedure for achieving results, what that American movie referred to as an offer one cannot refuse."

"That is not my way, Egidio. And I'm sure it would not be the way of the Holy Father."

"But Excellency, it has been necessary at times. And now, perhaps it is our responsibility to act. The Pope, of course, must not be involved. We must provide him with what the Americans call "rifiuto plausibili," plausibile deniability."

Among the items within the Stanza Speciale are thousands of original papyri and documents laboriously copied by hand during medieval times. There are even cuneiform clay tablets, anything and everything too valuable to destroy, yet too controversial to see the light of day, at least as far as the Catholic Church was concerned. Much of it came from the middens of Oxyrhynchus, but the majority from other places. Among the items are "rogue gospels," perhaps authentic, perhaps not, but potential support for heresy.

It was never the intent of the Church, nor of the Pontifical Biblical Institute, to hide truth or mislead the Flock. But truth, like beauty, is often in the eye of the beholder. The sequestering, or even destruction, of some artifacts has been the outcome of thoughtful decisions by theologians, to avoid confusion and the possible florescence of splinter groups, even well intentioned differences of opinion that might undermine the infrastructure and intellectual unity of Christ's church on earth. Like so many "facts," those that run counter to established doctrine are usually deemed to be either wrong or irrelevant. There is little within the stacks of the Stanza Speciale that might be considered more than interesting footnotes to reality, as viewed by Rome.

In matters of established doctrine the Church no longer demands that heretics recant under pain of corporal punishment, but now urges the maverick theologian to impose self-censorship. It had long been decided that the wisest men within the Church would determine what was to be seen and heard, not the masses whose opinions might dilute doctrine to the point of possible intellectual collapse.

A few, even among the most trusted of the Institute's hierarchy, had sometimes strayed from the Church's interpretation of the goal set by Christ at the Last Supper. In modern times, "free thinkers" were not punished with hot oil or the rack, but something far worse for a true believer, separation from Holy Mother, the Church, excommunication, damnation to Hell.

Even within the confines of the Stanza Speciale, there exists a still deeper layer of security. A wrought iron fence spans the entire east side of the room, from wall to wall. At its center is a locked gate. The key, and once again there is only one, is kept on the person of the Institute's Rector. It is a massive brass key kept on a chain that hangs from his neck. It often wakes him at night as he turns over in bed. It is said that Saint Ignacious Loyola, founder of the Jesuits, wore an undershirt of coarse hair to keep him in a constant state of torment. The annoyance of a heavy key shifting about in the night was small price to pay for the honor of being its custodian.

The fence and gate were once located elsewhere in Rome. They were moved to the Via della Pilotta in sections by horse drawn wagons a century ago. Once securely in place the items, formerly held safe behind them, were transported by hand to the Institute under the direct supervision of the Pope's Swiss Guard. The items all possessed a single theme. It was inscribed on a brass plate attached to the gate.

ELEMENTI RELATIVI AL CALICE DA CONSACRAZIONE

One can peer through the fence but there is little to see, only cases and cabinets, nothing more, except for a single marble pedestal. On it rests a crystal display case. Within the case is a gold pedestal, encrusted with diamonds, rubies, and emeralds. On top of it stands— nothing. The case has been empty for 1,599 years, ever since Visigoth, Alaric I, sacked Rome during the reign of Pope Innocent I, and made away with the Chalice. Where he took it, no one knows. Papyri found in the middens of Oxyrhynchus, and stored within the Stanza Speciale, suggest that it made its way to a Benedictine monastery in Egypt from which it was spirited away by an angel to keep it safe from invading Muslims during the Seventh Century. The angel, according to one papyrus, was disguised as a leper. He took it to an isolated cave in the desert inhabited by a religious hermit, and left it there.

From that point on, the documents in the Stanza Speciale provide only a scatter of unconnected, sometimes contradictory, accounts. One thing seemed certain, the Chalice found its way to the Egyptian desert. There it was kept safe from the marauding Muslims. Beyond that, the scraps of information were either discarded as false, or added little but hysterical exclamations of devotion without geographic references of any use.

Egidio Scarza was near apoplectic. With hands on his hips, he had begun to pace back and forth in front of the Rector's desk. He threatened to knock over a large crucifix on a cabinet with his elbows as he turned abruptly to face the Rector.

"Now, right under our very noses, it seems a Jewish epigrapher employed by Ryan Quinn, has stumbled on a papyrus that fills in an important gap in our record. No special literature trail, no painstaking research. According to our dumb priests, she just walked into an antique store and the wizened proprietor simply pulled it from a drawer and tried to sell it to her for a few pounds in case she wasn't interested in buying any of his phony, tourist trinkets."

"Egidio. You are becoming very angry and overlooking something very important."

"Excellency?"

"Perhaps the papyrus and the events surrounding it were not blind luck."

"What are you saying, Excellency?"

"Has it occurred to you that we might be dealing with a plan greater than ours?"

The Reverend Egidio Scarza, S.J. stopped dead and stared at the Rector. "Your Excellency, it is not my place to offer any contradiction to whatever you, as my superior, find worthy of consideration, but I hardly think..."

"Sia calmo. Relax. I am not telling you what to think, Egidio. I simply suggest that we may be dealing with events that rise to a level of importance even greater than the mission of our Institute."

Scarza was taken aback. Had his own Rector gone rogue? For two thousand years the secret message of the Chalice had been clearly seen by two-hundred-sixty-six consecutive popes to be a message too dangerous to be revealed to the Flock, much less to the Church's enemies.

What was in the mind of Habib Colophon? What might Pietro Gandolfo be thinking while he was slowly moving south in a third-class coach on a rickety Egyptian train? And now, what was the Rector implying, his own superior, the Reverend Clemente Brava, Rector of the Pontifical Biblical Institute and his own spiritual leader? He tried to maintain his composure.

"I will have to think quietly about this, Excellency."

"Good, Egidio. May I suggest you pay a visit to our patron saint's church on the Piazza San Ignazio. I'm sure you know, but to put things in perspective, remember that it was built where once the Temple of Isis stood in Imperial Rome."

"Of course, of course, your Excellency. But I don't see the relevance of pointing that out."

"Simply that history moves on and what seems vital at one time may take on new significance at a later date. And please, Egidio, no more talk of the Mano Nero. Come to see me in a few days when you've had time to think. I promise I will do the same."

"Of course, Excellency."

Egidio Scarza left, his strained smile unable to soften the set of his jaw. Once in his own office, he fished a cell phone from within his cassock and dialed the number of an old acquaintance, not a priest. It was a man he could count on to follow instructions without question. Suddenly he stopped, closed the phone, and tucked it back within his cassock. He would have to think this through as he promised. The issues at stake were too important to act in haste. Perhaps they involved his very own, immortal, soul. Time was short but he would follow his conscience, not his gut. After a few moments, he pulled the phone out again, and dialed. It wouldn't hurt to have things in place should drastic measures still seem appropriate after due deliberation.

"Ciao, Raffaello. Questo è Padre Scarza. Como stai? Buono. E la famiglia? Voglio chiederti un favore, amico mio— I need a favor, my friend."

Chapter Thirty-Nine

Ryan was flattered to think that Habib Colophon believed in his special abilities to unravel a riddle of great importance. As he read the old priest's words, they seemed to make no sense whatsoever.

Seek the prize where darkness rules within the kingdom of the sun. It rests unseen below the timeless home of one who would inhale the blood of the lotus rather than the fragrance of its blossom.

You will find the prize within the heart of a Shining One, but be not misled by Maa-atef-f, Kheri-beq-f, or Horus-Khenti-maa. Look rather to their fellow defenders of Osiris, the sons of Horus. But even then, reach beyond Imset, Hapi, and Duamutef— to Him who refreshes his brothers.

He will stand in the dark amongst them, waiting beyond the deceptive well of death, along the hidden path of holy sepulchers. You need not venture far, though the journey may seem so in the dark— merely five lengths of a pontiff's crook, then left for another five. The Shining One waits, the prize held safe in his heart, within a chamber above four others where sacred beasts still slumber undisturbed.

Now that everything was out in the open among his colleagues, he saw no violation of the old priest's wishes to call in reinforcements. Once again, he felt his best chance of getting scholarly help would be from the combined intellects of Sharon and James. He found them sitting together at a table in the library pouring over Habib's notes.

"I need your help."

The two looked up in unison as though activated by a single switch. Sharon, who had been pensively tapping a pencil on the pad in front of her, tried slowly to place it behind her ear. It wouldn't stay. She forgot she was wearing glasses.

It is a rare woman who can look that beautiful in glasses, thought Ryan. James sensed the almost subliminal hesitation as Ryan tore his attention from her.

"How can we help?"

"I'm afraid Habib's estimate of my intellect may have been overly optimistic. Friends are like that. So far, I recognize the words and names within the riddle he left me but the sense of it escapes me."

In the past few days James had dropped the formality he had always observed when speaking with Ryan. "Such modesty doesn't become you, Reverend Quinn."

"I'll second that, Ryan. Want a Twinkie? Lucky thing I brought a bunch. James has developed a taste for them. He says they put him in a gay mood."

Ryan shot a glance at James, but found the priest completely at ease. He had developed a close relationship with Sharon and was not offended by her joking reference to his sexual orientation. Ryan was relieved. He loved this man and would never allow anyone to ridicule him. No one, not even Sharon.

"If I get the urge, I'll share one with James," said Ryan. "I wouldn't want to risk trying to wrestle one from the vice-like grip of Queen Nefer-Twinkie."

Sharon smiled. "OK. Let's take a look at it. I like riddles. I won a contest once. The prize was a year's subscription to The Daily Forward. The contest was at my parent's synagogue.

"The Daily Forward?" James looked puzzled.

"It's a newspaper for Jews, James, and I was only eleven. It wasn't over my head but I wasn't interested in the Jewish point of view regarding current events, either. I wanted to be a linguist not the first female rabbi."

On a piece of posterboard, Ryan had made a copy of the riddle in large, capital letters with a Magic Marker, then propped it up on an easel he'd brought to the table. He put a piece of blank posterboard on a second easel. Ryan had watched episodes of the medical show, "House," on television. He liked to watch technical minds whittling away at clinical problems, seeking to understand the connections among a complex array of possibly interdependent variables. It was much like the problem of working with bits and pieces of archaeological evidence to reconstruct an ancient civilization, or religious truth from the ancient writings of possibly imaginative historians.

"Let's make a list of the things we think we recognize and understand, OK?"

"OK, Dr. House." Sharon had watched the show, too. James looked puzzled.

Ryan picked up the Magic Marker and drew a vertical line down the middle of the blank board. On one side he wrote the names in the riddle.

MAA-ATEFF-F
KHERI-BEQ-F
HORUS-KHENTI-MAA
IMSET
HAPI
DUAMUTEF

"Either of you know who these guys were?"

"Do I get a Twinkie? That was James. "I think Habib was just showing off and being redundant to make you think there was more to the riddle than there actually is."

"I agree with James, so he doesn't get one of my Twinkies. All these guys were brothers. And they were all known as the Shining Ones. Except there were seven of them, not six."

"Very good, Sharon. You get to keep one of your Twinkies, and another for trumping James. That makes two Twinkies."

"Hold on, Ryan. I already have all the Twinkies. This contest is no fun."

"OK. You get to keep three if you can name the seventh Shining One. James?"

"I'm not sure I remember."

"Sharon?"

"Me either."

"It was Qebhsenuf. I get a Twinkie. But why were the Shining Ones important?"

Bedu and Leila had come over when they heard Ryan and the others working on the riddle. Bedu joined in.

"They were the spirits who protected the body of Osiris."

Leila snickered, "They sure did a lousy job. Didn't the oxyrhynchus fish snip off his penis?"

Bedu gave her an irritated shove. He had never grown used to the openness of sexual speech that comes so easily to Western women these days.

"Well, that's the story."

"Yes. I know."

"OK," said Ryan. "So we have seven Shining Ones, whose job it was to protect the body of Osiris. So what?"

"But Habib says you shouldn't pay attention to the first four, right?"

"Yes. He goes on to make a point about the other four, yet says not to bother with the first three of them, either."

"What does that tell us?"

"That the four are important in figuring out the riddle, but the one he doesn't mention is the most important of all."

"That's what I figure," said Ryan.

They had all been chiming in. Now Megyn joined them. It was sounding like a party game. "Why are those four of significance in Egyptian mythology?"

"They're all mentioned in The Book of the Dead."

"That's no help. Almost every spirit and god they could imagine was mentioned in the Book of the Dead. But they all had special responsibilities. What did these guys do?"

Megyn went over to the wall and looked for a copy of the Book of the Dead. She found one in English, translated by the grand old linguist, E. Wallis Budge. It even had an index.

"It says that Imset took care of the liver. But then it says they thought the liver was responsible for emotion, the way we think of the heart."

"What about Hapi?"

"He was one of the Seven Dwarfs." Sharon couldn't resist.

"Thank you for your erudite contribution to the deliberations, Dr. Feinschutz."

"Sorry."

Megyn flipped through the pages. "Lungs," she said.

"Duamutef?"

"Stomach."

"And, Qebhsenuf?"

"Intestines."

"This doesn't seem to be getting us anywhere. What did these spirits look like?"

When James and Sharon had been working together earlier, he had brought over a book for children about Egyptian mythology. There were lots of pictures.

"Here we go. Duamutef had the head of a jackal. Hapi was a baboon, not a dwarf. Sorry, Sharon. Do you forfeit a Twinkie?"

"Go on, James."

"Sorry, Ryan. Qebhsenuf had the head of a falcon and Imset had a human head."

"You keep saying, head of this or that, James. What about their bodies?"

"Not in this book for kids, Ryan. The pictures are showing canopic jars. The lids are different but all the jars are the same."

Leila was embarrassed to ask, "What are canopic jars?"

"During the embalming, they would leave the heart in the body because they thought that was where the soul dwelt. And they liquefied the brain and pulled it out through the nose and threw it away."

"They threw it away? Why?"

"Have you ever had a head cold? They thought the brain did nothing but create mucus. They figured it would be useless in the afterlife."

"No comment." That was Sharon, the class comedienne again.

"The other parts, the ones that Megyn read to us, were considered important, the stomach, the lungs, the intestines, and the liver. So they put them in separate jars and put them in the tomb with the embalmed body."

"That's it! James blurted out. "It's not their heads or their jobs that are important. It's the fact that, of the seven Shining Ones, it was these four who were used to represent spirits as lids for the canopic jars."

"And of the four," said Bedu, it was in the jar with a falcon head, the jar with the head of Qebhsenuf, that Habib hid the Chalice."

"I think you're all right. I'm glad I asked you all to sit in on this. Just one problem. There must be thousands of canopic jars all over the world in museums, antiquities shops, and in Egypt, in one tomb after another. Some have been excavated and are on record. Others are known only to one archaeologist or another, in this case, Habib Colophon."

"At least we know what to look for," said Leila. "The rest of the riddle should tell us where."

"And I thought you were just beautiful," said Bedu.

"OK, guys. Let's look at the rest of the riddle."

Ryan erased the names of the Seven Shining Ones and prepared to write whatever came up next. Megyn was the first to speak.

"First of all, we know that Akhenaten was a sun worshipper. That's how he got into all the trouble with the priests. They always think they should be in control of what you think. Sorry James, I didn't mean you or Ryan."

"The heck you didn't. And if Ryan and I didn't always know better than the rest of the world, and tell them, it would be in really bad shape."

"It is."

"OK. So, when the riddle says "kingdom of the sun" we should assume he meant the ancient Middle Kingdom, where Akhenaten and Nefertiti played house, right? Well, that's where we are right now. Amarna is just down the river. We still have a lot of ground to consider. It's like saying, "look in the state of Nevada.""

"But he says, "where darkness rules." "I'd guess he is talking about a burial site or a catacomb, most likely a catacomb. That's where darkness is extensive, or rules. Not a single tomb."

Ryan took over. "Let me sum things up. We should look for the Chalice in a canopic jar with the head of a falcon, in a catacomb someplace near Amarna. Not bad, guys. The search is beginning to narrow. We know that Habib did work around here. Maybe it was more than just luck that I decided to get us all together in El Minya rather than Luxor and the Valley of the Kings. James is right. We priests usually have a handle on the truth. Was that snicker coming from you, Sharon?"

"Not me, boss."

"Good. I want your opinion as to where we go from here. Leila, as a geomorphologist, where would you look for ground that would be solid enough to support a catacomb, yet soft enough to allow excavation with primitive tools? And what should we look for on the surface?"

"I thought you were asking Sharon."

"That was just to scare her into shutting her Twinkie Trap."

"There is a rise in topographic level in the vicinity of Tuna el-Gebel. The surface displays typical, desert morphology, aeolian deposits, barchans, mers de sable, nefuds, medanos, draa, sandvelds, a qoz or two and so on. Typical ergs, salars, and playas."

"Please Leila. I'm sorry about the priest remark. Speak so I can understand you."

"Dunes."

"Thank you."

"But beneath the dunes, you think there's something worth looking for?"

"Not only I, but many others, if my research has been accurate. There are broken columns, arches, and various other artifacts on the surface. The geologic map simply says, "ruins." I know you archaeologists are never satisfied with what you see on the surface and start digging as soon as you can get a permit, often sooner, under the cover of darkness, or big tents."

"So now we have a target, am I right? We're looking for a canopic jar with the head of a falcon, in a catacomb, somewhere near Tuna el-Gebel. The search narrows."

"Father Holmes, may I make an observation?"

"Yes, Doctor Watson, or is it Feinschutz?"

"Sharon will do, Sherlock."

"Reverend Sherlock, to you."

"What's the observation?"

"With all due respects to Leila, the catacombs at Tuna el-Gebel are rather well known. They even take tourists through them. I doubt that Father Colophon would have hidden something so valuable where there was the possibility of accidental discovery."

"Good point, Sharon. Don't look so sad, Leila. It was a good suggestion and you may be on the right track. If there is an extensive catacomb in the area, what is the possibility that there is a lesser known, or unknown one, in the vicinity?"

Leila brightened a bit. "Very high, I would say. Barring the existence of a thrust fault, the same lithologic characteristics would persist laterally."

"Thanks. I think I understood that. Let's look at the rest of the riddle to see if there are any clues that provide a more narrow focus."

"Anybody here have a background in botany?"

"Me." It was Leila again. "Some desert forms are composed of loess."

"English?"

"Wind-blown soil. The organic content is a clue to origins. I made a specialty of botany, so I could understand loess deposits more from theories of sources than simple geologic position."

"Good. I knew I brought you along for something besides your good looks."

Leila blushed. Of all of them, she was essentially the most innocent, including the priests.

"It refers to the Lotus. What's special about a lotus, Leila? Particularly the Egyptian lotus?"

"In Egypt, two native species grow, the white lotus and the blue lotus. It was the blue lotus they considered sacred. That's the one you usually see in the hieroglyphs."

"Anything peculiar about the lotus? Habib didn't mention anything about the color."

"You bet. It's almost magical. The lotus closes at night and sinks underwater. In the morning it re-emerges and opens again, the perfect symbol for resurrection. You might say, metaphorically, it can breath under water, or that its life giving substance is water."

"Amazing, Leila. It seems you are both botanist and Egyptologist, besides geomorphologist. Thank you. Would you stretch your analogy to say that the blood of the lotus is water?"

"I think that's a bit of a stretch, but reasonable to a nopn-botanist. I don't know if Father Colophon knew botany."

"True, so let's go with it as a working hypothesis. Perhaps Habib was not as learned in this field as you. Perhaps he was just being poetic, the dear old soul, and talking about water as the blood of the lotus. In that case, what would it mean to inhale the blood of the lotus?"

Bedu spoke up. He was proud of Leila and wanted her to be impressed by him as well. "It would imply drowning."

"Good. And what if one tried to sample the fragrance of the lotus blossom at night."

"Same thing. With the blossom under water, any attempt to sample its perfume would again involve drowning."

"I agree. Now we've got something. What has drowning got to do with catacombs, mummies, and the area around Tuna el Gebel?"

"I think I've got it."

"Terrific, Sharon. But I think I do, too. You go first, or I will have to claim a Twinkie, and we don't want you to go desperately sniffing underwater blossoms if your supply runs out."

"Isadora!"

"Bingo! You keep the Twinkie."

The others looked back and forth between the two.

Sharon continued. "Poor Isadora was a romantic, young woman who fell in love with a young man who lived in Wadi el-Nakhla on the other side of the Nile. He was probably an embalmer, maybe even a priest." She shot a look at Ryan, then continued, "I deciphered a papyrus found there last year. It came from an embalming cache."

Leila wanted to learn more, "What's that?"

"Trash heaps, or middens, where embalmers dumped the refuse from the embalming process, natron, soiled linen strips, and rags. Being important technicians they tended to be neat. The stuff was mostly in jars, boxes, even coffins. The papyrus that came to me at the Brooklyn Museum was a fragment of instruction sheet. Embalming was a mix of technology and religious ritual, not easy for an apprentice to manage without a reference. And mistakes, considering the rank of the subjects, might be fatal."

"Great Sharon, but let's get back to Isadora."

"One night she was overcome by longing." Again she shot a glance at Ryan. This time she blushed and he didn't miss it. "She tried to swim across the Nile to look for him and didn't make it. She drowned."

Ryan picked up where Sharon left off. "Apparently her family recovered her body. They had it embalmed and built a small temple, a mausoleum I guess you'd call it, where she was laid to rest. It is in the vicinity of Tuna el-Gebel. I think we may have zeroed in on Colophon's secret location, or at least, close to it."

Megyn seemed lost in thought. Her beautiful face took on an expression of sweet sadness. She had spent her life living with a terrible affliction. She was created with an exceptional mind, an incredible body, and a face that captured the adoration of men. But with all that, she remained always locked within the prison of her perversion, young boys. Whenever she heard a story of a deep, natural romance, it depressed her. It was like those Christmas TV shows of happy families around decorated trees and piles of presents. Most people watched and wondered why their Christmases were never quite like that. She heard her own voice as the others turned to her.

"I wonder, when they found her and gave her over to be embalmed, did her young man have to perform the rituals? Did he have to remove her organs and place them in jars? When no one was looking, did he kiss her cold lips, and detect the scent of lotus blossom on her mouth?"

Everyone was silent for a long time as Megyn sat unaware of their attention. Finally she shook her head to chase away the sadness. James went over to her and gave her a kiss on the cheek. She looked at him and smiled. He was her friend and a priest. He had heard her confession once. He knew her physical dilemma and suspected she knew his.

"Thank you, James. I needed that."

Ryan broke the uncomfortable silence. "Tuna el-Gebel is a treasure house of unusual artifacts. It was a center for the manufacture of high quality faience, particularly chalices, fashioned in the form of either the blue or white lotus, decorated with scenes in relief that told stories, the way tomb paintings and reliefs did in other parts of ancient Egypt."

Sharon took up the narrative, "They also made faience beads, rings, and amulets, some in the forms of gods and spirits."

Bedu had gone over to the bookshelves while they were talking. He returned with a volume called, "Temples and Tombs of Ancient Egypt."

"I know the fellow who wrote this," said Bedu. "He came to visit us at the museum in Brooklyn. I think you met him, too, Sharon. His name is Preston Duncan. He's English, I think."

"Yes. I remember him— a travel writer, not really an Egyptologist. What does he have to say that caught your interest, Bedu?"

"He says, "The best known structure in the vicinity of Tuna el-Gebel, is the family tomb of Petosiris, a high priest of Thoth. It was constructed in the form of a temple with an entrance portico and a chapel behind."

Sounds a lot like the guest house we're in."

Sharon started to respond but Ryan held his finger to his lips to let Bedu continue.

"The burials are in decorated chambers beneath the tomb. South of it is a Greco-Egyptian city of the dead thought to date back to the first century AD, with tombs and mortuary houses constructed in a mix of Greek and Egyptian styles"

"Now here's the important part— Included among the mortuary dwellings of the dead is the tomb of Isadora, who drowned in the Nile about 150 AD. Her mummy is still here."

Ryan took over. "Who knows what we'll find or where circumstances will lead us, but I think we've found our immediate destination. Someone, call Wadid. We'll need to get rolling as soon as possible."

"Not necessary. I've been listening in for the past half hour. It has been interesting to watch you working together. I could have used you over the years."

Ryan conspicuously swept the huge library with his eyes, "You seem to have done quite well without us."

Wadid smiled. "I'll have the desert vehicles ready to go in the morning, and a small cadre of guards, trained in hand-to-hand combat."

"Do you think that's necessary, Wadid?"

"Necessary? Perhaps not. Prudent? Definitely. I have more experience at plundering tombs than you my friend."

That night, the guesthouse of Wadid Hamza was full of angels. Everyone slept despite the fluttering of wings everywhere. No one stirred. All were in a deep, restful sleep, marvelous dreams swimming through their heads, dreams unlikely to be mentioned to one another in the morning.

Chapter Forty

Raffaello D'Agostino was born in Roccastrada in the province of Grosseto in Tuscany. The D'Agostinos didn't live in the village, but on the outskirts, on a tiny farm. Their nearest neighbor was the Scarza family. Raffaello used to play in the mud and manure with their little boy, Egidio.

Growing up in Roccastrada, there were only three options: get married and continue farming, keep your pants zipped and become a priest, or catch a ride to a big city and look for work, honest or dishonest. The D'Agostino farm was tiny. Raffaello had four brothers so, even if he liked the idea, farming was out of the question. He was not "blessed with a vocation," as his mother put it, so as soon as he could, he moved out and went to Rome to seek his fortune. He found his way and made a good deal of money for a boy with no education. His activities did not bear scrutiny by parents, neighbors, or the law. He was tough and knew he must follow a ruthless path if he were to succeed in a tough environment. He never turned down an assignment, regardless of its nature. He rose rapidly until he was soon able to make others do what he'd rather not.

Raffaello never lost touch with his childhood playmate, Egidio, though they followed very different paths. Both understood what it took to make one's way in the world, and refrained from commenting on the path chosen by the other. It was Egidio who performed his friend's marriage ceremony when Raffaello chose a bride. On the other hand, it was Raffaello who helped Egidio rise within the ranks of the Church, at times making offers to influential people that they could not refuse.

When Raffaello received the phone call from Egidio, he was not surprised. They spoke from time to time. When his friend said he needed a favor, he knew the priest was not talking about money or a new suit.

"There are some people in Egypt who are causing trouble for the Church, Raffy. I'm sure you could make the situation go away."

"I understand, Egidio. Where are they and what's the problem? I don't work, personally, in North Africa, but I have connections."

"The problem is a bunch of archaeologists. It sounds innocent enough, but they are digging for something best not left in their hands. If they find a certain object, it would be very helpful were I to be the one to present it to the Holy Father."

"What is it?"

"An antique cup."

"You want them persuaded to hand it over?"

"Not just handed over. I'm afraid they must be stopped entirely, Raffy. There must not be any loose ends left dangling afterwards to complicate matters."

"I understand."

"But there is a further problem. They are being protected by a rich man who has his own, how should I say, forces."

"That's a problem Egidio, but not one I haven't dealt with before. How many?"

"I don't know. Worst of all, Raffy, I'm not sure I really want you to do this. It's complicated."

"That's up to you, my friend. Tell me the details and call me when you make up your mind."

Egidio explained most of the situation, not mentioning the true nature of the "antique cup," then fell silent. Finally, he let out a big sigh, and continued. "I must give this more thought, Raffy. In the meanwhile, my distance from the whole matter is essential. I will not talk to you again, unless I call to tell you to stop. You understand?"

"Of course."

"If I don't call, go ahead."

"I said, I understood, Egidio. You will not be involved."

"Grazie."

"Di niente. Ciao."

"Ciao."

✝ ✝ ✝

The rumbling of engines in Wadid Hamza's huge garage was deafening. Not one, but three half-track vehicles, were warming up for the mission. To add to the racket, Wadid had turned on the enormous ventilation fans he used to keep the air breathable. He often liked to sit in one of his fine machines and listen to the sound of its pistons slamming up and down, its valves clacking open and shut, its crankshaft whirling within its pool of oil. But rarely had he run three diesels at once. These were among the most powerful in his collection.

First of all, of course, was Rommel's command car. The second was an open-top, troop carrier. The third was similar to the last, but smaller and more maneuverable. He and Ryan would sit in the back seat of the command car. An armed driver would be at the wheel. He liked to drive, himself, but wanted to savor the impression he expected to see on Ryan's face beside him. The smaller troop carrier would be for Ryan's crew. The larger one was for the cadre of armed guards. There were more than ten of them in red turbans, knives slung across their chests, carbines resting on their laps. The large vehicle also carried food, water, tents, poles, ammunition, explosives, and various other provisions. Both the personnel carriers were armed with turret-mounted, machine guns.

Ryan hid his amusement. *Wadid is a little boy with a fat wallet*, he thought. It seemed they were off, not for a short trip into the desert, but to re-live one of Rommel's campaigns.

Everyone took their places in the vehicles. They roared through the gaping, garage door, and down a sand road that Wadid had built out to the desert. He did not want the tracked vehicles tearing up the regular roads through the green fields of his estate on their way to the desert.

✝ ✝ ✝

Egidio Scarza did not live in one of the Jesuit community enclaves. His rank permitted him a room in the Vatican. Because of his scholastic interests and special privilege, he was permitted a room in the Vatican Library. His accommodations created a unique situation given dispensation by the Pope, himself. His chamber was hardly big enough to warrant the name, room. I was not much bigger than the wooden bed and desk within it. But the honor! Egidio Scarza, farm boy from Roccastrada, slept a few steps from the library's Sistine Hall with its array of painted vaults and columns. Egidio could feel their presence each night as he drifted off to sleep. There was no plumbing in his chamber, but he gladly walked the black and white marble floor of the Sistine Hall at night when nature demanded that he relieve himself. Sometimes as he walked, he purposely slapped his sandals hard on the floor, like a child, to hear the echo off the ancient murals. It underscored the unique privilege he enjoyed.

None but the sandals of Egidio Scarza, he thought, *dare be heard at night within the Sistine Hall of the Bibliotheca Apostolica Vaticana.*

As he had, hundreds of times before, Egidio lay on his bed tonight, sensing history about him, and the importance of his position within it. What lay ahead? No one could say. If indeed, he could deliver the Chalice of the Last Supper to the Pontiff, he could name his own reward, perhaps plumbing, right here in his own chamber within the Bibliotheca Apostolica Vaticana. He liked to say the name of his library out loud.

The triviality of that last thought actually made him laugh. He chuckled at first, and then the idiocy of it filled his mouth with loud, boisterous laughter. If someone could hear him they would think he was utterly insane, laughing loudly in the middle of the night by himself in this august environment.

The sound of his own laughter startled Egidio. Was he truly insane? He had everything he could possibly want. Was he going to trade Christ's cup of the New Testament for a flush toilet? What was he doing? He lay silent for a long time. This was, indeed, a crazy venture. He would call Raffaello in the morning and tell him to stop. What had he been thinking?

Just then, he heard a rustling at his door. While he watched, with growing rage at the audacity of this intrusion, the door opened slowly. In it stood an incredibly beautiful woman. She was completely naked. Egidio's rage froze in wonderment as the woman spoke.

"Sono venuto a ricompensare la vostra stupende conquiste, Egidio Scarza." I have come to reward you for your marvelous achievements, Egidio Scarza. She spoke in an elegant, Florentine dialect, but with a slight speech impediment that lent her words a strange, clicking sound.

† † †

The performance of every human task is examined for quality. People who deserve recognition for good and faithful performance are generally rewarded. Signora Maria Delvecchio had been a Vatican maid for fifty years. With mop and pail she began when she turned eighteen. At sixty-eight, dressed in black, a white headscarf to hold her grey hair in place, she continued to perform her tasks with regularity, if no longer with any enthusiasm. She had mopped the floors of the Vatican faithfully, finally being given the honor of performing her simple task in the Pope's private quarters. She was proud of her achievement, but after an unfortunate event, she had been reassigned to work in the Vatican Library. Despite the magnificence of this place, she rarely raised her head to enjoy the murals and painted ceilings. Her demotion had been a devastating event in her simple life. The sadness lasted, but at least her work remained. Her job was, and remained, the floor. Bent over by age, it was no longer difficult to maintain her attention in that direction. She'd left miles of glistening Carrara marble floors behind her. Who knew how many still lay ahead? In the Vatican it all seemed the same, miles of marble, rarely soiled except after a rainstorm. It was just she, the glistening marble, her black shoes, and the swish, swish, swish of the wet mop from side to side, then a pause to dip and wring the mop before continuing. Even the water in the pail never seemed to grow dirty before she would resume the rhythm, swish, swish, swish.

This morning it was different, though not completely out of the ordinary. There were feathers scattered here and there. It happened. Once in a while, a bird came in through an open window and flew about in a frenzy, looking for a way out. In panic it would let loose drops of white excrement here and there. Worst was when the distraught bird might perch above columns, murals, or on doorjambs and sculptures, leaving white deposits that sometimes ran down, leaving trails behind. All of it needed to be removed at once before it could damage priceless objects. Though she looked carefully this morning, the old lady saw nothing that required special attention. Good. That made her job a little easier. Her old bones resisted the activity that once seemed so effortless.

Signora Delvecchio came to the door of Father Scarza's room. There was a scatter of feathers near it that fluttered erratically, escaping the broad sweep of her mop. She would have to gather them up by hand and that would be painful. Fortunately, she saw no white droppings anywhere, either on the doorjamb, or floor. At least she would be spared that. She knocked gently on the door. Father Scarza was always gone to the Biblical Institute by this time, but she always knocked. She knew better than to enter, unannounced, into the presence of high-ranking priests. They were rarely gentle with her if she surprised them.

There was no answer, so she opened the door. She was not a young woman, so her outcry was not a high-pitched scream, but an old woman's croak of horror. There on a chair facing her, sat Egidio Scarza, draped in black cloth, a crimson skullcap on his head, mouth agape in a bloodless face, eyes wide and staring.

It was not the first time Maria Delvecchio had encountered such a scene. The last time had been in the Pope's private quarters. It had been the Pope, himself, who sat there with white face and staring eyes. She had run to tell the Cardinal in attendance. Within hours she had been transferred to work elsewhere. Would it happen again? The scene was horrifying, but fear of another demotion even more so. This time she closed the door quietly and continued mopping down the hall— swish, swish, swish.

When Egidio's absense was finally noticed and his body discovered, the Rector of the Biblical Institute was informed. Except for him, no one else was told. The incident would not be reported anywhere. It would be as though Egidio Scarza had never existed. A sub-rector to assist the Reverend Clemente Brava, S.J. at the Biblical Institute was named at once. Neither he nor the Rector spoke of the matter.

Ritual executions like this one were an unbroken series down through Church history, a string of beads, a pater noster of angelic executions, as one. well-informed, cardinal put it in private to another. No one was ever witness to one, and no clues ever remained, except the feathers. No one dared discuss them either. It was a succession of bizarre events as unbroken through history as the succession of bishops to the papacy. In fact, they were connected. No pope had escaped. In secrecy, one theologian referred to the popes as Lambs of God, vicars of Christ, who follow His violent path to Heaven. Angels were always suspected but never identified as the executioners. The "why" of it was known, perhaps, only to the popes and to the few prelates who had access to the Stanza Speciale. Only occasionally, had there been ritual executions that involved persons other than those elected to wear the papal mitre.

Raffaello D'Agostino waited for a call from Egidio Scarza. He made no attempt to contact the priest. He had promised to maintain his anonymity. If Egidio changed his mind he would call. After a few days Raffaello shrugged and made a few calls of his own.

In Connecticut, the old lady heard a knock at the door. She rarely had company and wondered who it might be. She didn't even bother to look through the peephole, but opened the door. There stood a handsome man, tall and slim, dressed in black. There was a delicious aroma about him. *Some new cologne*, she thought.

"Excuse me for coming unannounced. I hope I'm not interrupting anything important."

He sounded as though he were from Boston, or perhaps England. His words sounded very elegant, but clicked as he spoke.

He's much too young to be wearing a denture, she thought. "Please come in. What can I do for you?"

"I was sent by the brother of one of your former tenants, Father Ryan Quinn."

"Oh yes, Spencer Quinn. A terrible tragedy. No one seems to have any idea what happened. You say you were sent by his brother?"

"Yes. The Jesuit, Ryan Quinn."

"Where is he these days? I know he is very important and has a big office in New York City. His brother adored him."

"He's in Egypt on a very special mission important to the Pope, and to a number of other important people."

"Oh, my. But I'm not surprised. What can I do for you?"

"It occurred to me, and my sister, who is involved in such things, that after Spencer's death you might have renovated his apartment and rented it again."

"No. The news of the bizarre killing had everyone spooked. I doubt I will ever be able to rent it again. I just cleaned it thoroughly and left it at that. Maybe in a few years someone will be brave enough to be interested. You aren't looking for a place, are you?. I'm ready to offer very attractive terms."

"I'm sorry. No. But thank you very much." He smiled sweetly and the old lady felt her heart flutter.

"My sister and I were wondering if you might have found anything while you were cleaning, a small medallion seems to be missing. It was very important to Spencer. A Jesuit friend of his brother had given it to Spencer. Father Quinn would love to have it as a keepsake."

"As a matter of fact, I did find something. I put it in a coffee can in the kitchen in case anyone missed it. I'll be right back."

The old lady left the young man in the living room, and returned a few moments later. Her eyesight was failing, but she thought the young man seemed to be floating a few inches above the floor. She rubbed her eyes and said nothing. He was so cute she really didn't want him to know how old and feeble she'd become.

"Here it is." She held out her hand. The medallion lay on her outstretched palm.

"May I?" He reached for the medallion, his fingers lightly touching her palm. A tingling ran through her whole body and she could swear, though she had not felt one for thirty years, she was beginning to experience an orgasm. She gasped and tried to hold onto the top of the couch.

"I think I need to sit down," she panted, embarrassed.

He closed his hand on the medallion and laughed. It was like the tinkling of bells, delicate, yet masculine.

"My sister will be so pleased. You have no idea. We will get it to Father Quinn as soon as possible. We will be sure to mention how helpful you were."

"I'm so glad," gasped the old lady. "Please come and visit again."

"We will see one another again, dear lady. You can be sure of it. Thank you."

Chapter Forty-One

After a number of name changes, the Necropolis of Khmun is now known as Tuna el-Gebel. It lies out in the desert, a little more than forty miles from El Minya. It is at the end of a pitted road that struggles to survive the heat of the sun and the scouring of wind-driven sands that wash incessantly back and forth across it. An occasional raptor flies the route in search of road kill. Most flights are a disappointment. There is little wildlife available to die on the road to Khmun and virtually no vehicles to perform the executions. In the still heat, the road tar exudes the pleasant aroma familiar to all who have walked desert roads anywhere in the world.

There is almost no vegetation and very little other life, yet there are tracks in the sand, little herringbone trails left by insects and larger patterns left by a few hardy reptiles that travel by night and bury themselves by day to avoid the blazing sun. Even these must be printed again and again each day if they are to survive the shifting sand.

Among the few signs of life that last for a while are footprints left by passing caravans. Strings of camels on their way to market can still be seen on the Egyptian horizon in places otherwise so obvioiusly hostile to life that they appear to be delusions, mirages that shimmer close to the surface and may not exist at all. A shake of the head and they usually dissolve.

Like everywhere on earth, there are signs of man. Here and there in the Egyptian desert one comes upon a lonely monument left by a long gone center of civilization. Today in the desert wastes, there are few signs of contemporary life, and those rather unpleasant. As light breezes caress the desert, they carry with them unexpected passengers. Every camel footprint seems to hold a cigarette butt, rolled along by the wind in search of a resting place. Yards of audio tape from broken cassettes hang from virtually every sprig of vegetation hardy enough to poke its head above the sea of sand.

Wadid Hamza's caravan of half-tracks left the floodland farm roads of El Minya and made its way noisily out onto the surreal sea of shifting sands. If tranquility is mistress of the desert, diesel half-tracks are rapists intent on penetration.

Vehicles on dry roads throw up clouds of dust. Not so in the desert. Tank treads, though they rip and tear, only throw sand into the air that falls back almost at once. Even their tracks, like those of desert beetles, are soon erased by the breezes. It is the noise of the half-track that is the rapist, the whining of pulleys, the clacking of tread plates, folding and unfolding, and the roaring of the diesel engines, that threaten to jar one's sanity. Wadid Hamza loved it.

Ryan, sitting beside him, was not happy with the mode of transportation. Wadid could see it on Ryan's face but did not want to ask him about it. In fact, he could not, even if he wanted to. The clamor was too great for any question to be heard without screaming, and just the act of cupping his hands around his mouth and yelling, would have underscored the problem Wadid would rather not acknowledge. Both he and Ryan understood the joy of peaceful, desert travel, sitting on a colorful, embroidery-clad saddle, atop a swift, silent, squishy-footed camel. He had hoped that Ryan might let the roar of magnificent, old machinery penetrate his soul as it did his. Apparently not. An old pick up truck would have taken a few hours to Tuna el-Gebel, even along the nearby, pock marked road. The Hamza caravan moved with a slowness that belied the great racket it was making. If they were doing five miles an hour, that would be stretching the truth.

Ryan tried to blot out the roar and let his mind take flight. He imagined the quiet of an ancient chariot, its wheels plowing light furrows in the sand behind a brace of panting horses, even their hoof beats muffled by the soft desert. For the moment he would be a pharaoh, dashing about this same landscape, enjoying the sun and flying sand, on a short gallop before lunch, looking forward to a poolside visit with a beautiful wife.

The rickety, third class train limped into El Minya Station on Sharia Saad Zaghioul, across the street from the Hotel Seety. A hand-written sign advertised, "Hot Water." The sign lied. It should have added, "sometimes." By now, Pietro Gandolfo would settle for a sign that just promised toilets.

As the exhausted Nuncio stood contemplating his options, a young man approached him. He was dressed in an immaculate, three-piece suit. He looked familiar, but didn't wait for formalities. He smiled and held out his hand.

"Here, take this." He took Pietro's hand and placed a coin in it."

"Please, my good man. I may look disheveled after my long train ride, but I am not in need of charity. But, thank you."

He tried to force the coin back into the other's hand but as he touched him, a tingling washed over his entire body that left him weak and gasping.

"Do I know you?"

"I believe you've met my sister."

"Oh, dear Lord. No more. What do you want with me?"

"I think you know, Pietro Gandolfo. Take the medallion. Father Quinn will need it. He is in the desert. He will soon be at the Necropolis of Khmun."

Gandolfo looked at the coin in his hand. He recognized it at once. It was not a coin at all, but as the man had said, a medallion. Pietro had seen drawings of it in an archive at the Biblical Institute in Rome, in the Stanza Speciale.

He jerked his head up to look at the young man, but he was gone. Pietro whirled around, but saw only small groups of people standing about laughing and talking. A few had begun to leave the station, moving toward the street. In a state of bewilderment, he followed them. He needed a coffee.

Still clutching the medallion, he found a street vendor. In a single gulp, he downed a cup of the thick, sweet, Egyptian brew. There was no time to think about anything. He headed across the Sharia Saad Zaghioul into the dusty lobby of the Hotel Seety. *Well named*, he thought.

Once in his room, Pietro sat on the bed. It was missing both legs at the foot end, and sloped in that direction. He took the medallion from his pocket and stared at it. It was the bas-relief of Judas he'd stared at years ago, the apostle's tongue hanging from his mouth as he dangled from the end of rope slung over a tree branch. Two ghouls in the foreground stared out at Gandolfo, their hands on the rope. It was the same scene reproduced from who knows what source, by the medieval sculptor, Gislebertus, that still decorated one of the capitals in the Cathedral of Lazarus in Autun, France. This was the medallion that had caused such controversy for two thousand years. Now it was in his fist as he sat on a broken bed, in a dump of a hotel, in El Minya, Egypt.

Providence certainly moves in mysterious ways, he thought. Was he a key player in the plans of the Almighty? Impossible! But here was evidence of it in his own, unworthy hand. Did the Patriarch Shenouda, his old friend, have anything to do with this? Questions, questions, questions.

The shower was cool, not cold. Water is rarely cold in Middle Egypt, just a bit cooler than the ambient temperature that is only chilly in February. The bar of soap was just the sliver left by the last occupant. It was hard to keep a grip on it, especially since Pietro still clutched the medallion, afraid to let it out of his sight.

After using one of the rough, grime-grey, towels to dry off, he let it fall to the floor. It smelled rancid, like a dish-towel, used too often and ready for the garbage pail. He put on a clean pair of boxer shorts, then pulled back the chenille bedspread and sheet. There was no blanket. The slope of the bed toward the missing legs was not a problem. If it sloped toward the head it might have led him to sleep with his head in the other direction. As it was, he was so exhausted he climbed onto the sloping bed, pulled the sheet over himself, and fell asleep at once. Even as he slept, he clutched the medallion tightly, unmindful of the orange glow of late afternoon that still crept around and under the window drapes.

The Nuncio's dreams were glorious. He flew with the angels across the land, wheeling with them in great sweeping turns, like the swallows he'd watched in his youth, moving in unison as though by a single command.

When he awoke he felt healthy and alive. The morning sun had turned his simple room into a palace of sparkling light. He knew, now, what he must do. With the reassurance that the medallion was still in his fist, he dressed quickly, paid his bill at the front desk, bought some bread, cheese, and bottled water at a neighborhood store, and went in search of a taxi.

In Egypt, one never has to look far for any kind of service. The natives sense a foreigner, and appear from nowhere to offer tours, perfume, jewelry, artifacts, or transportation. After a few moments wasted in bargaining, Pietro Gandolfo was soon headed into the desert on the rough road to

Khmun. The driver knew the archaeological name, but asked to be sure that Pietro knew where he really wanted to go.

"Most pleasing, sir, did you mean Tuna el-Gebel?"

"Yes, the Necropolis of Khmun."

"No one goes there, sir."

"I know. But I wish to."

With a crunch, the driver jammed the old Peugeot into first gear, popped the clutch, and off they went, belching clouds of black smoke.

Muhammed bin Abdullah lived like a king. He had more than enough wives. In truth he had far too many. It wasn't the expense. Money was no problem. They were a nuisance. The young ones didn't know how to do it, and the old ones wanted it all the time. His home was his palace— thick carpets, sometimes smaller ones on top of larger ones, gold plated chairs and tables, colorfully crocheted seat covers and pillows, a hidden collection of alcoholic beverages, the "waters of hell" he enjoyed so much.

At night he preferred the soft glow of the oil lamps that hung from the ornate ceiling of his abode. During the day he kept the carved shutters closed so the sun cast intricate designs on the marble floors. The patterns lost themselves among the designs of the oriental carpets. His home was cool in the day and just right in the humid, Alexandria nights. It was heaven. He sat back in an overstuffed chair and prepared to light a gold-tipped, black cigarette, when the phone rang.

"Shit!" He had learned the word from one of his hired assassins, a vulgar man he had saved from a US prison.

"Yes?" His greeting was irritable, but softened at once when he realized who was calling. "Oh, my dear friend Raffaello. So good to hear your voice. You are in Alexandria? No? In Italy? My poor fortune. Yes, of course I can take care of a problem for you. You have only to ask. You know that. Where? Out in the desert beyond El Minya? That is very primitive country, my friend. Not the sort of environment in which my people are accustomed to operating. Yes. Yes. Of course I am willing to help you. Have I ever refused? Tell me specifically what you need done."

As he listened, Muhammed fumbled awkwardly with his unlit cigarette, trying to reach for the lighter on the table, just beyond his reach. Finally, he interrupted Raffaello.

"It doesn't sound at all simple, my friend. Too much exposure. My people work most efficiently in crowded cities. They are not comfortable out of town. They are rats who strike and devour in their own sewers, not in the homes of clean-living neighbors."

He took the moment of silence at the other end to struggle out of his chair and retrieve the lighter. He lit the cigarette, inhaled deeply, and began to cough.

"No. No problem. Of course. And your offer is most generous, Raffaello. I will take care of it."

He had been offered a great deal of money, but he did not need money. On the other hand, he knew what it meant to say no to Raffaello D'Agostino, master of the offer no one dares refuse. He figured that five men with weapons would be more than enough, young brutes hoping to rise in the business, not yet aware that brains, not muscle, were the key to success.

After he hung up, he drained a bottle of American bourbon, then lay snoring in the soft chair for a long time before one of his old wives coaxed him into a sloppy coupling in the half light of evening.

Despite the sex and liquor, Muhammed bin Abdullah did not sleep well that night. He would put together a group of stupid killers in the morning and send them by train to El Minya. One of his people there would know the whereabouts of the archaeologists, hopefully still in El Minya where his thugs could do the job and get out of town quickly. If none of them came back alive it would be OK with him. He didn't need any more business from Italy and he could point to failure as an honest attempt to please D'Agostino. He would even waive the fee as a sign of true regret for his failure. It should satisfy that bloodthirsty farm boy. Abdullah did wonder, though, about the nature of any archaeological prize, some old cup that would prompt D'Agostino to call for such a bloodbath.

Chapter Forty-Two

Wadid Hamza had long since given up hope of making it to Tuna el-Gebel in a single day. In truth, he knew from the outset that it was impossible in his antique vehicles. It was all part of his plan, like the extravagant party for ancient goddesses at his home a few nights earlier. He loved pageantry. This was an opportunity that all his money could never buy, the finest Egyptologists, hand picked for the most interesting quest in two thousand years, many of them beautiful women, on a mission sanctioned by the Patriarch of his Church, all packed in, buttock-to-buttock, in one of his venerable half tracks headed for the catacombs beneath the City of the Dead, the Necropolis of Khmun. He was the Desert Fox, Field Marshal Erwin Rommel, at the head of a small strike force on a holy mission. He would have preferred he was buttock-to-buttock with one of those lovely professors back in the troop carrier, but sharing Rommel's command bench with the famous Egyptologist-priest, Ryan Quinn, would have to do. From tomb robber to crusader. It was an accomplishment he never dared imagine.

Leila was probably the only one immune to the roar and clatter of the vehicles. She was fascinated by the topography. This was the laboratory of her chosen specialty. They were roaring through a textbook panorama of Aeolian geomorphology. The khamsin, hot southerly wind of Egypt, was at their back as they plunged into arroyos, through ergs, only to climb barchans, medanos, nefuds, alabs, akles, then grind across one playa after another, and across sandvelds.

Bedu was beside her and used the opportunity of the pounding journey to hold her tight in public. She hardly noticed, but would not have resisted if she had. To Bedu, this was not an extraordinary landscape. It was home.

As the sun grew huge and orange near the horizon, Wadid threw up his arms in mock desperation. "We must make camp for the night."

Ryan was not fooled. He knew he was in the hands of a showman, but welcomed any break from the horrible beating they were all experiencing. Or were they? Was it perhaps that he was getting old and a bit delicate? He tried to act as though he were disappointed. A few minutes later, after Wadid had motioned the caravan to form a circle and halt, that Ryan attempted to hide his clumsy exit from the command car. His legs were numb and his knees hurt. Sharon didn't notice and he was thankful for that.

Wadid had been on the lookout and chose a small playa to make camp for the night, a dry lakebed surrounded by barchans, boomerang shaped dunes. They were protected from the wind and from view, in the unlikely case someone might be looking for them. They weren't. Not yet.

The red-turbaned guards would be performing double duty on this venture The first was as an armed force. The second was a job at which they were adept, and enjoyed, as expert desert campers. They were Bedouin and were born with a sense of desert survival. As the Chalice team sat about on the dunes above, tents began to rise on the level playa below. Bedu, despite his western doctorate and fascination with history, was a tent builder at heart. Leila had gone off by herself to see what desert mysteries of geologic interest she might uncover. She found nothing unusual but enjoyed refreshing her knowledge of desert phenomena. Everything was a product of wind and hot sun, the three-sided rocks, dreikanters, polished flat on one side, then flipped by the wind and polished again, over and over. The process would go on for centuries until all that was left would be a small grain to join billions of others as tiny nomads in a wandering dune. She looked for loess, wind-blown soil, but found none. She stood and calculated the direction of the region's prevailing wind from the orientation of the dunes. They would be heading into the wind on the way to Khmun. Thank God for that. A wind from behind would mean inhaling more diesel fumes. There were boulders, shiny with a coat of sun varnish. She turned a couple over and found a crust of caliche. There must be water somewhere down below to leach the minerals from the ground and redeposit it on the underside of the hot surface rocks. What looked like a desolate scene to most, was a storybook to Leila. Then she noticed Bedu. She had grown tremendously fond of this desert man, gone academic. She saw that he had not been content to sit with the others on the dunes, but had gone down to join the red-turbaned crew setting up tents and preparing a place to sit and make tea.

Ryan sat alone, reading his Office, the mandatory passage of daily prayer demanded of all priests. Not far from him, James was doing the same. Sharon looked at the two of them with mixed emotions. They could not see her as she peered from behind a sand ridge.

Despite what they had read in Habib Colophon's note, they remained true to their faith. Was it just routine, just two men clinging to ritual in the face of reality? They had read things that might shake the roots of the lives they had chosen. Here were two brilliant men, within sight of no one but God, toiling in the orange glow of the setting sun, at the boring task of reading prayers they'd read a hundred times before.

If they were two dunces, she thought, *I might scoff at their foolish obstinacy. But I have never known two more intelligent human beings. What am I missing? And if it is something that can be found, where do I look for it? I love the one man, and the other, too, in a different way. Are they both beyond the reach of my understanding?*

Bedu called to everyone. Camp was ready. The two priests closed their books and stood. Leila came wandering back. Sharon came out of hiding. They all descended to the floor of the playa, their feet sliding in the sand, sending tiny avalanches ahead of each step. Now the dunes were dotted with footprints, each bearing a little sand-beard below it. In a day, a week, no more than that, they would all be gone.

Wadid was already brewing tea in an ornate brass pot he always carried with him into the desert.

The campsite had been well chosen. Wadid Hamza wanted to maintain the romantic concept of a desert campaign far from modern conveniences. Although it was possible in many places in the Egyptian desert, the expedition camp was still too near El, Minya to be truly isolated. Wadid knew they were never very far from that miserable excuse for a road between El Minya and Tuna el-Gebel. If they had been riding camels they would have been high enough in their saddles to see it. Motor vehicles might have been heard, if there were any, but certainly not over the racket created by Wadid's half-tracks. Leila never looked in the right direction during her wanderings. So the aura of isolation held fast.

Inside the main tent, protected by the dunes around the playa, no one heard the old Peugeot pass a few miles away, as they stirred sugar into their tea, shelled hardboiled eggs, and broke round, flat loaves of bread into crusty wedges.

Pietro Gandolfo, inside the old sedan, rumbled by, hidden by the dunes and the early morning qobar, dry fog of the Nile. He fidgeted nervously. He had no idea what to expect ahead. He knew what he still held in his hand. He knew from which silver goblet it had come, and who had pried it off. He did not know why the man had done so, nor what he had done with the goblet. He knew that those of the highest ecclesiastical rank in Rome wanted the goblet and hoped it would never be exposed to public scrutiny. He also knew the reason for that. It was not the goblet itself, but the very medallion he now held in his hand, ancient symbol disclosed at the Last Supper, proposing an Eighth Sacrament, a death sentence placed upon all popes, and a reality that might devastate the political structure the apostle, Peter, intended to create, a structure that had, indeed, encircled the globe in the face of all odds and cruel persecution.

He, Pietro Gandolfo, had run from the site where Habib Colophon had been working to avoid all of this and, through his cowardice, had risen in eclesiastical rank as though a hero, suffering only a broken leg at the hands of an irritated angel.

In the chilly dawn of the Egyptian desert, in an old jalopy, he now sat near the vortex that whirled between Heaven and Earth. He was wedged squarely between the Church of Saint Peter and the possible design suggested by Christ, the Son of God. But then, God always intended that Man follow the dictates of his own free will. It was the dilemma of Good and Evil in a Universe ruled by an Omnipotent Presence. Who was he, Pietro Gandolfo, to play a pivotal part in a drama of this magnitude? Perhaps the goblet would answer all the questions. Was it here, somewhere in this desolate landscape, or beneath its surface?

The old Peugeot bumped along as he continued to fidget, turning the medallion over and over in his hand. His fingers were cold and stiff. The desert is a place of extremes. It is hot as a stovetop by day, chilly as a tomb by night. The sun had just risen and threatened to blind the driver as they headed east, the shadow of their decrepit automobile painted a long, black phantom, flat on the pavement behind them that flowed in and out of the potholes.

In most of the world, a cemetery is a place for the bodies of those whose souls have flown to Heaven. In ancient Egypt, the dead were not considered gone, but waiting. Houses were built in which they might pass the time, or in tombs filled with their favorite foods, furniture and other paraphernalia, necessary for the new life which they would be entering. Little statues, ushabti, were placed in with them, expected to come to life and care for the resting one. Sculptures of beetles were also wound into the linen wrappings with the embalmed bodies. One was placed on the tongue, in a ceremony known as the opening of the mouth, to aid conversation in the next life.

At Tuna el-Gebel, most of the houses in the City of the Dead had taken more sun and wind than they could withstand. Broken columns stand awash in an ocean of sand. It has invaded the roofless houses like a rising tide, covering doorjambs, floors, and windowsills. Only a few, particularly sturdy structures, endure. Those are the tombs of the very wealthy, or most revered. Among these is the tomb of Petosiris, the highpriest of the god, Thoth. On its interior walls, scenes of everyday life are carved into the stone, as well as passages from the Book of Gates that describe the homes and inhabitants of Am-Tuat, the underworld traversed each night by the sun god, Ra.

At Tuna el-Gebel, it is only below ground that the sea of sand has been kept at bay. There, a honeycomb of passages twist and turn in the dark, their walls carved into an endless succession of burial niches. In each lies the linen-wrapped mummy of a beast favored by the god, Thoth, baboons, ibis birds, and crocodiles. There are thousands of them.

Pietro saw no one as they arrived at the ancient necropolis. He had expected to see evidence of Ryan Quinn and his group.

"Stop anywhere. I want to look around. Stay here. I will pay you for your time."

Every Egyptian who lives near an ancient ruin, and that means virtually everyone, fancies himself an Egyptologist. Not only do they offer tours, but long discourses on the history of the region, emphasizing the more bizarre aspects, and filling gaps in their knowledge with fanciful versions of their own creation. The more romantic or bloody the story, the greater the fee expected.

"I am knowing a great deal about this place. You would like a tour? I will make you a special price that includes the trip back top El Minya."

"I thought we agreed on a price for the round trip before we left."

The driver shrugged and smiled. He was missing several front teeth. One is in a poor position to bargain with the driver of the only car in a deserted city of the dead in the middle of the desert.

"I will take you into the monkey mummy tunnels. No extra charge. I have a flashlight."

Once again, there was little room for negotiation. Pietro had been to Tuna el-Gebel many years ago with Habib Colophon. The archaeologist in him would love to visit the places he once knew so well. And he was talking to the man who not only had the only automobile in sight but undoubtedly, the only flashlight. A sum was offered and accepted. They set out on foot, leaving the car near a sand-engulfed temple.

Wadid's caravan of squeeking, grinding half-tracks pulled into the Necropolis of Khmun.

Enough noise to wake the dead, thought Ryan, but kept the silly thought to himself.

Wadid made sure they kept the vehicles in the sand. He loved Egypt and had no intention of shredding its already tattered roads for his own pleasure. If there had been a waiting crowd to watch his pharaonic entrance he might have driven down the main road and later paid to have it repaired. As it was, they appeared to be the only act in town. Almost. A lone car sat on the pavement near one of the sand-swamped tombs. There was no one in it.

Beneath the waves of sand and toppled columns, Pietro Gandolfo and the taxi driver made their way slowly through the catacombs. The tunnels were pitch black, with many twists, turns, and side passages. Pietro hoped the driver would remember the way back, and that the flashlight batteries would hold out. The tunnels varied little, thousands of niches, each occupied by a small, linen-wrapped mummy. Some were larger or longer than the others. The driver would shine his flashlight into a niche and make his pronouncement. If the niche was large, he said, "bahboon." If it were one of the smaller ones, "eebis." A longer one, he would identify as, "cocodrill." The constant repetition was starting to drive Pietro crazy. He began to blurt, si, si, si, in the darkness. Finally, in desperation he began to say bahboon, eebis, or cocodrill before the driver had a chance to open his mouth. But the tour continued, mostly in silence once the driver took the hint. Occasionally a side passage had been partially blocked with some boards. Pietro wondered what lay beyond the them, but when he took the driver's arm and directed the flashlight between the boards, it seemed there was nothing special, just another passage leading off into the dark with more niches carved into both sides.

Pietro mused to himself, *There must be a reason for such barriers, but what? Had they been erected within recent times or eons ago? Did they restrict visitors from special passages reserved for a human interment? Or were they forbidden, subterranean entrances to the basements of surface tombs or chapels? Perhaps they were simply protective devices to keep stray visitors from entering dangerous sections of the maze.*

Pietro found these blocked passages fascinating. *Forbidden fruit always offers the sweetest promise,* he thought. *It has been the same since the Garden of Eden.*

If he lived to return under less stressful conditions, Pietro, would try to learn the meaning of the barricades. For the moment, he nervously kept one fist tightly clutching the medallion. *Had it been here before?* That was a question to which he might learn the answer sooner than the last one. *What if he dropped the medallion here in the dark?* He decided to put it into his pocket in his fist, so he would have the reassurance of contact with it.

There was no way of telling where the two of them might be beneath the necropolis. They had come a long way.

Neither of them heard the racket on the surface as the half-track vehicles rumbled into the necropolis and came to a stop.

Chapter Forty-Three

The Tomb of Petosiris is easily visible from where Wadid ordered the half-tracks parked. It is the most impressive structure in the necropolis. Just a few yards away, much smaller but elegant in its simplicity of line, is the Tomb of Isadora. The lone automobile left by person or persons, unknown, was not near either of them.

Wadid ordered his armed guard to make camp near the spot where they had parked the vehicles. The men began at once to set up tents and prepare comfortable arrangements for the night, or for as long as necessary. A ring of stones for a fire to brew tea near the center of the small camp was high on their list of priorities. The two priests, Wadid, and the others, walked together toward the Tomb of Isadora. Ryan spoke quietly to Sharon and James, not to be secretive but out of respect for the dead in this lonely city of tombs and chapels.

"This all seems too easy, James."

"Remember, Ryan, we think we solved the riddle as far as the idea of a canopic jar and its association with the Tomb of Isadora. But there were other parts to the riddle that we never even discussed."

"Such as?"

"The well, for one."

Sharon joined in, "You mean the "deceptive well of death?"

"Exactly. And the slumbering beasts, for another."

"That one's easy," said Ryan. This place is crawling with slumbering beasts. From what I've read, there are thousands of mummified apes and birds buried in miles of tunnels beneath the ground. There may be some below us where we're walking right now."

"You're right," Wadid joined in, "but that may be more of a problem than help. With so many, how are we to find a single one?"

"That's why the so called, deceptive well of death, is the important factor," said James, drawing his hand across his throat to emphasize the word death. He had been picking up Wadid's sense of drama. "The well is the benchmark, to use a little surveying jargon. We don't know where we are or where we're going until we can put an *x* on a map and mark it, Deceptive Well of Death."

"You're absolutely right, James," said Sharon. By this time, they had reached the Tomb of Isadora.

As usual, the other members of the team spoke up when they thought they had something to offer. This time it was Leila.

"While I was scouting around last night's camp I found evidence of water, caliche on the bottoms of the rocks. There's nothing unexpected in that. Except where the substrata are fracture-free, crystalline rock, there is usually water. It may be very deep, and sometimes salty, but it's usually there."

"So?" That was Ryan.

"Actually, so— nothing," answered Leila. "I just wanted to sound like a geologist who had something to contribute in this Egyptologists-only club."

Ryan looked upset. "Is that the way we've been acting, Leila? I don't think any of us feel that way. We just get excited and start talking shop."

"I know that. Remember where I work back home. I'm used to it. I was just trying to push a dramatic wedge into the conversation before we got to Isadora's doorstep. The night before we came bouncing across the desert, I did a little library research about Tuna el-Gebel."

"And?"

"The Romans built a deep well here. I say, "built," because it was a major construction project, a huge dome of mud bricks, at least mud bricks above the phreatic zone."

Now they were standing on the steps of Isadora's Tomb. Sharon turned to Leila.

"The what zone?"

"It doesn't matter. It's the semi-saturated zone between the water table and the earth above. I was just trying to point out that the mud bricks would have to be above that zone or dissolve. Anyhow, the well structure is 120 feet deep before you even get to the level from which they would lower the buckets. The whole thing is deep and enormous. Does that qualify as a deceptive well of death?"

"I'm not sure, Leila," said James. "I get the "well" part, and if you fell into it I'm sure it would be a well of death, but why deceptive? I think it's referring to something else."

"Let's look around inside Isadora's Tomb," said Ryan. "That's the most obvious place to start. If that's no help, we'll go look for the Roman well but I tend to agree with James. Habib wasn't a geologist. He was trying to say something that would mean something to me. And I never heard of the phreatic zone. No offense, Leila."

"It's not too late to learn, Ryan." Bedu put his arm around Leila. He had never spoken like that to Quinn and immediately regretted it. But he probably would have spoken to the patriarch of his own church like that if he thought he was defending Leila.

"I'm sorry, both of you. I'm on edge. I suspect we all are. And I keep wondering who the people are who were in that car and where are they right now?"

With that, Ryan climbed the seven steps to the platform in front of the door to Isadora's Tomb. There was an iron gate and a hasp for a lock on it. The lock was missing. Ryan pulled on the gate. The old hinges complained, but gave way. The door behind it was not locked either. The small group followed as Ryan entered the windowless chamber.

Wadid had a flashlight. He cast the beam around the hot, dry interior. Nothing, but there was a door on the far side to another chamber. Wadid led the way. In the middle of the second room lay the mummy of Isadora. She was lying peacefully in a glass case to protect her from curious tourists.

Despite the drama of the scene, Ryan and the rest were disappointed. Neither chamber was big enough to hide anything. At Ryan's request, Wadid ran the flashlight over the floors of both chambers. There were no obviously loose paving stones, or even enough room to accommodate a "well of death." And it was apparent from Habib Colophon's diary that he was in a rush to find a hiding place for the Chalice. This couldn't be it.

In the dark, with the flashlight beam moving erratically about the chamber, Ryan spoke up. "What was it exactly that the riddle said? Can anyone remember the precise words?"

"It happens I have an eidetic memory." It was Leila. Wadid's flashlight beam darted to her face. She blinked in the sudden light. "Please, Wadid!"

"I'm sorry." He turned it back down onto the floor.

"It said— Seek the prize where darkness rules within the kingdom of the sun. It rests unseen below the timeless home of one who would inhale the blood of the lotus rather than the fragrance of its blossom. . . shall I go on, Ryan?"

"I said I was sorry, Leila. Again, you have proven to be very valuable to us. I thought it said in the timeless home, and so forth. Are you sure it said below? Never mind. I believe you. Let's get out of here."

Moments later they were all on the doorstop, blinking in the sun. Half to himself, Ryan mused out loud, "How do we get below the Tomb of Isadora if there are no loose paving blocks?" Then, more audibly, "C'mon. Let's walk around the building. Maybe there's an opening to a crawlway or basement, below the level of the floor.

There was none. In the frustrated silence after they had carefully inspected all sides of the small building, Leila spoke up again. "While I was checking the geohydrology of the necropolis, I came across, not only references to the Roman well, but a map of the Tomb of Petosiris. They called him Ptosiris. I guess it's the same thing."

"Did you bring it with you?"

"I didn't have to, boss. I told you about my memory. I've got it here." She tapped her pretty head with three fingers like a street magician calling a spirit voice from the ether.

The tomb of Petosiris, or Ptosiris, was just yards away. They all went to the front of it, a fascinating architectural blend of carved stone panels and papyrus columns. Again an unlocked iron gate presented no problem. They were in the antechamber, full of light from the large openings in the front façade. As they headed toward the back chamber, Leila called out. "Be careful. In the middle of the back room there's a deep pit with no railings or other markings."

"Of course," blurted Sharon. "Lots of Egyptian tombs had those pits to trap unsuspecting tomb robbers who might fall into them in the dark and be killed."

They all stopped as it hit them together. The Deceptive Well of Death!

"Wadid! Can you have one of your men bring us a rope or ladder?"

"Of course, Ryan." And to everyone's surprise, he fished a phone out of his safari jacket.

"I didn't think cell phones worked out here," said James.

"It's not a cell phone, Father McAndrew. It's a walkie-talkie. I use it for short distance communication with my men. I can talk to the command car where there's a short wave radio.

The half-tracks were not far away. In moments, two turbaned men came running up with the necessary equipment.

"Leila. Did the map show anything about the substructure below Petosiris?"

"Yes. I can see it clearly. There are a number of rooms and passages. It was apparently where the family members of the High Priest were laid to rest with him."

Bless Wadid Hamza, thought Ryan. His men had brought a wire ladder, the type used by speleologists to explore the underground.

"Let me go first," said Leila, "I've used these before. You can only put one foot on a rung at a time. You put your foot into the first rung, toe first, then the next one from around the ladder towards yourself, heel first. That way you keep the ladder from pushing out leaving you hanging by your hands."

"Did I mention you're getting a bonus when we return, Leila?"

"No. But I'm sure everyone heard you, Ryan." She laughed as she started her descent. Carefully, they all followed her doing the heel and toe thing. Soon they were all on the bottom.

"I'm sure I can figure it out, Leila, but could you repeat the riddle directions without another bonus?"

"Sure, boss, five lengths of a pontiff's crook, then left for another five. The Shining One waits, the prize held safe at his heart within a chamber above four others, where sacred beasts still slumber undisturbed."

"Hold that thought, Leila. James. How long is a pontiff's crook?"

For the sake of the others, James explained. "The shepherd's cane that hooks over at the top is what the pope uses as a staff during ceremonies. I've never measured one but it looks to be about a foot taller than the pope. I'd say it's about seven feet."

"So, straight from the wall we came down, about thirty to forty feet, right?"

No one answered the obvious but followed Ryan as he paced it off. At that point, there was a catacomb entrance to the left. They all followed him into it for another thirty-five feet. The passage continued on into the inky blackness, but Ryan stopped. There were a series of niches in the wall, about seven of them from floor to ceiling. He counted from the bottom. One, two, three, four. The fifth was just at his shoulder height.

"Shine your light here, Wadid."

There they were, the four sons of Horus, Tuamutef with the head of a jackal, Hapi with the head of a baboon, Imsety with the head of a man, and Qebhsenuf, with the head of a falcon.

With his hand shaking and fingers cold with excitement, Ryan reached for Qebhsenuf, but stopped suddenly. They all heard it too, the sound of voices from farther down the dark passage. They all fell silent, barely breathing, as a dim light came slowly into view. It grew closer but not brighter, the shaky beam of a flashlight about to fail. Wadid had extinguished his light as soon as he heard the voices. Now the seven stood as the voices grew louder. Each was aware of his own pulse. The voices grew more distinct but the words didn't seem to make any sense.

"Si, si, si. Eebis, Eebis, Eebis. Bahbone, Bahbone, Cocodrill, Cocodrill."

The voice sounded familiar to Ryan. He was sure of it when he heard the next words, "Do you have any idea where we are?" English with an Italian accent.

"Archbishop Gandolfo?"

"Ryan? Thank God!"

Chapter Forty-Four

Muhammed bin Abdullah's men were exactly what he thought of them, brainless thugs, not afraid to murder in plain sight, if they could run back to the safety of the Alexandria slums where they could comfortably lose themselves amidst the other human refuse. or threaten any witnesses or police informants into frightened silence.

Muhammed had given them substantial walking around money and gave them simple instructions, the only kind they would be capable of understanding.

"Buy clothes unlike the ones you usually wear. but bring your regular clothes with you in plastic grocery bags to put on later. Buy third class train tickets to El Minya. When you arrive, do not check into a hotel. Get a taxi immediately and go to number 14 Said Abo Khlafe. Write it down. It's near the river. There you will meet my friend, Abdul Gemel. You will make no mistake. He has only one eye. I have called ahead to tell him you're coming. He will tell you where to find the little group of priests and professors out in the desert. You will go there, ask no questions, simply leave them dead in the sand, and take the antique cup they have with them. I don't know why it's important, and you don't need to know either. Bring it to me. That's all. Do you understand? If you fail, you will each have only one eye like Abdul Gemel."

They all laughed but looked nervous. He handed each a wad of untraceable Egyptian pounds and sent them out the door, then heaved a sigh of relief. He had done his part. He had called Gemel and told him the men would be coming in a couple of days. He didn't want any progress reports.

"Just send them off into the desert and forget it." That was the end of it. He wanted no more assignments from that shit of an Italian in Rome.

He'd been there once and it made him nervous. Muhhamed bin Abdullah went to find one of his younger wives. Maybe she would be clumsy but he was in a mood to hear squeals of innocent surprise. There was a bulge in his pants as he thought of it.

✝ ✝ ✝

Two of Abdullah's hired guns were brothers— Mustafa and Hakim. The other three were cousins— Said, Ali, and Hussein. All had the same last name, Nouri. They used the money to buy expensive, pinstripe suits, all identical. The store clerk's eyes bugged out when he saw that each wore a shoulder holster but said nothing. They looked dangerous and this was a big sale.

As the five entered the railroad ticket office, all in identical suits, they looked like a group on tour with a cheap nightclub act, except for their luggage. Each carried a plastic, grocery bag full of old clothes. Despite that minor detail, they felt very elegant, too elegant to ride third class, so they all agreed that Hussein would purchase first class tickets on the express. It was waiting when they went out onto the platform. They would be in El Minya the next day.

The Nouri's tilted back the comfortable, coach seats and slept. They hadn't been pumped enough to buy tickets for roomettes, but the trip would take just one night.

They stirred a number of times as the train plummeted through small stations, slowing only slightly, sounding its high-pitched horn to warn people and livestock off the tracks. Over and over, through half open eyes, they saw platform lights shoot by, then darkness as the swaying rhythm of the train continued, clickety-click-click, up the Nile.

Overnight, the trip eventually became uncomfortable. Even a plush, parlor car seat was no substitute for a bed. Near dawn, the conductor finally came through the Nouri's car with a tray, handing out cups of Egyptian coffee. Not long after, he came through again, calling out, "Al Meen-yah, Al Meen-yah," and the train began to slow.

Dawn was just breaking as they came to a stop, with a screech of sandy brakes. The Nouri's stepped carefully down the metal stairs along with a few other passengers. Most had stayed on board, headed for destinations to the south, probably Luxor.

Even at such an early hour, finding a cab was no problem. "Take us to 14 Said Abo Khlafe. You know where it is?"

"Of course. Near the river."

The five Nouri's barely fit into the taxi. The driver argued for a bit about the fare, which he said should be double for a group of this size, but soon gave way when he noted the cruel set of their jaws and the fact that they were willing to pay in advance.

Number 14 was a high wall with an iron gate. The driver pulled up in front and ran around to open the back door for them. Hussein, who had ridden next to the driver, let himself out.

"You will wait for us here," he spoke to the driver who was still helping the others out.

"Of course, of course."

Beside the gate was an intercom with a button. Hussein pushed it. After what seemed a long time, the intercom crackled. "Yes? Who's there?"

"We have come to speak with Mr. Gemel."

"Mr. Gemel is sleeping. Please come back later."

"Tell him we are the Nouri's, sent to see him by Muhammed bin Abdullah."

Silence. "One moment." Another long silence, then, "You're early, but Mr. Gemel will see you." The lock on the gate buzzed and Hussein pushed it open. They all entered the walled garden.

As soon as they heard the gate click shut behind them, they heard the screech of tires as the driver took off in a cloud of piston smoke. The driver didn't need a second fare as much as wanted to see the sun rise the next day. He decided to stay away from the railroad station for a while. There were fares to be had at the hotels and downtown. He would spread the word that some dangerous city people had come to town, all five in new, pinstripe suits. The Nouri's would have some trouble catching taxis in El Minya.

A man in turban, short tunic, and puffed out pants, opened the door to the residence. "Please, gentlemen, follow me." He led them into a large sitting room.

"Someday," said Mustafa, "we will each have a home like this."

"And both eyes, my friends?" It was Abdul Gemel in a bathrobe and slippers, his good eye looking huge behind a thick lens. The other had been frosted to hide the empty socket.

"You are early. I didn't expect you for several more days. Neither Muhammed bin Abdullah nor I appreciate changes in plans. It makes us nervous."

Hussein, though far bigger than the one-eyed man, felt a shiver of apprehension as he answered. Many brutal and powerful men are small in stature. This man was powerful. No question.

"We felt that we cold do a better job if we took a faster train and got started early. If you want us to come back, we can do that."

"With no transportation? I heard your taxi leave. Why did you send him away?"

"We didn't. We told him to wait. He will pay for his bad hearing."

"No he won't. You look like a bunch of clowns. Probably every cab in El Minya will be on the lookout for you. I will have to provide you a vehicle to do your job."

"That is most generous, Abdul."

"Who said that?" Hussein turned, to Hakim. "You will address our host as Mr. Gemel." I apologize for my comrade's rudeness," he added, turning to face the huge eye.

"Let's not waste my time. You are early but I doubt it makes much difference. I will have a driver pull a van out front. He will take you to Tuna el-Gebel. It is in the desert a few hours from here. You know what you are to do. Do it, come back here, and get out of town on the next train. Understood?"

"Yes, sir."

The servant in the puffed out pants led them back to the front door and through the gate. He left them standing on the sidewalk looking like a Marx Brothers skit. Hussein looked as though he might slap one of his cousins on the head at any moment.

A van pulled up and they got in. What was intended as a fun trip, with a simple slaughter, had turned unpleasant. Gemel was hostile, the cab driver had dissed them, and the van had no windows. It was hot, noisy, and there were no seats. They had to sit on the floor. Their new suits were getting dirty. By the time they got to Tuna el-Gebel, two of them were carsick.

"Everybody out. This is it. I'll wait for you here."

Could they trust him? After the cab driver, they were suspicious. They should shoot him and take the van, but then they'd have to deal with Gemel, and eventually, bin Abdullah, back in Alexandria. They had no choice, and as it turned out, no chance, either. If ever there was an uneven match, this was it.

Wadid's men were on them in an instant. The Nouri's might have talked their way out of it, but Hakim pulled his gun. They all went down in a hail of rifle fire. The driver floor-boarded the van throwing up a cloud of sand and dust but only got a few hundred feet. Sniper shots took out all four tires. The van went swooping in circles, the flat tires flopping noisily, unable to carry the van in a straight line. The driver jumped out and started to run. He was doomed whether he ran or not. It made no difference.

The red turbans moved with precision. Six bodies were carried into a partially buried mausoleum. The van was a problem, but not a great one. Both of the half-tracks had towing hooks. The van was towed a few thousand feet into the desert to a spot between a couple of boomerang-shaped dunes where it would be out of site. A few days of sun, wind, and shifting sand, and it might never be seen again. The Necropolis of Khmun welcomed a handful of new residents.

Below ground, the search party never heard a thing. In El Minya, Abdul Gemel would miss his van but never go in search of it. In Alexandria, Muhammed bin Abdullah would grow more content with the passing of each day the exterminators failed to show up. He wouldn't call Gemel.

In Rome, Raffaello D'Agostino was concerned. He got no response when he made some discrete inquiries about Egidio Scarza. One evening, he received a visitor. His wife was in Naples visiting her mother. She took the kids along. The woman at the door smelled like orange blossoms, or was it white ginger?

What great timing, he thought. He had cheated often on his wife, but always when he was away from home. Now she was gone. He didn't mind if she found out. He could slap her around a bit and she would see reason. But the kids. Home was off limits, usually. This was home delivery. He wondered what the woman wanted. She wore a low cut dress, her throat white as an Easter lilly.

"May I come in, Signor D'Agostino?" She smiled when she caught him looking at her breasts. Then they locked eyes, just as he was imagining the rosy nipples that would crown those smooth, white breasts.

"You haven't asked me to come in, Mr. D'Agostino."

"Sì, sì. Per favore. Please come in."

Her question had sent his mind reeling. It had sounded like a musical phrase from a romantic opera, perhaps Verdi. *Perfect*, he thought, *except for a slight speech impediment.*

Chapter Forty-Five

Both parties in the catacombs were relieved to find that the other was not a threat.

"I was looking for you, Father Quinn. I was told you were in Tuna el-Gebel. As my driver and I were coming down this awful passage, I was thinking about the time I was here with Father Colophon so many years ago."

"You were here? I mean, you were down here in this catacomb, Archbishop?"

"Please. Pietro, not my title. It may not even be my title much longer. But that can wait. Let's get out of here. I'm beginning to get nervous. I never liked underground passages, bats, bugs, and I suffer from a bit of claustrophobia."

"Out of here? You don't know why we're down here? And who told you we were in Tuna el-Gebel? Someone in Rome?"

"No. I think I know why you are in Tuna el-Gebel, but not why you are down here. And no, it was not someone in Rome. This will sound strange, but it was a young man in the railroad station in El Minya. He gave me something for you."

The rest of the group listened quietly, hardly breathing. They had been about to make the find of the millennium, knew that priests from Rome were possible adversaries, and that this man was about as high in the Church as one could rise, except for Cardinal or Pope.

"I don't know the rest of you, except Father McAndrew and Dr. Corbet. That is you, two, isn't it? It's dark in here."

"Yes, your Excellency. We met in New York."

"What is it you have for me, Pietro?"

"Something very important, maybe as important as all of Rome. Perhaps a reason why I may not survive this trip. But I am prepared. Here."

The archbishop handed over the medallion, his hand relieved, at last, of its grip on the metal disk. Ryan took it. He asked Wadid to shine his flashlight into his palm.

Everyone gasped. They had all poured over Megyn's photos from the cave in Gebel al-Naqlun. James recognized it, not only from that scratched over image, but as a miniature of the Gislebertus sculpture atop a column in the Cathedral in Autun. It was Judas Iscariot in the act of being hanged from a tree by two winged figures. Angels? The gospels implied that Judas had hanged himself in remorse. The Gislebertus sculpture, and this medallion, suggested he had perhaps been executed by angels. *Do this in memory of Me,* thought James.

The heat and darkness had become unbearable. The cab driver's flashlight had dimmed to nothing, and finally gone out. Perhaps it was the heat and all of them consuming the oxygen, but Ryan thought he heard something coming from farther down the passage.

"Are there bats down here?" asked Sharon. Her voice was calm. She wasn't afraid of bats. Apparently only the archbishop was bothered by the thought of the creatures.

"Perhaps some of the ibis mummies are coming to life," said a voice in the dark. It was Bedu. He was joking, but not entirely comfortable with the idea, himself. Now they all listened. The fluttering had grown louder. With one flashlight dead and the others beginning to grow dim, they had a problem. They were too close to stop, but searching the crypt in the dark would be difficult.

"I've got candles," said Leila. "It's an old habit from my cave exploring days. I never go underground without a supply. The thing about old technology is that you can depend on it." She handed candles around to everyone.

"What about matches?" said Bedu. Leila gave him a jab in the ribs.

The fluttering noise was growing louder. Now they could feel a breeze coming from down the tunnel. Someone, or something, was coming. Megyn had heard that noise before, and had felt that breeze. *Angels!* She didn't say it out loud.

She began to dread the idea of having another sexual hallucination right here, surrounded by her friends. "I'll go back to the ladder and wait for you. This is making me nervous."

"No," said Ryan, "I don't want us to become separated."

The eight of them, including the Nuncio and his driver, were now huddled together in the cramped passage. They all held unlit candles like useless, wax spears.

Ryan was anxious to proceed with the mission. He handed his candle to Sharon, then reached with both hands for the falcon-headed, canopic jar, Qebhsenuf, son of Horus.

The base of the jar made a grinding sound across the sandy shelf as he carefully pulled it to the edge. From there, he lifted it gingerly and brought it down to his chest. It felt warm.

"James, would you please lift the lid?"

James handed his candle to the Archbishop and reached for it with both hands. The fluttering sound from down the tunnel was growing louder, and the breeze stronger.

Slowly, ceremoniously, he lifted the falcon head.

There it was, the Holy Grail, the Goblet of the Last Supper, the Cup that had once touched the Lips of Jesus, the Chalice of the New Covenant!

All at once the candles lighted by themselves. The flames played across the faces of the group as they peered in wonder at the exposed rim of the Goblet.

The breeze had grown strong now, but the candles didn't flicker. A low chant arose, not in their ears, but as though from within their own heads . No one said anything but all of them, even the cab driver, knelt in the dust.

Archbishop Pietro Gandolfo, Papal Nuncio to His Holiness, the Pope, began to sob, "Forgive me, Lord. I was ambitious and lost my way. It was my fault, my fault, my own most grievous fault."

Chapter Forty-Six

When James replaced the falcon lid on the canopic jar, the candles suddenly extinguished themselves. The group was in complete darkness again, and silence. The sound of chanting that had filled their heads, vanished as suddenly as it had come.

Ryan's voice broke the silence. "Leila. You said you had some matches. Now would be a great time to produce them."

"Right here, boss." An air of levity was needed and Leila supplied it in the dark. To everyone's relief she produced the promised matches and, one by one, relit the candles. Ryan decided to follow Gandolfo's route back to the exit rather than risk a climb up the wire ladder with the Chalice. The candles provided more than enough light for the group to find their way through the tunnels.

Gandolfo's cab driver led the way back. As they moved slowly, in single file, through the winding, mummy-lined passages, it struck Ryan that the group had assumed both the mood and appearance of a religious, candlelight procession. *What could be more appropriate?*

The Archbishop, though just one of nine in the procession, was easily identified by the bobbing of his candle as he limped down the tunnel, still bearing the scar dealt him for his cowardice so many years ago at the hand of a vengeful angel.

The sunlight was overwhelming as they emerged from the catacomb, Ryan clutching the canopic jar to his chest, the others encircling him as they walked.

Pietro Gandolfo paid the cab driver handsomely, and told him he would not be returning to El Minya with him. The driver seemed reluctant to leave. He had been witness to something he did not understand but had been deeply moved. He would speak of it only to close friends, but certainly never forget it.

From a pocket in his vest, Wadid fished out his walkie-talkie. In moments, the expedition vehicles came creaking and clanking into view. Wadid spoke briefly to the driver of the Rommel Command Car. He nodded solemnly and returned to the group.

"Apparently, there were some dumb militants sent here to intercept us. My guard took care of them. We will not be returning with my people. They have radio'd for a couple of limousines. Until they arrive, my men will prepare tea and biscuits.

Sharon gazed at Ryan, a mix of emotions raging within her. What happened in the catacombs threatened to change everything. She knew she had fallen in love with a priest. Now he stood looking out into the desert as though peering into Eternity. Had she lost him to his God? Had she ever had a chance with him at all? How could she compete with the Almighty?

Yes. She, too, had felt it, there in the catacombs. They were not just Egyptologists ecstatically involved in the wonder of a magnificent discovery. They had been in the presence of something far beyond that. Now, the man she loved was clutching something to his chest that she did not understand. And yet, she, too, felt reverence for that object she could not find within her intellect to comprehend. She had watched the crippled, old archbishop grovel in the dust pleading for forgiveness, and the hardened tomb robber, Wadid Hamza, grow subservient, anxious to serve in whatever way he could.

Ryan never let go of the canopic jar as they sat around the burning logs where one of Wadid's men was brewing tea in a brass kettle. Bedu and Leila sat together. So did James and Megyn. Only Sharon, Wadid, and Ryan, sat without partners.

Ryan is not alone, thought Sharon. *He is clutching his heart's devotion to his chest, and Wadid has a wife waiting for him at home. Only I am alone.* She felt a tear roll down her cheek. No one noticed.

After such a long and arduous trip in half-tracks across the desert, it was amazing how quickly two limousines could make the trip from El Minya to the Necropolis of Khmun. Wadid sent the half-tracks on their way. He knew the fate of the men who had been sent to assault them, but didn't share that information with the others. The bullet riddled van lay out of site behind a dune as the limousines sped back towards El Minya. Wadid was sure there would be more assassins to deal with sooner or later. He had no idea when, or how many. It would be no problem. He knew how to take care of that sort of thing.

Chapter Forty-Seven

The papal jet still sat in quiet dignity on the tarmac at Borg al Arab airport in Alexandria. The pilot-priests continued to enjoy the luxury of the El-Salamiek Palace Hotel. They had not heard from the Nuncio in days. They did not question his absence. Life was too pleasant. Despite their special training and expertise, in Rome they were little more than lowly, service personnel, limousine drivers with wings. In Alexandria, they were the honored representatives of His Holiness, the Pope. As such, they were extended every possible courtesy by the hotel staff, particularly the fawning clerk at the front desk.

"Good morning your graces. — Good evening your graces. — Are your rooms comfortable? — Did you enjoy the fruit baskets? — Our pleasure. — Have you received word from his Excellency, the Nuncio? — Of course, I'll be sure to let you know if he contacts the hotel."

In El Minya, installed once more in the luxurious guesthouse of Wadid Hamza, Pietro Gandolfo tried to reach the pilots by telephone. After a barrage of obsequious blather from the clerk, he was put through to their room.

"Father Stephen, I have had a change in plans. I would like you to fly to El Minya to pick me up. Is that a problem?"

"Of course not, Excellency. We have kept the plane fueled and ready.

Reverend Stephen Cullen, S.J. was an American who joined the Jesuit Order after a career in the US military. He had been a Strategic Air Command pilot, flying a BI-B bomber until his early retirement. He was happy with his decision to become a priest, but did regret the fact that the B-2 Stealth had become part of the SAC fleet after he left. Flying one of those would have been an airman's dream.

"Do you know anything about the airport at El Minya, your Excellency? Never mind. We have aeronautical maps that will tell us everything we need to know. Is there a number where you can be reached so we can inform you of our arrival time?"

"I'm afraid not. There will be a limousine at the airport when you arrive. My host will be in contact with the officials at the airport and will be aware of your arrival time. Understood?"

"Of course, Excellency. We will lift off in the morning and should be in El Minya before noon."

"Excellent." Then, with an impish grin, he added, "Please convey my blessings to the clerk at the front desk, and ask him to take no messages for any of us until we return to Alexandria."

The request seemed a strange one but a priest does not question the Papal Nuncio. "Of course, Excellency."

Pietro Gandolfo had no intentions of heading back to Alexandria, but no need to mention that. He put down the phone in Wadid's library and returned to the guesthouse where he found the others sitting about in brittle silence. Ryan had released his grip on the canopic jar, but only to set it on a table where he and the rest could see it. He did not lift the falcon head again. He had no intention of doing so until he felt he and the others could cope with the possible repetition of supernatural events like those they had experienced in the catacombs.

Pietro Gandolfo spoke directly to Ryan. "I suspect you will not be sleeping tonight, my friend. Here, take this seat." He pulled over a leather, Ekornes, recliner. "At least you can push back and doze within site of the jar."

"Thank you, Excellency."

"Though I asked you earlier to dispense with that title, now I demand that you stop. It is undeserved, and now sounds ridiculous to me. Please, Ryan. I am Pietro, a sinner who deserves no worldly respect, but hopes to regain the respect of the Almighty if given time to earn it."

"You have my respect, Archbishop. Respect is a human measure of value. You have not lost that in my eyes, though I think we have a lot to discuss."

"You are certainly right about that, my friend. Thank you." He pulled a straight back chair up close to Ryan who was now leaning back in the leather chair, one eye always on the ceramic effigy of Qebhsenuf, Son of Horus.

It would be a long night. No one made a move to retire. Only Wadid left to sleep with his wife and wonder about life. Bedu sat beside Leila, his arm circling her shoulders. James sat with Megyn, who persisted in looking incredibly beautiful, despite all the activity, mental and physical. Sharon sat alone, her eyes fixed on Ryan, the man she loved, but to whom she had little hope of being anything more than a mortal woman caught up in an unfair competition with God.

"I have spoken to the pilots in Alexandria," said Gandolfo. The plane will be here in the morning. I have also spoken with Mr. Hamza. He, in turn, spoke with the authorities and said we would be leaving the country with an artifact, an insignificant canopic jar from Tuna el-Gebel. He assured them that it would be returned to Egypt, unharmed, within a matter of weeks. He was transferred to the private line of the Secretary of Antiquities, Zahi Hawass. Hawass was particularly concerned, since it was at Tuna el-Gebel that he had done his first official archaeological work. In the end, however, he agreed to our host's request. Hawass loves Egypt, its artifacts, and the Egyptian museums that display it's proud history for all to see. God only knows what Wadid promised him in the way of museum donations to seal the bargain."

☥ ☥ ☥

"Borg al Arab, this is Ichthus One ready for take off."

"Ichthus One, you are cleared for take off. Say hello to Heaven for us."

"We will, Borg al Arab, Insha'Allah."

With the extra kick of dense, sea air, the Falcon 2000 EX's twin Pratt & Whitney engines were capable of delivering incredible thrust. The sleek jet hurtled down the runway and, at about the mid-point, no farther, yanked itself into the sky and soared out over the Mediterranean. In a wide, climbing arc, it circled back over Alexandria, the city already little more than a three-dimensional map below. The papal crest on the tail of the holy sky-fish glowed red and gold in the morning sun as the priests pointed the plane's nose south, up the Nile. The pyramids on the Giza plateau stood out like game board pieces in the low morning sun. White felucca sails dotted the mighty river in a string that disappeared at the horizon.

Deserts, mountains, open plains, and wetlands are only visible one at a time, as separate worlds. From the air, Egypt's brown landscape is a broad continuum with only a narrow ribbon to divide it, the twin floodplains of the Nile, the shining river at its middle.

The airport at El Minya was more than adequate. The runway, one hundred, twenty-eight feet above sea level, is almost two miles long. Traveling at just below the speed of sound, the Falcon was over the city within an hour.

The wheels gave a chirp and puff of smoke as Ichthus One touched down. The muezzin were still calling the faithful to prayer from their minarets. At one time, it took a powerful voice to blanket a city so all could hear. Now even the poorest communities broadcast their devotional messages from loudspeakers, but still not synchronized. They create a melodic cascade, one upon the next, mingled with the morning cries of roosters and barking dogs. The expression of religious tradition, regardless of one's own beliefs, is unifying. It is a declaration of man's brotherhood and insignificance before the Almighty.

As Ichthus One reversed thrust at the end of the runway, the brute force of its jets roared across a city accustomed to the gentler, medieval sounds of livestock and wagon wheels.

A black limousine waited on the tarmac, well away from the terminal building, as the jet approached slowly, engines whining. Two men stepped out of the car to greet the pilots. One was Archbishop Pietro Gandolfo. The other was Nazeer Gayeb, Pope Shenouda, Patriarch of Coptic Christianity. He had anticipated the events that were now taking place, and had taken the train from Alexandria. This time he had taken the overnight express, forgoing the pleasures of third class. This was a special occasion.

Chapter Forty-Eight

Now they were nine, seated around the conference table in Wadid's library, three Roman Catholic priests, three beautiful, brilliant, young women, three Coptic Christians, one the leader of the Orthodoxy, another just a scholar without portfolio, the third, a very rich tomb robber. The two pilots had been escorted to the main house where they were being entertained by a squadron of servants with exotic teas and sweet cakes. Ryan kept one hand on the canopic jar that sat on the conference table in front of him.

Archbishop Gandolfo spoke to his friend, the Patriarch. "We have the prize in our possession, your Holiness. He did a typical Italian flip of his chin toward the falcon headed jar. And now, Ryan, I suggest you remove the lid. We cannot leave it closed forever."

Ryan was hesitant, but despite the change in relationships, he was, by reflex, inclined to follow the orders of an archbishop. Hesitantly, he grasped the falcon head with both hands and lifted it slowly.

No choruses of angels. No fluttering of wings. Everyone breathed more easily as the rim of the chalice appeared. It was only then that Ryan remembered that he had placed the medallion in his pocket. Hastily he felt for it. He breathed a sigh of relief as he took it out and placed it on the table.

Now he stood and carefully took hold of the goblet. He pulled it up and out of its resting place. Almost as during the consecration at Mass, he held the Chalice high so all could see it. Everyone stood.

"Insert the medallion where it belongs," said Gandolfo.

Again, obediently, Ryan placed the Chalice on the table and picked up the medallion. He had not noted before that it had an oddly shaped nick in its perimeter. He found that the medallion fit perfectly into the place from which it had been pried, so long ago, by Habib Colophon. It was complete again, the goblet fashioned two thousand years earlier to the exact specifications laid out for a silversmith by Jesus of Nazareth.

They all stared at the goblet. It was magnificent, miraculously untarnished after millennia, its rim adorned with eight medallions, each representing a sacrament intended to constitute the core of Christian ritual and belief, now with the eighth sacrament represented for all to see, mortal sacrifice depicted by the hanging of Judas Iscariot with the help of two angels.

As Ryan withdrew his hands from the goblet, he noticed something he had not before, nor had anyone else, even in the photographs taken by Megyn in the cavern at Gebel al-Naqlun. It was the stem of the Chalice. It was not a simple stem, nor even one that might have been an afterthought, simply to provide a place for Jesus to hold it. It was very complex, two columns wrapped around one another, each composed of small, iridescent spheres of different shades.

Leila was the first to recognize what they were looking at. She gave a small gasp. "It's the DNA molecule!"

James felt the air go out of his lungs. Of course! He saw it too. Though a priest most of his life, he had always had a nagging thought lurking at the edge of his faith. Why had Christ not left a sign, something physical, to prove to doubters such as he, that He had been more than a man, an entity beyond the limitations of time and space? And now, before his very eyes, here it was. Christ had left the symbol of something undreamed of in His time, something that would not be recognized by a living soul for thousands of years to come, and then, only by humans who had finally caught up with the technology that Christ understood even as he walked across the surface of the Sea of Galilee.

Each person in the room dealt differently with the astounding revelation of divine precognition before them. None were more profoundly moved than Archbishop Pietro Gandolfo. As one of a handful of men in history privy to the secrets of the Stanza Speciale, he was aware of the Eighth Sacrament, of the unique relationship between Christ and Judas Iscariot, and of the bizarre fact that, for two thousand years, every pope had been executed in secret by heaven-sent angels. He had shared both the knowledge, and sin, of Habib Colophon, the denial of God's will in favor of the practical wishes of Peter's successors. Through his silence he had achieved one of the highest posts within the Roman Catholic Church but tossed at night with the guilty realization that it was his ambitious nature that had elevated him. He had joined with the world in its castigation of Judas Iscariot, perhaps the Lord's best friend. He truly believed that Peter had chosen the right path for the survival of Christ's Church in an imperfect world, but who was he to say? So he and Colophon, along with others through the centuries, made the choice to live with power, wealth— and guilt.

Until its theft during the sacking of Rome, the Chalice had rested safely atop its pedestal in the Vatican. Popes and other trusted church officials had seen it. A monk in the desert at Gebel al-Naqlun had seen it. And yet, none of them had seen it with the eyes of the 21ˢᵗ Century. Everyone had focused on the rim of the Chalice, on the medallions, and especially the medallion depicting the hanging of Judas. No one had given the stem of the Chalice any attention. Even if they had, it would have been with a jeweler's eye, not that of a 21st Century geneticist.

While everyone stood about, with no idea of what to do next, the pilots returned. It was a strange scene, nine brilliant men and women, standing around a conference table in silence, mesmerized by a headless canopic jar, its falcon lid to one side, and a beautiful goblet to the other.

Father Stephen Cullen, S.J., the jet captain, cleared his throat. Standing beside him was his copilot, Father Franco Pirelli, S.J., former Collonnello in the Aeronautica Militare, the Italian Air Force, whose last duty had been as first officer at the controls of a Panavia Tornado.

Everyone looked up as Stephen Cullen cleared his throat again. "I was told, Archbishop, that our mission was urgent and to be prepared for departure at any moment. Is that still the case?"

Pietro shook his head in an effort to clear it. "Yes. Yes. Even more so than I had thought when I spoke to you. When can we leave?"

"We fueled up in Alexandria. After such a short flight we can leave at any time. To where, Excellency?"

Ryan whispered something in Pietro's ear. He turned again to the pilot. "Just a moment, Father. Let me speak to Father Quinn."

Ryan and Pietro went to one of the carrels at the side of the library where they sat for a moment.

"There's no time to explain right now," said Ryan. "I'll explain my plans in more detail later, but I would like to take the Chalice to Los Alamos, New Mexico."

Pietro was no longer able to express surprise at anything. "Isn't that where they designed the first Atomic Bomb?"

"Yes, but that has nothing to do with it. Among Chalice Corporation's assets is a state of the art testing laboratory in Los Alamos. We have access there to the world's most powerful computer, and have been asked to verify the authenticity of various artifacts over the years, including the Shroud of Turin. I would like to perform some tests on the Chalice if you agree. The problem is, I'm not sure if we can get to New Mexico in secret, considering the probability that prying eyes will be following our movements, and perhaps trying to interrupt them."

Pietro nodded. He was entering Ryan's world— a technical world beyond his understanding. He beckoned the pilots to join them.

"We have a delicate problem, gentlemen, perhaps an impossible request. Is it possible to fly halfway around the word in secret?"

Father Cullen's response startled them, even his copilot. "No problem, Excellency. It's what I did for a living before I joined the priesthood."

Father Cullen's response put Ryan's concerns to rest. He didn't understand how the pilot expected to accomplish a secret flight from El Minya, Egypt, to Los Alamos, New Mexico, but the man had the assured air of one who had delivered the impossible before.

Wadid Hamza and Pope Shenouda, regretfully recused themselves from the ongoing adventure. Wadid could not leave his estate. Enemies were always on the lookout to sack his kingdom and perhaps even run away with his wife. Pope Shenouda could not leave millions of followers without the assurance of their leader occupying his seat in Alexandria.

The others threw a few things into bags. It was no problem. They had been packing and unpacking for days. They still didn't know where they were going, but if Ryan was in the lead, they would follow. He had carefully placed the Chalice back into the canopic jar and replaced the falcon head of Qebhsenuf.

Wadid was almost in tears as he ushered his new friends into two limousines he had ordered brought to the guest house. He loved adventure, and knew that this one might just be entering its most interesting and dramatic phase.

Pope Shenouda helped his limping old friend into one of the cars and kissed him on the cheek. "We are really all one, are we not, my friend?"

"I will miss you, Nazeer. Who knows if I shall come this way again?"

Minutes after the limousines arrived at El Minya airport, Ichthus One's jet fans were turning. A few more minutes, and it was sitting at the south end of the north-south runway, its powerful engines whining loudly. Except for the two priests up front, no one in the world knew where it was headed. Ryan had told his crew, New Mexico, but that was all he knew. In fact, they would touch down in a number of places with very strange names. The first stop would be Decimomannu, for fuel, then on to Kangerlussuaq, to spend the night.

"Ichthus One, you are cleared for take off. Have a nice flight, Insha'Allah."

The whine of the two engines grew until it became a deafening roar. The holy sky-fish hurtled north down the runway, then up into the sky. Moments later, it made a thirty-degree turn to the west above the desert, headed toward the Mediterranean, and on to Decimomanno Airfield in Sardinia.

The planned stops had one thing in common. At one time or another, each had been home to Colonel Stephen Cullen. All were US Strategic Air Command bases, accustomed to secret arrivals and departures, still manned by old friends of Father Cullen, always ready to extend hometown courtesies to old comrades, even if they had swapped Air Force blue for Jesuit black.

The cabin was quiet as the sleek jet sliced through the sky, a long, white, condensation trail across the heavens behind it. The plush, leather seats were not beds, but the next best thing. All but the pilots were asleep. Ryan had finally let go of the canopic jar. It wasn't going anywhere without the rest of them.

Leila and Bedu slept, her head on his shoulder, one leg across his. They no longer made any pretense about their relationship. James sat with the Archbishop, their heads nodding forward, then back, as they fought slumber at first. Megyn sat with Sharon, both so slender there might have been room for a third. While they dozed, Ryan placed the canopic jar carefully between them. He sat upright in the jump seat against the forward bulkhead.

No one stirred as they circled Decimomannu, and only came to drowsy, semi-awareness as they touched down. This would be a very short stop to take on fuel and a few moments for Father Cullen to greet a a handful of friends on the tarmac and walk around the aircraft to make a routine safety inspection.

Soon they were aloft again, following an approved, secret, military, flight plan across France and Ireland. After that, Father Cullen advised his copilot to sleep if he could. This leg would be long, and far from commercial routes. They would be crossing the North Atlantic, then the Greenland Ice Cap, just below the Arctic Circle, finally setting down at the eastern end of Sondrestrom Fiord, at Kangerlussuaq Airfield.

Sharon was restless and kept getting up to look out the window above Ryan's jump seat. She had to lean across him. He feigned sleep, but was acutely aware of her. He thought he could sense the warmth of her body. He could smell the soap she had used to wash her hair back in Egypt.

There was little to see from the windows. Night had fallen. The ocean below, was black. Then suddenly, a fiery emerald flowed into view. It was an iceberg, lit from the side by the low, northern sun. It sat amidst the black velvet of the ocean, glowing as though with inner fire. Sharon sucked in her breath at the magnificence of it. She could not help herself. She shook Ryan's shoulder.

"Look. Look, quickly, before it's gone." He had not been asleep and needed no time to recover. For a moment they were one in mind, body, and soul. To look out of the window, he had risen within the circle of her arms and squeezed his head in beside hers. Their cheeks were against one another's, both their noses pressed to the inner, plastic windowpane. He was enveloped both by the beauty of the sight below, and by the closeness of this woman who seemed to appreciate the world's beauties as much as he. She was the soul mate he had always longed for. Now she was here, and it was too late. Sharon felt the same, as they crouched at the window, pressed together. Without thinking, she heard herself whispering into his ear, "I love you, Ryan."

He didn't answer. Seconds went by, then minutes, neither saying a word, nor moving. Ryan stayed within the circle of Sharon's arms, his cheek pressed to hers, as the glowing emerald, thirty thousand feet below drifted slowly out of sight. Now nothing but an expanse of black filled the world outside the window. And still, they did not move.

"I love you, too, Sharon."

Ichthus One was over the Greenland Ice Cap. Nothing, now, but white lay below. But then, a bright, blue river of liquid sapphire came into view. Megyn was staring out the window, now, calling to the others. It had never occurred to her, or the rest, that there could be a liquid river across a landscape of solid ice. But there it was, branches reaching out from a main course that emptied into an irregularly shaped lake, brighter than anyone had ever seen on dry land. The sun was high and lit the improbable river, a molten gem beyond even the imagination of Carl Fabergé.

Ryan and Sharon sat together in silence. The mental confusion was over. It remained now for them to deal with something not of their design, but beyond their ability to dismiss.

Ichthus One flew out over the edge of Baffin Bay, then made a broad circle and descended slowly as it moved east-by-north-east up the fjord, back toward the Ice Cap. They could see the frothy, gray water of the Wattson River rushing past the airstrip as they floated lower and lower, finally touching down with a puff of rubber smoke.

Winter is brutal in Kangerlussuaq. Summer is ideal. Wildflowers abound, amid puffy blankets of arctic snow grass. Herds of shaggy muskox graze, unmindful of the nearby human activity. Caribou stand and stare at the noisy planes that come and go but seem never to pose any threat.

The village of Kangerlussuaq is much like most high-latitude, Danish settlements. But with financial support from the US military, this one supports a well-equipped airport. That has led to two unusual aspects to this tiny settlement, a tourist hotel for adventurers anxious to experience the phenomena of life so close to the Arctic Circle, and research laboratories run by various universities, anxious to do the same. Near the maintenance hangers, but far enough from the tarmac to permit some semblance of peace and quiet, there is a long, modular structure built by the US Air Force to house pilots, crews, and military research personnel. It provides snug, well-heated rooms, and a dining hall. It even has a hotel-style, front desk to check airmen in and out.

The crew and passengers of Ichthus One were given five rooms. Ryan, James, the Archbishop, and the canopic jar, were given one room. The two Jesuit pilots were given another. Megyn and Sharon shared a third. Leila and Bedu each had a room. Too many priests aboard to allow conspicuous cohabitation.

The rooms all had black, pull-down, window shades. Pilots sleep at various times of the day. At Kangerlussuaq, summer nights are never completely dark, still a pinkish twilight on the land, even at midnight. Sharon went to the window and pulled up the shade. Her mind was on

Ryan a few doors down. She stared out at the landscape, a typical glacial outwash mix of gray sand and small boulders. Absent mindedly, she watched an arctic fox raiding a pile of refuse out back. Megyn watched her standing motionless at the window.

"You're in love with him, aren't you?"

"Is it that obvious?" Sharon answered without turning.

"I'm afraid it is. The good and bad news is, I think he's in love with you, too."

Sharon whirled around. "He even told me so. But as you said, "good news and bad news." He also told me we could never be lovers. He had made a vow to God. The awful part is, I don't think I would love him as much as I do, if he didn't take such a vow seriously."

"You do have a problem. I have one, too, but I don't think I'm prepared to tell anyone about it."

"You mean, young boys?"

Megyn jumped off the bed in surprise. "You know?"

"Everyone knows, Megyn. We all think we lead such secret lives, but they're really not that secret at all. I'll bet James thinks none of us know he's gay."

Megyn laughed. "I thought I was the only one who suspected."

The two young women, beautiful, sexy, and yet strangely innocent, despite their personal problems and brilliant intellects, began to laugh like naughty children. Except for the walls and door, sound-proofed to permit flyers to rest beside a busy airstrip, their laughter would have been a strange sound bouncing across the glacial landscape that had grown pink and shadowless.

"Can I tell you another secret, Megyn? Or do you already know that this rapidly aging Jewish maiden is a virgin?"

"What?"

Sharon began to blush. "It's true. I've been saving myself for the right man. What a mess. I finally find the right man, and he's a Catholic priest, one who takes his vows seriously."

Megyn let out a burst of laughter. "No wonder you keep popping Twinkies. They're penis substitutes. You're a nut case. I guess it's much too late for me to say I hope you get over this and find the right man." She was choking with laughter. Then Sharon joined in and they both rocked with uncontrolled mirth.

Between gasps, Sharon managed to choke out, "And I suppose it's much too late for me to say, I hope you find the right boy! Have a Twinkie!"

That sent them into more spasms, laughing and choking so hard it seemed certain someone would hear them, sound-proofing or not. Finally the laughing was replaced with sporadic giggle spells as the two, now probably best friends, undressed and slid into the twin beds.

After a few moments, Sharon got up. She'd forgotten to pull the window shade back down. She slept naked. As Megyn watched her, she was fascinated by the slender beauty of Sharon's body, with firm, round breasts, a wasp waist, and rounded, youthful buttocks. *Poor Ryan*, she thought. *Men would kill for that.*

Down the hall, Pietro Gandolfo kept his roommates wide-eyed and tossing with his snoring. Ryan's thoughts were a torment anyhow, so it made little difference. He watched the canopic jar on the dresser near his bed.

At four AM, the sky still pink, Ichthus One was back on the runway, engines roaring as it hurtled east, and up into the arctic air toward Baffin Bay. Next stop, Offutt Field, Nebraska.

Chapter Forty-Nine

If anyone looked skyward from a fishing boat on Hudson Bay, or from a skiff out in the marshes of the Canadian Tundra, they would never have suspected that the dot, at the head of the long con trail, was a craft carrying five priests, three gorgeous Egyptologists, a Coptic Christian, and the Chalice from which Jesus Christ had once taken a sip of His own blood. Ichthus One, at near the speed of sound, was headed for the New World, with the Cup of the New Testament, to Los Alamos, birthplace of the New Physics, and the Atomic Age.

The twin engine, Falcon 2000EX, can fly three thousand, eight hundred miles, without re-fueling. To be safe, Father Cullen had elected to touch down in Nebraska for fuel. The layover was short. They were aloft again in less than an hour. Considering the length of the entire flight, the leg to New Mexico would be short. There were a number of possible landing places, but Ryan had been anxious to make as few stops as possible in populated areas, military or not.

The first nuclear detonation was not at Los Alamos. It was much farther to the south. But it was at Los Alamos they had turned theoretical physics into reality, and assembled the chain reaction test device. Los Alamos was chosen by Dr. J. Robert Oppenheimer to carry on the secret work because of its isolation. It had been an exclusive boy's ranch school before, far from regular travel routes when even the rest of New Mexico might have been considered wilderness.

Los Alamos Scientific Laboratory was a helter-skelter array of wooden shacks and barracks, hastily assembled on the flank of the extinct Jemez volcano. The crude laboratories and test facilities sat on long, sloping mesas, separated from one another by deep canyons, cut over eons by streams that ran, like points of a star, from the core of the volcano.

After almost seventy years, the rugged terrain remains the same but the shacks and barracks have been replaced with ultra-modern structures. One large one houses the world's fastest computer. The entire research complex is now known as Los Alamos National Laboratory. Despite the vital nature of its work, it fights for existence, tarred by the image of its initial mission, detested by those who have forgotten that it may have been the most important factor in saving the world from tyranny.

Thirty years ago, in an effort to soften its public relations image, the Lab instituted a program to share its scientific expertise with small businesses clever enough to take advantage of the offer. Ryan Quinn had been one of those. He founded Calix Corporation, a subsidiary of Chalice, to provide the high-tech capability to perform non-destructive tests on archaeological artifacts. The key to its unique capability was its access to the non-classified "partition" of the Lab's giant computer.

With a bit of dust from the interior of a sarcophagus, a whiff of air from a long-sealed vial, or a cuticle from the mummified hand of an ancient ruler, Calix technicians could generate volumes of verifiable ancient history. They could figure out what people wore, what they ate, to whom they were related, even perhaps, whom they had kissed, or even shaken hands with, thousands of years ago. It was a matter of chromatography, spectrometry, neutron activation, magnetic resonance imaging, bioluminescent analysis, and a host of other, high-tech, tools and procedures.

Using Calix Corporation's proprietary software, the data could now be "crunched" in "Roadrunner," Los Alamos' most recently developed hybrid supercomputer, capable of performing a thousand, trillion calculations per second. Its refrigeration units alone would aircondition five theaters the size of Radio City Music Hall. Thanks to the Los Alamos "technical outreach" program, Calix could offer formerly impossible analyses, and charge clients handsomely for its services.

It provided archaeological expertise in support of its high tech capabilities, making it a unique operation. It had also developed special specimen handling equipment to minimize contamination. One device it called, "Ammit," allowed small objects to be suspended in a crossfire of computer-controlled air jets. Ryan had named it after the mythical,

Egyptian beast, known as the gobbler, the beast that would devour the heart of the deceased if it did not prove to be lighter than a feather.

The Los Alamos airstrip lies on one of the narrow, sloping mesas that radiate from the volcano's core. The east end of the runway is a precipice that drops hundreds of feet to the canyon floor. There are similar drops on both sides of the runway, which is not very long. Landing is tricky business with little room for error. Crosswinds can be deadly.

Ryan asked the pilots to radio ahead for a Calix van to meet them. It was waiting at the west end of the strip when Ichthus One let out its mighty, reverse thrust roar to keep from over-running the short runway that ends at a cyclone fence just yards from a residential community. Space is too scarce on the slender mesas of Los Alamos to waste an inch.

East Road parallels the Los Alamos runway. It turns into Trinity Drive as it enters town. At that point a road sign says, "The Churches of Los Alamos Welcome You."

Trinity Drive was named in commemoration of the first nuclear test in the New Mexico desert. The name for the test, in turn, was chosen by scientist, J. Robert Oppenheimer, from a line in a poem by 16th Century poet, John Donne. Oppenhiemer liked to quote poetry as he watched the nuclear explosions he helped create.

Undoubtedly coincidental, but strange connections raced through Ryan's head as they drove. Here in the birthplace of the "New Physics," he and his comrades were carrying the Chalice of the New Testament, along Trinity Drive, to see if modern science would support Christ's claim to being part of the Big Trinity. New Genetics might play a part. Was this to be God's lesson to an increasingly arrogant and godless 21st Century?

Sharon, sitting close beside him, wondered what was going through his head. The others just stared out the windows. There was nothing spectacular to see, but this was a place that had changed history. It looked disarmingly benign. They passed neat, middle class houses with well-trimmed lawns, streets posted with incredibly low speed limits, 5 MPH in one case, and signs alerting drivers to watch for children at play.

They drove directly to the Calix lab where they were met by Chief Scientist, Dr. Gary Archer. Without ceremony, Ryan and Sharon transferred the canopic jar, and the parcel containing the old papyrus, to the company's walk-in safe. They left them there on a shelf, amidst a variety of other treasures awaiting analysis. There were bones, bits of pottery, leather-bound volumes, fossil fish, and lots of other stuff, too small or ill-defined to easily identify. After making sure the door was closed, and the time lock set for the morning, Ryan and Sharon rejoined the others in the limousine.

Calix, Inc. kept a comfortable guesthouse for visiting clients in the village of Los Alamos. It was not set up for large groups. Sharon, Ryan, James, and Pietro would stay there. The others were given rooms at a nearby motel. They planned to meet for dinner at the "Fabulous 50's Diner." Except for Pietro, everyone was anxious for hamburgers, French fries, and Bar BQ. Sharon had run out of Twinkies, but didn't want to mention it in public, especially in front of Megyn.

As expected, dinner was fun. Even Pietro had to admit that Bar BQ is not really offensive to the sophisticated Roman palate.

Everything was within walking distance, Calix, the guesthouse, the motel, and the restaurant. Ryan offered to walk Sharon to a grocery store. No one had said anything but he had not seen her pop a Twinkie since Greenland. He suspected she needed to stock up. She welcomed the chance to be alone with him.

If Los Alamos looks like average America during the day, it is magic after dark. The stars, in a jet black sky, are bright pinholes that fight for identity with the lights of Santa Fe, on the horizon forty miles away. And then, there's the mysterious trail of lights along the rim of the next canyon. They mark the length of LAMPF, the Lab's linear particle accelerator.

With the stars bright overhead and the summer evening chilly, they walked along in silence for a long time. Ryan finally broke the spell.

"You know this can never be, Sharon."

"I know no such thing, big mouth! I love you and you love me. What is more sacred than that? We both read Habib's notes and the papyrus. It's not a matter of God versus woman, Ryan. We both know that. It is Church versus woman, and a Church that has been at war with God for two thousand years. You know it. James knows it. And I'd swear the Archbishop, who's probably hitting the sack right now, has known it for at least fifteen years."

"That's not the problem, Sharon."

"Are you saying you don't love me, Ryan?"

"No. I'm not saying that. I have never loved any woman more. I find you delightful in every way. I love your mind. I love your sense of humor. I even love your lust for Twinkies, you adorable woman. Have I left anything out?"

"Yes. You didn't mention my ass."

"I do, Sharon. I love your exquisite ass."

"Then what, you jackass?"

"First of all, I'm not sure the Church has actually been at war with God. Christ put His Church in the hands of Peter. We know that Peter didn't follow the plan laid out by Christ on the Chalice, but He did say to him that it was his job to make the rules on earth."

"Look, Ryan. I'm not a theologian but I'm not stupid either. Habib Colophon thought he had disregarded the wishes of God. Pietro Gandolfo seems to agree that he did the same. I suspect James may be having second thoughts. Come on. Tell me what your God said that trumps Peter's sin in unilaterally overruling the wishes of Jesus Christ?"

"You just said it, Dr. Smartypants Feinschutz, the wishes, not the command of Jesus Christ."

Sharon was feeling desperate and was beginning to get angry. "Fine. How do you know all that, Father Cold Showers, S.J.?"

"I don't want to quote scripture at you, Sharon."

"Do it. Do it. I can handle it."

"OK. According to the scriptures, that I believe to be authentic, Christ said to Peter, "whatever you bind on earth shall be bound in heaven, and whatever you loose on earth shall be loosed in heaven.""

Sharon was really angry now. "I'll bet I can find that passage written fifteen different ways. Don't tell me about scripture. I'm an epigrapher. Every time one of us translates something, a hundred other know-it-alls tell us we're wrong. And often, they're right. Translations are like beauty, their truth seems to lie in the bias of the translator. I don't buy it, Ryan. Your loss."

"Please forgive me, Sharon. I do love you. I can't just throw my conscience to the winds because of that. If my faith is well founded, not only would I be at war with God, but you would be damned as the one who took me from Him."

"Drivel."

A long silence, then Ryan began to laugh. It was at the silly sound of that word. Sharon looked hurt, then started to laugh, too.

"Drivel," she said again.

"Drivel," he repeated.

Then they both said it again, and laughed. They said it over and over as they began to skip down the sidewalk, hand in hand, beneath the starlit sky.

"Drivel, drivel, drivel."

They came to the grocery. Sharon suspected she was going to need a large supply of Twinkies.

Chapter Fifty

Analysis of the Chalice was priority, one. Test results came back quickly. Not surprisingly, they revealed nothing unexpected. Archer and his technicians used a technique known as "laser ablation inductively coupled spectrometry" to measure impurities within the silver alloy of the goblet. They compared the spectrum of impurities found against a set of reference spectra kept at Calix for artifact dating. They had developed the reference set by analyzing a large sample of silver coins whose ages were known from numismatic records of minting dates and design characteristics.

Ryan was not concerned with details of the method used. The answer was simple. The Chalice was made of a silver alloy that contained a variety of impurities in relative amounts consistent with alloys used in coins minted between the times of Julius Caesar and Emperor Claudius. In short, the Chalice had been fashioned from silver in use around the time of Christ. Samples examined from the eight medallions, the rim, the base and the stem were all consistent with the same time range.

Ryan was not disappointed. All archaeological data indicated that this was the Chalice of the Last Supper. Now science had verified its age as appropriate, essentially ruling out the likelihood it was a forgery, fabricated at a later time. That put the matter back in his, and his team's hands, as an intellectual and theological problem. Was there anything more to the Chalice that could be determined in a lab?

Pietro, James, and Sharon sat in the Calix conference room discussing the problem with Ryan. Leila, Megyn, and Bedu had taken off with the two pilots to look at a place Ryan asked them to visit. He had an idea.

Descending from the Los Alamos plateau, the "away team" was fascinated to see that the volcanic rock, just below the rim, was riddled with hand-dug caves, former dwellings of a prehistoric people known as the Anasazi, the Ancients. To Megyn, as they drove past Tsankawi, the cliffs looked disturbingly like those of Gabel al-Naqlun. To Leila, they were a delightful, geology, textbook illustration of "friable, semi-indurated, volcanic tuff." To Bedu, it looked like home.

There is a striking similarity between New Mexico and Egypt, including the fertile green strip down the middle of each, the Nile in Egypt, the Rio Grande in New Mexico. From space, you can see that the Jemez Mountains are not a linear chain, but an immense circle. They are the rim of a million year old volcanic field, with a collapsed crater at its center, the Valles Caldera. Los Alamos is on the volcano's eroded, southeastern slope. Northeast of the volcanic field is an area known as Abiquiu. Although there is a village by that name where artist, Georgia O'Keeffe, once lived. The strange name also applies to the huge, surrounding region, including a deep canyon carved by the Chama River.

The drive up the paved road through Abiquiu did nothing but reinforce the team's impression that the area looked like Egypt. On the horizon to the north of the main road, is the Muslim community of Dar al Islam, with a madressa housed in the largest example of North African architecture in America. It was designed by an Egyptian architect, funded by a Saudi prince. Five miles farther, is Ghost Ranch, a Presbyterian Conference Center, also the site of recent discoveries of dinosaur bones. A few more miles, and a dirt road cuts, cross-country, to the east and the Chama River.

A rutted, single-lane road runs up the river canyon, sometimes hanging from sheer cliffs, a hundred feet above the raging torrent. The primitive road dead-ends at a parcel of private land, the Monastery of Christ in the Desert. It was to this isolated, Benedictine outpost, that Ryan had sent them. Pilot-priest, Father Cullen, was at the wheel, unperturbed by the cliff-hanging road. The others held their breaths. Leila clung to Bedu. He didn't object. The monastery, once again, might well be in the Western Desert of Egypt. A sign advises people, who have braved the canyon, to park their vehicles and walk the final half mile. The monks, in their silent isolation, are to be spared the noise and distractions of the 21st Century.

As the group walked to the cloister, a bell began to toll, calling the monks to prayer. Inside the chapel, Megyn began to tremble at the sight of the stone altar standing before a Byzantine mural. She had a flash back to Naqlun. The aroma of frankincense brought her back to the present. This was a holy place for contemporary monks, a warm environment, medieval in flavor, but nothing whatever to connect it with Gabel al-Naqlun. The sound of Gregorian chant rose as the monks entered from behind the mural

Back in Los Alamos, in the presence of a Catholic archbishop and two Jesuits, the Jewish virgin, Sharon Feinschutz, made an observation that startled them all.

"My children's catechism says that, with the words of consecration, the priest turns the bread into the true body of Jesus. OK. So you guys believe that. I asked you, Ryan, and you said yes. You said you could have done it right there in the hotel room in El Minya, right?"

Ryan shifted nervously in his seat and Pietro gave him a funny look. James looked amused. Sharon continued, "If that's true, the bread should be plain bread before the consecration, and human flesh after. Right?"

The priests looked uncomfortable. She was nailing them to the wall. It was theological, "put up or shut up," time. Ryan nodded in the affirmative. The others left him to handle it.

"Well, what if the handle of the Chalice was your God's, and mine, if you're right— what if the handle was a sign left for the 21st Century skeptics to tell them to check the consecrated bread for human DNA?"

An electric silence enveloped the room. It sizzled like the air just after the explosion of bomb. It seemed to go on forever, so Sharon continued. "Test the bread before and after you do your thing. Maybe that was what Christ had in mind. If not, you come with me and my parents and we'll go look for the Ark of the Covenant. Fair? Incidentally, that kid's catechism also said that the transformed bread was left by Christ to keep humans company until Christ returned. I believe you guys call it, The Second Coming. My parents would think it was the First Coming. I've got some ideas about that, too. We can talk about it later. Meanwhile, ever hear of cloning?"

Chapter Fifty-One

The group had returned from the monastery in Abiquiu. None of them realized there were still places in the United States where men lived and prayed in a style considered medieval by a TV watching, video game playing world. The ones who remained in Los Almos had come to a decision.

Ryan would let the Archbishop do the priestly honors when the time came to say Mass and perform the Transubstantiation. The day before, he had given the wafer that would be used, to Dr. Archer. Now they were waiting for his report. In the meanwhile, Pietro Gandolfo and Ryan each had an important phone call to make.

Pietro placed his to Reverend Clemente Brava, S. J., Rector of the Pontifical Biblical Institute in Rome. "Father Brava, this is Archbishop Pietro Gandolfo. Don't speak, please. Just listen. I am in a very unusual place and I have the Chalice. Please. I asked you not to speak. I do have the papal jet with me. You may tell the Holy Father I will be returning to Rome within a few weeks with his jet and probably with the Chalice. I suggest you keep in mind, and remind him as well, that I have made no effort to make public the nature of the medallions on the goblet nor do I intend to. Should he wish to interrupt my mission here, I will be forced to make public both the discovery of the Chalice, and all that it represents. Do you understand? Yes. Yes. Now you may speak."

Father Brava had nothing to say except that he understood. The whole matter took less than three minutes. Ryan, waiting to use the phone, was within earshot.

"Pietro, did you just threaten the Pope?"

Pietro let out a long sigh. "I would prefer to think that I simply applied an old Italian business procedure. I made him an offer he couldn't refuse."

Ryan chuckled and took the phone. His call was just as short. "Hello. Dr. Hawass? This is Father Ryan Quinn. Yes. I do have the canopic jar and will return it to Egypt as soon as possible. I truly appreciate your generosity in allowing us to borrow it. Yes. I know that Wadid Hamza is an old friend and an Egyptian patriot. He is a good man and dear friend, but I have another favor to ask. No. I don't want to borrow anything else. I want to return something that perhaps you had no knowledge of, a papyrus. It was in the possession of a dear and dedicated Egyptian archaeologist in El Minya named Gawdat al-Meskeen. I wish to donate it to the Cairo Museum and ask that you display it with a plaque that says, "A Gift to the Egyptian People From the Private Collection of Gawdat al-Meskeen." Yes, I can testify to its authenticity but you are free, of course, to make that determination yourself. If there are any expenses involved, contact El Azmi Bank in Alexandria. They handle the Chalice Corporation account. I will inform them to honor any request you make in this regard. No, Dr. Hawass. It is I who am grateful to you."

This time, it was Sharon who was eavesdropping. Listening to him take care of the old shopkeeper, as he had promised, made her eyes grow misty. She walked past Ryan, as casually as though she had heard nothing, and whispered, "I love you, Reverend Coldshower."

☥ ☥ ☥

Archer found the group in the conference room. His report was probably thirty pages long. The only part that mattered to the assembled group was his summary.

"We examined the wafer, Father Ryan. We found a number of DNA signatures, all belonging to various sub-species of triticum aestivum. Wheat. Nothing else."

"Thank you, Dr. Archer. Did you place the wafer in a sealed, sterile container as I requested?"

"I did. The container is in the vault. Would you like me to bring it to you?"

Pietro interrupted. "Not yet. I have decided that neither Father Quinn, nor I, take part personally in the proposed experiment. We will need it in the morning."

Ryan understood. He and Gandolfo had discussed the matter. James was confused.

"Why the change in plans, Excellency?"

"I could give you a scientifically plausible explanation, Father McAndrew, or the real one. Which would you like?"

"Try the scientific one first."

"As you wish. The experiment should be a blind test, not conducted by someone with a personal interest in the result."

"That makes a little sense, but not much, begging your pardon, Excellency. Who is there in the world that doesn't have a personal stake in this? Now, the real reason?"

"The idea of being the key instrument in this momentous experiment, that crosses science, religion, and eternity, scares me to death."

Ryan had to smile. He was not anxious to play the key role in this, either.

James McAndrew said, "I understand, so please don't ask me, either. What is your plan?"

"We will take the wafer to the monastery just visited by our companions. Without providing any details, we will ask an ordained, Benedictine priest, isolated from outside influences of any sort, to celebrate Mass, using our wafer for the consecration. He will do so before a congregation of equally isolated monks, unlikely to delve deeper into matters than their usual emotional involvement with the miracle of Transubstantiation."

"Well put, Your Excellency."

The idea appealed to all concerned. It combined an unbiased, technical objective, within a framework of pure scientific methodology. With a splash of drama. It projected the perfect "proof of concept" sought in scientific proposals, albeit with an ecclesiastical aura of ritual to stir the hearts and minds of any who might be called upon to critique the methodology later. It would be a ceremony undoubtedly acceptable to all, to Jesus, to Simon Peter, even to Judas Iscariot. Failure would be undeniable, whether before the College of Cardinals, or a host of angels. Success would be undeniable everywhere in the universe.

"One thing," Ryan added, "We will ask the Benedictine priest to say Mass using The Chalice. Dr. Archer, please make sure the goblet is totally free of dust and every other possible contaminant. When you are certain, place the wafer in it and seal the top."

† † †

The black, all-wheel-drive SUV made its way carefully along the narrow road, a plume of dust rising behind it. In places the car slowed to a crawl as it negotiated some of the tight curves that loop in and out of side canons. Again, Father Cullen was behind the wheel. In the back sat Ryan and the Archbishop. Between them, was an air-tight, Pelican travel case, the goblet and its wafer of bread, cradled within it by sterile foam core.

The last part of the journey on foot was not easy for the Archbishop. He was limping badly along the uneven terrain. He gladly accepted Ryan's help. Father McAndrew carried the case with the goblet.

A monk in black cassock, skullcap, and sandals, greeted them as they approached the chapel, a moving sight against the rugged desert cliffs. The monk had no idea who the visitors were, although they had chosen to wear their clerical garb. Undoubtedly, Pietro was the first Papal Nuncio ever to set foot on the monastery grounds. It made no difference. The monk, aware of Pietro's limp, took over for Ryan, and helped the priest, whoever he was, toward the chapel door.

As they climbed the final incline, Ryan explained to the monk who they were. The monk, from Monterey, Mexico, was impressed but his was a world of the spirit, not the pomp of Rome. He accepted them as they presented themselves, and brought them to the abbot, who was donning his vestments to celebrate Mass.

The abbot was more aware of the outside world. His duties often took him beyond the Chama Valley to raise funds for his monastery. He made no objection to the request that he use the chalice and wafer they brought. He was somewhat taken aback by the demand that he use a hand disinfectant before touching the wafer during the ceremony, but submitted gently. Whether Church officials or not, he was used to the peculiarities of Italians. He had been to the Vatican on a number of occasions. He waited until all the monks had entered quietly from behind the Byzantine mural, wearing white cowls, and began.

"Gratia Domini nostri Jesu Christi et caritas Dei, et communicatio Sancti Spiritus sit cum omnibus vobis . . ."

Perhaps it was his imagination, but when he came to the consecration of the wafer, the tinkling of the bells shaken by the monk who assisted him, seemed drowned out by a chiming that seemed to come from the cliffs above the chapel.

As requested, he enunciated the words spoken at every Mass, in a thousand languages around the world each day.

"Hic est enim Corpus Meum," and placed the wafer back into the chalice his visitors had brought. Then, proceeding with his usual ceremonial chalice and sacramental wine, he went on with the rest of the ceremony.

The monks in white cowls, filed up to the altar, one-by-one, and knelt to receive the Body of Christ. Ryan, head bowed in reverence, collected the Chalice, took it to the back of the chapel, and returned it to the travel case. After a few moments, when the monks had retuned to their pews, he, James, and the archbishop left, Pietro limping badly. As the abbot watched them go he felt he had witnessed something very special, but then, to him, every Mass and Consecration was a special event, blessed by the Almighty. A limping Nuncio made it no more sacred than yesterday's Mass, or tomorrow's.

Chapter Fifty-Two

D r. Archer used the device developed by Calix to hold the wafer in mid-air, without touching it, while simultaneously taking five infinitesimal samples from different locations. The objective was to avoid human contact, and to provide redundant samples to confirm reliability of the results. The next day, he asked all the group members to assemble in the conference room.

"I have some stunning information. In examining the samples, expecting to simply look for DNA strands and extract them for more detailed analysis, we found much more. Scientifically important, from a proof of concept point of view, we found identical DNA strands in all five samples. In essence, that means we performed five analyses with absolutely, reproducible results. The DNA is human."

The room assumed that same sizzling, electrical silence that had descended on them once before.

"That was fascinating," Archer continued, "but uniform, cross-sample reproducibility did not surprise us given the sample was presumed to be homogeneous."

"What, then?" Ryan was holding his breath. With the exception of Leila, probably only he had sufficient background in biology to understand Archer.

"We found cells. Adult cells. Do you know what that means?"

Ryan let out his breath slowly and turned to Leila. Her expression said that she understood perfectly. The others were turning to one another in confusion. Sharon was the first one to speak, "OK. Why don't you tell everybody, Ryan? What _does_ it mean?"

"It means," he spoke slowly and carefully, "your verbal poke at me about cloning was on the mark. There is the distinct possibility that a clone is possible using material from the wafer. In fact there is enough for five clones."

Everyone, including Archer, was silent. There was so much going on in this room that facts threatened to challenge reality. How could tables, chairs, a couch, and a small group of people be appropriate witnesses to the immensity of what was about to be discussed?

Again, it was Sharon who was the first to recover and ask, "Is that all there is to it? Now we can just put a wafer in a petrie dish and, presto— a new Savior? My people will be confused, but delighted. They never accepted Christ as the Annointed One, and are still waiting for the Moshiach, the Messiah. Maybe this one will fly, or with five of them, maybe it'll be a squadron of Moshiachs."

The Archbishop was taken aback by the flippancy of Sharon's remarks, but quickly thought better of it. She was a young woman and spoke like a young woman. He was an old man and thought with the sclerotic brain of one. The same thought had occurred to him. *What about five Christs?*

Ryan brought them back to earth, so to speak. "No, Sharon. That's not all there is to it. It just means it may be technically possible."

With the tacit agreement of both Leila and Dr. Archer, he tried to clarify, "In a process called "somatic cell nuclear transfer," technicians can transfer genetic material from the nucleus of an adult cell to an egg whose nucleus, and thus its own genetic material, has been removed. The reconstructed egg containing the DNA from the donor cell must be treated with chemicals or electric current to stimulate cell division. If the process is successful, it will generate a cloned embryo, which if it survives to a suitable stage, must be transferred to the uterus of a female host where it can continue to develop until birth. Have I got all that right, Dr. Archer?"

"Essentially, Father Quinn. A bit simplified, but basically correct. However, you left out two important things— first, it's only been done with animals, never with humans, despite rumors. And second, in the United States, it's against the law."

"So," Ryan turned to Archbishop Gandolfo and Father McAndrew, "are we on a holy mission or a mission from Hell? As for the law, isn't it man-made laws in defiance of the wishes of God that got us all here? I believe that was the conclusion of Father Habib Colophon and yours, too, Nuncio. I believe that King Herod was in charge of the law two thousand years ago and would have had the Christ Child killed."

"Your point is well taken, as far as US law is concerned. As to heavenly mission, or Satanic, that's another matter. I suggest we take a few days to think this through."

✝ ✝ ✝

The stars were bright above Los Alamos as Ryan and Sharon went in search of more Twinkies.

"Ryan, I have a proposal. Here are the facts. I love you, and you said you love me. You are sworn to celibacy, and I respect that. It happens, I'm a virgin. No. Let me finish. I want to spend my life with you. I can't imagine life without you. You can keep your damned celibacy, and I'll keep my undamaged hymen. No. I said, let me finish. Will you marry me? It doesn't have to be public, and we can live our distorted, sexless lives together in what may turn out to be a delightful journey worthy of history books."

"What does that mean, Sharon?"

"It means I want to be the host for the developing Embryo. I want to give birth to the Child, and I want you to be His foster father. How are you at carpentry?"

Ryan was stunned into thoughtful silence as the two walked, hand-in-hand, beneath the stars. A light breeze rose and scattered a carpet of feathers that had fallen to the ground around them.

Dr. Barnett has written about science for Smithsonian Magazine and elsewhere. His biography is listed in *Who's Who in the World*. He lives in Santa Fe, NM with a tiny poodle who rules him with an iron paw. Charles' interests in theology, archaeology, and travel were the inspiration for *Iscariot*.

CPSIA information can be obtained
at www.ICGtesting.com
Printed in the USA
LVHW091611041119
636284LV00001B/84/P